CURVEBALL YEAR ONE: DEATH OF A HERO

ISBN 978-1-939633-28-6

Curveball archives, news, and series information can be found at:

http://www.curveball.xyz

More of Garth Graham's work can be found at:

http://www.gcgstudios.com

More of Jeff Darlington's work can be found at:

http://www.gpf-comics.com

Arpista Editing can be found at:

http://www.arpistaediting.com

Licensing Information

CONTENTS

DEDICATIONS

Patricia, who never once told me to get a real job

Matt, for patiently being my sounding-board as I natter on

Chris and **Thuy**, who bear more responsibility for these stories than either might care to admit

PART ONE: LIBERTY

The clear, untarnished melody of *In The Mood* starts up again for what must be the tenth, eleventh time—Alex has lost track at this point. It's a good thing he doesn't have neighbors: this is exactly the sort of thing that would get on his nerves, if he wasn't the one doing it. He feels sentimental tonight, and the music is comforting. He doesn't hate new music, not like some of the other guys his age, but he prefers brass and string instruments over computers. It reminds him of... happier days? No, not happier, necessarily, but more hopeful.

Once upon a time people believed that by coming together they could change the world. Things are different now—people don't like to pitch in, because they feel the ones asking for sacrifice aren't telling the whole truth. The worst part, he thinks, is that people aren't necessarily wrong. Too many leaders prefer saying what they think people want to hear instead of telling the truth.

The thought pains him.

This isn't new, Alex reminds himself. *It happened back in the day, too. More than we knew.*

He leans back in his chair and stares at the empty message window sitting open on his computer monitor. He sips his coffee, listens to the music, and notes the occasional rumble of thunder echoing off the Manhattan skyline. It will rain soon. An ache in his shoulder—the remnant of an old wound—suggests it will rain pretty hard.

Alex likes the rain. He likes the sound of rain striking stone, wood, glass, likes the sound of thunder rumbling across the sky. It's a good sound. This night it will rain, a proper thunderstorm from the sound and feel of it, and Alex is at peace. The last few days have been a mess, but he's on top of it now. He doesn't like the solution, but it's the only one with a chance at success. Alex is a tactician: he always maneuvers for the best possible advantage, if not for himself, then for his side. In this scenario his side needs to sacrifice a pawn. It's his turn.

This is the last time I'll ever hear the rain.

He almost slides from sentiment to self-pity, but he sets his jaw and pushes those thoughts aside. He has a job to do: he looks at the blank message window on his monitor and begins to type.

I know you're going to get this, no matter what they try, because it's you. Sorry to dump this on you kid, but you're the only one I know who has a shot. You know how I always tell you to tone things down? How you need to show restraint?

Not this time. Give 'em hell. It's no less than they deserve.

Capt. Alexander Morgan, Ret. (liberty@guardians.tti)

"Give Me Liberty or Give Me Death"

He stares at the message briefly, wondering if there's anything else he needs to say. Words fail. He almost slides into self-pity again.

He sighs, and forces himself to focus. He clicks the "attach" icon in the email window, navigates to the attachment folder, and double-clicks the file. He smiles briefly: teaching himself to encrypt that file was quite an achievement. *Jenny will be proud*, he thinks. *If she ever finds out.*

He hopes she never finds out.

His hands tremble, ever so slightly, as he types in the email address, then steady as the mouse pointer hovers over the send button. He takes a breath. Clicks the button.

A progress bar displays: *sending, 2%.* Alex sighs again, and waits.

He moved into his penthouse in the 90s, when floor plans favored open rooms and lots of large windows. It's a luxury apartment, and he still feels a little guilty that he lives there, especially since he doesn't pay for it himself. But he loves the openness, and loves the view, and considers it his refuge from the rest of the world. His sanctum. Which makes it all the more galling to him that it's about to be intruded on in such an ugly manner.

The progress bar reaches 12% as he hears the soft *click* of the balcony door latch. The intruder is very good; he hardly makes a sound. Most people wouldn't notice.

Alex notices.

His computer desk sits at the far side of the living room, next to a hall that leads to the bathroom, bedrooms, and laundry. A large L-shaped sofa separates the desk from the rest of the room. Alex reaches for a tray sitting on an ottoman wedged between the desk and sofa. His right hand grips the tray firmly as he carefully lifts it off the ottoman, testing its weight.

When the French doors burst open, Alex is ready.

The tray flies through the air, humming as it streaks across the room, smashing into a shadowy figure looming in the doorway. The tray ricochets off the figure with a loud *twang* and the figure staggers back, crying out in pain. Alex slides out of his seat and crouches to the ground, taking cover behind the couch as the *fwip fwip fwip* of silenced pistols is followed by shells bursting into drywall and shattering glass.

Alex calmly pushes a button set into the wall behind his desk.

He hears another volley of *fwip fwip fwip* as his assailants fire into the couch. He doesn't flinch—the muzzle velocities of the silenced weapons are too low to pierce through the back. Better, he thinks, to let them waste their ammo. He glances up at the monitor, untouched in the firefight.

24%.

One of the French doors swings wildly, crashing against the wall with a *bang*. Cool, humid air seeps into the living room. Thunder rumbles in the distance. The shooting stops; Alex hears indistinct muttering outside. Then:

"I confess, *Herr Morgan*, I hoped the weather would mask the sound of the latch."

Clear, precise English. Unmistakable German accent. Alex's jaw tightens.

"Richter..."

36%.

He hears a loud *crack* as the front door buckles. At the same time, a shout goes up from the balcony, and the glass windows on either side of the door shatter. Alex rolls back out of the living room and into the kitchen. He stands, hidden from the living room by a half-wall, and sees the front door splinter into pieces. Men clad in tactical gear enter the room.

Not soldiers, he thinks. *I will not dignify them with the name soldier.*

Alex reaches for his carving knife. It is a quality weapon: well-balanced, full tang blade, always kept sharp. Two men fill the broken doorframe. One kneels and brings his rifle to bear. Without hesitation, Alex throws the blade—it flies through the air with deadly precision, piercing the target's goggles with a loud *crack* and entering the left eye with a sickening *schlict*. The man slumps over, dead.

Alex doesn't like killing. He avoids it whenever possible. But today he is at war, and in war prisoners are taken only when your enemy surrenders. No one will surrender tonight.

He moves faster than any human should, leaping onto a counter as gunfire rips through the wood cabinets beneath him. He's still almost in peak form, even after decades, but he can feel the aches start to pile up, feel the sluggishness in his limbs. He's getting old, he realizes, and although a part of him feels it's about time, at the moment it's inconvenient.

He launches himself across the room toward the attacker. He feels, rather than hears, the bullets flying past him. He tackles the masked figure, propelling him outside the door, into the elevator foyer. The man grunts as he hits the ground, then twitches once as Alex twists the man's head farther than it is meant to go, breaking his neck. Alex grabs the man's rifle, reaches down to his belt, and draws forth a bayonet.

He turns back to the door. Richter will already be reconsidering his options. He doesn't like public displays—he probably hoped this action would be over in seconds. It isn't over; it's now more complicated. There's a chance, Alex thinks, that if he runs Richter won't bother to follow...

...but he has to make sure the email goes through.

He stands back, pokes the rifle around the corner, and fires blindly into the living room until he empties the magazine. He drops the rifle and runs, crouching low until he whips through the kitchen and emerges from the other side, back into the living room.

He glances at the monitor. 58%.

Alex vaults over the back of the couch, flying feet-first into someone emerging from the balcony. The man falls back and Alex rolls past, through the French doors and onto the balcony.

It's raining now, hard; sheets of rain falling from the sky, muffling every sound but their own. Three armed men stare at Alex, startled, and attempt to raise their weapons.

None of them are Richter.

Alex lashes out with his foot, undercutting one man's stance. The man falls flat on his back, his rifle discharging into the air. Immediately Alex throws the bayonet at another. The bayonet is crude compared to his carving knife, but capable. He doesn't bother to watch the man fall.

The third assailant hesitates. Alex springs to his feet and leaps toward him, striking him in the solar plexus, then kneeing him in the face as he doubles over. He feels goggles crunch as he breaks the lenses, then feels blood on his knuckles as he viciously strikes at the man's temple. In seconds all three are down.

Alex scans the area quickly. There is nothing but rain.

"Richter!"

No reply. He hears sirens in the distance, occasionally swallowed up by the thunder booming through Manhattan.

He steps over the broken glass into his living room and glances at the monitor. 89%. He sighs in relief.

Almost over, he thinks. *For me, at any rate...*

"Do not move, *Herr Morgan*."

Alex freezes. He hears the *click* of a very distinctive gun's hammer drawing back into its cocked position.

"Now raise your arms. Keep them away from your body, if you please."

Alex obeys. "I didn't expect you to be a part of this, Richter."

Low laughter rumbles behind him. "No? I find that strange. I have always been dedicated to the ideals of the Third Reich. Even after it fell, the beacon lit by *Mein Fuhrer* always led me on my path. And now I find the ideals are but a reflection of a greater design. A Fourth Reich? A map for all mankind. It is my honor to serve."

Out of the corner of his eye, Alex sees 97% on the monitor.

"Never understood your honor, Richter. You take it so seriously, but you tie your honor to madmen. Despots. Tyrants..."

Richter's voice hardens. "Turn around, *Herr Morgan*."

Alex turns to face Richter for the last time.

They are so alike they could be brothers: blond, blue-eyed, strong, clean-shaven, full of resolve... both warriors from a bygone age, making their way in a world that says "never forget" but can no longer remember why. Richter's gun points directly at Alex's head. His hand doesn't waver. Alex knows he won't miss.

"Tell me the name of your contact, *Herr Morgan*."

Alex shakes his head. "Not going to happen."

Richter smiles slightly. "Such arrogance. You have a choice: you may tell me now, or you *will* tell me later. I recommend the former."

"There isn't going to be a later." Alex's voice is flat. "If you don't kill me now, I'm going to kill you."

Richter's smile falters. "You do not kill."

Alex narrows his eyes. "You know better than that. I was a soldier. I fought, I killed. Your men in the hall are dead. At least two of the men on the balcony are dead. Not the legacy I wanted to leave behind, but I don't have the luxury of choice tonight."

Richter looks at Alex thoughtfully. "How much do you know?"

"Enough," Alex says. "Enough to know the truth."

Richter frowns. "No... no, I believe you are bluffing. As you did in '42? Remember your little gambit in Paris? I remember it quite well."

"Project Recall," Alex says.

Richter's hand tightens on the grip of his gun. "You should not have told me that." His voice is stern, harsh, tinged with... something else. Regret.

Alex's computer beeps.

"It doesn't matter," Alex says. "It's too late now, Richter. I *win*."

Alex leaps toward Richter, a study in balance, grace, power and speed. His movement is perfect—nothing wasted, no flourish, nothing that would detract from his ability to fight or kill. His fighting style is often studied, often imitated, and has no equal. By the time most people notice he's moving, there's little if anything to be done.

A light flashes between the two men. Richter steps backward as Alex falls to the floor, dead. He stares at the body, mesmerized by the red stain rapidly spreading across the back of Alex's head.

"I am sorry, Captain. Truly."

He *is* sorry. Yet another piece of his past has been torn away, sent hurtling into the shadows of memory. In the nights to come he will be haunted by the face of his oldest enemy leaping to his death: no malice, only resolve and a calm acceptance of what they both knew would happen.

Richter knows that look. It is the look of a man who knows his enemy has failed. That look concerns him.

He calmly unscrews the silencer from his pistol and pulls a black, eyeless mask over his face. He touches the earpiece embedded in his mask.

"This is Richter. Morgan is dead. However... we may have been too late." Richter frowns as he notices the email window open on Alex's monitor. "I believe he managed to contact someone."

He walks to the computer. An open dialog box reports *Message Sent.*

Richter tilts his head as someone on the other end asks him a question.

"I do not know," he says. "Hold on."

He grabs the mouse, closes the dialog, then clicks the "Sent Messages" folder in the email program. "Yes, he emailed someone. I do not recognize the address. The account is *cb@chaos.tti.*"

He listens a moment. "Yes, I believe that is a Thorpe domain. That will make it harder to track, but not impossible... and it narrows the list of potential recipients."

Sirens. They are very loud now—Richter can hear them quite clearly above the storm. "I must leave now," he says quickly, "or risk discovery. I am headed to the extraction point. I will make following this trail my next priority."

He steps out to the balcony, ignoring the rain, and pulls a second gun out from under his coat. He aims quickly, and fires—the grappling hook flies across the night sky, bonding instantly to the wall of a nearby building. He steps off the edge of the balcony, swinging in an arc toward the building. He shakes from the impact as he hits the building wall—the impact would shatter the legs of an ordinary man, but to him it is merely uncomfortable—then allows his grappling gun to pull him up the side of the building to the roof.

The wind dies down for a moment, and he hears the police as they storm the penthouse: shouts of challenge, of recognition, of alarm... then, finally, shouts of grief.

PART TWO: CURVEBALL

Afternoon sunlight streams through the Gothic windows in the bank lobby, highlighting motes of dust swirling through the air. CB stifles a yawn and waits, mostly patiently, in the cavernous room's only line. It looks more like a church than a bank, and some might consider that appropriate—a church to Mammon, perhaps.

"Here comes trouble..."

CB looks over his shoulder and grins at the smiling, elderly man in the security uniform. "Heya Frank."

"Back again," Frank says. "I told myself 'it's the third Thursday of the month. That young fella should be in today.' And don't you know it, here you are."

"You know me pretty well, Frank."

"I know all the regulars." Frank is obviously proud of this fact. "They never surprise me. Not any more. For example, I'd bet money you're going to refuse to open an account. Again."

CB laughs. "That's money you'd win. Just here to cash a check..."

"Every month," Frank says. "Just here to cash a check. And you get off the bus to do it! Don't they have banks where you live?"

"I don't live in a good neighborhood," CB says.

Frank grins broadly. "Then you should open an account. Keep your money in the bank instead of carrying it in your pockets all the time. It's safer."

"I'm OK," CB says.

"Well, it's a new girl today. Just started last week. She's going to try to talk you into opening an account."

"Is she now?" CB grins again. "Is she pretty?"

"She's married."

"I might let her talk me into it if she's pretty."

"You leave that poor girl alone. She's sweet." Frank shakes his head, torn between amusement and disapproval.

CB shrugs. "Guess I'll just cash my check, then. Keep holding out for the girl of my dreams."

"Girl of your dreams?" Frank asks. "What kind of girl would that be?"

"Depends on what I ate the night before..."

Frank laughs.

The line moves up one spot. CB yawns again, then grins at the woman in front of him, who tries to pretend she wasn't glancing furtively in his direction. He doesn't look like your typical bank patron: matted, spiky hair, a day's growth of beard, trenchcoat, heavy boots and a Clash t-shirt make him look more like someone intending to rob it.

He briefly considers trying to strike up a conversation with the woman, just to see exactly how uncomfortable he can make her, but the thought of the effort involved makes him tired. He sighs, slips on his earbuds, and chooses a random track from his iPod. He closes his eyes, lets the screeching vocals of the Hives surround him, and is completely oblivious when the front of the bank explodes.

The front wall blows inward, showering the patrons with a hailstorm of concrete rock, shards of glass, and a powdery mixture of both. Larger pieces of concrete litter the front of the lobby like man-made boulders; exposed support beams twist out from the intact portions of the wall like bonsai trees.

The line dissolves as people scatter, shrieking and yelling in alarm. Some hide behind desks or booths, others run to the restrooms or look for the back exit. Frank runs to a man half-pinned under a broken concrete slab and tries to push the slab away; he's too old, it's too large.

Dozens of silhouettes appear in the billowing cloud of concrete dust. Moments later they emerge: soldiers in gold armor, carrying rifles of unknown design and wearing gold helmets that obscure their faces entirely. They begin shouting commands in perfectly modulated tones, separating the frightened patrons into small, manageable groups against three remaining walls. Frank is forced away from the man he's trying to help, stripped of his sidearm and herded into one of the groups. More men in gold armor appear, pulling large, floating containers behind them.

CB wonders how Pelle Almqvist manages to get his voice to sound like that. It sounds *amazing*.

Frank does his best to calm the hostages, but he's only one man. They're in various stages of distress: some, tight-faced and unblinking, manage to hold it together. Others are hysterical: a small girl is screaming uncontrollably at the sight of a man with his face covered in cuts, a byproduct of all the glass flying through the air moments before. They're superficial wounds, but the girl doesn't know that—to her the man is bleeding to death and nobody cares.

CB inhales dust and coughs. He frowns, wonders why the room smells like burning cinderblock, and opens one eye. His frown deepens, and he opens his other eye. He looks around the room, sighs slightly, and reaches into one of his trenchcoat pockets. He pulls out a carton of cigarettes.

The gold figures—CB automatically classifies them as "minions"—are going from group to group, going through the personal belongings of each adult hostage, collecting driver's licenses and taking down names when a driver's license isn't available. CB rhythmically beats the back of his carton, watching the soldiers go about their work, idly wondering why none of them have noticed him yet.

At that moment, one of the soldiers notices him. He barks out an order, and three more advance on CB, weapons drawn.

"What do you think you're doing?"

CB looks at the soldier asking the question; the phrase *Disco Stormtrooper* flashes through his mind. He manages to keep a straight face.

"Packing," he says. "Makes it taste better."

"Get out of the way," another says, and gestures with his rifle.

CB flips open the top of the carton and pulls out a cigarette. "Nah."

The soldier hesitates. "Get out of the way," he repeats, obviously hoping for a different response.

CB shrugs. "I'd rather wait for your boss. You do have one, right? I'm assuming you do, since you're all wearing the same uniform, and you don't seem to have a hive mind—"

The floor trembles as a massive silhouette looms in the gaping hole where a bank wall used to stand. Easily ten feet tall and three times wider than a full-grown man, it's a hulking construct of gold-tinted steel and polymer. A large, still-smoking gun is affixed to its right arm—similar in design to the rifles the soldiers carry, but significantly larger.

"Do not move!" The figure's voice is modulated and artificial, similar to the soldiers' voices but significantly deeper in pitch. "This bank is currently under my possession. It will be released when we take what we need. Obey Doctor AEvil and live!"

CB rolls his eyes. The soldiers facing him thrust their rifles out menacingly. CB ignores them, places the filter of a cigarette between his lips, and fishes around his pockets for a lighter.

"You!" The soldier's voice is even louder. "Get over against the wall. NOW!"

"Can't." CB pulls out a silver Zippo from his pocket. The movement makes one of the soldiers twitch nervously, but none of them fire. "Doctor 'AEvil' over there told us not to move. I think he outranks you."

The soldier hesitates. "Do not move!"

"Well, I have to move a *little*..." CB flips open the Zippo, producing a tiny, orange flame. He brings the lighter up to the end of his cigarette and inhales sharply. The cherry glows bright orange, and with a second flip the lighter is doused. "Autonomic whatsits and other bodily functions, right? I mean, you wouldn't want us to drop *dead*. That would make the hostage negotiation portion of your evening a real drag."

"What is this?" Doctor AEvil notices the soldiers surrounding the lone man in the middle of the lobby and advances on them. The ground shakes with each step. "Why isn't this man contained against the wall?"

The soldiers hesitate again. "You..."

"Not their fault," CB says. "They were telling me to move when you told everyone *not* to move. I figured you were the guy I should be listening to. Am I right? Doctor... AEvil, is it?"

A burst of modulated noise that might have been a garbled *harrumph* emerges from a grille positioned on the helmet that roughly approximates the location of a mouth. CB can see a speaker vibrating behind the grille. "Yes. I am Doctor AEvil. And SOON THE WORLD WILL—"

"Will what?" CB takes a drag from his cigarette, casually blowing smoke in the direction of one of the soldiers. "Tremble in fear? Fear that name? No, wait, don't tell me. I think I have this figured out."

Ignoring the soldiers, he walks up to the hulking armored figure, gesturing with his lit cigarette. "They mocked you. They called you *mad*. They told you not to meddle in forces humanity didn't understand. They tried to ruin you—*ruin* you! But you swore, you swore you'd show them, you'd show them all! ... am I close?"

Doctor AEvil's helmet swivels down to regard him. "Who are you?"

"Don't get me wrong," CB says, "I'm not, you know, *mocking* you. I appreciate when a guy has a grasp of the classics. I know some think they're old hat, but me, I think it's *damned refreshing* to meet someone who's rejected the whole postmodern, angst-ridden personae and gone straight for revenge as a motivator. But... robbing a bank? Seriously? A scientist? Shouldn't you be constructing a death ray, or a killer robot?"

Doctor AEvil stares down at CB in silence.

"Or *something*?"

Doctor AEvil considers the question. "Science is... expensive."

"Well, I'll have to grant you that one," CB says. "And again I have to compliment you on the practicality of your motives. We're not *brooding*, we're not working through *daddy issues*, we're just *solving a problem*. Science is expensive, so we rob a bank. That pretty much paints the entire picture. Except for the name thing."

"What about my name?" If it's possible for a modulated, electronic voice to sound stiff and defensive, Doctor AEvil manages to pull it off.

"Well, come on. 'AEvil?' You were so fixated on 'Doctor Evil' that you just couldn't let it go? I mean, it's better than DocEvil666 or xXxDoctorEvilxXx—going with the diphthong is creative, I'll grant you that—but why not 'Doctor Destroyer?' Or 'Doctor Destruction?' Or something else entirely? And why is 'evil' so important, anyway? I mean, so far I see greed and a desire for revenge. That's a little on the selfish side, but—"

"DO NOT MOCK ME!" Doctor AEvil bellows. "Tell me who you are at once!"

CB shrugs. "Everyone calls me CB. Pleasure's all mine, by the way. I like your armor. Big. Got a mecha kind of vibe, am I right? Gold is a nice touch, though. Most guys would go with gray, or crimson red, or maybe olive green. The gold definitely makes it more... *sciency*."

"Hey, feller." CB and Doctor AEvil turn to face Frank, who's standing apart from the rest of his group and frowning at CB. "You're not allowed to smoke in here."

CB raises an eyebrow. "*Really*, Frank? Is that the biggest violation of bank rules you see in this room right now?"

Frank shakes his head. "No, but I figure it's the one I can do something about."

CB laughs. "Fair enough. I'll get rid of it." He turns back to Doctor AEvil. "Frank's had a rough day. I figure he deserves a little consideration on my part, you know? The thing is, though..." CB looks around casually. "I don't see any ash trays in here. Probably because it's a smoke-free building, right? But... well. I don't suppose you'd let me go outside to put it out?"

Doctor AEvil doesn't reply.

"Right. That's what I thought." CB sighs. "Oh well, I guess it's a flip of the coin, then."

He flicks his wrist, and the still-lit cigarette flies straight up into the air, sailing up to the ceiling with unusual speed, where it embeds itself in one of the ceiling-mounted sprinklers.

CB whistles. "I never did that before. That's a first for me. I mean, I know it doesn't reach the level of designing powered armor or putting together a small army to rob banks with, but hey, I gotta take my kudos where I can, you know?"

CB winks. Somewhere in the lobby, something makes a small popping sound. Seconds later the ceiling sprinklers activate, dousing the lobby in water.

The minute water hits Doctor AEvil's gun it sparks. CB casually steps back as a shower of sparks erupt from the barrel, transforming it into an elaborate sparkler. Doctor AEvil shouts in alarm, starts to turn, then stops cold. A puff of smoke emerges from the back of the armor; Doctor AEvil stands stone-still, frozen in place.

The soldiers stare in mute amazement at Doctor AEvil's now-motionless form. The sprinklers stop, and for a few seconds the only sound in the room is the soft, rhythmic dripping of condensation falling from the ceiling to the floor.

CB grins.

"Get him!" One of the soldiers takes command of the situation and raises his rifle, taking aim. CB winks. Something pops, then the soldier's rifle erupts in a shower of sparks. The soldier jumps back, throwing the rifle down in alarm. It begins to spin on the ground like one of the fancier fireworks you can buy on holidays.

CB runs back to where he'd stood in line, passing the three soldiers who originally accosted him. They stare at him, unmoving, then as the other soldiers begin to open fire they start after him. CB crouches into a slide as bolts of energy streak above him. The soldiers are shooting at him freely, and the rifles are definitely a cut above the norm.

He slides under one of the velvet ropes set up to corral patrons into a single open line. He falls to his knees and leans back, letting the rope pass over him like a limbo pole; as he slides under he reaches up, grabs the rope by the middle, and jerks sharply. The weighted posts wobble, and CB twists around, comes up to one knee, then stands. A bolt of energy severs the rope from the right post, streaks by CB with only inches to spare, and leaves a scorch mark on the far wall.

CB jerks on the rope a second time. The remaining post revolves around its base in a wide circle, tips over, and knocks into a second. That post falls, and its rope goes taut as it pulls the third post down, right into the path of the first soldier. He trips, gets tangled in the rope, and falls on his face. The impact reverberates through the room with a loud *clang*.

The second soldier tries to sidestep the first. CB winks, and the first soldier twitches, kicking one of the fallen posts. It spins around in place and stops directly beneath the second soldier's foot as it comes down. He trips, turns, and falls backward on another velvet rope, pulling both of its weighted posts directly on his helmet. A second, deafening *clang* fills the room. He twitches, then lies still.

"Boss skimped on the padding, didn't he?" CB casually kicks a third weighted post over. As it falls, it drags the second post down, and the velvet rope tangles itself around another weighted post, which also falls. The cascading effect resembles a very complicated combination of dominoes and cirque du soleil, ending in the third soldier getting hopelessly ensnared in four separate velvet ropes wrapped completely around him.

The room is silent.

CB frowns. The room shouldn't be silent. He vaguely remembers people shooting at him, and wonders why it stopped. Looking around, he realizes the other soldiers have been overpowered, immobilized, and disarmed by the bank patrons. The patrons begin to cheer as they realize they helped stop a bank robbery.

CB grins, runs his fingers through his hair to try to salvage what he can of his spike, then walks up to the teller's booth where a young, pretty woman stands gaping at the scene.

"'Scuse me, miss," CB says, reaching into his pocket and pulling out a slightly damp check, "I know you've been through a lot, and I suppose it's a little inconvenient right now, but do you think you could cash this for me? I could really use the dough..."

PART THREE: FARRADAY CITY BOARDWALK

In the nineties Farraday City was poised to become the next successful beach resort: middle-class and white-collar professionals flocked to its shores, looking to spend a few weeks of their precious holiday time somewhere far enough away to feel like a break, but not so far they couldn't rush back to the office in an emergency. Then the recession hit, and people stopped coming. Farraday City's economy tanked, the high-rise building projects stopped, the motel resorts were condemned, and it quickly turned into a metropolitan ghost town.

That's when organized crime moved in.

They wanted a new Vegas: instead of building one from scratch, they bought a fixer-upper. They restored the buildings, brought in their own politicians, bought the police force, and got the city running again—their way. It is, depending on who you ask, either an East Coast oceanside paradise, or a festering pit of corruption. It's consistently listed as the "Most Corrupt City in the United States," as well as the "Most Dangerous City to Live In," and, in one article that secures its infamy, it's described as "the only place in America where being a resident is grounds for probable cause."

There's very little in the way of "Family Entertainment" in the new Farraday City, unless you use "Family" to mean "organized crime." The remnants of the old city that were intended for families have been repurposed and adapted to new things. The Boardwalk, once a favorite spot for families to stroll along when they were taking a break from sunbathing, surfing, or building sand castles, has turned into a skid row strip with an oceanfront view.

That's where CB lives. He has decidedly mixed feelings about his neighbors.

Despite the change in demographic, the Boardwalk remains a popular spot. The wooden strip that travels down the shoreline is the main thoroughfare between all the bars, pool halls, brothels, and flop houses that replaced the restaurants, surf shops, souvenir shops, and other tourist attractions from the old days. During the day—the Boardwalk is much safer to traverse in the day than it is at night—you can still see some of the charm it had in better days. If you squint, and cock your head to the side.

And if you're drunk.

As CB walks down the Boardwalk he keeps a protective hand over the roll of bills stashed in his pocket. Tom Waits plays on his iPod as he tries very hard to ignore the smell. The Boardwalk can be an assault on the senses—in some situations, in a very literal way—but this is something new. He doesn't know what it is, but it's vile, and it's coming from below.

He tries not to think too much about it. As a general rule, the only people who go under the Boardwalk are homeless and deranged. It's not his problem, and he doesn't need any new ones. When he arrives at his favorite bar and realizes the smell isn't going away—it is, in fact, stronger than before—he decides he's going to have to make it his problem after all.

He sighs, walks over to the seaside edge of the Boardwalk, and peers down. The drop is about twelve, thirteen feet. CB sighs again, hitches one leg over the rail, then the other, and drops to the beach below. He lands on his feet, bends his knees to absorb the shock, and straightens, turning to face the underside of the Boardwalk. The smell is even stronger now, and he wrinkles his nose in disgust. It's definitely something dead, and he doubts it's fish.

It's afternoon, and the sun's high enough in the sky that there isn't any light getting in under the Boardwalk. CB fumbles with his cigarettes and hastily lights one, puffing quickly, hoping the smell of burning tobacco will cut into the stench of decay. Finally he pulls out a small Mag-lite from his trenchcoat, twists it on, and peers into the darkness.

He finds the bodies immediately. Twelve of them: all male, from what he can tell, though the corpses are so swollen it's difficult to say for certain. All are bound hand and foot, all are gagged, and it looks as if their throats have been cut. It's a methodical job, and everything about it says *reprisal*.

Except, CB thinks, that reprisals are usually put on public display. He isn't sure this counts. The bodies aren't hidden, exactly, but they are out of view. On the other hand, they're placed in a location where someone will find them eventually. There are too many people top-side, and if the stench hadn't driven CB down to investigate, one of the locals would have come. Eventually.

He decides the killer wants the bodies found, but not immediately. For what purpose? A chance to skip town? A chance to establish an alibi? He plays his flashlight over the swollen corpses, looking for anything obvious, and sees nothing. No clues, no hunches. He turns off the Mag-lite, walks down the beach until he finds a way back onto the Boardwalk, and makes his way back to his original destination.

Once upon a time the Swordfish was a seafood restaurant—now it's a bar with a swordfish motif. CB walks into the dimly-lit main room and nods to the bartender, a burly man with a twice-broken nose, playing solitaire at the far end of the bar.

"Jerry."

The bartender doesn't look up. "Here to pay your tab?"

"Among other things…"

Jerry looks up and smiles broadly at him. "CB! My favorite customer! How can I help you today?"

CB fishes for the roll of bills and counts out what he owes as he crosses the room. Jerry stares at the money with intense interest, and when CB places what he owes on the bar, he carefully counts it out on his own. When he's satisfied, Jerry goes over to the wall, opens up a small safe sitting next to a wood carving of a flounder, and stuffs the money inside.

The Swordfish is empty and dark. A few committed drunks sit at the bar, and two men engaging in serious conversation sit in a booth in a shadowy corner. Most of the light comes from the one TV set up high behind the bar. The sound is turned down too low to hear, but it looks like a game show.

"OK," Jerry says. "We're square."

"Yeah, good. Look, I need to use your phone."

Jerry narrows his eyes. "Use your own."

CB shrugs. "Don't have one."

Jerry snorts. "*Right*. You don't have a phone. Hell, even the *homeless* have phones these days."

CB shrugs again.

"Yeah, well, forget it," Jerry says. "My phone ain't for personal calls."

"This isn't personal. It's about that smell. Or hadn't you noticed?"

Jerry looks at CB steadily. "I don't want to get involved."

"Yeah? OK. You want your regulars to spend their money somewhere else tonight? Because that smell is going to get worse before it gets better."

Jerry frowns, struggling between a healthy desire for self-preservation and an unhealthy desire to make money. Eventually greed wins over; Jerry pulls a cordless phone out from under the bar, sliding it over to him.

CB picks up the phone, dials, and waits.

"Farraday PD." The voice on the other end of the phone sounds grumpy and vaguely ill.

"Larry!" CB acts like he's greeting a friend he hasn't seen in years.

"Oh, *Christ*." The voice, if anything, sounds grumpier. "Damn it all CB, stop calling me."

"Calm down, Larry, I'm just doing my civic duty."

The voice grows a little hostile. "I thought we already had that talk. We don't want your charitable contributions."

"Twelve corpses stinking up the Boardwalk, right under the Swordfish."

"Sounds like a personal problem."

"It's personal to someone," CB agrees. "Arms and legs bound, gagged, throats cut..."

"Stop." The hostility is gone, replaced with a sharpness that indicates CB has his full attention. "You saw this yourself?"

"Yeah, I saw it myself. It's not pleasant and it stinks. It might make a good story for the paper though. I bet I could make a few bucks if I—"

"Stop talking right damn now. And you don't mention this to *anyone* till our guys get there."

"When is that going to be, Larry? You know me. I get bored and I'm easily distracted..."

"Just sit tight. We'll be there in half an hour, tops." The phone clicks. CB hears a dial tone.

"That was fast," CB says.

"Shouldn't have mentioned the Swordfish," Jerry complains. "Now they're going to think I had something to do with it."

"No they won't. Larry was a little too interested in this one. I think this has probably happened before, and someone made the case a priority. That means it didn't happen on the Boardwalk, because the police don't care what happens here. And everyone knows you don't leave the Boardwalk."

"They might want to use me as a patsy," Jerry says.

CB shakes his head. "Not Larry. He'll lean on you, tell you all the nasty things the department will do if you talk about this—and I recommend not talking about it, pretty much for that reason—but other than that he'll leave you alone. Maybe even bribe you to shut up, if you play it right."

Jerry looks thoughtful as he tries to figure out how to play it right.

CB laughs. "Get me a beer, will you? Put it on my *new* tab."

The police arrive half an hour later, led by one Lieutenant Larry Hoydt: a rail-thin, bespectacled, balding man who radiates contempt for everything around him. He is flanked by two officers who look more like thugs than policemen: large, muscular, thick-necked men. When he sees CB at the bar, he shouts "You!" and gestures. The officers flank CB, one on each side.

CB casually finishes his drink, nods to each in turn, then spins around on his stool, hooks his elbows on the back of the bar, and grins at Hoydt. "Heya Larry. Got here faster than I expected."

"Are you gonna show me these twelve bodies, or am I gonna have to improvise and settle for one?" Larry has a direct approach that makes him intimidating despite his meek appearance.

CB likes him. He can't tell if Larry is dirty but not committed to it, or if he's clean but he's given up trying. In Farraday City, that's a plus: most of the FCPD display great enthusiasm for corruption.

"Why Larry, it's wonderful to see you too," CB says. "OK, follow me. Your corpses are at sea level."

CB steps outside, the Lieutenant and his officers in tow. No one is outside but the police. They've closed off the area—roughly two blocks of the Boardwalk in all—and the Swordfish's parking lot is full of squad cars.

CB turns to the Lieutenant. "You guys had nothing else to do today?"

"Shut up," Hoydt says. "Habeas corpus."

CB takes them down to the beach, and back to the crime scene. Much to his surprise, he sees the police are already there: a forensics team stoops over one of the bodies, other uniformed men are strapping other bodies to gurneys, and someone is filming the entire crime scene.

They're still a few hundred feet from the spot when Hoydt says, "Let's stop right here."

"OK..." CB turns to the Lieutenant, confused. "Looks like your boys managed to find the stiffs without any help from me. Why did you want me to show you this spot again?"

"Because," Hoydt says, "I didn't want anyone to overhear us have this little conversation."

The two officers at his side look at CB with an aura of cool menace.

CB looks from officer to officer to Hoydt. "Didn't think it would go this way, Larry."

"Shut up," the Lieutenant snaps, then lowers his voice so it's barely audible over the surf. "They're just for *show*. My bosses think I'm threatening to make your life a living hell unless you pretend like this never happened."

CB nods slowly. "I see. And what are you really doing, Larry?"

"Oh, I'm still going to do that," he says. "I know better than to piss *them* off. But just between you, me, Marty and Pete here—and it *better* stay between us—my heart just won't be in it. There are things I might do in other situations that I just won't be able to bring myself to do here, because this thing is way the hell outta my league."

CB frowns. "What thing?"

"I can't tell you that!" Lieutenant Hoydt looks over CB's shoulder at the team processing the scene. "It'll take longer to explain this than it will to tell you to keep your nose out of it. Understand?"

CB nods again. The Lieutenant is trying to tell him the conversation is being watched.

"What I can tell you is that these corpses are going to be taken to the city morgue for quick identification, and that some of us will be there to compare notes on the case... and it *just might come to pass* that after we go home, say at eight or nine o'clock tonight, *someone* might accidentally leave his notes behind. And then a few hours later—let's say around eleven—he might *suddenly* remember and come back to pick them up, because it'd be bad news if he didn't show up at work with that information the next day." Hoydt stares straight at CB and raises his voice. "That was the *polite* request, asshole. And you really want to keep this polite. Got it?"

CB throws up his hands in mock surrender. "Got it, Lieutenant. Clear. Crystal. Now if you don't mind, I gotta go make good with Jerry. No way he's gonna get any decent business tonight now that the *police have him surrounded.*"

PART FOUR: FARRADAY CITY MORGUE

The Farraday City Morgue is a modern building, built when the crime families moved in and started renovating the city. The police stations, hospitals, and morgue are all state-of-the-art facilities. CB is amused that a city government so thoroughly owned by organized crime will spend so much money on a crime-fighting infrastructure—it seems counter-intuitive. Still, there's a difference between "well-run" and "honest"—the city faithfully protects the people who can afford to pay for that protection.

He finds the room where the bodies are stored by calling the morgue from a payphone and pretending to be one of the Mayor's aides, berating a nervous orderly who doesn't want to offend City Hall. An autopsy room is reserved for that case, and it's always kept locked and under armed guard. It's an interesting complication.

He arrives at the morgue at 8:30 PM. It's closed to the public by then, but it's trivial to get in—he loiters around one of the smoking areas until an orderly comes out for a smoke break, banters with his fellow smoker for a while, then sticks his foot in the door when the orderly goes back inside. Once inside, it's easy to stay out of sight: the evening shift is lightly staffed, and entire parts of the building are completely empty. Nobody expects to see him, so nobody does.

He makes his way to the room the nervous orderly described. Sure enough, when he peers around the last corner he sees a bored uniformed officer standing in front of the door, talking on a cell phone.

"Yeah, I don't know. All I know is, if I don't get her something this time I'm going to catch all kinds of hell, and I don't want to deal with it any more. You know? I mean, it's not like she's my wife or anything..."

CB looks at the cell phone and winks. It pops. The officer frowns, then starts shaking the phone.

"Crap..." The officer turns it over in his hands and pries open the back. "Oh, come on, I know it had more of a charge than that!" He looks down the hall apprehensively, and CB pulls back to stay out of sight. A second later, the officer swears again, and muttering under his breath about a spare battery, he disappears down a side hall.

CB waits a moment for the officer's footsteps to fade, then runs up to the locked door. He pulls out a thin, flat piece of metal from his trenchcoat pocket, wedges it between the door and frame, and pulls down forcefully. The door clicks, and pulls open easily. CB steps inside, pulls the door closed behind him, and re-locks it. A few moments later he hears the officer resume his post.

I'll have to figure that out later, CB thinks.

It's dark, so he fishes out his Mag-lite. He's in an office with four desks. Each desk has a computer. One of the desks has a stack of folders on it. Swinging double doors sit at the other end of the room.

CB picks up the folders and walks across the room, swinging open one of the doors and stepping through. It's the Autopsy Room, and it's large: rows upon rows of cold chambers are set into the walls. He lets the door swing shut behind him, then flips the light switch. Cold fluorescent lights flicker on, and he sees that all but six of the cold chambers have name tags—the room is almost full.

How long has this been going on?

The last twelve tagged chambers are John Does—those are the ones CB discovered today—but the others are identified. A quick scan of names suggests that all of the victims are men.

The autopsy table is empty and clean, so CB spreads out the folders, going through each in turn. The police reports go back as far as six months. Going through the folders, he realizes the bodies in this room are only for the recent crimes.

A serial killer, then. They're always cheerful cases.

Six months ago, the first known victims appeared—three men found laid out in an alleyway, arms and legs bound, gagged, throats cut. A month later, five more victims. Three weeks after that, another five. A month later, two more bodies, and for the last three months bodies have been popping up with increasing regularity, and in ever greater numbers. Seventy-three dead in all so far.

Toxicity reports show each victim had a form of anesthesia in their system, and the coroner suspects they were completely anesthetized before they were killed. The victims have little in common. There are victims with different races, different ages, different heights, different weights, and the brief background check added to each file suggests they're from different economic, political and religious backgrounds as well.

"In other words," CB mutters to himself, "other than being men, the only thing they have in common is the way they died."

He wonders about the anesthesia. It's an odd choice.

One of the folders holds a collection of police notes from each crime scene. CB studies these closely, trying to memorize every detail. Locations. Dates. Names of witnesses, possible suspects, possible motives, everything.

When he finishes the file he checks his watch—it's close to the time Larry said he'd be coming back for his notes. He hastily gathers each set and puts them back on the desk where he found them. He puts his ear next to the outer door, listening. He hears the guard humming to himself tonelessly.

Right.

Back in the autopsy room he rummages through some of the bins under the autopsy table until he finds a set of clean scrubs. He changes into them quickly, placing his trenchcoat into a large orange contaminated waste bag, then turns off the light as he leaves. He unlocks the outer door, opens it, and deliberately walks into the officer.

"Sorry," CB mutters.

"Hey!" The officer whirls around in alarm, hand on his pistol. "Who the hell are you?"

CB stares at the guard blankly, then laughs bitterly. "I'm the guy who drew the short straw. Make the new guy do it, right? I better not get screwed over on this overtime, that's all I'm saying." He stifles a yawn. "I hope you guys appreciate this. I don't see the rush myself. It's not like the jokers in there are suddenly going to get more dead."

The officer relaxes slightly. "I didn't know anyone was in there."

"Oh, that's just perfect. They tell me to stay late and then they forget to tell the guy with the gun."

The officer smirks. "Sounds right. Find anything?"

"No," CB says, "I didn't. Which, by an amazing coincidence, is what I told everybody I'd find. Same MO, same cause of death, same everything. Only now there's sand. Look... can I go?"

The guard laughs and waves him away. CB stalks off, still muttering to himself about bosses and overtime. When he's out of the officer's sight he grins, pulls off the scrubs, puts on his trenchcoat, and makes his way to the exit.

The police aren't blockading the Swordfish any more, but the news of the day's events has thinned the evening crowd considerably. When he walks into the bar, CB is greeted by one or two of the regulars and by Jerry's frosty stare.

CB sits at one of the empty stools at the bar and smiles brightly. "How's it going, Jerry?"

Jerry growls.

"That well? Great. How about a beer? Put it on my tab."

"No tabs tonight," Jerry says. "I'm losing a lot of business because of you."

"They'll be back tomorrow."

"I'm still losing money tonight."

"The hell you are," CB says. "I'll bet any odds you want that Lieutenant Hoydt paid you hush money to keep quiet about everything. It's probably more money than you'd make in a week."

He doesn't actually know any of this, but Jerry grunts in agreement.

"It's still a pain in the ass, though," Jerry says. "And don't you go spreading that around, either. If people hear the police are paying me money, they're going to start thinking I'm informing on them, and—"

"Shut up a minute." CB holds his hand up, cutting Jerry off. He stares hard at the TV. "Turn up the sound, OK?"

Jerry snorts. "What, the news? Why the hell would I—"

"Turn. Up. The. Sound." Something about the tone in CB's voice makes Jerry forget what he's going to say next. He turns up the TV.

"Everybody shut up a minute!" CB shouts, and the patrons in the bar settle down to stare at him curiously. CB ignores them. He stares up at the screen, transfixed, his expression a mix of interest and concern.

The TV shows the interior of an apartment—a posh one, from the look of it, with a view of what has to be Manhattan. Lots of glass and carpet—only the carpet is stained with blood, most of the glass is broken, and the furniture—nice furniture—is upended.

"...half an hour ago," a woman's voice says. "Police responded to the alarm and found the bodies of men in paramilitary uniforms, each armed with military-grade weapons. There are reports of another body on the scene who does not appear to have been associated with the attackers..."

"What's wrong, CB?" Jerry whispers.

"Shut up," CB says.

Then: "I recognize that apartment."

The picture cuts back to the newsroom, where an attractive, well-manicured anchorwoman gazes serenely into the camera. "We do not currently have any information on the identity of the victim, but we expect to hear a statement from the police any minute now—hold on please—I'm getting a report the police are issuing a statement now. We're switching to our team on location to report this statement live."

The camera changes to show a small podium erected in front of a building CB doesn't recognize. Police line both sides of the podium, and an older man—CB recognizes him as the New York City Chief of Police—walks past the men and takes position behind the podium.

"I'm going to get right to the point," the Chief says.

The entire bar is silent. CB hears his heart beating in his chest.

"I know you all have questions, but I'm not going to answer them now. I'm going to issue a brief statement now, with a more thorough press conference in the following days. This evening, roughly an hour ago, armed men stormed the private residence of retired Army Captain Alexander Morgan, better known as the hero Liberty..."

CB tenses. A wave of whispers roll through the bar, countered by frantic shushing noises until the bar quiets again.

"Based on an initial assessment of the crime scene, it appears that Captain Morgan was taken by surprise. He was able to fight off most of his attackers..."

The bar patrons mutter their approval. Even in Farraday City, Liberty is admired.

"Unfortunately..." The Chief's voice catches. The room falls silent. "Unfortunately, Captain Morgan was not..." His voice catches again, and he clears his throat huskily. "Was not able to defend himself against all attackers. While he drove them off, he was wounded in the assault, and..."

The Chief looks up from his prepared statement. His eyes glisten in the camera lights.

"It is my solemn and unfortunate duty to report that Captain Alexander Morgan was pronounced dead at Mercy Hospital at 10:37 PM. Apparent cause of death was a gunshot wound to the head. This has been ruled as homicide and no expense will be spared by this department to find the responsible party."

The TV switches back to the anchorwoman. She's trying to keep up a professional facade, but it's not going to last. Her right hand grips a pen so tightly her knuckles are white.

"We'll... we'll return after these messages with more updates and analysis on this tragic event," she says.

The screen fades to black, then cuts to commercial. The bar sits in stunned silence. Finally, CB stands, expression unreadable.

"Jerry."

Jerry looks at him nervously. "Yeah."

"I'm going to need to borrow your phone again."

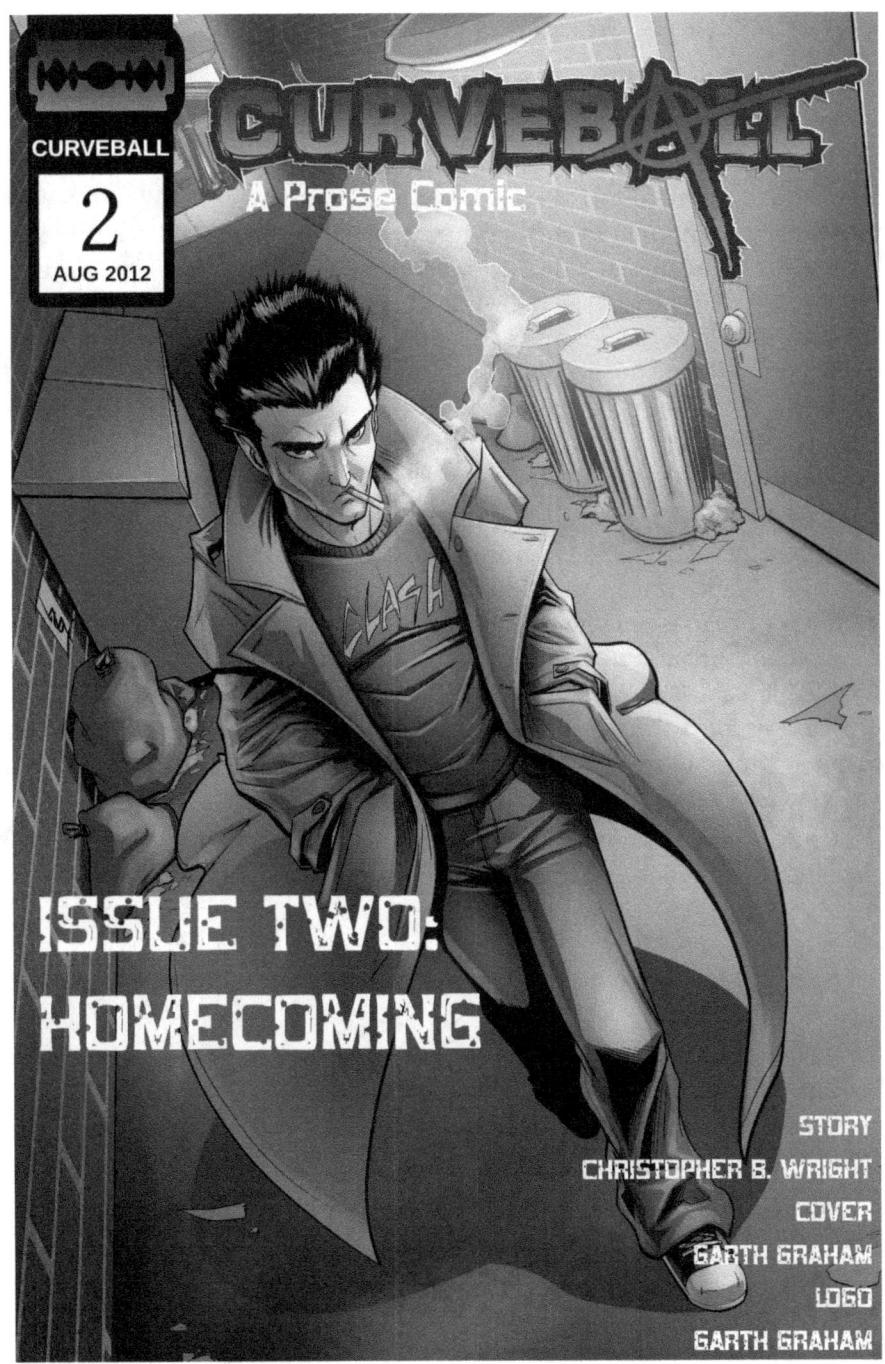

PART ONE: OBITUARY

ALEXANDER THOMAS MORGAN, 1920-2011. Soldier, hero, and humanitarian, he died at the age of 91.

Alexander Morgan, son of Ira and Adelle Morgan, born February 17, 1920 in Baltimore, MD. His father was a sailor and veteran of World War I. Morgan was raised to love his country, and had often said his father's example instilled in him a desire to serve in the Armed Forces from a very early age. At the age of 18 he joined the Army, and immediately volunteered for the now-famous Project Paragon, the United States' response to Germany's Ubermann Initiative. As the most successful and visible "byproduct" of Project Paragon, he fought on the front lines against the Axis and became a rallying figure for many of the soldiers across all Allied forces, not just American, but British, French, even Russian.

During the war Morgan was promoted to Lieutenant and finally to Captain. After the war he intended to settle down, but it was at this point that the "atomic humans"—a phrase eventually replaced by the term "meta-humans"—began to emerge. Morgan found himself called out of civilian life in order to combat a new menace, this time largely civilian, consisting of atomic humans who used their abilities to gain wealth and power by force. Morgan resumed the mantle of Liberty and joined forces with the Living Flame, Titan, and the Whispering Man to form the Protectors, the first hero group to receive official government sanction.

This sanction proved to be short-lived. The House Un-American Activities Committee began to investigate charges that some self-styled heroes were communists, and while Liberty was never charged or investigated, the Whispering Man was called to testify. When the Whispering Man refused and turned vigilante, the Protectors were forced to disband.

It was during the post-Protector era that the effects of Project Paragon became apparent: Morgan was now in his late thirties but still had the physique of a man in his early twenties. By the 1960s it became apparent that his aging process had slowed drastically.

The 60s showed a decline in public opinion toward Morgan's role as the hero Liberty. Changes in society and the emergence of the youth counterculture led to a growing distrust in authority figures, and Liberty was seen as part of "the system." Still, even when his popularity was at its ebb he had unexpected admirers: Abbie Hoffman once said, "when you meet Liberty you remember why this America thing sounded like a good deal in the first place. Then you look around, and you realize he's the only part of the deal that's left."

In the 60s and 70s Liberty took stances on social issues that, for a time, alienated him from the establishment he was so closely associated with. He supported the Civil Rights Movement, though he remained an outspoken critic of its militant fringes such as the Weathermen and the Black Panthers. He was deeply opposed to the Vietnam war, primarily because he felt the draft had been manipulated in a way that disproportionately chose the poor. His opposition to the war made him very unpopular with Presidents Lyndon Johnson and Richard Nixon. One of the more famous Nixon tapes features a nineteen-minute rant where the President accuses Liberty of collaborating with Jewish and Homosexual co-conspirators to undermine his presidency.

In the mid-70s, Liberty joined another hero group, the New Vanguard. The New Vanguard focused on disrupting the drug trade in New York City, and was responsible for thwarting a plot to destroy the United Nations by the Reichstaadt, a meta-human Neo-Nazi group. The New Vanguard disbanded in the early 80s, and Liberty resumed a career as a solo hero until he partnered with reformed villain Curveball for the last half of the 80s and through the 90s. In 1989, Liberty and Curveball joined the Guardians of Justice, another New York hero group led by Robert Thorpe, the high-tech hero Gladiator. The Guardians disbanded shortly after 9/11 when Thorpe refused to allow the newly-formed Department of Homeland Security to take control of the group.

After the Guardians disbanded, Morgan returned to civilian life and devoted himself to humanitarian work. He refused to make any public statements concerning the divisive and turbulent political division that characterized the first decade of the 21st century.

Morgan is survived by two children, Juliet and Alexander Jr, five grandchildren, and fourteen great-grandchildren.

A private memorial service will be held for family and close friends, with a public service following. The family requests that in lieu of flowers or other sympathy offerings, donations be made to the American Legion.

PART TWO: MANHATTAN, 1977

It's October in Manhattan, and it's cold. The wind is cutting today—it races down man-made tunnels, towering walls of concrete and steel channeling it. Shaping it. Focusing it. Stories above the ground the wind is truly fierce and cold: birds keep to their perches, apartment dwellers keep their windows closed, and window washers take the day off. At ground level, the wind isn't as fierce, but it still carries a sting. It feels more like mid-November than early October, and the pedestrians hurrying down the street wrap their coats tightly around them in an effort to beat back the chill.

CB, Sin and Billy lean against a chain link fence separating a back alley from the sidewalk. The fence is cold, but the trio sport expressions of disinterest and unconcern. CB is a thin, tall, lanky young man with thick, spiky hair. He watches each pedestrian as they pass hurriedly by, his cigarette drooping out the side of his mouth in a sneering fashion. His hands are thrust into the pockets of a ragged gray German pea coat covered in makeshift patches and safety pins. Sin, a heavyset, bald Asian, wears a thick green army jacket and an utterly bored expression. He tilts his head back against the fence and watches people passing by through mostly-closed eyes. Billy, the shortest of the three, wears a worn leather jacket two sizes too small. His bleach-white hair is combed into a "v" shape that falls down over his forehead.

"I'm bored," Sin says. A woman passing in front of them sidesteps three paces at the sound of his voice, looks at them nervously, and hurries on.

CB grins. "Just wait. They'll be here any minute."

"Hope so," Billy grumbles. "I'm *cold*."

CB glances at Billy, annoyed. "Nobody's making you stay."

"Shut up, CB. It's cold is all I'm saying. And don't tell me you don't feel it, even with that coat."

CB shrugs. "They should show up soon. Yeah, there we go. Look down there. That's the van."

Sin and Billy look. A black-and-gold custom Dodge van drives slowly down the street toward them. It has smoke-tinted windows, revealing only a vague, indistinct shape in the driver's seat.

Sin arches an eyebrow. "That?"

CB frowns. "Yes, *that*. What?"

"It seems sort of..." Sin trails off, looks hard at the van, then shrugs. "It seems sort of hip for something a villain would drive."

"Why would a meta even drive?" Billy asks. "I mean, don't they all fly or something?"

"God, Billy, just *shut up*," CB says. "They don't *all* fly. Moron."

Billy glowers. "Well what do they do, then?"

"No clue," CB says. "Some kind of mental crap, I think. Buddy's working a new bar and he overheard two guys talking about these guys." He gestures to the van. "Said they were going to rob the S&L."

Directly across the street is a large concrete building. The sign *Manhattan Thrift* sits above a set of large double doors. The van slows down and comes to a stop a block from the building, engine idling.

"This is *fucking stupid*," Billy says. "A Savings & Loan? Why the fuck would you rob a Savings & Loan? I mean, if you're a meta. Shouldn't you be trying to take over the world with giant robots and ray guns or something?"

"Yeah," CB says. "If you're a mad scientist. These guys aren't mad scientists. Like I said, I don't know what they do. Maybe they make zombie slaves. But Buddy said they're totally strung out. They're so deep into horse it's all they can think about. They're robbing the place to feed their habit."

"We're here to watch *junkies*?" Sin's voice drips with contempt. "How is this not a big waste of time?"

"Well first it's better than being *in school*," CB snaps. "And they're not just junkies. They're junkies with *super powers*. But also Liberty is five blocks away from us right now."

Sin and Billy fall silent. They watch the van with interest.

"How do you know?" Billy asks.

CB rolls his eyes. "Hell, Billy, *everybody* knows that."

"I didn't know that," Sin says.

"Everybody who bothers to read the *newspaper* knows that. He's at a convention giving a speech. But if he hears metas are attacking a bank? Come on, you *know* he's going to show up."

The gold-and-black van moves again, pulling out into traffic and traveling a block until it once again pulls over to the curb and slows to a halt—this time, right in front of the S&L.

"Who do we want to win?" Sin asks abruptly.

CB frowns. "Hard to say. I mean, on the one hand, it'd be kind of awesome if a van full of junkies just happened to kick Captain Flagpants' ass up and down the street, you know? On the other hand... he's going to be outnumbered."

"Yeah," Billy says. "If he took on the odds and won, that'd be pretty awesome."

"But he's The Man," Sin protests.

"True," Billy says.

"Yeah," CB says, "but it's not like they're the vanguard of the revolution. It's a van full of junkies. All they do is suck up air I could be breathing."

"I hear it's really cool to watch Liberty fight," Billy says.

"Hope we find out." CB tenses with excitement as he sees the driver-side door open. "Hold on. I think they're getting out of the van."

A white man with very kinky, curly hair, sideburns, sunglasses, a paisley-print shirt and flared jeans gets out and walks around the front of the van to the other side.

"God damn it." CB flicks ash from his cigarette in irritation, then carelessly discards the still-glowing remainder on the sidewalk. "They would have to park right in front of the bank. We're not going to be able to see a thing. Come on."

He propels himself off the fence and starts across the street.

Sin's eyes go wide. "Really? That's—OK, wait up." He grabs Billy by the collar and pulls him along.

"Hey!" Billy squawks, stumbles, and hurries in order to regain his footing. "I'm coming! Let go!"

CB jogs catty-corner across the street, ignoring the honking from the cars rushing past in both directions as he dodges traffic with the practiced ease of a native. When he reaches the other side he's twenty or thirty feet from the van, and has an unobstructed view. Four men stand in front of the van, all facing each other. They're all dressed like the driver: big hair, sunglasses, sideburns, flared jeans, paisley shirts.

CB shakes his head in disbelief. "Is that supposed to be their uniform, or something?"

"Is *what* supposed to be their uniform?" Sin asks. He steps up to the curb to join CB, puffing slightly from the effort of dodging traffic while pulling Billy helplessly along in his wake, then turns to look down the sidewalk, toward the van. "What are you talking—oh. Huh."

Billy manages to pry himself free of Sin's grip, looks at the four men standing in front of the van, and laughs. "*Hippies?* Jesus, CB."

"Shut up. I didn't dress them. What are they doing?"

Sin shakes his head. "They're standing in a circle holding hands. *Kum ba yah* is next, right?"

"No... look!" CB's voice is tight with excitement. "There's some kind of glow. You see the glow?"

It's faint at first—a slight ripple in the air around the outlines of the men, all standing in a circle, holding hands, heads bowed. It looks like the shimmer of a hot sidewalk in summer, but it's too cold for that. Seconds pass, the shimmering solidifies, until all at once a nimbus of blue energy surrounds them, translucent, obscuring their features.

"Holy shit," Billy whispers.

The glow intensifies, brightens, until it's so strong their features are completely hidden by light. All at once the light flares, bright enough to create new shadows on the ground from the objects around it.

"What are they *doing*?" Sin asks.

The glow is so bright CB has to throw his arm across his eyes. The four men are completely obscured by the light, and CB is dimly aware of the sound of cars screeching to a halt, crashing into each other, steel smashing into steel.

"Power to the people!" one of them shouts.

"Power to the people!" the others shout back.

All at once the air *ripples* and fills with an intense *thummm*. The men are gone; in their place is a single humanoid shape, glowing with blinding radiance. It's nearly nine feet in height, roughly the shape of a man but flatter and wider, like a paper cutout with burning edges.

It looks like light set on fire.

"God damn it, CB," Sin growls.

The creature whips around toward the sound of Sin's voice. CB, Sin and Billy all take an involuntary step back. It stares at them for a moment. CB can't breathe. He can feel *heat* radiating from it, heat and power. It could kill them, he realizes—all of them, easily. He tenses and wonders if he can dive behind the green Oldsmobile station wagon to his right before it strikes. Then, slowly, it turns away to face the Savings & Loan. It emits a low, rumbling growl.

CB hears Billy exhale sharply, Sin swear softly under his breath. They all crouch behind the Oldsmobile and watch.

The rumbling growl escalates quickly, shifting into a high-pitched shriek of rage. It's not a sound made by men. CB doesn't know what happened to the four men who created this thing, but there's no trace of humanity in it now. It lashes out with its arms, striking toward the side of the S&L: energy streams out of its fiery, paper-thin arms and burrows into the wall. CB feels a wave of intense heat as some of the concrete shatters from the force of the strike, and the rest actually begins to *melt*.

Burrrrrrrrrrrn. The word is barely understandable, but the creature repeats it over and over like a mantra. More of the wall melts. CB can hear people screaming in terror. He hears the sound of horns, frantically honking to no effect. He doesn't bother to look behind him—he can't. He stares at the glowing thing, fascinated.

"This doesn't look like a bunch of junkies robbing a bank," Billy says.

"No," CB agrees. "Really doesn't."

The building is starting to sag on one side. The heat isn't just affecting the S&L, it's damaging the buildings on either side of it as well. *Burrrrrrrrrn*. CB wonders if it's trying to burn through the wall or is deliberately trying to collapse the building. It shouldn't be too much longer before it collapses. *Burrrrrrrrn*.

"Where's Liberty?" Sin asks. "That thing is going to kill a lot of people. I don't want to see that."

An explosion erupts from the door of the Savings & Loan. No, not an explosion—a gunshot. An armed guard carrying a heavy-caliber revolver stands in the doorway, firing at the glowing creature. The noise is deafening—CB has never heard a gun fired so close to him before, and he's surprised at how loud it is. The bullets flash and disappear before they reach the creature, but it too hears the noise, and turns.

Burrrrrn. One arm extends to the guard, and energy covers him. The guard screams, but only briefly. Then he *disappears*. CB recoils in horror as he smells burning ash.

"Holy shit," Sin says. "They killed that guy! They just killed him!"

Sin bolts from behind the Oldsmobile and darts across the street. Traffic is at a complete standstill. A four-car pileup blocks both lanes, but nobody cares about that—not even the people in the accident. There aren't many onlookers—most have run away at this point, and the few who remain look like they won't be hanging around much longer. Sin leaps over the hood of a car and runs to the other side of the street, then takes off down the sidewalk as fast as he can run.

"Sin! Wait!" CB calls out after his friend, but Sin doesn't look back. A moment later, Billy follows in kind. CB is alone behind the car.

The creature returns its attention to the bank, focusing its energies on the wall. CB smells smoke—the blast that killed the security guard also melted through the glass doors and set the interior of the building ablaze. He can hear cries for help inside, but nobody runs out.

He hopes there's a back door. He hopes they use it.

And then, suddenly, a streak of motion—something races past CB's field of vision and streaks toward the creature in a blur. It's not until the object begins to melt that CB realizes it's a manhole cover. It doesn't get close enough to touch the creature, but it is noticed all the same. The creature turns.

"Stop what you're doing. *Now!*" The voice is loud and commanding.

CB turns to look. Standing on one of the abandoned cars in the middle of the street is a man wearing blue-and-brown body armor. On his chest is a stylized flag with a single star. Hanging from his belt, where most people would expect to see a gun, is a large truncheon.

Liberty is here.

He's clean-shaven, blonde-haired, blue-eyed, and has a classically strong jaw. CB immediately dislikes him. He's holding something—CB can't tell exactly what it is, but it reminds him of a harpoon. Liberty looks at the creature without fear.

The air around the creature surges with power as it continues to repeat the word *Burrrrrrn*.

"I have its attention," Liberty says. He doesn't sound entirely happy about this. "Ready?"

"Ready!" The voice comes from above. CB looks up and gapes. Floating about thirty feet in the air is something that looks like a flattened pontoon boat without a top. A man in his early twenties stands on it, grasping what looks like a radio receiver in his right hand.

Liberty steels himself, then hefts the "harpoon" in his right hand and throws. It flies through the air toward the creature, and to CB's surprise it does *not* melt—it tears through the creature with a flash of blue and sinks into the bubbling, melted concrete.

The creature roars and lashes out, a wave of energy surging toward Liberty. At the same time, Liberty leaps to one side—the energy washes over the car where he'd originally stood, and the car is torn to pieces, parts of it melted into slag before his eyes. CB smells gasoline, but there's no time for it to ignite.

Something glints off the light. A line, a cable so thin CB didn't see it originally, connects to the end of the harpoon, travels through the creature, then attaches itself to the floating sky platform at the other end.

The creature doesn't notice—it's too intent on destroying Liberty. It sweeps the energy toward him, and he runs. The ground bubbles and melts behind him as he runs toward the thing. The creature howls in rage and a patch of sidewalk behind Liberty turns into a pool of liquid concrete.

CB is sweating now. The side of the Oldsmobile he's hiding behind is almost too hot to touch.

Liberty carries a second harpoon. Now that CB knows what to look for he sees that it, too, has a thin cable attaching it to the floating platform. He's wincing—CB can only imagine how hot it must be, as close to the creature as he is—and as he darts past the glowing thing parts of his costume begin to smolder. The creature raises its arms to strike again, but Liberty throws himself toward the melted portion of the wall, touches the end of his harpoon against the exposed metal of the first, and shouts "Now!"

The man on the platform closes his fist over the thing that looks like a radio receiver. The air crackles with energy, fills with the smell of ozone, and hairs stand up on the back of CB's neck.

The creature screams in a mixture of pain and rage. The current—whatever it is—passes through the cable, and thus through it. Immediately it starts to flicker, like a light bulb burning through its filament, and then all at once it falls apart into four separate man-sized pieces. The glow fades, the humming stops, and four men dressed in flared jeans and paisley shirts lie motionless on the ground. A short distance from them, Liberty slumps over as he drops the second harpoon. It falls to the concrete with a dull *clang*.

"Ouch," Liberty says.

The floating platform lowers, emitting a strange pulsing, buzzing noise as it does, and when it's about five feet off the ground the young man leaps off it and runs toward him.

"Are you all right?" the man asks.

"Don't worry about me." Liberty picks himself up off the ground. "We need to get into that building and help the—"

"No we don't," the other man says. "Fire and Rescue went in the back and got everyone out of the building. I was in contact with the dispatcher while you were fighting... them. Are you sure you're OK?"

Liberty nods and waves him away. "Take care of those," he says, motioning toward the four prone men. "I'm fine."

He doesn't look fine to CB, but he does look alive. That's impressive enough.

The other man obediently stops at each of the unconscious figures and turns them on their stomachs, puts their hands behind their backs, and places a pair of handcuffs on each of them. "I told you not to touch the metal." His voice is tight with worry. "I told you that if you were touching the metal when the two bars made contact—which you were—you would complete the circuit—which you did. You could have died."

"I didn't die," Liberty says, and stands. "Sorry, Doc. The first bar was half-sunk in the wall. I had to hold the second to make sure they kept contact. I figured I could handle the surge."

The other man stands and walks over to Liberty, frowning. "Well, we'd better fly you to a hospital and get you checked out."

Liberty shakes his head. "We need to get these four in the Pit," he says. "We can check up on me later. We don't want them... doing... that again."

Liberty frowns, then turns to look straight at CB. The second man follows his gaze and his eyes widen in surprise. CB is standing not much more than ten feet from them, listening to their conversation with undisguised interest.

"Shouldn't you be in school, son?" Liberty asks.

Immediately the finger goes up. It's purely instinctive, and it takes a moment for CB to realize he's just flipped the greatest hero of World War II the bird. He puts his hands in his jacket pockets, but doesn't bother looking embarrassed. Instead, he looks over his shoulder at the floating platform.

"What the hell is that thing?"

"It's my car," the other man says. "And you are...?"

CB doesn't reply. "It's just floating there," he observes. "No engines on it that I can see. It's not like the hoverjets they're talking about at Skylar Industries. Those would be setting small cars on fire right now..."

"Uh..." The younger man is clearly thrown off by the observation.

"That's right, they're not jets. It's new. Who *are* you?"

"Son," Liberty cuts in smoothly, "the police are going to be here pretty soon. If you are, in fact, supposed to be in school, I expect being a witness to a crime scene will make your life inconvenient."

CB turns away from the floating platform to look at Liberty, considering his words. "Good fight," he says finally. "Neat trick with the hooks." With that he starts walking down the sidewalk, away from the smoking S&L and away from the scene of the crime.

"Why did you let him go?" the other man asks. "He *was* a witness, right? Aren't we supposed to question him or something?"

"He was hiding behind that Oldsmobile when we got here," Liberty says. "Trying not to get killed. I couldn't get to him without putting him in more danger, and I don't feel like making his day any worse. The important thing is we got Abel and his boys. Now let's make sure they don't cause any more problems..."

PART THREE: ARRIVAL, NYC

The Greyhound bus comes to a shuddering halt at the 42nd Street Port Authority Bus Terminal, rocking slightly in place before the bus doors open and passengers shuffle out one by one. CB steps down onto the curb, rubbing his neck as he tries to work out all the kinks that come from sleeping hunched over on a bus bench. He waits silently as the driver opens up the baggage area, then joins the mob of other passengers as they fish through the luggage, finally picking up his own: an old green army bag. He throws the bag over his shoulder and makes his way down 8th Avenue, grateful for a chance to stretch his legs.

It's the middle of the day; the street is filled with people. It's a far cry from Farraday City, where almost everything important happens at night. But he knows it will be just as busy at night as it is during the day. There's a reason it's called "the city that never sleeps."

He stops at the corner of 8th and 42nd a moment, taking everything in. He's right on the corner of the Theater District; to the west, eventually, is Hell's Kitchen. That doesn't mean quite what it did in the 80s and 90s. Even then, it didn't mean what it had in the 70s.

He hears a loud *thooom* in the distance, followed by the sound of sirens. The people around him don't break step, don't look up. They're used to it by now. It's probably a "spandex fight" and will cost New York City a small fortune to clean up after it. CB looks at the locals and grins. They'd be a lot less jaded if it were happening right in front of them, but the one thing you have to say about New Yorkers is that they're adaptable.

He adjusts his duffel bag and steps off the curb, intending to head to one of the hot dog stands on the other side of the street. Instead, he feels something twist and fold over onto itself—a familiar sensation—as reality rearranges itself, ever so slightly. A second later he hears the screech of tires and frantic honking.

CB looks to his right and sees a silver Toyota stopped mere inches from him. The driver-side door opens, and an agitated woman climbs out.

"What the hell is your problem?" She sounds more alarmed than angry. "Didn't you see the light?"

CB looks up and sees the pedestrian light is green, the letters WALK blinking above it. The woman, a blonde-haired, pretty twenty-something sees it as well, and shakes her head in confusion: her traffic light is also green.

So that's the way it's going to be then.

"Sorry," CB says. He frowns. She looks vaguely familiar. "Have we met?"

The woman narrows her eyes. "Nice try, creep. Why don't you take your retro-stalker self and go—*CB*?"

CB cocks his head to one side and studies her more closely. "*Jenny?*"

The woman colors slightly. It is her. For a moment CB actually feels his age.

They stare at each other in shock. A car honks impatiently behind hers.

"Get in," Jenny says. "I'll give you a lift."

CB doesn't hesitate. As Jenny climbs back into the driver's seat, he jogs over to the passenger side, throws his bag in the back, and climbs in.

The car behind them honks again, but the light has already turned red. He hears someone swearing at them. Jenny doesn't react.

"I didn't think you were going to come," she says. "Nobody did."

"Of course I was going to come." CB sounds a little hurt. "He was my best friend."

"Funny way of showing it," Jenny says, then blushes. "Sorry."

CB shrugs. "It's fair."

"You stopped visiting." She sounds angry and hurt.

"Yeah," he says. "Figured it was for the best. And for the record, your great-grandfather agreed with me."

Jenny looks like she doesn't believe him. CB shrugs again. "What happened, anyway? When did you grow up? I mean... when did you lose your braces?"

Jenny laughs. "I'm out of college now, old man." The light turns green and they set off down 42nd Street. "I have a job and everything. And why don't you have the decency to look your age? Mom is going to be *pissed* about that. How is that even possible?"

"Hell if I know," CB says. "Alex was 91 and he looked almost exactly the way he did when World War II ended. How does *that* work?"

"That's Project Paragon," Jenny says. "We have an explanation for him. Nobody even really knows what it is you *do*."

CB grins. "And for the record... 'retro-stalker self?' What the *hell*."

Jenny's grin looks a little bit like his. She drives much faster than the speed limit, weaving in and out of traffic with expert precision and control. They turn right on Park Avenue, and she glances over at him, expression unreadable.

"Something wrong?" CB asks.

"Depends," Jenny says.

"Should I have stayed away?"

"No." Jenny frowns. "It's not that. I mean, we'll all be glad to see you. And apparently he wanted you to deliver his eulogy."

"Yeah..." CB stares out the window and absently reaches for a cigarette.

"Don't even think of it." Jenny's voice is sharp. "And while you're at it, put on a seatbelt. We get fined now."

They cross 17th Street. Park Avenue becomes Union Square East. The light is green.

CB puts the cigarette away, but makes no move to buckle up.

"Jesus, CB, what's your problem? Death wish? Nobody smokes any more. It's not even considered cool. And do you want to go hurtling through a windshield at 80 miles an hour?"

"Not really," CB says, "it hurts like hell."

Jenny snorts. They cross 14th Street. Union Square East becomes Broadway. The light is green.

"So what is it?" CB asks. "Do I have a kid?"

Jenny laughs. "Not that I know of. Were you expecting one?"

"I don't know," CB says, "but the way you're looking at me, I figure it's something *bad*."

"Not bad," Jenny says, "just weird. I haven't seen you in ten years. You look exactly the same now as you did then, and then you looked fifteen years younger than you should have."

"How do you think I feel?" CB asks. "Ten years later and you're not a kid any more."

"I'm supposed to get older, CB. You're not supposed to stay young."

"Guess so," CB says. He stares out the window, brooding.

They turn left onto Canal St. The light is green. Jenny takes them across the Manhattan Bridge into Brooklyn.

"The government's here," Jenny says.

"Ah." CB's mouth twists into a bitter smile, then he shrugs. "Well, that makes sense. And it's not like I'm a fugitive or anything."

"Pete Travers is here."

"Pete? Damn." CB sighs, starts to reach for a cigarette, and stops. "Well. That makes sense. It could be worse."

"Could it?" Jenny looks at him curiously. "That's not the impression I got ten years ago."

"I was *really pissed off* ten years ago. Ten years ago the government tried to eminent domain my ass and turn me into some kind of goddamn... I don't know what. It wasn't Pete's fault. He was just the messenger."

"Is that why you broke his jaw?" Jenny asks softly.

CB sighs again. "Like I said. I was *really pissed off*."

Jenny turns sharply into a private alley, and comes to a sudden stop alongside a familiar-looking brownstone town house. CB looks at it in surprise. "I thought your dad was going to sell this thing."

"He couldn't bring himself to do it," Jenny says. "Come on, everyone should be inside."

CB leaves his bag in the back. The gravel crunches beneath his boots as he stands in front of Jenny's car and stares at the house.

"Well?" Jenny waits expectantly. CB doesn't move.

Jenny frowns slightly. "You OK?"

CB doesn't answer. He stares at the house.

"They're going to be happy to see you," Jenny says reassuringly.

"Yeah," CB says. "I guess."

"Maybe I should go in first," Jenny says. "Tell everyone you're here."

CB nods slowly. Jenny stares at him a moment longer, then turns to the front of the house. She disappears around the corner, leaving CB alone with his ghosts.

CB pulls the cigarette out of his pocket. His hands tremble as he lights it.

They're going to be old.

He hadn't expected that. He feels stupid for not expecting that. He stares down at the gravel and smokes in silence.

The sound of a car coming up the gravel drive breaks him out of his reverie. He looks up to see a charcoal gray Subaru Forrester come to a halt just behind Jenny's car. The door opens almost before the engine is turned off, and CB hears a strangled yell of surprise and excitement as a well-polished leather shoe sets down on the gravel from behind the door.

"CB?"

CB looks up sharply as the figure gets out of the car. A young man with short-cropped blond hair and ice-blue eyes stares at him, grinning in astonishment.

CB blinks twice, then puts a name to the face. "*Andy*? Dammit, you got older too?"

Andrew Stuart Forrest, Jenny's older brother, slams the door shut and barrels toward CB, crushing him in a massive bear hug. He laughs as he lifts CB a full foot off the ground.

"I didn't think you were coming!" Andy says. "I mean, we hoped. But we figured you wouldn't want to. When did you get here?"

He sets CB back down on the ground, and CB tries to remember how to breathe. Eventually he notices Andy's wearing the dress blue uniform of an Army Captain.

"What are you staring at?" Andy asks, looking defensive.

"When did you enlist?" CB asks.

"ROTC in college," Alex says, "just like I always said I would."

"You look just like your great-grandfather," CB says. "Just damn like him."

Andy beams.

"And you have his grip, too…"

"When did you get here?" Andy asks. "How long are you staying?"

"Just got here," CB says. "Ran into your sister getting off the bus. Almost literally. She's inside telling your folks I'm here."

"And you're smoking up the courage to go in after," Andy says. Andy was always good at noticing things like that.

CB shrugs. "At any rate. I'm here for the service, at least. I might stick around a little after that."

"Are you going to look into who did it?" Andy asks.

"I think it's probably better for everyone if he doesn't answer that question," a voice behind CB says.

CB turns. A slightly overweight, balding man in a cheap gray suit looks at them both, a polite, slightly friendly, carefully neutral expression on his face.

Andy coughs, and shifts uneasily. CB and the other man stare at each other in silence.

"Pete Travers," CB says finally.

"CB," Travers says.

The silence that follows is even more awkward than the first. Finally, Travers sticks out his hand. CB takes it, and they shake.

"You're pretty quiet for an old fat guy," CB says. "You managed to get right behind me. And I didn't even see you come round the corner."

Travers barks a laugh. "There's a back door, remember? Asshole." His hand goes up to his jaw. It's an unconscious gesture, but CB looks away.

"There he is!" Another familiar voice booms out from the front of the house, and CB turns to see Martin Forrest, Alexander Morgan's favorite grandson-in-law, step around the corner, grinning wide.

"Heya Marty!" CB drops the rest of his cigarette and grinds it into the gravel with the heel of his boot.

Martin is taller than CB, and wider. He's in pretty good shape for his age, and he still has the briskly cheerful no-nonsense demeanor he had when he was on the force... but he's softer around the middle than he was ten years ago, and his hair is mostly white.

Martin claps his son on the shoulder as he passes, then shakes CB's hand warmly. "When my daughter told us you were outside it caused something of a stir. The Junior Senator from New York finds himself in a dilemma."

"Ah," CB says. "I was hoping Toby wouldn't be here."

"Well the feeling is mutual." Martin laughs. "He wishes he wasn't here too. But..." He sobers for a moment. "He loves his grandfather too."

CB sighs. "Yeah."

"Anyway," Martin says, "I'm damned glad to see you, and you need to pick up that bag out of the back of Jenny's car, because you're staying here."

CB starts to protest, but Martin waves him off. "Get the bag. And hurry up. It's cold out here, and Juliet wants to see you."

CB laughs and gets his bag from the car.

PART FOUR: HARUSPEX ANALYTICS, TOP FLOOR

The boardroom is large and windowless. It's the first time Jason Kline has ever been in it, and something feels off balance. He fidgets in his seat, occasionally rubbing his eyes, chastising himself for not getting enough sleep the night before.

"Mr. Kline, how long have you been employed at Haruspex Analytics?"

The room is dimly lit, and the Chairman is almost covered in shadow. Jason can see him at the far end of the table, but not clearly. He's leaning back in his chair, chin resting on his hand. The light is too dim to see his expression. Jason expects that's intentional.

The other members of the board are easier to see, but they stare at him impassively, waiting for his answer. They're not your usual board—there's a pretty good mix of sexes, races, even ages. One of the board members actually looks younger than Jason. But they all stare at him impassively, betraying no emotion, waiting for his response. It adds to the unevenness of the room.

"Five years, sir." Jason's voice cracks slightly. There's something wrong with the room and he can't figure out what it is.

The Chairman waves slightly with his free hand, and a holographic image displays in the middle of the table. Jason has seen this once or twice, and the technology is fascinating: it always looks like you're looking directly at a flat display, no matter what angle you view it from. It appears to be his personnel file.

"Five years," the Chairman says. His voice is strong and rich. There's experience in that voice, experience tinged with humor and anger both. It doesn't speak to a specific age, though Jason suspects he's older. In his fifties, perhaps. "And you've done very well for us. According to this file your service has been exemplary."

"Yes sir," Jason says. He's not an arrogant man, but he doesn't believe in false modesty. "I have." He forces himself to acknowledge this: he has done incredible work in the last five years. Whatever they're doing in this room to put him off balance, reminding himself of that helps him regain his focus.

"Tell us about your latest project."

Jason steels himself. He doesn't like delivering bad news. "My group was tasked with locating and gaining access to an email account. To date we have been unable to do so. We've only been working on it for a few days, and we certainly haven't run out of options, but in my professional opinion we probably aren't going to be able to do it."

"I don't want excuses, Mr. Kline." The Chairman's outline doesn't move, but his voice is flinty. "I want results."

"I'm not giving you an excuse, sir." Jason allows his voice to harden a little in return—just a little. "I'm giving you my professional tactical analysis based on our experiences so far."

The room is silent. The board members continue to stare at him without expression. The Chairman doesn't move, elbow still on armrest, chin still on hand.

Jason realizes what's wrong with the room: it appears to be a circle, but it's actually a slight oval—so slight you can barely notice in the dim light— and the table is turned clockwise about ten degrees off from the length of the room. That's why nothing seems to line up correctly, and why his mind keeps trying to make it line up when it won't.

"Go on," the Chairman says. "Give us your *tactical analysis*."

Now that he knows the trick, the room has lost its power over him. Jason feels his confidence return, and he leans forward to address the board.

"The email address makes the subject relatively easy to identify," Jason says. "TTI is a Thorpe domain. Dr. Thorpe was a member of the New York City Guardians before he moved Thorpe Industries out of the United States. Liberty was using his own *guardians.tti* address to send the email. The address *cb@chaos.tti* obviously belongs to the hero Curveball..."

"Obviously?" The voice is female—one of the members of the board. "Why is this obvious?"

"He's the only member of that group who would use 'chaos' as his domain name," Jason says. "And he was Liberty's... partner? Sidekick? They worked together for a long time, even before the Guardians. And they were *enemies* before that. Liberty's email was sent to someone he knows, someone he's close to, someone he shares a history with. It fits."

He waits. No one replies, so he pushes ahead. "Unfortunately, knowing the identity of the recipient isn't helpful from a purely technical perspective. We don't understand enough about ThorpeNet to figure out how to crack it."

"ThorpeNet?" A man's voice this time. A very old voice, to his right.

"Dr. Thorpe is something of a prodigy in... well. In a lot of things. Cold fusion, cellular regeneration, alloys... and computer technology. Thorpe Industries uses its own high speed network for communication, and *tti* is the domain extension used to link that network to the Internet. And we can't get past it. The man is decades ahead of us, sir. There are things we're coming up against that I simply don't understand, and I don't know how to start understanding them."

Jason relaxes slightly. It's not good news, but he's more comfortable now. "The file Liberty sent was encrypted. We haven't been able to open it yet, and I'm not optimistic we ever will. The message Liberty sent was also encrypted—the only reason your people were able to read it in the first place was because they found it on Liberty's own machine, which had the key."

"But it didn't have the key for the attached file," the Chairman says.

"That's right," Jason says. "Obviously he had the key at one point, because he needed it to encrypt it in the first place. But he didn't have it on that machine, and without it... it's going to take a long time to break the encryption."

"How long?" the Chairman asks, impatience seeping into his voice again.

"Years, sir. Years." Jason takes a deep breath. "I don't like admitting it, but we don't have the hardware we need to brute force it."

The room falls silent again. A soft sigh escapes the Chairman as he shifts in his seat.

"This is not the news I wanted to hear," the Chairman admits. "But your failure isn't a result of laziness, or incompetence... and I don't punish my employees for honest failure. Are there any other options?"

"There are, generally speaking, three ways to get into an account," Jason says. "The first is the way I described—trying to get in from the outside. The equivalent of trying to force a door open to break into a house. The second is to try to access it from the intended recipient's computer."

"Is that easier?" the Chairman asks.

"Sometimes," Jason says. "It all depends on how paranoid the intended recipient is. All the security protocols in the world won't do any good if Curveball is sloppy. But I don't think he's sloppy. He's been off the grid for ten years. Nobody's seen him. The Department of Homeland Security sends him an Abstention of Service check every month and they still can't figure out where he lives."

"Abstention of Service?" The old man again.

"The government essentially pays him a pension as long as he agrees not to... get involved," Jason says. "I don't know the specifics of it, but it appears to have something to do with the Prodigy scandal."

That actually provokes a reaction from the board. Looks of genuine surprise appear on the board members' faces as they begin murmuring to each other in low voices. The Chairman clears his voice, and the board falls silent. Their masks return.

"You said there was a third option," the Chairman says.

"Social engineering," Jason says. "Essentially you find someone who can access the email account and you con them out of the information. Unfortunately, I don't know how to approach it."

"What do we know about Curveball?" It's the woman who questioned him earlier.

"I can speak to that." The board member to his immediate right, a distinguished-looking middle-aged man with salt and pepper hair, opens a dossier sitting in front of him. "With your permission, Chairman."

The Chairman nods.

Jason looks over the board member's shoulder at the dossier. The name CURVEBALL is hand-written in faded blue ink on a white label, and the words PROPRIETARY and SECRET are stamped on the front—literally *stamped*, from an ink stamp. Nobody uses those any more, and he realizes this information is at least twenty years old.

"We have very little information on Curveball," the board member says. "The most we have was acquired from the Federal Bureau of Metahuman Affairs when the Guardians first sought government sanction in 1989. All of the founding members were required to go through a complete battery of tests, including the metahuman classification tests."

"How accurate were the tests in 1989?" the Chairman asks.

"They were very crude, compared to what we have now," the board member says. "It was at the beginning of that program, and they were looking for baseline data. But they were able to determine some very general things. They could detect whether someone genuinely was psychic, for example, as opposed to someone simply using misdirection to convince people they were. They could detect specific DNA markers that accompanied metahuman mutation. All of Curveball's tests were negative. He was the only founding member that tested within standard human norms, across the board. His IQ was high, but still within human norms."

"That's hard to believe," Jason says, then mentally kicks himself for speaking out of turn.

If the board member is angry, he doesn't show it. "I agree," he says. "We have film footage of Curveball doing things that... normal people shouldn't be able to do. But there was nothing in his physiology that explained it. No genetic abnormalities. No trace of psychic ability. Even Gladiator tested as a mutant, and his only innate 'power' is his intellect..."

"So," the Chairman muses, "the recipient of Liberty's email—assuming Mr. Kline's theory is correct, which I believe to be the case—is, for all intents and purposes, an unknown quantity."

Jason feels the topic of the conversation is going to move away from his area of expertise, and, potentially, to drift into areas he might not be authorized to overhear. He clears his throat, then says, "If you have no further need of me, Mr. Chairman, I'll return to my work."

"Ah," the Chairman says, "yes... Mr. Kline."

The board members return their attention to Jason. He tenses slightly.

"Your record with this company is excellent," the Chairman says.

"Thank you, sir," Jason says.

"You had a rather extensive career in the intelligence community before joining our group, didn't you?"

Jason nods. "Yes sir."

The Chairman turns in his chair to look at someone to Jason's left. "Mara, has he been vetted?"

"Fully." It's the woman from before. "He's quite suitable. As is the rest of his team."

The Chairman nods. "Excellent. Mr. Kline, don't leave just yet. We're going to bring your team more fully into this affair. In the next few days your team will be read in, but if the Board agrees I think we should bring you up to speed now."

A murmur of assent echoes through the room.

"Very good," the Chairman says. "Mr. Kline, the email Liberty sent to Curveball is of great concern to me, but an even greater concern is that he was able to gather enough information to prompt him to send that email to begin with. We have a security problem at Haruspex Analytics, and I believe we'll need the services of you and your team to locate the source of that problem."

"I see," Jason says. "I'll do everything I can, sir."

"I know you will," the Chairman says, "but first you need to understand exactly why this is so important." He gestures with his free hand, and the holographic image on the table shifts, replacing Jason's personnel file with a presentation slide.

"Project Recall?" Jason stares at the words and frowns. "What's that?"

"It's the single most important event in human history," the Chairman says. "Now pay attention. I'm only going to say this once..."

PART ONE: FORREST BROWNSTONE, ROOF

The roof of the Forrests' brownstone can't be called a commanding view, not by New York City standards, but CB likes it. It's night, but there's enough light to see over the tops of the other brownstones in the neighborhood and into a small park located behind the houses across the street. In the distance he can see taller buildings rise up into the sky.

It's chilly tonight. The wind is almost sharp enough to convince CB to go back inside. But he wants to smoke, and the house is strictly smoke-free.

"Hey."

CB looks over his left shoulder. Leaning out the window that opens into his stretch of roof is an attractive middle-aged woman, smiling at him.

CB smiles back. "Juliet."

"You left the window open again," she says. She sounds more amused than angry.

"Old habits," CB says.

"Bad habits," Juliet counters. She's blond, fair-skinned, with only a few wrinkles around the corners of her eyes. She holds out a green thermos. "Coffee?"

"Sure," CB says.

Juliet crawls out through the window and awkwardly slides down the roof, dragging the thermos and a blanket behind her. When she slides down next to CB she stops, hands him the thermos, and wraps the blanket around her shoulders.

"Not surprised to see you here," she says. "This is where you and grandpa would go to talk."

"And smoke," CB says, waving his cigarette in the air.

"That was just you." There's a hint of disapproval in her voice.

CB snorts. "Alex smoked like a chimney. He just never did it around you."

Juliet looks at him sideways. She's not sure she believes him.

"Not kidding," CB says. "Hey, until the... 80s? Early 90s? Smoking was pretty much *everywhere*. A lot of people did it. And Alex was born in 1920. *Everybody* smoked back then. Hell, in World War II he was convinced it was good for his health, and *so were his doctors*. The doctors at Project Paragon actually prescribed him cigarettes to counteract the nausea from his treatments."

"Hmmm." Juliet's voice is noncommittal. "And you? Did you think it was healthy?"

"Nah." CB takes another drag. "I just thought it made me look tough."

Juliet laughs. She still has that carefree laugh, the one that makes him want to laugh too, even when he doesn't really know why she's laughing. "You're a bad man," she says. "A terrible influence."

"That must be why they never used me in one of those 'Just say No' campaigns."

"Weren't you on the FBI's Most Wanted list during most of those campaigns?"

CB thinks back. "Yeah," he says finally. "That probably had more to do with it."

Juliet laughs again. "Are you going to drink any of that coffee?"

CB looks down at the thermos. "After the cigarette," he says.

"Then pass it over here."

CB hands her the thermos.

"Saw you and Peter talking earlier today." Juliet unscrews the lid and pours some coffee into the screw-top cup. Steam rises into the night. She holds the cup under her face, breathing in the warmth. "Nice to see you talking again. I thought it was terrible the way things ended up."

"I was pretty mad," CB says, "but I never hated him."

"You broke his jaw."

"Everyone keeps bringing that up." CB flicks the ash from his cigarette into the gutter. "I don't know what you were expecting me to do to the guy telling me that my choices were to either sign myself over to the government or go to jail."

"It wasn't his decision," Juliet says.

"Which is why I only broke his jaw."

Juliet *hmmmms* and lets the matter drop. "What were you talking about?"

"Alex's will, mostly. He made a few requests that are making some of Pete's bosses uncomfortable."

"Oh really?" Juliet sounds intrigued. "What requests were those?"

"Well, he wanted me to speak at his funeral."

"We already knew that," Juliet says.

CB shakes his head. "Not the real one. The one they're going to put on TV."

Juliet chokes back laughter.

The curtains at the window draw back, and Martin sticks his head out, peering down at CB and Juliet. "Hah! Knew I'd find you two here. Room for one more?"

CB waves him down. A minute later the three of them sit side by side on the roof.

"I think I need to put rails up here," Martin says. "And maybe a few ashtrays."

"Joykiller," CB says, grinning.

"That's my job," Martin says.

"Pete says grandpa wanted CB to speak at the national service," Juliet says. She adjusts her blanket so it drapes over her husband as well. "And here's some coffee."

"Hmm." Martin takes the thermos. "I can think of a few people who won't like that. Your brother. The governor. Most of the DHS..."

"I know," CB says. "Alex must have known too. I guess I was rubbing off on him after all."

Everyone laughs. An awkward silence follows.

"I'm sorry," CB says. "I'm sorry about Alex, and I'm sorry I haven't been around. I missed you guys."

"We know why you couldn't be here," Juliet says softly.

CB snorts. "That's one up on me. I don't have a clue."

"Liar," Martin says cheerfully. "You were always good at that. Lying. Especially to yourself."

CB doesn't reply.

Martin unscrews the thermos and drinks from it directly. He makes a face. "Instant? Julie. Instant?"

Juliet sighs. "It's all I could find. We used the last of the real stuff this afternoon."

"I'll pick some more up tomorrow. Is there anything else we need? I could turn it into a proper trip if you want."

"Good idea." Juliet stretches and shrugs off the blanket. "I think I'll make a list now. Don't freeze to death, boys."

She climbs over Martin, gives him a quick peck on the cheek as she passes, then climbs back through the window into the house.

CB frowns, then reaches for another cigarette. "That was weird."

Martin chuckles. "What's weird? I wanted to talk to you in private, so she made an excuse and went inside."

CB stares at Martin and shakes his head in disbelief. "You wanted to talk to me in private."

"That's right."

"All you said was you were going to buy coffee tomorrow."

"She knew what I meant."

CB laughs. "That's creepy, Marty. Only telepaths should be allowed to talk like that."

Martin shrugs. "Years of marriage. Mind reading. Same thing." He takes another swig of coffee and winces. "This really is terrible."

"I'll stick to smoking, then." CB lights his cigarette. "What do you want to talk about?"

"Oh, I've got a list," Martin says cheerfully, "but it boils down to 'are you going to be all right?' and 'what trouble are you going to stir up when you start looking into Alex's death?'"

"I'll be fine," CB says tonelessly.

"Don't bullshit me," Martin says. He says it casually, as if he were complimenting a woman's hat. "I'm not Julie. You don't have to play-act in front of me, remember? You had a hell of a day today."

"We *all* had a hell of a—"

"Hey, guess what?" Martin interrupts. "I'm getting *old*."

CB falls silent.

"And so are you," Martin continues, "but you don't show it. You're like Alex. You saw how it affected him, you're here after being gone ten years, and suddenly I have gray hair, Julie has wrinkles, and Jenny and Andy are the age we were when we first met. Suddenly you don't know if you have more in common with them or with us. It's freaking you out."

CB flicks ash off the side of the house and watches as bits of it, still glowing, disappear into the darkness. "Yeah."

"So you're trying not to think about it," Martin continues, "but your best friend in the world—the one guy who would understand more than anyone—isn't here any more. So now you're sitting in the spot where the two of you used to sit for hours talking about... I don't know, everything. And you're trying not to wonder what it's going to be like in ten more years, but you can't help it."

His voice is still cheerful and kind, and it doesn't let up. CB remembers seeing hardened criminals crumble just by listening to that man lay out all the evidence they had in exactly the same voice he'd use to tell his daughter a bedtime story. That's just how Martin is—he's the nicest guy CB's ever known, and he's brutal when it comes to telling the truth. Mr. Rogers, the Grand Inquisitor.

"You know how it was with Julie's dad," Martin adds.

CB sighs. "Yeah."

"I've been thinking about that a lot," Martin says. "It's morbid, I know, but... that hit him pretty hard. After that I saw him watching us grow old every time he stopped by to visit. You know? He was steeling himself for the day he'd have to go to one of our funerals. He ever talk about that with you?"

CB blows streams of smoke out of his nostrils. "Just once. I don't want to talk about it. No offense."

"None taken," Martin says. "I don't have to deal with it. I get to grow old and die like everyone else in the world. You're the one getting left behind. I'm sorry about that."

CB wraps his trenchcoat a little tighter around him.

"Is that why you left the first time?" Martin asks.

CB shrugs. "Pretty much," he admits. "I mean, I was pretty much disgusted with the world at the time and wanted to hide anyway, but... that just made it easier. Other than you guys, I don't really have a family. A few friends. That's about it."

"That doesn't sound easier to me," Martin says.

CB doesn't reply.

"Are there any others?"

"Other what?" CB looks over at Martin. "Any other Peter Pans? Yeah, actually. A few."

"Well?" It's the first hint of exasperation Martin's shown all night. "Have you thought of *talking* to them?"

"About what?" CB narrows his eyes. "You might find it hard to believe, but 'hey guys, we might be immortal' isn't much of a common bond."

"It might be as soon as everyone else around you starts dying off," Martin points out.

"Jesus, Marty..." CB laughs bitterly. "I know two guys, OK? But trust me, there's nothing—"

"You keep making excuses," Martin says. "Are you shy? I'm going to answer that for you: you're not shy."

"Are you finished?" CB asks, irritation rising. "Vigilante is an interesting guy, but aside from having the *single least creative name in the business*, he's also considered a criminal by the government. And that's only when he's not considered a *terrorist* by the government. The body count around him is a little high for my taste."

Martin frowns. "Vigilante. Right. I thought he died."

"Yeah," CB says. "More than once. But it doesn't take."

"OK," Martin says, "Vigilante is probably not the guy you want to kick back and have a beer with. What about the other guy?"

"Fella named Jack Barrow," CB says. "Great guy, to be honest. Pretty down to earth and laid-back, when he's not on the job."

"So what's the problem?"

"He works for the Mob," CB says.

Martin's eyes narrow. "He works for the...? Wait. *Scrapper Jack?*"

CB shrugs. "His life is complicated."

"A life of crime will do that."

"A life of law-abiding behavior will do that, too," CB points out.

Martin *harrumphs*, takes another swig of coffee, and winces yet again.

"Anyway," CB says, "you can see how it might be difficult to strike up a regular friendship with either of them."

They both lapse into silence. CB finishes his cigarette. Martin tries to finish the coffee, but gives up in disgust.

"You ever miss the force, Marty?" CB flicks the rest of his cigarette off the roof.

Martin shrugs slightly. "I'd never pass the physical."

"Not what I asked. Do you regret retiring?"

"I didn't exactly *retire*," Martin says. "Not by choice. I went on disability and saw the writing on the wall. But yeah, I regret it now and then. What about you? Do *you* regret retiring?"

CB raises an eyebrow. "Who says I did?"

"Pete Travers," Martin says. "He says the government is actually paying you to retire."

CB laughs. "Yeah. They actually put me on a... I forget what it's called. Abstention something. It's a pension. All I have to do is stay out of the game."

"Have you stayed out of the game?" Martin asks.

"Sort of," CB says. "But I told 'em when it started that if I didn't cash a check in thirty days they better take me off payroll."

"So you never ruled out coming back." Martin thinks it over, then grins. "Who am I kidding? You probably never left to begin with."

"I cashed their checks," CB says. "And I stuck to the letter of the agreement."

"What about this month's check?"

CB doesn't reply.

"CB?"

CB sighs. "Cashed it the day Alex died. Before I found out. Guess I'm going to have to give Uncle Sam a refund."

Martin nods slowly. "You're going to look into the murder." It's not a question.

"Hell *yes* I'm going to look into it. Marty, nobody puts a bullet right between Alex's eyes in a fair fight. Not even in an *unfair* fight. And it sure wasn't a bunch of random hooligans in commando gear."

"You don't buy the official story?"

CB laughs bitterly. "Do you? You know what he could do. There are only a few people I can think of who could pull this off. They're all bad news, but they don't do vendettas. This wasn't a whim, it wasn't an accident, and it wasn't a revenge killing. My money is on a contract killing. Someone wanted Alex dead. I don't know why, but I'm going to find out."

Silence.

"I want in," Martin says.

"I'll take all the help I can get," CB replies. "And since you're offering, I need you to call in some favors and get me access to Alex's apartment. I want to see where it happened up close."

Martin nods. "Can do. You want me to smooth things over with Pete? I expect he's supposed to be keeping you off the job and all that."

CB shakes his head. "Pete's a smart guy. He knows why I'm here."

"So when are you going to get started?"

CB thinks. "Well, there's the viewing in the morning, then the service..."

Martin nods. "And then in the evening we'll have everyone over here."

CB hesitates. "The whole family?"

"Every last one."

"Well," CB says, "that settles that. I'll get started tomorrow night."

PART TWO: PARK SLOPE UNITED METHODIST CHURCH

"This is sick," Jenny mutters.

The sidewalks are so full of people CB can't imagine how anyone is able to breathe in those crowds, let alone move. Lined up along the curb are the paparazzi, jostling with each other and with the occasional aggressive tourist in an attempt to get a money-making shot. Police are everywhere, trying to keep the crowd on the curb so that cars can continue down the street unimpeded. This is met with only mixed success: as often as not a car is mobbed by photographers, and the streets are gridlocked until the police can wade in and force open a path.

This is for a wake, CB thinks.

"Yeah," he agrees. "Pretty sick."

"I hope Mom and Dad made it through," Jenny says. She grips the steering wheel so tightly CB can see the veins in the backs of her hands rise up.

"They'll be fine," CB says. "And so will we."

They inch their way up 4th Avenue. CB keeps his eyes forward, pretending not to notice the chaos on the sidewalks. He thinks he sees a street vendor selling merchandise that he's positive Alex's estate never licensed or authorized. He resists the urge to get out of the car and make a scene.

A piece of the crowd behind them swells, and a mass of photographers break free, rushing to surround the car behind them. The car ahead of them turns left and there's a gap in the road. Jenny sighs in relief and accelerates, temporarily leaving the crowd behind as a new group of police dressed in riot gear descends on the mob of photographers, trying to force them back onto the curb.

"It's a nightmare," Jenny adds. "And it's not right. A funeral shouldn't be treated like a Hollywood premier."

"This isn't the funeral," CB points out. "It's a viewing. And the public isn't allowed in, so there's a lot of interest in it. The funeral itself won't be an issue. We'll all be traveling together and the route's already set. This is nuts because we're all arriving separately."

A few seconds later he adds, "...though it's times like this I wish I could fly."

Jenny snorts. "You'd abandon me?"

"In a heartbeat."

CB tugs at his collar. It feels about half a size too small. He unbuttons the top button and tightens his tie a bit.

"That never works," Jenny says.

"What never works?"

"The whole 'I'll tighten my tie so no one will notice I unbuttoned my collar' thing. Everyone knows."

"Good to know," CB says. He loosens his tie. "This is the first time I've worn a suit in... a long time."

"Oh? When was the last time?" Jenny's voice turns playful. "Mom and Dad's wedding?"

CB shakes his head. "It was another funeral."

They fall silent.

The traffic and the crowds thin a bit as they near the police checkpoint. 8th Street is blocked off with police cars and glow-paint sawhorses. CB sees Pete Travers talking to one of the police officers. He looks tired.

Jenny drives up to the blocked-off road and rolls down her window. An officer leans down to look in the car.

"We're family," Jenny says.

The officer looks up at Travers questioningly. The officer he's talking to nudges him. He glances over quickly, recognizes the car and its occupants, and nods once. The officer at the car waves at some of the other men who pick up the sawhorse and move it aside.

"Up two blocks on the left," the officer says. "You'll see all the cars lined up on 6th Avenue. Someone will show you where to park."

"Thank you officer," Jenny says, and they turn onto 8th Street. She sighs in relief as the crowd drops away.

Normally 8th Street is a one-way street going the other direction. It's a pleasant drive. Charming row houses line one side of the street, the other side looks like something is being either built up or torn down... it's a mix of concrete buildings and empty, dirt-filled lots. Cars line the side of the street along the residential areas.

CB winces. "I feel sorry for the folks who actually live here," he says.

"I'm trying not to think about it," Jenny agrees. "Great-grandfather loved this church, and the neighborhood. And they get locked down because of it."

"And there's... I guess there's a school next to it?"

"Across the street," Jenny says. "Yeah. They shut it down today. Because schoolkids are a threat to national security."

"Well," CB says, "I was."

Park Slope United Methodist Church is a small community church located on the corner of 8th Street and 6th Avenue. It looks vaguely old to CB, with an a-frame roof, arched windows (complete with stained glass), and something that looks like battlements atop the bell tower. It's the church Alex attended for the last twenty years, but it's not used to the amount of attention it's receiving. Law enforcement is everywhere: local, Federal, even the Secret Service. There are police posted outside each of the red doors leading into the church. There are police keeping watch over the church's garden, enclosed in a wrought-iron fence sitting to the right of the church.

In front of the church is a long line of cars, starting with the hearse. Behind it they see a black car with government plates.

"That'd be Uncle Toby," Jenny says. Her voice is studied neutrality.

"What'd you expect?" CB says. "He's a Senator. I see your Dad's car. And Andy's. And it looks like we're going to get valet parking."

A man in a dark suit wearing dark sunglasses runs up to them, waving his arms. Jenny stops the car and unrolls the window.

"I'm Agent Fredericks," the man says. "If you don't mind, we'd like to go ahead and get you inside as soon as possible. You're Mr. Forrest's daughter?"

Jenny nods.

"Well, just go on in. I'll get your car in the line."

"Thanks," Jenny says. They get out of the car, the agent hops in and her car pulls away as they go into the church.

It's a private affair, but it's a large family and an even larger extended family. The narthex is full of people standing around in small groups, talking in low voices. They're greeted at the entrance by a harried-looking man wearing a long black robe and a purple sash.

"Welcome," he says. His voice is tired, but kind. "He is in the sanctuary, if you would like to pay your last respects."

"Thank you," Jenny says. CB shifts his weight uncomfortably and looks away.

The double doors separating the narthex from the sanctuary are open. The sanctuary is softly lit, the pews are dark and mostly empty. The coffin sits in front of the podium, positioned lengthwise down the aisle. A lone figure, his back to the sanctuary door, stands beside the body.

Jenny grabs CB's arm and tugs urgently. "They brought grandfather."

Her voice is strained. CB looks at her, then looks to where she's pointing.

Off in a corner of the room is an old man with thick, white hair. He sits in a wheelchair, and a young, pretty nurse stands next to him trying to look as inconspicuous as possible. The man stares around him with a blank, slightly bewildered expression on his face.

"Why is he here?" Jenny asks.

"How could he not be here?" CB says. "It's his dad's funeral."

"He doesn't know that!" she says fiercely.

"How do you know?" CB says. "How does anyone know? I can't think of a single reason to keep him away."

"It's just..." Jenny sighs, frustrated. "It's going to hurt mom. Again. And if he's not going to understand what's going on, I just don't see any reason for him to—"

At that moment a side door opens, and men in dark suits enter the room. They're with the Secret Service, and a moment later a distinguished-looking man with dark, gray-tinged hair enters, followed by a camera crew.

CB suppresses a scowl. "There's your uncle," he murmurs to Jenny. "And he brought his own *press*."

The room quiets down. People awkwardly move aside to let the Junior Senator from New York through. He sees his father, hesitates a moment, then spies Martin and Juliet standing at the other side of the room. He flashes a brilliant, practiced smile and walks over to them.

"I guess I should say hello." Jenny voice is flat.

"I think your mom and dad would appreciate the assist," CB says. "I'm... going to pay my last respects."

Jenny mutters something that sounds like *lucky bastard* and reluctantly walks over to her parents. CB walks into the sanctuary.

He doesn't want to be there, but he doesn't want to be there less than he doesn't want to be in the other room, where the most self-serving politician CB has ever met is making sure his re-election campaign gets plenty of images of him commiserating with his family over the loss of the man whose name he spent his entire career profiting off of. The coffin is open, so he has to move around the right side to look in. The man standing at the coffin is at the head, blocking off CB's view.

"Excuse me," CB says.

The man steps down the aisle immediately, turning as he does so he can continue to regard the body. He's an older man, in his mid-sixties, refined and elegant, a little shorter than average, with sharp, bright eyes. His snow-white hair is thinning but not gone. There's something vaguely familiar about him.

"Ah," the man says. "Curveball. I apologize, that was thoughtless of me. I was... lost in memory."

An alarm goes off in the back of CB's head. He stares at the old man, hard, trying to figure out why. "Have we met?"

"Oh yes," the man says, "many times I daresay. Of course, we were much younger. Well. *I* was much younger. That's terribly unfair of you, I must say."

"That seems to be the general consensus," CB says. "And you are...?"

The man raises an eyebrow. "Ah, yes, well. I suppose I shouldn't be surprised. I'm... out of uniform. Artemis LaFleur. A pleasure as always."

CB tenses. "LaFleur."

The old man raises his hands in a placating fashion. "I come in peace," he says. "I genuinely mean no ill will to anyone here in this place. I have come to pay my respects to the greatest man I have ever met."

CB studies the old man for a moment, then shrugs. "I thought you were taller."

"I might be," LaFleur says.

CB snorts, then looks down. His retort is abandoned the moment he sees the body.

He's familiar with the cliche "he looks like he's sleeping" but he's never actually seen a body that looks like it's sleeping. It wasn't true the last time he was at a funeral of a good friend, and it isn't true now. Nonetheless, he's astonished. There's no question that he's looking at a corpse, but even in death he can see Alex. His jaw is still set the way it was when he was about to go into a tough fight, with one corner of his mouth turned up ever so slightly, as if he were tempted to mock his enemy but was too polite to actually do it. And although CB knows that Alex had been shot in the head, he can find no trace of the wound anywhere.

"I don't know who prepared the body," LaFleur says quietly, "but whoever it was did an outstanding job."

CB nods wordlessly.

A moment later LaFleur sighs. "It seems the Senator has decided to view his grandfather's body. I suggest taking one of the side doors out into the narthex so you can avoid his... entourage."

"I don't have any beef with the Secret Service," CB says.

"I was referring to his ego," LaFleur says.

CB smirks. He doesn't want to, but he can't help it.

"Curveball."

CB looks up to see LaFleur studying him, hand outstretched, holding a business card.

"I don't need to be who I am to know what you're planning to do," LaFleur says. "I can tell you that none of my associates are involved. I've looked into it personally. I don't expect you to... trust me, not yet, but the deeper you look into it the more you will, I think. Over time. In this matter at least."

CB reaches out to take the card from LaFleur's hand. It's a business card, but completely blank. A phone number is written at the bottom in clean, sharp lines.

"My inability to learn *anything at all* carries certain implications that don't sit well with me," LaFleur continues. "With that in mind, and out of my deepest respect and regard for the man who lies before us, should you need... assistance, and find you lack resources from the *traditional quarters*, please do use this number."

CB stares at the number, frowns, and puts it in his shirt pocket. "I'm gonna hope it doesn't come to that," he says. "No offense."

"None taken," LaFleur replies, then disappears into thin air.

CB hates that trick. He takes the side door out.

PART THREE: SCHAEF EARTH GARDEN

The room is even more crowded than it was before. Someone let in select members of the press—CB is pretty sure whose bright idea that was—and the small groups are now besieged with reporters trying to interview them during a wake. The reverend of the church has closed the doors to the sanctuary and is stating in loud, plain terms that under no circumstances will the press be permitted in there. CB smiles slightly as a very startled Senator Tobias Morgan is told, in somewhat more strident language, that if he attempts to bring his cameramen into the sanctuary the reverend will have him ejected immediately.

CB steps out the front door and takes a deep breath. He turns left, and walks down into the garden. A few of the Secret Service are there. He waves as he makes his way over to a bench, sits down, lays his head back, and closes his eyes. He sighs heavily as he tries to gather his wits.

"You too?"

CB opens one eye. A tall, solidly-built, dark-skinned man looms over him, looking down. CB squints while his eyes adjust to the light, then breaks out into a grin. "Roger!"

Roger Whitman is six and a half feet tall. Even in his suit—a relatively inexpensive two-piece with a too-thin tie that was obviously purchased in the 80s—it's plain that he's a solid mass of muscle. His dark curly hair is cut short, and his sideburns are showing white. Other than the white in his hair he looks like a man in his late thirties or early forties.

Roger grins in return. "Figured you couldn't stay in there for long. I was waiting for you to get out of the sanctuary to say hi, but the Senator started making up his own rules and invited the press. I cleared out before things came to a head."

"Yeah, I walked into a madhouse," CB says. He stands and holds out his hand. Roger's grin widens, and he wraps CB up in a bear hug that lifts him off the ground for the second time in two days. CB hears his back crack.

"Ow." It's the only word he manages to say, but it's enough. Roger puts him down quickly.

"Sorry," Roger says. "Been awhile. Nice to see you."

"You been in hiding too?" CB twists his upper torso to make sure it still works.

"No, nothing like that," Roger says. "I have a 9-to-5, pretty simple stuff.

Retirement's boring. I have to do something with my time."

"You're still in the city?" CB asks dubiously. "And they leave you alone?"

Roger shrugs. "From time to time the government sends someone by to see if I'm 'available' for 'a problem they could really use my help with.' I remind them that they're the ones that wanted us to retire in the first place."

"I'm sure they appreciate that reminder."

Roger chuckles. "They act like I'm the most unreasonable person on Earth. But now I know I'm not, because you're still alive."

CB laughs.

"So where have you been?" Roger asks. "I keep in touch with everyone, but nobody knew where you were. Well. Alex knew, but he wouldn't say. You doing a thing?"

"Yeah," CB says. "I'm doing a thing."

Roger nods slowly. "Well let me know when it starts to spiral out of control and you need someone to haul your ass out of the fire. I seem to remember being pretty good at that."

"Yeah," CB says. "I seem to remember that too."

They both sit on the bench in silence for a while. CB looks at Roger and frowns.

Roger narrows his eyes. "What?"

"How do you feel, man?"

Roger shrugs. "Dunno. Pretty good."

"Yeah. You look better than you did. A *lot* better. You looked haggard at the end of everything."

"I didn't feel too good," Roger admits.

"You were always going on about feeling old. I started calling you 'Mr. Glover' for a while."

"Yes you did, you little bastard," Roger says, laughing. "I'd forgotten all about that. I was actually in pretty bad shape. Doctors said I was on the verge of a massive heart attack, and there was nothing they could do to stop it."

CB stares at Roger in shock.

"Yeah," he says, "it was pretty bad. Ironic, too. Theoretically the surgery they needed to do was pretty standard stuff, but they couldn't do it. Nobody knew how to crack me open."

"Well what happened?" CB asks. "You didn't die, obviously."

"I went to Robert. I didn't know what else to do. Explained the whole thing to him. He flew me to his island, ran a few tests. Turns out I needed some kind of... amino acid, or something. I don't exactly know what. I know he said 'amino acid' five or six times, but I'm not sure whether he was telling me I needed an amino acid or if he was saying 'I can't explain this to you, I might as well just say amino acid over and over again.' Anyway, he... gave me a pill. I took it pretty regularly for a few years. I'm pretty much back to normal now."

"Huh." CB looks at Roger again and shakes his head. "I thought I had problems."

"Oh, you have problems all right," Roger says. "No question there."

They lapse into silence again.

"Have you seen the body yet?" CB asks.

"Yeah," Roger says. He shakes his head. "I don't believe that story for a second. The one they're saying on TV? No way it happened like that."

"Yeah," CB says.

"You tell me when it's time," Roger adds.

"Time for what?" CB asks.

Roger just looks at him.

"Yeah, I'll tell you," CB says. "Believe me. When the time comes, I'm definitely getting the band back together."

PART FOUR: PENTHOUSE APARTMENT

"Here we are."

A uniformed police officer steps into the elevator foyer outside Alex's apartment. CB steps out after him, looking around once, noting two tape outlines on the floor and the broken remains of a door hanging in the doorframe.

"Forensics has been over this place three or four times," the officer says. "There's not a lot left to see. We didn't move anything, but they did take a few things. Some kitchen knives and the computer are the ones I remember."

"Sure," CB says, "makes sense. Shame about the computer, though. I would have liked to see it."

"Nothing there, from what I hear," the officer says. "I got a buddy in the lab, and he says somebody wiped it."

CB frowns. "Wiped it?"

"Yeah, some kind of magnet or EMP or something. Hard drive is toast; can't read anything off it, and my buddy tells me the tricks they use to get around that aren't working. You figure Liberty did that?"

CB shakes his head. "Can't think why he would."

"Well, look around as much as you want, but if you find anything please let us know." There's a sullen tint to the officer's voice—CB is here because he's a "hero" connected to Liberty, and in his experience, "heroes" don't share information.

"I'm not trying to steal a collar," CB says. "I just want to help catch the son of a bitch who killed my friend."

The officer nods, satisfied. "Well, I won't get in your way. The elevator doesn't lock from up here, so you can let yourself down when you're finished."

CB nods. The detective steps back into the elevator and the doors close with a soft *ping*. CB walks into the apartment.

He stands in the living room, trying to focus. He doesn't know what he's looking for, and he doesn't know where to start. He stares down at the white tape that outlines where the police found Alex's body. There's a red stain on the carpet—Alex's blood. CB frowns.

Alex was found face down on the floor. According to the tape outline, he fell toward the balcony door. CB walks over to the French doors and opens them, stepping out onto the balcony. He glances at the outlines where the other bodies were found, but doesn't pay much attention to them.

The attack came from two directions. That would have made more sense if Alex hadn't lived at the very top of a very tall building.

CB leaps up on the balcony rail, then somersaults up over the lip of the balcony onto the roof of the apartment. It's been a long time since he had to do something like that, but immediately the body takes over: long-forgotten instincts remember when to stretch, when to jump, pull, flip, and almost effortlessly he's over the top.

It was raining the night they murdered Alex. They probably counted on that to cover most of their tracks, but CB notices a few things. Cigarette butts litter the roof near the side overlooking the balcony. Along the opposite side of the building he finds indentations in the concrete about three feet from the edge. He kneels, sticks a finger into one, notes the angle, then lies on his side and looks up in the direction of the angle.

There's a rooftop. It's a little farther than he'd like if he were using a zip line, but it's doable. He doesn't know what building it is, so he makes a mental note of its location and decides to follow up later.

CB slips over the edge back onto the balcony, then returns to the living room. He glances at the couch, turned on its back, then settles on the now-empty desk sitting against the wall. Computer, keyboard, mouse, and monitor all taken. There's a shattered coffee cup on the floor.

He walks over to the table and looks under it. There's the "panic switch." He remembers Alex talking about it when he first set up the security. He remembers a few of the other things he said as well.

He looks up and scans the walls. From time to time he stops when he thinks he sees a piece of wall that is, perhaps, a little too smooth compared to the rest. Six cameras so far, evenly spaced around the living room. A bird's eye view, in fact. CB smiles grimly and walks down the hall, past the bathroom, past the guest room, into Alex's bedroom.

Alex's room is spare, almost austere. A double bed, neatly made—CB is convinced that, if he tried, he could probably bounce a quarter off it—and a lone dresser set across from it are the only pieces of furniture. CB goes straight to the closet, opens the door, and pulls the chain to the light. Alex's shirts and pants are folded neatly on their hangers, the cuffs of the pants all hanging at exactly the same distance from the floor. He shoves the hangers to one side and examines the back wall. A few moments later he sees it—a slight hump on one part of the wall, the faintest of irregularities over the surface.

CB reaches into his trenchcoat pocket and fishes out a pocket knife. He pries open the blade, then pushes it into the sheet rock around the hump.

The blade sinks in easily—it's not sheet rock at all. He carefully works the bade around the hump, prying bits of covering away, until finally the entire thing pops out into his hand.

It's a hard drive. It's a solid state drive, pretty expensive but easier to hide. CB blows the dust away from the device as best he can before he places it in his other trenchcoat pocket. He pats it once, satisfied. It's time to leave.

He reaches up to pull the closet light chain and freezes. He hears a soft squeak from the hall just outside the bedroom. He glances back. He's relieved to see he shut the bedroom door behind him.

The doorknob starts to turn. Very, very slowly.

CB looks for something, anything, and sees a clothes basket—a white sack draped over a thin wire frame—and decides it will have to do. He pulls the light chain and waits in the closet.

The doorknob continues turning. Seconds later the door opens slightly— just a crack—and then stops. It opens a little more, then a little more, until finally CB sees a gloved hand grip the side of the door.

CB kicks; the wire-framed basket flies through the air and strikes the hand on the knuckles. CB hears a loud, muffled curse. He doesn't hesitate: he runs out of the closet and kicks the door, hard. The door slams on the hand, and he hears a crunch as a knuckle is caught between door and doorframe. A voice on the other side shouts in pain for a moment, but then the door is kicked open, forcefully. The edge of it catches CB on the side of the head, and he reels.

Someone leaps toward him. CB steps to one side, vision still clearing, and manages to get his guard up as a thick-soled boot smashes into the dresser, splintering the wood. He latches onto the leg and pulls up, intending to force his attacker to the ground, but the other leg whips around, hooks behind CB's neck, and the next thing he knows he's flat on his back, breath rushing out of him.

He can see his attacker now. Male, he thinks, dressed in a body suit with kevlar armor over most of the tender parts. The man is wearing a solid face mask—no eyeholes. CB has seen masks like that before. It's an optical illusion: the weave of the mask is wide enough that whoever wears it can see fine. The man leaps to his feet in a single, fluid motion—not a move just anyone can do, even with extensive training.

The man takes a step back. CB hates it when they step back. He rolls to one side as a bullet *thwips* into the floor where he lay just moments before.

The wire basket sits on its side, still rolling back and forth from its landing. CB sees his attacker's shadow in the doorway and does a quick calculation as to his location. If he were being honest with himself, he'd call it a "guess" instead of a "calculation."

He kicks the basket again. It bounces off the door and hurtles down the hall. He sees the thready shadow of the basket disappear into the shadow of his attacker, and hears a muffled curse. It's in a foreign language—German, he thinks—but he can't quite make it out. CB rolls to his feet and launches himself through the door. His attacker reacts, trying to bring his gun up in time, but CB grabs the wrist and buries his shoulder in the man's chest. They go hurtling into the wall, sheet rock cracks, and the attacker's hand smashes against the molding around the bathroom door. The hand opens involuntarily and the gun falls to the ground. CB sees the gun clearly for the first time, and his blood runs cold.

He recognizes that gun. It's a very distinctive gun. He's not going to win this fight.

Richter throws CB off him with one arm, pushing him into the opposite wall. CB tries to ignore the pain as the entire wall cracks from the impact, and kicks, striking right below the man's armpit. He hits kevlar—of course he does—but that doesn't negate the full force of a steel-toed boot. Richter jerks back, giving CB just enough time to get to his feet and kick that damned gun as far down the hall as he can.

Just enough time, but no more. He hears Richter move, and turns to see the glint of a knife. He twists, lashes out with his hand, and hits Richter's wrist, knocking the blade aside. He grabs the arm and turns further, forcing Richter's arm to twist with him. Richter drops the knife, and utters a genuine cry of pain. CB tries to follow up with a throw. Instead, Richter's other hand grabs him by the back of his neck, lifts him off the ground, then throws him down the hall into the living room.

CB skids across the carpet and rolls out of the way, barely avoiding Richter's kick. He doesn't do so well with the second, and pain explodes as Richter's boot lands on his chest.

Richter sees his gun. He dives; CB rolls, and by the time Richter can raise his weapon and fire, CB has run out through the French doors, onto the balcony, and leapt over the rail.

This is the part of daring escapes from the tops of buildings that CB hates the most. It's a long way down, and he doesn't fly.

He reaches into a trenchcoat pocket and pulls out a coil of high-tension wire, quickly looping one end around his trenchcoat sleeve, then throwing the other end toward a passing balcony. The other end bonds instantly with the stone—CB makes a note to thank Robert for that gadget, assuming he lives long enough to do so—and then the coil is unspooling at an alarming rate.

He has just enough time to figure out what that means when suddenly it goes taut, and he screams as the loop closes on his sleeve, almost jerking his arm completely out of its socket. Almost. Thankfully his sleeve keeps the loop from tearing away his flesh.

He's about halfway down the building at this point, dangling about a foot from a balcony rail. There's a nagging little voice in the back of his head lecturing him about physics, and velocity, and how there's no way in hell he should be alive. He tells that nagging little voice to shut its goddamn mouth and give him time to think.

"What?"

CB looks down. A middle-aged man in a Hawaiian shirt and shorts, and a middle-aged woman in a t-shirt and jeans, are staring up at him in amazement.

"Sorry?" CB smiles at them in what he hopes is a reassuring fashion.

"Did you just tell me to shut my goddamn mouth?" The man sounds a bit bewildered.

"Er..." CB looks up. He doesn't see anyone falling off the side of the building after him. "Uh... hi. No, sorry about that. I was... talking to myself..."

The man just stares at him. The woman leans over the balcony to stare up at the line CB is dangling from.

"Are you all right?" she asks.

"Well now that you mention it..." CB kicks his feet, starting to swing. He grabs the line with his free hand and lifts, just a little, relieving some of the tension in his right arm. "Uh, look, I'm going to swing over a bit and land on your balcony, OK? I mean, if it's all right with you."

The man says nothing. The woman blinks rapidly a few times, then says in a faint voice, "I guess so."

"Great." CB lifts himself up with his left arm and starts to flex his right. It hurts, but it works. He loosens the loop enough so that his right arm slips free. Immediately pain shoots up and down the arm, but he forces himself to ignore it. He pulls on the line, swinging to and fro, until finally he gains enough momentum to swing past the balcony rail. He lets go, tumbling semi-gracefully through the air until he lands on the balcony in only a slightly overdramatic fashion.

CB grunts as his feet hit the stone balcony floor, then grins. "Good evening!"

The couple stares back.

"So..." CB looks at the two of them as he fishes out a pack of cigarettes. "Either of you mind if I smoke?"

PART FIVE: THE BOWERY, NYC

He rides the trains for hours, switching from line to line just to make sure he's not being followed. When he decides it's safe he gets out at the corner of Bleecker and Mulberry, more out of habit than anything else.

An old habit. A very old habit. So old he wouldn't have considered it a habit at all.

It's dark when he climbs out of the subway. It's not the way it used to be. It was definitely dirtier then, but it's not just that: he feels like a tourist now. Back then he was just a kid who got swept up in something the older kids were doing that he knew was the coolest damn thing on the planet. Now he sees little echoes of all that, but he doesn't recognize much of it.

He feels old, just for a second, then it goes away.

He starts walking toward the Bowery, the way he always did. He and Sin and Billy would walk down the street, meet up with friends, hurl taunts at whoever they felt like taunting at the time, occasionally get into fights... all the usual crap. And eventually they'd hear the music, and they'd quicken their steps a little, until eventually they'd get to Bowery, and right across the street there'd be CBGB, and the music would be pouring out of it like an ocean.

Talking Heads, Blondie, Television, the Voidoids, the Ramones, and a million other bands nobody remembers any more.

The closer he gets to the Bowery the deeper he frowns. He doesn't hear any music.

He lights a cigarette and quickens his step. The rain picks up. It's now a steady drizzle, and unpleasantly cold.

When he reaches the intersection of Bowery and Bleecker he doesn't quite understand what he's looking at. He crosses the street, ignoring traffic, and stops in front of a place he should recognize instantly. A place that should be as familiar to him as any other place he's ever considered home. Instead he sees:

john varvatos

315 bowery

"What the *hell*?" CB snarls. He whirls around and glares at a random passer-by—a college student, from the look of him.

"*What the hell happened to CBGB?*" he shouts.

The student stumbles back in alarm. "What? Hey, it's cool. You want money? I don't want trouble."

CB grabs the kid by his shirt. "Listen to my words," he says. "What. Happened. To. CBGB."

He tries to get away, but CB won't let go. He shuts his eyes, whimpering. A second later they snap open and he looks at CB in utter confusion. "Wait. The club? The music club?"

"Yes! The fucking music club!" CB shouts.

"It closed!" The student's voice is desperate and shrill. "Five years ago! It closed five years ago. They put up a... that." He gestures frantically to the store behind them. "Please let me go, man, I don't want any trouble!"

The student's words finally sink in. CB loosens his grip on his shirt. "Sorry," he says. "Look, hey, I'm sorry about—"

The student doesn't bother to listen. He runs off down the street as fast as he can go.

CB looks around. A few people who'd stopped to gawk suddenly decide they have better things to do. He turns back to the storefront and stares at it in astonishment.

Ten years. Ten years in Farraday City, trying to figure out what made it tick, trying to learn how to bring it down. And he never knew. He paid attention to the news, but... not that kind of news. He'd been too busy. Too busy, and it'd been gone for five years, and he never knew.

It's at that moment, as he's standing in the rain, staring at something he used to love, something that no longer exists, that's he's forced to confront the one thing he's been trying to ignore ever since he got off the bus at Port Authority.

Alex is gone.

Alex is really gone.

PART ONE: LOFT APARTMENT, QUEENS

The sound is quiet, even in the near-total silence of the room: the faint sound of crickets chirruping on a summer night. It does not, however, go overlooked. The man throws off his covers, rolls out of bed, and lurches toward the jacket thrown over the back of an office chair. The room is dark, the curtains drawn, the only light comes from an old digital clock displaying 2:25 on a red LED. He fumbles for the inside pocket of the jacket and pulls out a smartphone. It's not a model you can buy on the market.

The light radiating from the slab illuminates the tired features of Jason Kline. He's only been home for a few hours. He and his team have been busy. Looking at the number on the display, it looks like he's going to have to be busy again.

He turns on the phone, says "Two minutes, please," then puts it on hold. He sets it down on his desk, reaches over to turn on the desk light, and slips into his chair. He shivers as bare skin touches cold leather—he's only wearing boxers—but he ignores the cold as he places his smartphone in a cradle to the right of his computer monitor, then turns his computer on.

Almost immediately the monitor flickers to life, numbers scrolling up the screen like they did in *the Matrix*. Jason hates that movie, but he likes the screensaver.

Half a minute later his phone beeps, and the monitor displays the Haruspex Analytics login screen. One username, one password. He places his thumb on the screen of his smartphone and leans in to the monitor so that his eye lines up with the webcam attached to the side. The smartphone screen flashes, a light runs down the length of his phone. A small white light shines over the webcam, illuminating Jason's right eye. A second later the monitor blinks and displays the profile for the incoming call. No identity is shown, but the security credentials are higher than his own, even now that he's been read in to Project Recall. It takes a moment for the computer to verify that the connection is secure, then a green bar displays under the profile.

Jason takes the phone off hold. "This is Kline. Line is secure."

"*Herr Kline.*" A German accent. Not very thick, but noticeable. "I apologize for the time of night. I expect you were asleep."

Jason stifles a yawn. "That's okay," he says. "I was told to expect a call. I... I'm sorry, I'm not sure what protocol we should use."

The voice on the other end of the line hesitates. "How secure is your home?"

"Haruspex is taking every precaution," Jason says. "Under most circumstances, I'd say this line is as secure as it could possibly be."

"Most circumstances?"

Jason frowns. This line can only be used by personnel with the highest levels of access—the Chairman, certain members of the Board, and a very few high-placed employees. It's only used when the highest levels of security are absolutely necessary. Which means, in theory, it's almost as secure as meeting face to face in a SCIF. But "almost" is one of those words that gets people in trouble.

"We still haven't found the source of the security breach," Jason says. "Until we do, I can't guarantee this connection. Our mole could be one of the people involved in setting it up."

The other end of the line is silent. Jason waits.

"We will have to take the risk," the man says. "I need you to work on this now."

"OK," Jason says. "Let's get started. Am I authorized to know your name?"

"Richter," the man says. "You may call me Richter."

Jason blinks. *Johann Richter.* The man who killed Liberty. "All right. Mr. Richter. What can I do for you?"

"This morning I returned to Captain Morgan's penthouse. I wanted to... I wasn't convinced we'd made a clean exit. The police have, as yet, found nothing, but I suspected there was more."

"Oh?" Jason leans closer. "What did you find?"

"Morgan had a security system. The EMP sweeper should have destroyed everything, but... there was a hard drive."

Jason frowns, keys in a few commands, and calls up a file on Alexander Morgan. "You think it survived?"

"Perhaps," Richter says. "It was in a different room, down the hall. There may have been enough space between it and the device to have survived the blast."

"Do you have it?" Jason asks.

A small sigh escapes the other end. "No," Richter admits. "When I arrived someone had already retrieved it. He... evaded my attempts to subdue him."

Jason hesitates and stares at the screen, frowning. "So he was a metahuman? Was he a *hero*?" An alarm goes off in the back of his head.

"Oh yes," Richter says. "Well... after a fashion. And one who trained with Morgan. The influence is unmistakable. It was our mutual friend."

Curveball.

"He was in town for the funeral," Jason says. A few keystrokes later and the profile for Curveball—a new file he'd finished keying in himself, not eight hours ago—displays next to Morgan.

"I know," Richter says. "He delivered the eulogy. I found it quite moving."

"OK," Jason says, "so we have two, maybe three problems. First, you think Liberty's security system may have recorded the attack, and that there's a possibility it might have survived the EMP."

"Yes."

"Second, someone has already taken the hard drive. You think it's Curveball."

"He was in the room where the drive was kept," Richter confirms. "What is the third problem?"

"Do you think he recognized you?"

There's a long silence on the other end of the connection. For a second Jason thinks they've been disconnected—it's irrational, because the monitor still shows the blinking light that identifies an active connection, but the silence is unnerving.

"Yes," Richter says. "His tactics—the way he fought—they changed. At the start it was very aggressive. He was fighting to win. But during the fight he changed his mind, decided to run. I believe he recognized me."

A list of Morgan's known associates begins to scroll down the screen under his profile. Jason's new program flags entries that are also known associates of Curveball, and then flags suspected associates in a different color. "How did he escape?"

"He… jumped off the balcony."

Liberty's penthouse is on the top floor. Jason's eyes widen. "Do you have any idea where he went?"

"No," Richter says. "He has a legitimate reputation for being able to avoid capture. Ten years ago the United States Government branded him a fugitive and marshaled every resource they had to try and track him down. They failed miserably. And he uncovered a government conspiracy in the process. A very embarrassing three months for the United States."

Jason exhales, a long, slow breath. "Okay. That's not good. If he knows who you are and he's in the wind, then he's had the opportunity to tell others. If word gets out you were involved in Liberty's death—"

"That will not be the end of the world," Richter interrupts. "That is one of the reasons I was chosen to do it. I am, after all, his oldest enemy."

"As soon as you're connected with Liberty's death we're going to have every hero in the city gunning for you," Jason says. "The registered heroes we can manage, but there are others..."

He hears Richter sigh in frustration. "You are probably right. We cannot afford to have groups like Crossfire involved. I will prepare to leave immediately. You will handle the hard drive?"

"I'll do what I can," Jason says. "I'll contact my team, and we'll get started."

Jason waits for the connection light to turn red. It stays green.

"Are you a Jew, *Herr Kline?*"

Jason blinks. "What?"

"Kline is a Jewish name. Or, at least, it is an American bastardization of a Jewish name. Americans insist on changing everything. But if I am not mistaken, Kline is Yiddish for 'little.'"

Jason tries to keep his voice steady. "I didn't know that."

"You didn't?"

"I'm not Jewish."

"I see." Richter sounds almost disappointed. "Well. I will leave you to your work."

The connection light turns red.

Jason sighs in relief. He reaches for his phone, preparing to contact the rest of his team, but a name on the screen catches his eye. It's one of Curveball's "suspected associates." He frowns, clicks on the name, then swears in amazement as he sees the picture for the first time.

"Jenny?"

Jennifer Forrest. Daughter of Martin and Juliet Forrest. Great-granddaughter of Captain Alexander Morgan.

"She never mentioned *that*," he mutters. Not that he would have expected her to. Still... is it something he can use to his advantage?

Maybe.

He reaches for his phone, calls his team, and plans out the rest of his day.

PART TWO: FORREST BROWNSTONE

It's almost 3 AM when CB finally stumbles through the front door of the Forrest's brownstone. He still aches from his encounter with Richter. The adrenaline has worn off, leaving him exhausted.

"CB?" Martin is in the living room, sitting in his easy chair, reading a newspaper. He's still dressed.

"Jesus, Marty…" CB manages a half-rictus grin, then stumbles over to the couch, collapsing onto it. "Did you wait up for me?"

Martin shrugs.

CB laughs weakly. "I'm not your kid, you know."

"I know," Martin says. "If you were my kid you'd know to call if you were going to be out this late." CB can hear the relief in his voice. "What the hell happened to you?"

CB shrugs with the shoulder that wasn't almost ripped out of his body. "Got into a fight. Jumped off a balcony. Fell about forty feet. Jerked my arm pretty bad. Landed on concrete… oh. And I got shot."

Martin's eyes widen. "You got *shot*?" His voice is sharp, full of alarm.

CB closes his eyes and thinks. "No," he says. "Sorry. *At.* I got shot *at.*"

"You smell terrible," Martin observes.

"That'd be from all the sweat," CB says. "And the blood."

"You'd better hope you're not bleeding on that couch." Juliet walks into the living room wearing a thick, white cloth bathrobe, cotton pajamas and fuzzy slippers. "I just had that cleaned."

CB waves half-heartedly in her direction. "Sorry," he says. "I'm pretty sure the blood's dry."

"You sure know how to put a girl at ease." Juliet's voice is much drier than the blood.

"What are you doing up?" CB asks.

"I heard my husband say 'you got shot,'" she says. "I assumed he was talking to you."

CB laughs.

"He got shot *at*," Martin clarifies. "He's not communicating very well."

"I'm tired," CB says.

Juliet studies CB for a moment. "Go to bed," she says finally. "We can talk about it in the morning."

"No..." CB forces himself to stand. "I found something. It's probably important... Marty, do you have a computer? I need to borrow a computer."

"What's going on?" Jenny enters the living room, frowning, wearing an oversized t-shirt and biking shorts. "Who needs a computer?"

"Pack of light sleepers in this house," CB grumbles.

"CB needs a computer for something," Martin says. Everyone looks at CB expectantly.

CB reaches into his trenchcoat pocket and pulls out the hard drive. "I took this from Alex's apartment. It was the hard drive to his security system."

Jenny stares at the drive thoughtfully. Juliet and Martin look surprised.

"I didn't know he had one," Martin says.

"I did," CB says. "He talked a lot about it after he had it installed. He was pretty proud of it. Anyway, I need to hook it up to a computer to see what's on it."

"No problem," Jenny says. "I'll get my laptop."

"Jenny is a hacker," Juliet says.

Jenny narrows her eyes. "No, mom. I'm not. I'm a *security analyst.*" The tone in her voice suggests they've had this conversation before. "So what's on the drive?"

CB hesitates.

Jenny frowns. "Well?"

CB looks at the hard drive and frowns. "The night he died."

Nobody says anything.

"Yeah," CB says. "Maybe you should give this a pass."

The silence stretches on.

"No," Juliet says softly. "If that thing has the last moments of my grandfather on this earth... I want to see it."

"Really?" CB looks at her incredulously. "Because I *really don't.*"

Juliet tilts her head back and looks CB straight in the eyes. "Really."

"... I'll get my stuff," Jenny says, and heads back upstairs.

"Bring it into the kitchen," Martin says. "I think CB needs some coffee."

"God yes," CB mutters. He follows Martin and Juliet into the kitchen.

The kitchen is a long room with a ceramic tile floor and an island butcher block table in the center. CB sets the hard drive on the table, shakes off his trenchcoat, and drapes it over one of the stools set around the table. His Black Flag t-shirt is stained with blood. His right arm is covered in bruises, with swollen, angry welts around his wrist. He climbs up on another stool and leans over the table, head in his hands.

Juliet notices his arm. "That looks bad," she says. "I'll get the first aid kit."

CB shrugs. He listens to the coffee maker boiling water, listens to the sound of water passing through the filter into the carafe, and feels his eyes close.

Moments later Martin places a hot cup of coffee under his nose. CB's eyes open, and his left hand curls around the mug. He feels the heat seep into his fingers. He leans over and breathes in. It's strong. He takes a sip and sighs.

"Thanks."

"So what happened?" Martin asks.

"Someone else had the same idea I did," CB says. "Luckily I got there first."

Juliet returns with bandages, a bag of cotton, and a few bottles. CB automatically extends his arm and sits patiently as she cleans his arm and bandages it up. It's an old routine, and they fall into it naturally.

CB is halfway through his second cup of coffee when Jenny returns with a large laptop bag, followed by a sleepy and confused Andy, dressed in a t-shirt and sweat pants, carrying two more.

"Black Flag?" Jenny asks. "How old is that shirt?"

"Older than you," CB says. "What's all this?"

Jenny sets her bag down on the table. "My stuff. Andy, just set the others down by me."

Andy shrugs and sets the other two bags down on the floor next to her stool.

"This should cover just about any contingency," Jenny explains. "I didn't want to have to go back upstairs."

She picks up the hard drive, studies it briefly, then opens up one of the other laptop bags and rummages around inside it. A few minutes later the hard drive is connected to Jenny's laptop, which is so large CB thinks it really doesn't deserve the name.

"It's good," Jenny says finally. "Considering the shape CB was in, I was half-afraid the drive would be too knocked up to work, but it's good."

They all gather around Jenny to get a better look at the laptop screen.

"OK," CB says. "Go on."

There's no sound, only an image—rather, six images, one from each camera, each showing a different angle. In one frame Alex's apartment looks completely empty. In another, he can be seen crouching behind his couch, reaching under his computer desk. In another the front door shudders, then splinters. In another, the windows on each side of the French doors shatter and men start to enter the room.

"These angles are terrible," Jenny says. "He's got six cameras and he's still not getting the French doors. Who set this up?"

"Alex did," CB says. "He was proud of that. In his defense the cameras were hidden pretty well."

"He should have called me," Jenny grumbles.

It's not easy to figure out which screen to pay attention to at first. There are men coming into the living room, and men coming in through the door. Alex moves so quickly he's nothing but a blur to the camera, and seconds later the men in the door are down. Seconds after that, the men in the living room rush back out of the view of the camera, to the balcony, as the muzzle flash of a rifle erupts from the front door. Seconds after that, Alex flies across the living room camera and disappears out of view.

Everyone is silent as they watch. There is no movement from any of the cameras for what feels like eternity. Then, finally, Alex reappears, soaking wet. He leans over the computer, staring at something on the monitor.

Then he stiffens, straightens, and raises his hands over his head.

Juliet tenses. Martin puts his hand on her shoulder.

Alex turns around. His mouth moves, but there's no sound. CB grinds his teeth in frustration—none of the cameras show who he's talking to. Then Alex's head cocks to one side—very slightly, as if he'd heard a noise—and seconds later he leaps through the air... and falls to the ground, dead.

Juliet sobs and buries her head in Martin's chest. Martin, watery-eyed, tries to comfort her. Andy stands by his mother, a mix of emotions running across his face, and while Jenny doesn't show any emotion at all, her hands are shaking so badly she has to fold them in her lap.

Another man walks into the picture.

"That's him," CB snarls. "That son of a bitch."

Everyone turns their attention back to the monitor. A man dressed in commando gear is staring down at the body, then turns toward the computer.

"Who?" Juliet asks. "Who killed him?"

"Johann Richter," CB says.

"Never heard of him," Jenny says. "Who is he?"

"He was a lot more famous in World War II," CB says. "He was the reason the US started Project Paragon."

Jenny's eyes widen. "*That* Richter? I thought he died. That's what they taught us in history class."

"I'm not surprised," CB says. "He likes to keep a very low profile. Why is he looking at Alex's computer?"

Jenny squints at the screen. "I can't tell. It looks like he's reading something on the screen."

"I don't suppose you can..." CB waves his hands in the air. "You know, do some kind of Hollywood computer magic to get us a clearer picture?"

"No," Jenny says tersely. "Hollywood computer magic isn't real."

"Don't get her started on that," Andy warns. "She'll go on for hours."

"Is it important?" Martin asks. "What's on the computer, I mean."

CB nods. "Probably."

"If I could get my hands on that computer's hard drive I bet I could recover it," Jenny says.

CB looks at her and raises an eyebrow. "Yeah?"

"Yeah," Jenny says. "Dad, maybe you could make a few calls? I really want to know what he thought was so important."

"Hold on a moment," CB says. "I just had a notion. Does this thing have Internet?" He gestures to Jenny's laptop.

"Wireless," Jenny says.

"Is it on now?"

"Yes..." Jenny looks at CB curiously. "It is 'on' now."

"Scoot over and let me drive a minute."

Jenny hesitates, then climbs off the stool and stands aside. CB hunches over the table and starts typing.

"None of you are watching me do this," he says. "If asked, you don't know what the hell anyone is talking about."

"So what *are* you doing?" Jenny asks.

"Checking my email," CB says.

"Wait... you have an email address?" Andy sounds incredulous. "All this time? And you never contacted anyone?"

"It's not for social calls."

"No kidding," Jenny says. "Andy, it's a TTI domain."

Andy's eyes widen. "You have a Thorpe account?"

"Of course I have a Thorpe account," CB says. "I worked with the guy for years! We're friends. Mostly."

Jenny frowns. "What do you mean by that? Either you're friends or you aren't."

"No," CB says, "'mostly' friends is pretty standard for me."

"Yeah," Martin agrees. "That's about right."

Juliet makes a disapproving noise in the back of her throat.

"OK, so..." CB's voice trails off as he looks at his inbox for the first time in weeks. There's only one message.

"Holy shit," Andy breathes.

"Open it," Jenny urges.

CB clicks the title.

I know you're going to get this, no matter what they try, because it's you...

CB reads the email in silence.

"There's an attachment," Jenny says. "Open it."

CB clicks the attachment and is completely unsurprised when it fails to open.

"Looks like Alex was being careful," he says. "Encrypted."

"Do you have the key?" Jenny asks.

CB shrugs.

"No," Jenny says impatiently, "that isn't something you answer with a shrug. Encrypted files require a key. If he sent you an encrypted file, that means you have to have a key."

"Then I guess I have a key," CB says. "Damned if I know what it is, though. I won't be able to open it here, at any rate. I need something to save it to..." He rummages through his pockets and pulls out a USB thumb drive. "This should do it."

"What's that for?" Jenny asks.

"I don't actually have a computer," CB says. "I use the ones at the public library, mostly. If I want to make backups I put 'em on this."

"You don't have a *computer*?" Jenny shakes her head in disbelief.

"Why should I? The ones at the library work fine."

"Never mind that," Martin says. "CB, do you know what's in the file?"

"Not a clue," CB says, "but I bet whatever's in it has something to do with why Alex died. Richter sure seemed interested in what Alex was doing on his..."

CB's voice trails off. Then he frowns. "Oh, *fuck.*"

Everyone looks at him curiously, except for Juliet, who looks at him in alarm.

"Martin." CB keeps his voice deliberately casual. "I can't help but notice how well you've kept up the house. It doesn't really look like much has changed since I was here last."

Martin frowns. "Not much has. We refinished a few surfaces and had the floors polished. That's about it."

"Yeah..." CB pushes away from the table, walks around to the other side, and picks up his trenchcoat. "I was wondering if you still had that panic room."

There's a slight pause. "We still have it."

CB puts on his trenchcoat. "Good. Go there. Right now. All four of you."

"Right..." Martin exchanges a knowing glance with Juliet. "How bad?"

"I apologize in advance."

Martin looks around his kitchen and sighs. "Damn it. You're sure?"

"I'm tired," CB says. "It's going to get messy."

"Right," Juliet says in a businesslike voice. "Well, you heard the man. Everyone into the panic room, double-time."

Jenny starts packing up her laptop. Andrew hesitates. "Can I help?"

"No," CB says. "Sorry. I'll get you when it's over."

"Come on, son," Martin says. "He knows what he's talking about."

Jenny finishes packing up her laptop and they all file out of the kitchen. Jenny stops at the door and turns back. "Be careful," she says.

CB grins. "The hell I will."

Jenny shudders.

"Oh, Juliet," CB calls down the hall after them. "I have to apologize for something else."

"What's that?" Juliet's voice is stronger now. She was always good about bouncing back.

"I'm going to smoke in your house."

Sharp laughter echoes down the hall.

"I guess you might as well."

PART THREE: ASSAULT

CB sits in Martin's easy chair, smoking and waiting. All the lights in the house are off. All the curtains are drawn, the blinds are closed, and the house, for the moment, is silent.

He clenches and unclenches his right fist, forcing his arm to limber up. It wants to hurt. Now is not the time.

He sits up slightly as he hears the sound of a vehicle slowing, then coming to a stop a few houses down. Then he hears it again, and then a third time. CB gets up, walks to the front door, then peers through the peephole. He doesn't see much, but he hears the sliding door of a van.

Three vans in front. Assume three vans in back. How many per van? They need room for gear. Four? Assume six. Assume thirty-six in all...

Will Richter be part of this? He shudders at the thought and pushes it out of his mind. *Six vans full of bad guys in a residential area is messy. Richter doesn't like to work messy.*

But he's been known to make exceptions in the past.

CB backs away from the front door, into a hallway that separates the living room from the dining room, with stairs leading up to the second floor and down to the basement. He hears the steady, rhythmic pulse of blades slicing through the air.

Helicopter.

CB takes a deep breath and closes his eyes. He feels the world whirling around him, fragments sliding over each other, around each other, like misshapen puzzle pieces that almost, but don't quite, fit. All of reality pulses, rises up, crests, and comes crashing down around him, washing over him. Then—all at once—the whirling stops, the pieces come together, and the world snaps into focus.

He's ready, and he's angry. He's angrier than he's been in a long time.

He reaches into his trenchcoat pocket and pulls out a pair of welding goggles. He puts them on, making sure there's a proper seal around each eye, then lights another cigarette. He stands in the hall and smokes, feeling the tension around him tighten until it reaches a breaking point, and everything unravels into chaos.

The gas comes first. He hears the living room windows shatter as tear gas hits the back wall with a thud, and hears the hiss as the canisters discharge. His lungs are stinging, but he's been around tear gas enough to handle that. It was the involuntary tearing he needed to deal with. He hears glass shattering in the kitchen—the window in the back door, and the window over the kitchen sink—and imagines the scene is repeating in there.

Flashbang grenades follow almost immediately. He hears the bang and sees an echo of the light through the living room entrance. After that, the front door crashes in, and heavy boots run through the room. The boots stop before anyone comes through. He can imagine what's next—a man on each side of the door, someone silently counting down to three...

CB steps directly into the doorway and kicks.

His boot connects with a gas mask to his left—a black-clad soldier (no, he corrects himself, this is definitely an *operative*) falls back, his rifle discharging into the air. He hears a truncated cry as another operative, crouched on the other side of the entrance, is hit by friendly fire. He's not five feet away from a man dressed in a black commando uniform and body armor, head covered with a gas mask, carrying an assault rifle. The man doesn't hesitate—he opens fire. A three-shot burst, aimed directly at CB's center of mass.

He misses.

CB leaps at him. The operative is still shooting—three bursts, three bursts, three bursts—but each shot goes wild. The television explodes, a picture frame shatters, furniture splinters, but CB is untouched. He tackles the operative and they both fall, hard. The operative lets go of his rifle and reaches for a knife. CB hits him in the neck, and all the man can do from that point forward is choke for air.

More people are coming through the door. CB examines the fallen operative quickly. He has a pistol.

You know how I always tell you to tone things down? How you need to show restraint?

Not this time. Give 'em hell. It's no less than they deserve.

Right.

The pistol slides smoothly out of its holster into his hand. He stands, facing the shattered doorway, as more men storm the house. He can see figures on the sidewalk, in the street, can see a searchlight from the helicopter playing over the road, trying to shine into the house. He hears footsteps behind him, and knows more are coming through the hallway. He releases the safety, closes his eyes, focuses his will, and *pushes out.*

Every gun in the room jams at the same time. Every gun but his.

CB starts shooting. He doesn't bother to aim; he points the gun in whatever direction *feels right*. He points the gun at the front door, pulls the trigger three times. He turns, fires at the wall, from left to right, five times. He turns, fires out the front window, four times. He turns, fires at the back wall two times, then the gun clicks as he empties the magazine. He drops the gun, runs to the hall entrance, and nearly trips over bodies as he turns the corner.

Seven bodies. Three have holstered pistols; CB retrieves two, then rushes down the hall.

An operative steps through the dining room entrance. CB fires once, and the man collapses; a second steps over the body and turns, bringing a rifle to bear. CB fires again, and the operative falls, sideways into the wall.

The grenades come next. He hears something roll into the hallway through the living room entrance and sees two tumble through the dining room entrance. He pushes, the world shifts, and the grenades sit on the floor, doing absolutely nothing at all.

CB runs into the dining room. It's a long room; the table still stands upright but it's been pushed out of the way, leaving scratches across the floor. Water seeps in from under the swinging doors separating the dining room from the kitchen, and five men crouch on either side of the door, three on the left, two on the right. All five are distracted: they're waiting for something that's not happening.

CB happens instead.

He charges forward, opening up with both pistols. Immediately two twitch and fall; the remaining three scatter, raising their rifles. CB *pushes*, and one rifle slips free of an operative's grasp at the same moment the firing mechanism malfunctions, causing it to discharge uncontrollably until the magazine is empty. The rifle twists in its sling, spraying the entire room as it discharges. CB is untouched, and the other two operatives fall. He shoots the third. Just as CB passes through the swinging doors into the kitchen, the grenades in the hallway remember what they're supposed to do. The thin walls are torn apart from the force of the blasts. The wall between the kitchen and dining room shakes as shrapnel tears into it, but it stands.

There are four operatives in the kitchen, with one more coming through what remains of the back door. The tile floor is covered in an inch of water—a pipe burst under the sink. CB slides across the wet floor, firing into the room. Three operatives fall, two in the room and the one in the doorway. The two left in the kitchen train their rifles on him. He tucks into a sideways roll, pushes off the butcher block table, and slides into the legs of one, who tumbles on top of him. CB strikes the operative on the head with the butt of his pistol, hard, and as he feels the man slump he fires both pistols into the second.

Nothing happens. Both guns jam simultaneously.

Time to improvise: CB *throws* the pistols at the second operative. One strikes the barrel of the rifle just as he pulls the trigger, and the rifle discharges into the ceiling. A chunk of plaster falls to the ground as CB picks himself up off the floor and charges the operative, throwing his shoulder into the operative's armored gut and shoving him backward until the small of his back hits the corner of the kitchen sink. The man cries out and they both sink to the ground, the operative from pain and CB from exhaustion. CB slams the operative's head through the cabinet doors under the sink—one door already askew from all the water pouring through—and the operative stops moving.

CB is breathing hard. The fight with Richter is catching up to him; the tear gas is finally starting to slow him down. He hears heavy boots coming through the dining room.

The remnants of the cabinet doors under the sink hang uselessly on broken hinges. Through the scraps of wood, just over the operative's head, CB sees a fire extinguisher, apparently intact. He grabs it just as the swinging doors burst open and the first of maybe four operatives burst into the kitchen.

CB pulls the safety pin out of the extinguisher and throws. It flies through the air, hitting the first operative squarely in the face, spraying foam across the room. The operative staggers back and falls into the man behind him—as he does, the fire extinguisher rolls over the first and sprays the second man directly in the face, covering his gas mask with a thick layer of fire-retardant foam. He curses and shoves the first operative to one side, then staggers forward, trying to wipe the foam off his mask.

CB gets to his feet, takes a deep breath—coughs—then leaps onto the electric stove, leaps from the stove to the butcher block table, then runs the length of the table, leaping across the room to land, feet first, on the second operative's face. He staggers back into the third, and the third into the fourth. They collapse like dominoes; CB drops to the floor in front of them, cushions his fall with his arms, and gets to his feet just in time to kick an operative as he tries to get back on his feet. Then CB leans against the doorframe, panting heavily.

CB hears the sound of boots splashing in water; out of the corner of his eye he sees one more operative, standing in the frame of the back door, rifle trained on him. CB tries to *push*, but he's tired. He can't concentrate. He laughs weakly as he turns, too exhausted to do anything but watch the operative pull the trigger.

He hears a *thoom* in the distance, and by the time he figures out it's something moving faster than the speed of sound he's covered in glass and bits of brick as an adult-sized blur of motion races through the already-shattered kitchen window and stops between CB and the operative. As soon as it stops moving, CB recognizes it immediately.

It's Roger.

The bullets ricochet off Roger as if he were made out of stone—they even spark when they hit his body. A moment later he blurs again, and in the blink of an eye he's right in front of the operative, where he gives him the slightest tap on the chest, and sends him flying backward into the night.

Roger blurs again, disappears, and reappears moments later in the center of the kitchen, just to the left of the table. He wears faded jeans, tennis shoes, and a t-shirt now riddled with holes.

"All clear," Roger says.

"Good timing." CB grins wearily. "Faster than a speeding bullet."

The corner of Roger's mouth curls up ever so slightly. "Tryin' to get me sued?"

CB coughs once and makes his way over the refrigerator. He has to kick the body of an operative out of the way to open it, but he's pleasantly surprised to discover the light still comes on. "Want a beer?"

"It's a little late for me."

CB shrugs and grabs two, slipping one into his pocket. "Guess we better wait for the police."

The walls separating the dining room from the hall and the hall from the living room are completely gone. The dining room table is now in pieces, the living room furniture is barely recognizable, and the front door is now just a gaping hole in the brick. As CB steps out onto the front porch he sees every light in every house in the neighborhood is on. Neighbors are standing on their doorsteps, some gawking, some on their cell phones calling friends or relatives, some taking pictures—and probably putting them on Facebook, or whatever it is people are using for that these days.

For all the attention, no one is willing to approach the house. Not yet.

CB settles down on the front step and opens his beer. Roger sits down next to him.

"There are a hell of a lot of dead bodies in this house," Roger says quietly.

CB sighs. "Yeah."

"It's gonna be real awkward when the police get here."

"Couldn't help it," CB says. "I had to push."

Roger doesn't say anything.

"Also, those are the bastards who got Alex."

Roger looks at him sharply. "Yeah?"

CB shrugs. "I don't know how they tie in, exactly, but yeah. How did you know to come?"

"Marty called. Where are they?"

"Oh. Shit." CB hauls himself to his feet. "They're in the panic room. I guess we should let 'em out."

"You sure you want to do that?" Roger asks. "Juliet is going to be *pissed*."

CB hesitates. "I'll finish my beer first." He sits back down.

Roger laughs.

PART FOUR: AFTERMATH

It all goes down pretty much the way CB expects, with one exception: the police arrive before the press. This is a positive development. Still, the arrival of the Fire Department, followed by the local police, followed by the press, followed by the EMTs, followed by CSI, followed by the FBI, followed by the Army, and then, finally, followed by the Federal Bureau of Metahuman Affairs makes the entire cleanup a mess. The police cordon off the block, forcing the press to either retreat or make hasty business agreements with some of Martin and Juliet's neighbors, but other than that nothing is getting done: everyone is too busy arguing over what to do.

The FBMA insists on taking charge, since metahumans were involved in the fight. The FBI insists on taking charge, since the attackers look like foreign nationals, and terrorism is a concern. The Brooklyn PD points out that this took place in their jurisdiction, the Fire Department insists on making sure the house won't explode or burn to the ground, and the EMTs just want to look for survivors and make sure they get medical treatment. Things are just about to get interesting when Pete Travers shows up.

Travers is one of the only people CB has ever met who can get different government agencies to work together willingly. It's an impressive skill to have, and even if Travers had been an idiot it would have made him indispensable to his superiors. As it happens, Travers isn't an idiot. As soon as he shows up everyone who was fighting the moment before falls silent, and *waits*: most of them have worked with him before, those who haven't know him by reputation, and every one of them trusts that whatever decision he makes will be the right call.

CB wonders if Travers might be metahuman after all.

In short order Travers has all the groups working together like a semi-well-ordered machine: as soon as he's convinced there's no longer a human threat in the area, he sends in the Army to dispose of the unexploded ordinance, then the Fire Department to make sure the house isn't about to spontaneously combust and burn to the ground. Finally CSI goes in to collect evidence, tag the bodies, and move them to the morgue. Meanwhile, the FBMA questions the survivors.

CB doesn't get much of a chance to talk to Martin, Juliet, Jenny or Andrew. He gets a tight smile and a nod from Martin, and Juliet says, "Well, it could have been worse" before they're intercepted by the FBMA. Jenny and Andrew don't say anything. They're in shock at the state of their house. And there's something else with Jenny—CB isn't sure what, exactly, but she looks fierce.

FBMA standard procedure is to question everyone separately, but there's not a lot of free space. Martin's next-door neighbors volunteer their living room, so he sees everyone being called into the house next door one at a time, only to come out a little later looking vaguely chastened. When it's his turn, he finds himself sitting on a comfortable overstuffed chair, facing four FBMA agents in dark suits, one working recording equipment while another is typing something into a field laptop. There's hot tea sitting on the coffee table. If you ignore the recording equipment it's unusually comfortable for an interrogation room.

The agent in charge, a tall, thin, bearded man named Hollin, asks CB what happened. CB gives him the edited version: they were talking in the kitchen, he heard vehicles idling outside, it didn't feel right, he told the family to get into the panic room.

Agent Hollin doesn't react to anything. He has a good poker face—CB suspects his interrogations usually go pretty well. "Can you tell me what you were all doing up at 3 AM?"

CB shrugs. "I was out late. It was a difficult day. When I got in, everyone else woke up. We were drinking coffee and talking."

Hollin nods. "Do you know why the Forrests would be attacked? Do you think they were the targets?"

CB shrugs. "I really wouldn't know. I mean, I guess it's not really a big secret that Juliet is Liberty's granddaughter. And we'd just had the funeral."

"So you think they were attacked because she was related to Liberty?"

"I didn't say that," CB says. "I mean, it could just as easily have been intended for me. I was his partner for a long time."

Eventually the FBMA gets everything it wants, tells him to stay in town for a few days, and CB leaves the neighbor's house, looking suitably chastened.

He's greeted by Roger at the front step.

"They get you yet?" CB asks.

Roger nods. "I didn't have much to tell them. Hell, I didn't even do much when I got here, other than take a bullet for you. You made most of this mess yourself."

"Did you get the helicopter?" CB asks.

Roger shakes his head. "I passed it on the way in, but it was gone when

I did my perimeter search. Which means it's pretty fast."

"Too bad," CB says. "Still, I appreciate your priorities."

Roger chuckles. "Well, look. They're releasing me, so I'm turning in. I have a spare room if you need it."

"Thanks, Roger," CB says, "but I think I'm going to have to lie low."

Roger nods and extends his hand. CB shakes it. "You let me know what you need," Roger says.

"You bet."

Roger shoots into the sky like a rocket and disappears into the night. CB hears a faint *thoom* in the distance.

Technically CB isn't allowed back in the house—it's a crime scene now, and no one has quite decided if CB is a witness or a suspect. That said, everyone in the house is very busy, and nobody looks up when he makes his way through the living room, climbs up the remnants of the stairs, and makes his way to the guest bedroom on the second floor. The second floor is in much better shape than the first. If it weren't for the lingering smell of smoke and tear gas he wouldn't have known anything had happened at all.

His duffel bag, already packed, sits at the foot of his bed. He picks up the bag, turns around, and sees Jenny standing in the doorway, looking at him.

"What's up?" CB asks.

Jenny doesn't answer. She looks at the duffel bag.

"Yeah," CB says. "This isn't exactly the way I planned it, but it looks like I—"

"I'm coming with you," she says.

CB frowns. "No, you're not."

Jenny's jaw tightens. "Yes I am."

"No," CB repeats. "You really aren't."

"Look," Jenny says, "you're going to need someone to figure out how to crack that encryption. Unless you already have the key. Do you have the key? No? I didn't think so. But I can do it. Hell, CB, I'm *really good* at doing that sort of thing. I can help you, and it's my great-grandfather we're talking about here."

CB stares at Jenny. She meets his gaze, unflinching.

"Seen your house lately?" CB asks.

Jenny narrows her eyes.

"The guys who did this? They were good. They were very well trained, very well armed, and very well organized. They're also not the ones who killed Alex. The one who killed Alex was *significantly better than them*. And I expect there are others like him involved."

Jenny looks at the floor.

CB sighs. "Look. I *might* be able to protect you if we run into more of these mercenaries. But... it's hard to say. The higher the stakes, the harder it is for me to guarantee anything, other than your insurance company jacking up their fees. Downstairs is mostly my doing, and that was against normal, well-trained men."

"*You* did this?" Jenny's voice sharpens. "Why the hell would you...?"

"I didn't do it on *purpose*," CB snaps. "It's the way... it's the way my talent works. It *scales* and *escalates*. A lot of people think it scales disproportionately to the situation, favoring overkill."

"I don't care," Jenny says. "Besides, you're going to need a ride out of here."

"Well," CB says, "I was thinking maybe I'd just steal a car..."

"You will *not*!" Jenny says, scandalized. "First of all, don't you *dare* do that to Mom and Dad right now. Second... *steal a car*?"

"Fine!" CB throws up his hands in exasperation. "You can drive me around, and you can help with the encryption. But if I tell you to stay behind at some point, it's because I'm pretty damn sure that if you don't you're either going to wind up getting killed, or I'm going to get killed trying to keep you from getting killed. At which point, you'll probably get killed anyway. Understood?"

"Fine," Jenny says. "But you're still not smoking in my car."

"Christ," CB mutters. "All right, let's go."

They agree to meet two blocks down, leaving separately to attract less attention. Jenny ducks into the alley to get her car, and CB walks up to Martin and Juliet, both sitting beside an ambulance, wrapped in blankets, drinking coffee out of a thermos.

"I keep forgetting how expensive your visits can be," Martin says dryly.

"And you were always such a cheap date," Juliet adds.

CB grins. "Sorry. I should have done all this somewhere else. I didn't want to drag you guys into it."

Martin shakes his head. "We were already in it. We know what it means to be part of this world."

"And we stick around anyway," Juliet says, smiling slightly.

"Of course," Martin adds, "it helps that I'm rich."

CB laughs out loud. "I guess it would at that."

Martin nods to the duffel bag slung over CB's shoulder. "Moving on?"

CB nods. "I'm going to have to poke around a little, and staying here... well. Bad idea. Especially since it looks like things are going to scale up."

Martin frowns. "I see."

Juliet looks around, suddenly worried. "Where's Jenny? I see Andy, but I don't see Jenny anywhere."

CB looks at her steadily.

Juliet's eyes widen. "No!"

"It wasn't my idea," CB says. "She takes after her mother."

Martin places a reassuring hand on Juliet's shoulder. "She's an adult," he says. "She can make her own decisions."

"No she *can't*," Juliet mutters.

"I'll keep her out of the thick of it," CB promises. "I'm half-tempted to give her the slip and leave her behind, but she has that look. You know the one, Juliet, don't even *try* to pretend you have no idea what I'm talking about. If I ditched her, she'd just find a way to follow me, attracting all sorts of attention along the way. At least I got her to agree to stay put when I tell her."

"Did you really?" Martin looks surprised.

"Well that's what I'm telling myself. Try to keep Andy out of this, will you? I can't handle both."

"He's not going to go AWOL," Martin says. "He'll be tempted, but he won't actually do it."

"Well," CB says, "that's something, anyway."

"Oh," Juliet adds, "Pete's looking for you. He wanted me to let you know."

"Ah," CB says. "Well... I might have forgotten to pack something. I'm going to head back upstairs for a few minutes."

"Good luck," Martin says. "Keep my little girl safe."

"Please," Juliet adds. CB sees pain and fear on her face.

"I'll do what I can," CB says.

There's not much else to say after that. He heads back upstairs into the guest room and waits. A few minutes later Travers walks in.

"We don't have a lot of time," Travers says.

CB raises an eyebrow.

"Fortunately my reputation for promoting cooperation between agencies has prevented any single agency from getting control of the situation," Travers says. "Which means nobody is listening in just yet."

"Why do you think that's a concern?" CB asks.

Travers sighs. "I think Alex's death was an inside job."

CB feels his jaw drop. "The hell you say."

"Not *completely* inside, but a few things happened in the last few weeks that make me think someone inside was involved in his death... and that they used me to help make it happen."

Travers looks as calm and mildly polite as he ever has, but his voice is thick with anger. "A few weeks ago Alex called me out of the blue. He wanted to know if I knew anything about the old Project Paragon archives—if they still existed, and if he could get a look at them. I told him I'd look into it. I made a few calls. The people I called wanted to know who wanted to know... and I told them Liberty wanted to know, because... well, hell, CB, because it was *Liberty*. I didn't think anything about it."

CB nods.

"Every call came back with an apology and a statement that Project Paragon files were still classified. One or two said they'd be happy to research specific questions, if Liberty had any. That's what I told Alex, and he said he wasn't surprised by the answer, thanked me, and that was that. Except that a few weeks later I got a call from a man following up on my inquiry with a bunch of questions about what Liberty had been looking for. Did he tell me anything further? Did I know if he'd been in contact with any of his old teammates? I thought it was odd, and when I asked the guy to identify himself he gave me a name that was flagged as an active alias for someone used in a covert operation. A few days later Alex was murdered. And now... suddenly I'm getting a lot of calls about you. A *lot* of calls."

"I see," CB says.

"Yeah," Travers says. "Calls from people I don't know, but who apparently have enough pull to get my bosses on my case. My bosses want 'full cooperation.' And you know what? It's all starting to feel very familiar to me."

CB nods again.

"Did you know we put a watch on this house?" Travers continues. "Yeah, we've had people watching this house nonstop, 24/7, ever since Alex's death was reported on the news. Only tonight, for some *mysterious* reason, the watch rotation gets screwed up, and the agents on watch were relieved a full hour before their replacements showed up. Someone arranged that lapse on our end, CB, and that was the window these guys used to attack the house. There's no getting around it, we've been compromised."

"Again?" CB asks.

Travers shakes his head. "More like 'still.' I think it's the same people from ten years ago. I always felt like parts of the investigation were too easy. And parts of the job—parts that should have been routine—were close to impossible." He pulls out a USB thumb drive and a cell phone, and hands them to CB. "The drive has everything I know. I don't know how useful that'll be, but maybe we'll get lucky. The phone will contact me directly. Don't use it until you have something important to tell me: you get one call, then it's in the system. I recommend ditching it after that."

"OK," CB says. "Thanks."

Travers nods. "Good luck." They shake hands, then Travers heads back down the stairs.

CB looks at the thumb drive and the cell phone, puts them in his trenchcoat pocket, then heads outside.

One of the fire engines has moved closer to the house to make it easier for the firemen to unload some equipment. It very conveniently blocks all the good camera shots the news team holed up in the house across the street was hoping to get. CB gets to the police tape without attracting a single flash, ducks under, and keeps walking.

Two blocks down he opens the passenger-side door of Jenny's car, throws his army bag in the back, and climbs in.

"You stink." Jenny wrinkles her nose. "I didn't notice outside."

"Fighting will do that," CB says.

"I'd almost decided you'd ditched me."

CB shakes his head. "Just had to talk to your parents. And Travers."

"Am I in trouble?" She tries to make it sound like a joke, but she sounds legitimately worried.

"Oh hell yes," CB says, "but not from your parents. Though your mom isn't happy you've decided to follow in her footsteps."

"So... what, I'm in trouble with *Travers*?" Jenny frowns. "That doesn't make sense."

"No," CB says, "you're not in trouble with Travers. He just wanted to talk to me. You're in trouble because you decided to put yourself in the middle of something incredibly dangerous—which, for the record, is *stupid*—and putting yourself in the middle of something incredibly dangerous puts you in trouble pretty much by definition."

"So why did Travers want to talk to you?" Jenny ignores everything CB says that she finds inconvenient. *Just like her mother*. He finds it awfully inconvenient that he admires that.

"He gave me some information he thought I might find useful," CB says. "Start driving."

Jenny turns on the ignition. "Where are we going?"

"For the moment we want to put as much distance between us and your house as possible. Other than that, I don't know yet."

"OK," Jenny says, "I'll take us uptown. So what exactly did I get myself into?"

"Hell if I know," CB says. "I hate conspiracies. I really, really, hate conspiracies."

"Conspiracy?" Jenny sounds a little alarmed. "What kind of conspiracy are we talking about?"

"I don't know yet." CB reaches into his trenchcoat pocket for a cigarette, looks sideways at Jenny, sighs, and gives up on the idea. "That's the problem with a conspiracy. The one time out of ten that you actually figure it out, you have to let the bad guys chase you relentlessly across the country first."

Jenny glances at CB. "One time out of ten? What about the other nine times?"

"Hm. Well." CB looks out the passenger-side window. "Nine times out of ten you don't actually figure anything out. They just kill you instead."

PART ONE: HARUSPEX ANALYTICS, TOP FLOOR

"I want to know exactly what happened in that house."

The Chairman isn't shouting; he doesn't even sound angry. But the crispness in his voice is unpleasant. It's the sound of command unfettered by social convention: there's no attempt to soften it with politeness or pleasantry. He's not rude, and he's not overbearing, but there's no question that he's giving an order, and he expects to be obeyed.

It's very early in the morning, but most of the members of the Board are there, sitting around the table, staring at Jason with the same blank expressions they wore the first time he was in the room. If Jason were more arrogant, or less paranoid, he might think the Chairman chose them because they didn't think for themselves. They certainly looked like mindless corporate drones, waiting to be told what they thought by their superior. But Haruspex Analytics isn't that kind of company, and the people who run it don't get promoted for being yes-men. What Jason is looking at isn't stupidity, it's a poker face.

Jason clears his throat nervously. "I don't know."

"That's a very unfortunate admission." There's a noticeable edge to the Chairman's voice now.

Jason tries not to squirm—he wasn't offered a seat at the table as before. He's standing before them, being called to account for something he's only vaguely aware of.

"Mr. Chairman, with all due respect, I don't know what you expect to hear from me. I received a report that someone had accessed Curveball's email account and downloaded the file, of course, but I had nothing to do with that assault team. I didn't even learn there *was* an assault team until after it had been sent in." Jason stares at the shadowy figure in the corner and tries to focus on the spot where he thinks his eyes are.

The Chairman tips his head to one side. "Mr. Kline, I very recently gave you significant operational control over parts of Project Recall that were specific to the security breach."

"Yes sir," Jason says.

"And the email attachment Alexander Morgan sent out before he was 'retired' falls under the parameters of your authority."

"Yes sir," Jason says again. "It does."

"How do you expect me to believe you weren't involved in this unmitigated disaster? We didn't just lose operatives. Some of them were *captured*. They are now security risks."

The members of the Board continue to stare at him blankly. It wasn't this unnerving before. Then again, the last time he wasn't being accused of gross incompetence.

"There is no way I could have organized this assault," Jason insists. "I was still assembling my team in response to an emergency call from Richter earlier this morning."

"Richter?" The Chairman appears startled by this information.

"He had an encounter with Curveball the night before. He believed Curveball had recovered a piece of intelligence that could tie him to the assassination..." Jason deliberately chooses not to use the euphemism. "He decided he had been compromised, and wanted to know what to do next."

"What intelligence?" the Chairman asks.

"Digital footage of the whole thing,'" Jason says.

A low murmur ripples through the back of the boardroom. The Chairman leans over as another board member, also hidden in shadow, murmurs something in his ear.

"The initial report Richter sent indicated he deployed a small EMP when he left the scene," the Chairman says finally.

Jason nods. "He confirmed that in his conversation with me. But it only affected the immediate area. The hard drive was in another room. The EMP ended the transmission from the cameras, but if the hard drive is unaffected it will have a record of everything up to that point."

"And that's why you were assembling your team?"

Jason nods again. "We had to get Richter out of the area. If that information goes public—at this point I'm not sure how to contain it—then everyone will know that Richter was involved. We were arranging travel and resources, as well as tracking down another lead—"

The main doors to the boardroom open behind him. Jason turns, caught off guard, and sees "Mara," the board member who vetted him.

She takes in the room. "I apologize for being late."

"Where were you, Mara?" The Chairman's voice is crisply neutral once more.

Mara keeps her cool. "I was investigating the deployment of the assault team. I can confirm that Mr. Kline was not responsible for that action."

"Oh?" The Chairman's voice doesn't change. There's not the slightest hint as to whether he believes her. "Then who *was* responsible for it?"

"No one, sir."

The Chairman is silent. Jason frowns, looking visibly confused.

"That is to say," Mara continues, "the assault team was automatically deployed as the result of a protocol put in place when intelligence classified 'Threat Red' is distributed without authorization. Mr. Kline placed surveillance on attempts to access Curveball's ThorpeNet account, and the routines were able to trace it back to the Forrest residence in Brooklyn. It also recognized the encrypted package as it was being retrieved. The recognition automatically triggered the protocol."

"So it *was* my fault," Jason says.

Mara looks at him.

"In a way," Jason continues. "Because I set up that surveillance but I didn't check to see if any protocols were assigned to the encrypted package."

"No," Mara says, "it is not your fault."

She turns back to face the board. "The protocol was put in place long before Mr. Kline was added to the project, and while he has been briefed on many parts of Project Omega, this was omitted. His role is analysis, this protocol was military. It was an oversight on my part. I take full responsibility."

There is a slight tremor in her voice as she finishes, but she looks as calm and untroubled as she ever has.

The Chairman is silent a moment longer, then sighs. "All right, Mara. Take your seat."

Mara walks around the table to her empty seat, and sits.

"Mr. Kline," the Chairman says. "It appears I assumed incorrectly concerning your role in this mess. Please accept my apology."

Jason tries not to look surprised. He's not used to his bosses apologizing to him. "Thank you, sir."

"Now let's go back to something you were saying when Mara walked in," the Chairman says. "You were tracking down another lead?"

Jason takes a breath. "Yes, sir. When Richter called me and said he found Curveball in Captain Morgan's condo I began to run an analysis on both of their files, trying to find commonalities between them. One of the matches was Martin Forrest and his family. Forrest married Captain Morgan's granddaughter."

"I'm familiar with Martin Forrest," the Chairman says. "And we already know Curveball associates with that family."

"Yes," Jason says, "but this isn't about Curveball. It's about me. As it turns out, I'm familiar with Mr. Forrest's daughter Jennifer."

"Really?" The Chairman leans forward slightly. "Explain."

"I met her at a security conference last year," Jason says. "She'd just been hired as a computer security analyst for DataComm Industries. She hasn't been in the industry long, but she's quite talented."

"How well do you know her?" the Chairman asks.

"Well..." Jason shifts uncomfortably. "It was a week-long conference, and we enjoyed each other's company. But we didn't talk about our personal lives. I knew her last name, but I didn't realize she was part of that family until this morning. I got to know a great deal about her skill with computers, though... and the equipment she used. And based on the preliminary report I received about the email, I think it was her laptop that was used to retrieve it."

"Are you certain?" Mara cuts in, voice sharp. "Are you absolutely sure?"

"Well... no," Jason says. "I'm not. But at that conference, I remember her talking about the model she was planning to get. It was a high-end model, one sold by a manufacturer who doesn't go through normal retail channels. It's too big a coincidence for me to ignore."

Immediately the board members start conferring among themselves. The Chairman raises a shadowy hand, the room falls silent.

"What does this mean?" the Chairman asks.

"It could mean a number of things," Jason says. "Since Jennifer's computer was used, I'm inclined to assume she was present when Curveball downloaded the file. Since she was present, I have to assume she's a strong candidate for continuing to be involved. We can use that to our advantage."

"I see," the Chairman says. "So how do we do that?"

"We put her under surveillance. We tap her phone, we tap her computer, we put a tracker on her car. We monitor everything she does to see if she's working with Curveball. If she is, she's probably our best way to get to him."

"How so?" Jason can't tell who asks the question, but whoever it is has a hoarse, husky voice. "I thought you said she was competent."

Cigarettes and shouting, Jason thinks.

"She is," Jason says, "but she's a civilian. Her background is in computer security, not espionage. We know Curveball is good at staying off the radar, but if Jennifer wants to use her skill set, she's always going to run the risk of being noticed by people who are just as good as she is. Or better."

Jason stops talking. The room is silent. The only sound comes from the vent as it blows warm air into the room. The Chairman's silhouette is still, head tilted down, as if he is either deep in thought or asleep. Most of the other board members look at the Chairman expectantly. A few of them glance at Jason, their expressions still unreadable in their studied neutrality.

Finally the Chairman speaks. "This is what we're going to do."

All eyes are on his silhouette now. He has full command of the room.

"First: we had a bad night tonight. Some of our people are in custody. They will resist interrogation for as long as possible, but we need to make sure we can get access to them, debrief them, and then take what steps we must to preserve our secrecy. Second: we will have to re-examine our protocols to make sure it doesn't happen again. Mara, I want you on that."

Mara nods.

"Third: we will follow Mr. Kline's recommendation and begin surveillance on Jennifer Forrest. Mr. Kline, I want you to oversee that."

Jason nods.

"Finally: the Forrest family may have a digital record of Captain Morgan's 'retirement.' They may also have knowledge of the encrypted file Curveball received from Morgan. This means we now risk exposure to the civilian world."

A low murmur of concern rolls across the room.

"Unfortunately," the Chairman continues, "we are not in a position to silence the Forrest family. They're too high-profile, too close to Liberty in the public eye... and such actions would not be supported by key allies. So I want options. If there are ways to discredit them, or discredit the information they have, I want to know those scenarios. If there are ways to completely insulate ourselves from that information, or use a third party as scapegoat, I want those scenarios as well."

The Chairman leans back. His head disappears entirely into shadow. "Things are starting to wobble. I want balance restored. Let's get it done."

PART TWO: DRIVING, MANHATTAN TO JERSEY

"... so Travers thinks the Federal Government is compromised, and he doesn't know how far up it goes," CB says.

Jenny says nothing for a moment. CB watches the lights play off her face as she guides the car down the streets of New York City.

"Damn," she says finally.

"Yeah," CB says. "At the moment we're on our own. Travers can't help until we help him first. We need to figure out what the conspiracy *is*, so he knows how to look for it on his end."

"Damn," Jenny says again.

"Well you wanted to come along," CB points out.

Jenny laughs bitterly. "I get the feeling I'm going to regret that."

"There's still time to go home," CB says.

"No," Jenny says. "I want to find out who killed my great-grandfather."

CB shrugs and settles back in the passenger seat. "Your choice."

The lights in Manhattan are pretty tonight. Most of the time CB doesn't notice; tonight he does. Maybe it's because he's tired. He's suddenly acutely aware of every bruise, every ache, every cut on his body. He has a lot of them.

"I'm beat," CB says. He closes his eyes.

"No way," Jenny says firmly. "You're not sleeping until you answer some questions."

CB opens one eye and glares at her. "So today I got into a fight with a Nazi supersoldier, leaped off a tall building, then got into a fight with a small army. What'd you do?"

"I went to a funeral," Jenny says.

"I also went to a funeral. Where I had to deliver a eulogy."

"Yeah, OK," Jenny says, "sorry. Fair point. You're tired. But before you get some sleep you have to answer some questions."

CB groans. "What questions do you have that can't wait till later?"

"Where do you want me to drive to?"

"Oh," CB says. "That. OK, I guess that's a fair question."

"Well I'm glad you approve," Jenny says. "Do you have an answer?"

CB thinks. "Go to Jersey. If you manage to get through Jersey before I wake up, go to... hell, get on 95 South and just keep going. I'll be awake before you have to do anything else."

"Jersey it is," Jenny says. She turns down a side street. "Lincoln Tunnel OK?"

"Fabulous," CB says. "Can I sleep now?"

"I have more questions."

"*Christ*. Fine. Ask."

"What's your name?"

CB raises an eyebrow. "Uhhh... CB?"

"No," Jenny says, "your *name*. Your *real* one. I mean, your handle was 'Curveball' and I know you said that was a nickname, and that everyone always called you CB, but what's the name on your birth certificate?"

CB shrugs. "Don't have a birth certificate."

"Very funny."

"I'm serious," CB says. "I'm an orphan."

Jenny rolls her eyes. "Come on."

"I know, right?" CB sits up in his seat and rubs his eyes. "But I'm serious. I was deposited rather unceremoniously at an orphanage. There was a card with the letters 'C' and 'B' on it—nobody knew what the hell that meant. It could have been my mother's initials, my father's initials, my mother's and father's initials, my initials—anything. Nobody knew. The orphanage had to call me something, and that was the only thing associated with me, so that's what they put down. They always told me I could decide for myself what it stood for, and I decided it stood for 'Curveball.'"

"Seriously?" Jenny shakes her head. "You're trying to tell me that your legal name is—"

"CB," CB says. "My Social Security number is assigned to 'CB.' First name 'C,' last name 'B.' It makes filling out forms awkward. Which is why I mostly don't."

"I can't believe you don't have a real name," Jenny says.

"It's real enough. I answer to it. Everybody went by their nicknames when I was growing up anyway. My best friend was a guy named Sin."

"Your best friend's nickname was *Sin*?"

"It was the 70s! Are we done?"

"No..." Jenny sees a sign for the Lincoln Tunnel and turns. "What is it you actually do?"

"Do?" CB stares at her with a blank expression on his face. "What do you mean?"

"Your power," Jenny says. "Superpower. Whatever. Andy and I never knew. We figured you were just really, really well trained. Like a commando, or something. But that doesn't make sense, since you were a villain. Which is very interesting, by the way!"

CB keeps staring.

Jenny colors. "When I was in college I found a website that was devoted to the Guardians of Justice. It was pretty popular. It had a whole section devoted to you and the forum had a huge debate over whether you actually had any powers at all."

"Oh yeah?" CB smiles slightly. "What did it say?"

"Split 50/50. One group thought you were just a really good athlete, who maybe—maybe—went through some version of Project Paragon, sort of like a 'Liberty Lite.' The other theory was that you were psychic, and your power was to confuse people."

CB laughs.

"Well I'll tell you what," Jenny says, a little sharpness creeping back into her voice, "I'd be willing to believe that. Because you confuse the hell out of everyone you meet."

CB laughs again. "It's not a bad guess. It's not right, but it's not a bad guess."

"So tell me," Jenny says. "What is it you do? You said earlier it 'scaled.' What does that mean?"

CB stares at the half-formed reflection of himself in the passenger-seat window. It disappears every time they drive by a street lamp, then reforms when the street grows darker.

"I make things happen," he says.

"Oh," Jenny says. "Well. Thanks for that. Now I feel much better."

"I can't explain it," CB says. "I don't know how it works. Sorry I can't be more specific. But I make things happen. Good things to people I want good things to happen to, bad things to people I want bad things to happen to. If I let go and slip into the moment, I can make good and bad things happen at the same time."

"What kind of things?"

"Well, when someone tries to shoot me they usually miss," CB says. "No matter how close they are, no matter how good a shot. They miss, or the gun jams, or misfires... nine times out of ten. Back at the house, they tried to blow me up with grenades. They were all duds, until I got out of blast radius. Then they took out your living room."

"That was your fault?" Jenny asks.

"Yeah. Sorry. At first I thought basically that I was manipulating the laws of probability. But Gladiator keeps saying that the laws of probability aren't like the laws of gravity, because probability isn't a force, it's just a mathematical expression of how other forces interact with each other."

Jenny laughs. "So if it's not that, what is it?"

CB shrugs. "'Manipulating the laws of probability' was all I had. The smart guy took it away from me."

"And when you say it 'scales?'"

"Hard to explain," CB says. "But the bigger the stakes, the bigger the side effects. If I'm fighting a... mugger, or a shoplifter, not much happens. Maybe he trips on a shoelace. When the stakes go up—when the fight is harder, when the situation is more dangerous—the effects are more noticeable. And there's usually more property damage."

"So tonight..."

"Tonight was a lot more dangerous than a mugger," CB says. "I was also pretty angry. When I'm angry it scales higher."

"So," Jenny says, "you don't fire laser beams out of your eyes, you can't pick up a car, but you 'make things happen,' and when the stakes are high you make them happen *more*... you just don't know exactly *how*."

"That's right," CB says.

Jenny sighs. "The ultimate slacker hero. Fine. Last question: what do we do next?"

"Well... we've got two USB drives with information on them." CB pats a trenchcoat pocket. "I don't think anyone knows about the information Travers sent us. The information Alex emailed me, though... someone tried to level your house in order to get it back. We need to figure out what's on those. We need to figure out who we can trust. Then we need to round up the people we can trust, form a posse, and bring the hurt to whoever's behind this."

"So who *can* we trust?" Jenny's question sounds plaintive. She scowls after she asks it.

"Good question," CB says. "The people I know we can trust can't help us right now. There are a few people I think we might be able to trust, but I'm not sure how to contact them... and getting a few of them to trust *me* might be a challenge..."

"Why?" Jenny asks. "What did you do to them?"

"Well..." CB pushes the passenger seat back as far as it will go and closes his eyes. "We have basic philosophical differences about fundamentally important things."

"Doesn't that describe your relationship with pretty much everyone in the world?"

CB laughs softly. "Yeah, it does. Good point."

They pass through the Lincoln Tunnel. They've been in New Jersey for five minutes when Jenny says, "OK, I lied. I have one more question. Why were you a villain?"

CB doesn't answer. He's asleep.

PART THREE: NEW YEAR'S EVE, 1983

It's 20 degrees Fahrenheit at 11 PM. Occasionally snow drifts down out of the sky, depositing itself unceremoniously on cars, sidewalks, roofs, trash cans, awnings, and the homeless. The snow has been intermittent throughout the day, so it doesn't stick to the streets. The sidewalks are slippery—the snow that fell there has been ground down to thin sheets of ice, almost invisible on the concrete, and it's not uncommon to see people randomly grabbing at trees, benches, mailboxes, and handrails in an attempt to keep from falling over backward. Of course, most people aren't on the sidewalks in Times Square: they're in the street. It's New Year's Eve, it's Saturday night, they're outside, they're drunk, and they're waiting for the ball to drop.

The scene at the East Village—specifically, the part that everyone calls "Little Dresden"—is a little different. It's called Little Dresden because it has so many burnt-out and abandoned buildings, sort of a mini-wasteland in the middle of the city. It's not a friendly neighborhood. The ruins of Little Dresden are mostly abandoned by their owners, but they're all claimed by someone, in some capacity. Squats, crack houses, hideouts, party spots, havens for runaways, they can all be found here. And tonight, most of them are full of people trying to keep out of the wind. Trash cans full of trash are lit, people huddle around the fires, and everyone seems on edge.

Except in the club.

8BC is located on Eighth Street, between Avenues B and C. It opened in October, and has hosted all manner of mayhem since. Bands play frequently, but they do other kinds of shows as well: performance art and experimental theater are as common as punk bands. It's not terribly warm inside—the heat isn't always reliable—but it's better than you'd think, because it's full of people, and most of those people are drinking. The walls stop the wind, the people radiate heat, and the club is infinitely preferable to the weather outside.

Also, CB thinks, the band is seriously kicking ass.

Sin has been going on and on about a band, Indestroy, for weeks. He has a bootleg demo tape that he plays constantly, and CB has to admit they sound good. They're loud, they're angry, and they're pretty shamelessly political. Their singer has a lot of charisma and a lot of energy, their guitarists are tight, their drummer is always on—it's a great sound.

CB, Sin and Billy are sitting at a table decorated (as always) with a kitschy chipmunk table lamp. CB and Sin are gasping from exhaustion. They aren't fifteen any more. Moshing is getting harder to do for any length of time.

"Let's go in again," Billy urges, grinning.

Billy seems impervious to exhaustion. He's managed to turn into a proper bruiser over the years, with a physique that makes him look like a big, white-haired Conan the Barbarian. Some nights he works as a bouncer for the club, but tonight he's hanging out with his friends.

"God," CB says, "*no.*" He fumbles for his trenchcoat, thrown over the back of his chair, reaches into its pocket and gets out a pack of cigarettes. He offers one to Sin, who takes it wordlessly, and then puts one in his own mouth. As he lights up, he watches the singer appreciatively. The guy really knows how to sell his music. CB wishes he could do something like that.

It's a small club. The official occupancy is two hundred. Unofficially, it's possible to squeeze more people in. It's pretty crowded tonight. The stage is huge, especially for a club this small. When the place was being built one of the owners had dreams of it being a proper theater. He changed his mind, eventually, but he kept the stage. The floors are covered in dirt, and there are live chickens pecking about, for some reason no one has ever been able to explain. Dozens of inflatable Ronald Reagan dolls line up against one wall; on another is a painting of Greek women, struggling to hold up the side of a building as if they were the columns, while wolves tear at their feet.

CB likes that painting. It's called "Civilization Teeters."

"Come on," Billy urges. "This is a great song. Get in the pit."

"Damn it Billy, I'm *tired*," CB says. "What kind of drugs are you on tonight?"

Billy grins wider. "I'm just glad I'm not working tonight. Sin was right, this band is *awesome.*"

CB nods in agreement.

"Also," Billy adds, "you bums would be in a lot better shape if you weren't smoking all the time."

CB flicks his ash in Billy's direction. Billy laughs. "Come *on!* It only turns 1984 once. Get in the pit for Big Brother!"

Six years ago Billy's enthusiasm would have driven CB crazy. Now it's fun. "All right," he says. "But, for the record, you are a rat bastard and I hate you very much."

"Save it for the pit, girlie," Billy says cheerfully. He makes his way back to the stage.

CB looks over at Sin. "Coming?"

"Hell no," Sin says. "I'm going to drink Billy's beer. Yours too, if you're going to be stupid."

CB laughs. "You owe me a beer. Asshole." With that, he launches himself out of his chair, and with a new burst of energy throws himself back into the crowd.

Music and elbows, music and elbows... CB spends the next few songs getting friendly concussions from his fellow man. After the third song CB has definitely had it; his head is throbbing from being knocked around, and his lungs are burning from the exertion of it all. He makes his way back to the table, where Sin is talking to a pretty girl he recognizes from somewhere. He collapses into his chair and fishes for a cigarette in his trenchcoat pocket. He can't find anything.

Sin looks over at him. "Oh, I smoked the last one. And I drank your beer. Sorry."

Sin is trying very hard not to smile.

CB laughs between gasping breaths. "You... son of a..."

"You know Annie?" Sin cuts in, gesturing to his left.

Annie has hair almost as white as Billy's, cut very short. She doesn't wear any makeup, but she is very pretty. CB waves, not quite in her general direction, as he stares semi-sightlessly at the ceiling. "Hey. I think I've seen you around..."

"I think you're out of shape," she says.

CB laughs.

Billy makes his way back, takes one look at the table, and announces, "Sin, you son of a bitch, you drank my beer." He goes over to the bar, buys four, and brings them back, one for each of them. "I don't know you," he says to Annie, "but you get one anyway."

"LADIES AND GENTLEMEN!" The singer for Indestroy is screaming into his microphone. "IF I MIGHT HAVE YOUR ATTENTION FOR A MOMENT I HAVE IT ON GOOD AUTHORITY THAT IT IS NOW **NINETEEN EIGHTY-FOUR!**"

Everyone cheers. CB raises his beer to toast the new year. Sin and Billy do the same. The band launches into another song, and the crowd responds with renewed vigor.

Sin whispers into Annie's ear. She smiles slightly and stands, he follows suit. "Later guys."

CB and Billy watch in amusement as they head out together. Billy shakes his head. "How does he do it?"

"He's charming," CB says. "I don't know what that means, exactly, but I hear women like it."

They lapse into silence and watch the band.

Another year gone, another year ahead. Four more years of the Gipper, four more years of Just Say No, four more years of Yuppies and the Moral Majority and Voodoo Economics and the Cold War and Nuclear Armageddon on the horizon and now, on top of all that, it's the year of Big Brother.

"Hey."

CB looks up to see Billy peering at him over his beer.

"You're brooding again," Billy says.

CB gives him a half-smile. "Blame the beer," he says. "I think maybe I—"

A slim hand falls on his shoulder. CB turns in his chair and sees Annie standing in front of him, swaying unsteadily.

"Annie?"

Her eyes are glazed and unfocused. She's trying to speak, but she isn't saying anything coherent. CB notices her lip is bloody, and there's a bruise on her cheek that is rapidly turning purple.

Billy is around the table in a second. "Hey, are you OK? You look hurt. Where's Sin?"

Annie looks over her shoulder at nothing. Her lips are still moving, but she isn't talking.

"Hey Billy, what's up?" one of the bartenders calls over.

"She's hurt," Billy says. "She left with Sin and I think something happened—"

Annie's eyes clear for a moment, and she focuses her gaze on CB. "Sin is in trouble," she says. "It's the NAA."

Seconds later CB and Billy are running out the door and down the street.

There are many different kinds of skinheads in the world. Not all are racist, and even a lot of the ones that claim to be are usually just bullies who use race as their excuse. But the New Aryan Army is bad news: they go beyond bullies and dive deep into scary territory. They mean business. They train for what they believe is an inevitable war of racial cleansing. They terrorize blacks, Jews, and anyone else who doesn't have white skin—and even then, if you don't have blond hair there's a 50/50 chance they'll go after you because you're "mixed." They're vicious animals, and they kill people.

Sin is a Korean who was walking with a white woman alone at night.

CB and Billy round a corner and see Sin's car parked on the curb. The passenger door is ajar, the overhead light is on. Sin isn't there.

"Sin? Sin!" CB's voice echoes off the gutted buildings. There's no response. He didn't expect there to be, but he hoped...

"Be quiet a second," Billy whispers. "Listen."

CB shuts his mouth and listens carefully. Very faintly he hears a repetitive *thud*, followed by a breathless grunt, followed by mocking laughter.

"This way!" Billy runs off past the car, and darts down along one of the abandoned buildings. CB follows him, breathing hard.

Billy turns around to the back of the house and stops short; CB almost runs into him.

Four neo-Nazis wearing jeans, braces, flight jackets, and thick work boots with white laces are standing around Sin, sprawled out on the ground, retching and gasping for air. Blood streams from his nose and mouth. One eye is swollen. A thick boot kicks down hard into the back of his head, and he pitches forward, smashing into the concrete ground. He doesn't move.

Billy yells, incoherent with rage, and throws himself at them. The four turn, looks of surprise on their faces. Surprise turns to confidence when they see it's only one guy—then confidence turns to alarm when Billy hits the first neo-Nazi and the force of the blow actually lifts him off the ground.

CB hangs back, torn. He's not much good in a fight. The last time he tried to help Billy, despite his best intentions, he actually wound up making things worse. Billy has tried, over the years, to teach him to fight, but for some reason he can't get it. Billy complains he tries to fight "like a cartoon," and that he's always overextending his balance. The lessons never go well.

He considers running to get help, but he doesn't want to. His friend is lying in a heap on the ground. Those bastards were trying to beat him to death. He's not a coward, and he won't run out on his friends, but he doesn't want to screw this up for Billy... so he waits.

It isn't a kung-fu movie, where each attacker waits his turn. They all jump on Billy at the same time, and they move like they've done this before. As Billy knocks the first guy to the ground, the second tries to take Billy's legs out from under him, the third tries to knock him down on his back, and the fourth just takes a swing. Billy knows what's coming, but he can't counter all of it, so he mitigates. He grabs the arm of the fourth skinhead, and as he falls over backward he takes the guy down with him. When the two left standing go in for the kick, one boot hits Billy in the side, but the other boot hits the fourth skinhead in the small of his back.

Still, Billy's in a bad spot, and he won't be able to get out of it on his own. CB takes a deep breath and runs straight at skinhead number two, shouting at the top of his lungs.

The skinhead looks up, startled, just as CB crashes into him at full speed. It's not a tactic that requires finesse to work, and they both go tumbling to the ground. The key to momentum is keeping it, so CB does everything he can to keep the skinhead down: hitting, biting, poking him in the eyes. It works for a while, but eventually the skinhead recovers enough to kick CB, hard, and suddenly he can't breathe.

The kicks keep coming after that. CB twists and turns as best he can, trying to dodge the blows, and to his credit he probably keeps them from landing in the places that would hurt the most, but they keep hurting. One after another, to the point that CB is starting to feel a little numb. Something in the back of his head tells him *that is not a good sign*, but he can't do much more than keep trying to roll, and dodge, and finally all he can do is curl up in a ball and wait for it to stop...

... and then it stops.

CB doesn't understand it at first, but after a second he realizes that he's not being kicked any more. He lifts his head up, and sees the blurry figure of Billy standing over him, panting heavily. Billy reaches down his hand. CB grabs it, and Billy hauls him to his feet.

CB yells in panic and pain as his ribs protest, but that's all they do. He doesn't think anything is broken.

"Not bad," Billy says as he wipes blood off his face. "You weren't totally useless."

CB tries to grin. He thinks it probably looks more like a facial tic. "Notice how I distracted him," he says between gasps. "Making him kick me all those times."

"Yeah," Billy says. "I noticed that. Can you walk?"

CB nods.

"We need to get Sin to a hospital. He's in bad shape."

CB nods again and stumbles over to Sin. He's moaning softly, but can't do much more than that.

"I'll get him up, you put an arm around your shoulder, we'll drag him to his car," Billy says.

"OK," CB says.

Billy drops to one knee and grabs Sin by one arm. "Hold on, man. We're going to—"

"Well, well, well. What have we here?"

Billy lets go of Sin, stands, and turns around. CB turns as well, then his blood turns to ice.

Nine. There's no way they can fight nine.

The leader stands in the middle. He's dressed like the others—jeans, boots, braces, a white t-shirt—but he's not wearing a jacket, and he doesn't seem the least bit cold. He's massively built. CB thinks he's bigger than Billy.

"See fellas, this is a perfect example of how dirtied the white race has become." The leader talks easily, casually. His eyes are sharp and cold. "These two are trying to help their friend, there. You see that? They're actually *friends*."

The man steps forward. Billy and CB tense, ready to fight, but the man actually *turns his back on them* and starts to lecture his own people.

"But you can't be friends with an animal," he says. "Not in the same way you're friends with another man. Oh, sure, you can say dogs are man's best friend, but that's the other way. Dogs are *our* friends. We love them, but they're *dogs*. We don't think they're people. We don't think they're equal. If a man came up to me and told me his dog was a person, I'd think he was crazy. And so would you."

Billy coughs nervously. Sin moans.

"The problem with lowering yourself like this—well, where do I start? But the main problem is that it makes you weak. It *diminishes* you. It makes you *sick*, in body and in mind."

CB notices that Sin is starting to twitch involuntarily. "Billy," he hisses, and then notices that Billy is sweating profusely.

"Billy?"

"They're like cancer," the leader says. "They fool you into thinking you're like them. They get you to treat them just like you... and then you get weak. And then you fall."

Billy's eyes roll back, his head tilts up, and he collapses to the ground.

"Billy!" CB kneels over him, ignoring the skinheads for a moment, and places his hand on Billy's forehead. Billy is consumed by a fever. Sin starts twitching more noticeably, and the sweat on his forehead glistens in the night.

CB looks up at the leader. "Cut it out."

The leader turns around and looks at CB, a strange expression on his face.

"I mean it," CB says. "Whatever you're doing. Stop it *now*."

"No," the leader says. "I won't. I can't. Purity doesn't hesitate, and it doesn't step back. It only marches on..."

CB gets to his feet. He feels pressure building in his head. It's rage—pure, seething rage. And it's mixed with something else. Something he doesn't quite understand.

The leader reaches for something behind him and pulls out a gun. CB doesn't know what type it is—it's not a revolver, but that's about as far as his experience with guns goes.

"But I can be merciful," the leader says. "Just because something's an animal, that doesn't mean it deserves to suffer."

"No," CB says.

The leader points the gun at Sin. "Sometimes the only white thing to do is to put an animal out of its misery."

All of a sudden CB feels the world come crashing down on him—the full force of everything in the world, all the pieces of it, whirling around him in incomprehensible patterns. And then, a moment later, *everything* clicks. All the pieces fall to the ground and he knows that he can grab them and move them anywhere he wants. He can see the gun, he can feel the trajectory the bullet will take as it exits the muzzle, he knows where it will enter Sin's body, where it will exit. He knows what will happen if he doesn't stop it, and more important, *he knows that he can stop it.*

In an instant, he feels like the most powerful man on earth. It's liberating.

"I said no," CB says... then he winks. Somewhere, off in the distance, something makes a soft popping sound. Then the skinhead leader pulls the trigger, and the gun makes a sound it's not supposed to make—a grinding, grating noise—and nothing happens. The gun jams.

And then CB moves.

He runs toward the leader with a yell. The leader's eyes widen in surprise, and he takes a step back, preparing to meet CB head on. But CB stops, changes direction, and throws an elbow into one of the other skinheads. Elbow to neck—the only thing that skinhead will do is gag and claw at his throat for the next several minutes.

And then there are eight.

The suddenness of his attack catches everyone off guard. The leader recovers fastest, realizes what's going on, and immediately charges into the fray, but the other skinheads were expecting CB to go after their leader and still can't understand why he didn't. This gives CB time. One fist, one kick, a second elbow—all to soft spots, all dirty shots, three more incapacitations.

And then there are five.

The leader closes on him then, and hits CB in the face, hard. Stars explode, and CB staggers back. He tastes blood. But he keeps his wits about him, and when the leader follows up with a left, CB grabs the arm with both hands, and falls backward, pulling the leader along with him. Before the leader can fall on him, CB's foot buries into his stomach, and as he rolls back he kicks up—and the leader goes flying over him, *just like Shatner used to do in all those old Star Trek shows*. CB vaguely remembers attempting that when Billy was trying to teach him.

Billy told him that would never, ever work.

The leader snarls and climbs to his feet, but CB ignores him for the moment. The skinheads are now even more confused—they apparently find it inconceivable that anyone would be able to lay a finger on their boss. Three more dirty blows, three more incapacitated skinheads, and when the last man standing comes to his senses, he runs away.

CB turns just in time to see the leader's right hook, but not in enough time to dodge out of the way. He staggers back again, stunned, and this time can't counter the left. He trips over his feet and falls to the ground. The leader stands over him, furious.

"*Why didn't you get sick?*" The leader spits out the question, voice dripping with rage. And then, a moment later, Billy hits him in the back of the head with a brick.

The leader crumples to the ground.

Billy helps CB up again. He looks at CB strangely. "You... did a lot better, that time around."

"Yeah," CB says. "I know."

"What the hell happened?"

CB shrugs. "How do you feel?"

"I felt like shit," Billy says. "Like my insides were on fire. Until you started fighting him, then it went away."

"Good," CB says. "Let's get Sin to that doctor."

Billy nods. Together they lift Sin up, throw his arms around their shoulders, and drag him off to his car.

PART FOUR: PLANS AND ACTIONS

CB wakes up suddenly, disoriented. He's staring at the roof of Jenny's car. He can hear the motor, feel the car vibrating as it rushes down the highway. The radio is playing softly—he focuses on that for a moment, realizes who's playing, and instantly regrets it. He hates Jenny's music. He hated it ten years ago, and her tastes haven't improved.

"Good morning," Jenny says.

CB doesn't reply. He still feels an odd, aggressive exhilaration that he hasn't felt in a long time.

"CB?" Jenny glances over at him quickly, frowning. "You awake? You were having a hell of a dream."

"I was?" CB's tongue feels thick. He half-remembers tasting blood. He wipes his sleeve across his mouth, but it's dry.

"Yeah," Jenny says. "You were tossing around on the seat, muttering something under your breath. I couldn't tell what it was. You sounded pretty mad, though."

CB connects the exhilaration to a memory. New Year's Eve, New Year's Day. 1984. He feels a sudden thrill of freedom—the same thrill he felt when he made his first important decision.

And made the wrong decision, he reminds himself. But a little voice in the back of his head says *was it?* And he doesn't know the answer to that.

"Yeah," CB says. He sits up in his seat, adjusting the back so it's in the upright position. "Dreams about the past. They're not always fun."

"You sound like great-grandfather," Jenny says. "He didn't like his dreams either."

"I know." CB yawns and stretches. "His were much worse than mine. He saw concentration camps. I got to see the Talking Heads."

"Who?"

CB forces himself not to answer.

"You were only asleep for about an hour," Jenny says. "We're almost to Trenton."

"We... wait, we've been through tolls?" CB is wide awake now.

"Yeah..." Jenny says, looking confused. "You said take 95..."

"Yeah, I did. And I screwed up. God damn it!"

"What?" Jenny looks at him in alarm. "What's wrong?"

"They know where we are," CB says.

"Who knows where we are?"

"The bad guys. The bad guys know where we are. I was tired and not paying attention, but I'm pretty damned sure they were."

"Paying attention to *what*?" Jenny snaps. "For Christ's sake, CB. I know I'm new at this, but I'd appreciate a little detail..."

"Travers said his group was compromised, right? Well Metahuman Affairs was on the scene, questioning all of us about how I... you know. Totaled your dad's house. In self defense." CB adds the last bit somewhat defensively.

"You think someone in the FBMA is working for the bad guys?" Jenny asks, looking shocked.

"It doesn't have to be one of the ones at the scene," CB says. "It just has to be someone with access to the reports. At this point they know I'm not around, and they know you're not around. And if they're not stupid—which they aren't—they probably *also* know that the EZ-Pass registered to your car paid a toll to get into Jersey."

CB points at the tiny box mounted on Jenny's windshield.

"Shit," Jenny says.

"Yeah," CB agrees. "So... they know we're in New Jersey. We've got to make sure they don't learn anything else."

Jenny reaches into her back pocket and pulls out a smartphone. She turns it off, then sets it in one of the cupholders. "Do you have a cell?"

"Yeah," CB says. "The one Travers gave me. It's turned off."

"Right..." Jenny rolls down her window, pulls the EZ Pass off the windshield, and throws it out onto the road. "Battery's welded to the motherboard. Guess I'll have to report it stolen."

CB grins.

"I guess I won't be using credit for purchases," Jenny adds. "Not for a while. Which is a problem, actually. I don't have a lot of cash, and we'll need gas and toll money."

"No problem," CB says. "Pull into the next gas station."

Jenny frowns. "You're not going to rob it, are you?"

"What the hell, Jenny? No. Just pull into a gas station. Or a rest area. Or something."

They pull into a rest area. It looks like a small shopping mall, complete with a food court. Most of the shops are closed, but one still has a guy sitting behind the cash register, nose buried in a book. He looks up once as they walk in, decides they aren't worth paying attention to, and returns to his reading.

CB grabs two cokes out of the soda dispenser and takes them up to the counter. The man reluctantly puts his book down and swipes both cokes through the scanner.

"That it?" The man sounds tired and grumpy.

"Yeah," CB says. "Well, wait. I'll take three of those 'Insta-Win' tickets." He points to a lottery display sitting to the left of the cash register.

"Seriously?" Jenny wrinkles her nose disdainfully. "I thought you were smarter than that."

"Quiet, you," CB says good-naturedly. "It's harmless fun."

The guy behind the counter smirks, then dutifully tears off three instant lottery tickets from the display, scanning each in turn.

CB hands the guy a ten-dollar bill, then waits patiently as the clerk counts out his change. He takes one of the coins and begins to rub out the first ticket.

"Can't wait to lose, I guess," the guy says to Jenny in a half-amused, half-annoyed voice.

"What's the point?" CB says. "I'm addicted to 'em, but I never win. Might as well get it over wi— well, look at that."

Jenny leans over the counter to look, then laughs in surprise. "You just won a hundred dollars."

"Huh?" The clerk looks down at the ticket. "Well damn. You did. Congratulations, I guess."

CB laughs. "Shows what you know," he says to Jenny. "Hey, buddy, where do I have to go cash this in?"

"For a hundred dollars? I think we pay out here. Hold on, I have to look it up."

The clerk picks up a small pamphlet that says LOTTERY on the front, and starts paging through it. CB starts scratching away at the second ticket.

"Nothing," he says. "Big shock. One more, then." He starts scratching away at the third.

"For cash prizes of $100 and under we pay out here," the clerk says. "You're lucky, I guess. If it was any higher you'd have to wait till Monday and go to one of the lottery offices."

"Not *that* lucky," CB says. "If I won ten thousand dollars I'd be willing to wait till—hey, look. I did it again!"

The clerk's eyes widen. "Another hundred dollars?"

"Well... no," CB says. "It's fifty. But I'm not complaining!"

"Uh... well, I need you to fill out some paperwork," the clerk says. "And show me a valid ID. Then I can redeem those for you."

"OK," CB says. "Uh... if it's not too much trouble, I'd like twenties and two fives."

Twenty minutes later they drive away from the rest area one hundred and fifty dollars richer. Jenny laughs.

"Do you do that a lot?" she asks.

"I don't usually win twice." CB grins and shakes his head. "That was unusual. But now we've got enough cash to get through the tolls and stop for gas again. We can keep doing that until we get to wherever we need to go."

"How does that solve anything?" Jenny asks. "You still need to show an ID and fill out paperwork, remember? If the bad guys have access to EZ-Pass, they have access to the Lottery. They can track you by your wins."

"Probably not," CB says, "since I used a fake ID."

"... you have a fake ID?" Jenny asks incredulously.

"I do," CB says.

"What are you, sixteen?"

"Oi!" CB says. "Fake IDs weren't invented by teenagers. There's lots of good reasons to have official-looking identification that doesn't trace back to the real you in any way."

"It just doesn't seem very heroic," Jenny says.

"Maybe," CB says, "but people tell me I don't either. And back in the day I was the Guardians' deep cover guy, when they needed one."

Jenny snorts. "The deep cover guy with a hairstyle thirty years out of fashion?"

"Geez," CB says, "this is a tough crowd... Back then it was only fifteen. And it's just gel, *it washes out.*"

"It's weird," Jenny insists.

"Every hero with a secret identity carries a fake ID," CB says. "Either the hero identity or the mild-mannered reporter identity."

Jenny shakes her head. "I never thought about that."

"That's good," CB says. "The guys with secret identities want people thinking about it as little as possible. Anyway, *this* ID, and others like it, is what let me stay out of sight for ten years. That and one other thing."

"What's the other thing?" Jenny asks.

CB frowns. "Location." His frown deepens. "Damn you, location..."

"What are you complaining about now?" Jenny rolls her eyes in exasperation. "Compared to what's already going on, it can't be that bad, can it?"

"Don't ever say things like that," CB says. "It can *always* be that bad. It can often be worse. In this case, I just figured out where we need to go."

"Where?"

"You're not going to like it."

"I'm a big girl," Jenny insists. "Where to?"

CB sighs. "Farraday City."

Jenny's knuckles tighten on the steering wheel. "Seriously?"

"That's where I've been for the last ten years. I have some contacts we can use to lie low and start poking around. Also, I'm pretty sure no one expects us to go there."

"OK," Jenny says, trying to keep her voice steady. "I've just heard some stories about the place, is all."

"They're probably true," CB says. "Even if whoever told the stories was making them up at the time. Still, it's not like you're immediately stepping into a war zone. There are parts of the city that are pretty safe, where life goes on and you almost can't see the corruption. Then there are parts of the city that look like a post-apocalyptic movie set, where people take Darwin's name in vain on a regular basis."

"Which part are we going to?"

"... well, the bad part," CB admits. "But we won't be mixing with the locals much. It should be OK. Also there's a hacker community who might be able to get you the things you need if you're going to work on decrypting Alex's file."

Jenny takes a deep breath. "OK. If you say so. Will we be safe?"

CB snorts. "*Fuck* no. If your mother knew I was taking you there she'd kill me. Maybe twice." CB settles back into his seat and gazes out the window. "I'd probably feel obligated to let her do it, too..."

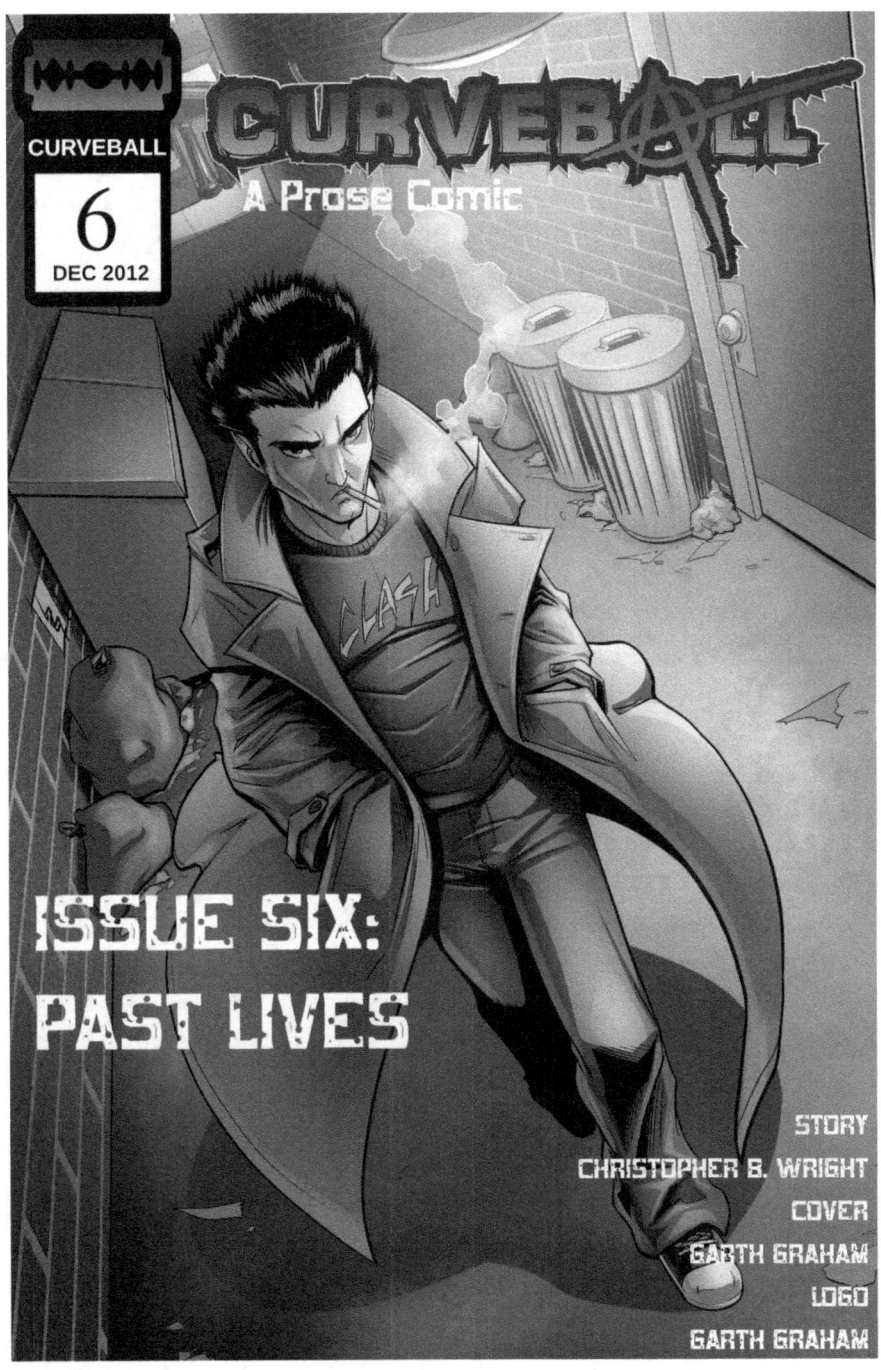

PART ONE: SOUTHBOUND

"We're going to have to ditch your car."

"What?" The car swerves as Jenny turns her head to glare at him. Neither of them has had much sleep, and Jenny refuses to let CB take a turn behind the wheel. She's obviously exhausted, and the stress from last night's violence combined with their current situation is starting to seriously fray her nerves.

CB sighs. "Sorry, Jenny. You have a very nice car, and having nice things makes you a target in Farraday City."

"We're *already* a target," Jenny says. "I mean, we are, right? We're being chased by bad guys, so what's new?"

"Well," CB says, "those guys aren't interested in stealing your car. And the crime families in Farraday City probably aren't, either... but there are lots of lower-level outfits who will be, and they won't necessarily wait till you get out before they try to take it."

"So, what, there's no honor among thieves? Didn't our guys call it first? I thought criminals didn't step on each other's territories."

CB shrugs. "Depends on the criminal. Some are very polite."

Jenny laughs. Then she looks at him nervously. "You're kidding, right?"

"Nope. Depends on the criminal. Overmind is always unfailingly polite, even when he's trying to kill you. Scrapper Jack would actually stop fighting for a minute in order to get out of the way of rescue services, or drive the fight away from whatever building they wanted to get to."

Jenny shakes her head. "That doesn't sound like a villain to me."

"He also crippled his arch-nemesis by crushing his spine."

"...OK, that sounds pretty bad," Jenny says.

"It was for Mach," CB agrees. "He was a dick, but he did the job. Jack had a legitimate beef with him, but it went way too far."

Jenny looks outraged. "'Jack?' You're on a first name basis with villains? And he had 'legitimate beef?' What, are you defending him?"

CB sighs. "It's complicated, Jenny. I used to work with the guy."

"You used to work with Mach?"

"No," CB says, "not Mach."

"Then what are you—" Jenny stops and reddens. "Oh. Scrapper Jack."

"Yeah. For about a year we were on the same crew. I liked him. We were friends. Mach screwed him over, big time, and payback was hell. But it was over the line. Scary how well planned it was, too."

"What happened?" Jenny asks.

"Well," CB says, "Jack used to work in a—no. Not right now, look, Jenny, we have to ditch your car."

"I'll risk Farraday City," Jenny says. "If someone steals it, well, that's better than just throwing it away."

CB rolls his eyes. "We're not going to throw it away, we're going to park it and walk away from it. Well, we're going to take a bus. Go the rest of the way by Greyhound. We'll get a chance to sleep, a little, though sleeping on a bus isn't really comfortable..."

"But I *love* this car." Jenny's voice is small and plaintive. CB thinks she might actually burst into tears. "It's the first new car I've ever owned. *Ever.*"

"My heart is *breaking.*" Sarcasm drips from his voice. "Look, Jenny, forget Farraday City for a second. The people who are chasing us—or who *will* be chasing us, if they're not chasing us *now*—know exactly what car you drive. Make, model, color, License Plate, VIN, and probably a bunch of things I'm not familiar with. That car *belongs to you,* and if one of their people spots it they'll assume you're there with it. So we can't take it with us. We're trying not to get ourselves *killed,* and the fact that we're headed toward the murder capital of the United States in order to *improve our chances of staying alive* should tell you exactly how screwed we are right now."

Jenny hisses through her teeth in frustration. "Fine. Look, I know, CB, okay? I'm sorry. I'm just... tired. And a little scared. OK, more than a little..."

"You're the one who wanted to come along," CB points out. "I told you to stay home."

"Yeah," Jenny says, "you did. Stop throwing that in my face. *I want to help,* and what's more important, I'm pretty sure I actually *can.* But I'm allowed to be scared!"

Jenny glares at him. CB opens his mouth, ready to retort, then lets it go.

"Yeah," he says. "OK. I'm sorry too. Just... trust that I'm trying to keep us alive, OK? I'm not saying ditch the car because I want to make you miserable."

"You're not going to insist that I obey you unquestioningly, are you?"

CB laughs. "Mindless obedience is not a family trait."

Jenny grins ruefully. "Was mom a pain in the ass when you first met?"

"Sure," CB says. "I used to call her Lois."

Jenny laughs.

"But Alex was just as bad," CB says. "He was almost court-martialed before he became Liberty. For mutiny, no less."

"What?" Jenny laughs incredulously. "You're making that up. He was in the Army. You can't mutiny in the Army, there's no ship."

"Honest to God, I don't know what they call it in the Army but that's what he did. He was a sergeant at the time. His Lieutenant, who he never described in flattering terms, received orders that he managed to completely mix up and he wound up giving every wrong order you could think of. So Alex went all Fletcher Christian, had his Lieutenant hog tied and gagged, and proceeded to do what their Captain actually wanted them to do. They won the day, Alex untied his superior officer who immediately placed him under arrest."

"I've *never* heard this story," Jenny says.

"How many war stories did Alex ever tell you?"

Jenny frowns thoughtfully.

"Yeah. He almost never talked about it, even to me. And I'm pretty sure he didn't want the world to know about that point in his life. He thought that was it for him as a soldier."

"Well what happened?"

"His Captain was smarter than his Lieutenant. He asked Alex what happened, Alex told him the truth, and the Captain believed him. Actually, according to Alex, the Captain sighed and said 'it figures.' A few days later a bunch of MPs showed up and carted Alex away. He thought he was going to the stockade, but they dumped him off at Project Paragon. The Captain pulled a few strings."

"Wow," Jenny says. "Sneaky Captain."

"Military guys are like that. They talk a lot about discipline, and following the rules, but don't let them fool you. They study *tactics*, and part of being a good tactician is *knowing when to lie*."

Jenny is silent a moment. "I miss him," she says finally.

"Yeah." CB looks out his window and keeps his hands folded in his lap. He really wants a cigarette.

"Well, never mind that right now," Jenny says briskly. "So we have to ditch my car. How do we find a bus station?"

CB points down the road. Off to the side they see a large green sign with the words FOOD - TRANSPORTATION displayed in reflective white text.

Jenny shakes her head. "Does that happen to you a lot?"

CB shrugs. "I don't have anything to compare it to."

They pull onto the exit ramp and merge onto a state highway.

"OK, question," Jenny says. "How do we know the bad guys aren't going to guess you're going to Farraday City? That's where you live, right? So won't they be expecting you to go home?"

"I haven't exactly told anyone," CB says. "Not until recently. And your parents aren't going to tell anyone willingly, and the bad guys aren't going to torture them to find out."

"That's... good to know." It hadn't occurred to her that torture might be a possibility. "Why do you figure?"

"They're famous," CB says. "Your mom and your dad and your uncle are all public figures, and they're getting a lot of attention these days. The bad guys don't like attention. They're allergic to it. And their very public raid on your father's house blew up in their face quite spectacularly. So they're not going to do anything that will attract attention."

"Good," Jenny says.

"*You*, on the other hand..." CB shrugs. "They probably figure you know too much at this point."

"Great," Jenny says. "Guess I'm stuck with you, then."

They drive into the parking lot of a small, nondescript diner. CB climbs out, grateful for the chance to properly stretch his legs. "You go in and order some food," CB says. "I'll walk down to the bus station and get us some tickets."

"Do we have money for both?" Jenny asks. "We only have about forty dollars left."

"You take the money. Order me an omelet and some coffee. Take your stuff, we're not coming back to the car."

Jenny nods, grabs her cell phone and her laptop bag, then opens the trunk of her car. She pulls out two small bags.

"You brought clothes," CB says. "I'm impressed, since you didn't know we were going on a road trip."

"I always keep a bag in my car. Sometimes I have to travel." Jenny smacks her forehead. "Crap! I forgot about my job. I guess I'm probably going to get fired this week."

"Probably," CB says. "But if we survive this I'm pretty sure there are going to be a lot of people interested in hiring the woman who decrypted Liberty's final message exposing a worldwide conspiracy against mankind."

Jenny laughs. "Right. I'll meet you in the diner."

Twenty minutes later CB sits down at her table holding two tickets.

"How much did they cost?" Jenny asks. "I had the money..."

CB shrugs, and sits just as the waitress arrives with his coffee and omelet. "I had coupons."

Jenny frowns.

"Seriously. Greyhound had a promotion five, six years ago. The prize was prepaid tickets. They never expired. The lady at the booth was surprised to see them, but they were still good. All I had to do was choose a destination. I still have a few more."

"How many times did you win this promotion?" Jenny asks.

"A few times," CB admits. "I thought it would be useful someday."

Jenny shakes her head. "You cheat."

"I sure do. Eat up. Bus leaves in an hour."

When they leave the diner they see a police car parked next to Jenny's. A policeman stands behind Jenny's car, staring at her license plate and talking into a handheld radio.

"And so it begins," CB says. "Come on. Don't pay any attention to the cop. Just follow me."

They get to the bus right when the driver is starting to let people in. They make their way to the back and sit together, Jenny sitting next to the window, CB by the aisle. Waiting for the bus to leave is excruciating.

"I think I'm going to freak out," Jenny says.

"This is the part I don't like," CB admits. "The cop already found your car. You're nowhere to be found. There's a bus station within walking distance. They're not stupid. They're going to guess we've taken the bus. They might try to stop it."

"Can they do it?" Jenny asks.

"It depends. I'm working on a few assumptions at this point, and if any of them are wrong we're probably screwed."

"Great," Jenny says. "Please, do go on."

"Well..." CB glances past Jenny, out the window. "First, I'm assuming they're still playing by the rules. They want to know where we are, but they don't want to attract any attention, so they're not going to take direct action, and they're not going to pull any strings with law enforcement that will make people ask questions. This means they'll go through normal channels to get things done, and they're not going to open with 'Jenny Forrest is a wanted fugitive, please apprehend.' If I were them, I'd give the police a request to call in any car matching a certain description, and give them a partial license plate. That compartmentalizes everything nicely. And it buys us a little time, because the officer is going to wait for further instructions."

"What's your next assumption?" Jenny asks.

"That they're going to need an order from a judge to stop the bus," CB says.

Jenny winces. "I don't think that's the case."

"I really hope it is," CB says.

Jenny shakes her head. "I don't think so. I mean, I don't know how it was in the 90s, but these days all law enforcement has to do is say 'we think they might be terrorists' and they can search pretty much anything they want."

"Well God Bless America," CB says. "Still, I don't think they're quite ready to pin us as criminals. Not just yet. I think *they* think they can get to you by playing the 'concerned Federal Agency' card. 'Miss Forrest, we just want to make sure you're OK, and we want to make sure the men who did this to your family, and to your great-grandfather, pay for all of it.' That kind of thing."

Jenny thinks it over. "That might have worked," she admits.

"Sure it would have. Almost worked on me, ten years ago, and I'm a *lot* more paranoid than you are. Hopefully they're still planning to do that, because it means they aren't going to pull out all the stops to try and get us. They'll probably try to figure out where we're going, and meet us there."

"Well that doesn't help," Jenny says. "They'll learn that someone used a six-year-old coupon to get two free tickets to Farraday City. There's no way they'll believe that *isn't* you."

CB grins.

"What?"

"Look at your ticket," CB says.

Jenny pulls out her ticket and examines it closely. "Jackson, Mississippi?"

CB chuckles. "Farraday is on the route."

Jenny grins back. "Why CB, one would almost think you've done this before."

"Time to time..."

"Time to go!" The bus driver climbs into his seat, and pulls the doors closed. Jenny and CB breathe a sigh of relief as he starts the engine and pulls out onto the highway.

A few minutes later, CB starts to relax. "I think we're good," he says.

Jenny yawns. "All that terror really takes a lot out of you."

"Get some sleep," CB says. "It's going to be a while."

"OK," Jenny says. She leans her head on his shoulder, and closes her eyes.

"Um..." CB looks down at her uneasily.

"Why Farraday City?" Jenny asks sleepily.

"I told you," CB says. "I think it's the last place they'll think to look."

"I don't mean now," Jenny says, "I mean when you first moved there. Why did you move there in the first place?"

"Oh..." CB hesitates. "I went to help an old girlfriend."

"Who was she?" Jenny asks.

"An old girlfriend," CB repeats.

Jenny sighs. "Fine. Tell me another time." A few seconds later, she's asleep.

He sinks down onto the bench a bit, trying to get more comfortable without knocking Jenny's head off his shoulder. He's only moderately successful, and sighs in irritation as he realizes he's probably not going to get a lot of sleep. He reaches into his trenchcoat pocket, pulls out a cigarette, and puts it in his mouth. That's when he sees the no smoking sign.

"God damn it."

PART TWO: 8BC, JANUARY 6, 1984

8BC on a Friday night is usually full of people. Tonight is an exception—there are maybe a quarter of the people CB expected, and he's not sure how long they're going to stay. It's empty enough that CB has a table all to himself. He drinks, he smokes, he pretends to listen to the band; more fundamentally than that, he tries, unsuccessfully, to ignore the world around him.

A few years ago CB, Sin and Billy wound up playing pool with a bona-fide pool shark named Ray—a friendly game where the winner got his drinks for free. They wound up paying for Ray's drinks all night, but they didn't mind—he was a riot. He had great stories about all the cities where he played pool, games where he won big, games where he lost big. He had his own pool cue that he'd named "Maureen." CB is thinking about Ray tonight, because he can't stop thinking about pool.

He's been thinking about pool for days. It's been gnawing at him since New Year's Day, specifically since the fight with the New Aryan Army skinheads. He didn't realize what it was at first, he just felt like there was something happening right under his nose and if only he'd been paying attention he'd see what it was. But then, out of the blue, he remembered asking Ray how he got so good at pool, and what Ray had said: "I dunno kid. I can see the shots. I can see all the shots."

From that point forward, CB has been seeing all the shots. He can't stop seeing them.

He stares across the table looking at four beer bottles arranged in such a way that he knows, if he flicked his thumb at just the right angle, he could get a bottle cap to ricochet off them and dead center into the forehead of the guy at the next table. He doesn't know why he knows that, but he knows he can do it, and he knows it'd be easy. Slightly more difficult is kicking the chair out behind him at just the right moment so that someone will step through the back, get tangled up, and fall, possibly breaking an ankle in the process. At one point during the night he sees a guy stumble while trying to carry four beers, and in an instant he knows everything he would have to do in order to catch each beer, before they fell, not spilling a drop. He also knows he doesn't have the kind of balance and speed it would take to actually pull it off—but he knows what he needs to do in order to do it.

Everything he sees tells him how to do something—or how he *might* do something, if he were in the kind of shape he'd need to be to do it. Somersault backflip off the table, landing on the next table in just such a way so as to make one end flip up under someone's jaw. How to kick off a wall in just the right way, to add more momentum to a spinning roundkick. On top of that he sees possibilities that he can't even understand. He *feels*, rather than *comprehends*, the potential to do things that he can't even keep clear in his head, much less put into words. And on top of *that* is another layer: a vague notion that, if he wanted to, he could reach out and push the world into a shape that would make some of those ridiculously impossible notions easier.

He can see all the shots, all the time. But it's a very specific game of pool he's playing. A very violent game: most of what he sees has to do with fighting. Occasionally it's just something weird, like how to save the beer, but most of the time it's about fighting in ways that he's only ever seen in Kung Fu movies.

He finishes his beer. Even as he drinks he can tell it's not going to do what he wants. He knows, even as he drinks, that it's not possible to drink enough to make it stop. He sets the bottle down on the table and immediately realizes exactly how he needs to throw it in order to knock over someone on the other side of the room.

Why is it always fighting? Why isn't he figuring out exactly what he needs to do to convince the pretty brunette two tables down to go home with him? He glances at her and immediately sees at least three ways he could disarm her, if she were carrying a weapon. Which she's not, as far as he can tell, but it doesn't matter. For some reason every time he looks at someone he sees scenarios in which they're armed: with knives, with pistols, with rifles, occasionally with swords.

CB grits his teeth and stares down at the table. Focusing on a single thing helps, though when he does that he feels himself starting to pay attention to *sounds* and *smells* and occasionally piece together scenarios that deal with both. He grinds the butt of his cigarette on the table, pulls out another cigarette, and lights it, trying to pretend he isn't suddenly aware of three ways to quickly burn down the club with his Zippo.

"Why is what always fighting?"

CB looks up from the table and finds himself staring at a wide, black leather belt with a heavy iron buckle. He looks up further, and frowns. It's the pretty brunette from two tables down. Only up close, "pretty" isn't the right word. "Pretty" is too soft, and she isn't soft. Her brown hair is pulled back into a tight ponytail, revealing sharp, clean features. Scars run down her jawline on both sides of her face—something he didn't notice earlier. It seems to suit her—the scars are fierce, and *she* is fierce. He gapes at her, even as he finds himself assessing whether it would be more effective to try to break an arm or a leg first. If it came down to it.

"What?" It's the only thing he can think of to say. It sounds stupid.

Her mouth curves into a sharp, sardonic smile. "I said, 'why is *what* always fighting?' You were muttering that to yourself while you were defacing Dennis' table."

CB frowns, staring at her blankly. "What?"

She hesitates for a moment, then pulls out the empty chair to his right and sits down, uninvited. She moves two beer bottles out of the way and points.

CB looks down at the table as if seeing it for the first time: he was using a bottle cap to meticulously carve an anarchy symbol into the layers of dirt and cigarette smoke and resin and cheap wood of the tabletop. He stares at it, uncomprehending. He wasn't aware he was doing it.

"Are you high?" She doesn't accuse him, she's just curious.

CB shakes his head. "Trying to get drunk," he says finally.

"How's that working out?"

"Not so good," he says. "Uh... hi."

Her smile softens a bit, a hint of genuine amusement behind it. "Hi. I'm Joan. You're CB, right?"

He shrugs, trying not to appear tense as he forces aside the part of him that's evaluating how much effort it would take to kick her chair from under her, and whether it would be more practical to simply break one of the chair legs, causing the whole thing to collapse under her weight. "Yeah. That's me."

"You're pretty famous," Joan says.

"Yeah," CB says. "I'm a goddamn celebrity." He stuffs the remains of his cigarette into an empty beer bottle and fishes in his trenchcoat for his pack.

"The way I hear it, you beat the crap out of Plague and his crew. That makes you a goddamn celebrity this week."

CB looks at her blankly. "What plague?"

"The leader of the New Aryan Army," Joan says. "What are you, thick? He calls himself 'Plague.'"

"That's stupid," CB says. "That's a stupid fucking name."

Joan stares at him levelly. "Your friend—the one they beat up—his name is Sin, right?"

CB grumbles and lights his cigarette, pondering the effectiveness of cigarette ash being flicked into someone's eye. He grimaces and pushes the thought aside.

"Is he going to be OK?" Joan cocks her head to one side. "I heard it was pretty bad."

"He's gonna limp for the rest of his life," CB says. "Doctors saved his life. That's about it."

"No insurance," Joan says. "If you're not in, you're out."

"Yeah. Something like that. Are you serious about me being a celebrity?" He can't keep the incredulity out of his voice, and it makes Joan laugh. He likes the way she laughs.

"Celebrity is a shallow word," she says. "I'm going to go with hero. Seriously. Plague is bad news. It's rare to find people who stand up to him. It's even rarer to find someone who can kick his ass."

CB shifts uneasily. "Billy did most of that."

"That's not how he tells it," Joan says matter-of-factly. "He says you took out eight of Plague's boys all on your own, then you threw his ass across the yard."

"And then Plague kicked the crap out of me until Billy clocked him," CB says. "He's being modest."

"Bull." Joan leans in to CB, eyes locked on his. "Billy says he sucker punched Plague, and never would have been able to do it if you hadn't pissed him off so very, very much. I'm going to let you in on a little secret: Plague doesn't get angry very easily. You have to hurt him to do that. You hurt him. And that's not easy to do. He's a *metahuman*."

"Right..." CB smirks and settles back in his chair. "I fought a metahuman and lived."

"Yes." Joan's voice has none of the sneer CB has in his. "Plague can make people sick. Anyone he wants. Makes them too weak to fight. Sometimes he can even kill them. And he's strong, and he's tough, and despite the fact that he's a worthless racist shit he's also not stupid. He's what most people would call a *villain*, CB. And you kicked his ass. Which means most people would call you a *hero*. Or they would, if they gave a damn about any of us. Which they don't."

"Wow." CB keeps his voice light and dismissive. "At least you're not bitter."

Joan's voice is tight with anger. "Why shouldn't I be bitter? Why aren't *you* bitter? We live in a fucking police state, only most people don't realize it, because it hasn't reached them yet. I thought maybe you'd understand." She points at the anarchy symbol carved into the table. "But I guess you're just a poser who's in it for fashion and music, right?"

"And the sex," CB says casually. "You forgot about all that sex."

Irritation flashes across Joan's face for a moment. Then her mouth curves into a sly smile. "Fair enough. Spare a smoke?"

CB fishes into his pocket and pulls out his pack. He frowns; there are only five left. He shrugs, then slides the pack and his lighter across the table.

She fumbles with the lighter, and for a moment CB can see the scars on her jawline very clearly. They're angry purple scars that start where the jaw meets the neck, and travel down to the chin on both sides.

"Let's talk about something else," she says.

"I'm... pretty lousy at conversation tonight," CB says. "Maybe you noticed."

"I don't have anything to compare it to," Joan says. "For all I know, this is you at your most charming."

"No." CB stares at the end of his cigarette and watches it slowly burn down. "This is me going nuts."

"Yeah," Joan says. CB looks up, and is surprised to see genuine sympathy on her face. "Something happened that night, didn't it? Something you haven't been able to shake since."

CB looks down at the table.

"Hey." Joan's voice is soft. It sounds completely at odds with her. "CB."

CB looks up. For an instant, for one desperate instant, he almost tries to tell her. All he does is grimace, and shift uneasily in his chair.

Joan holds up his Zippo. "This is a nice lighter. I expect you'd like it back."

She places the Zippo down on the table in front of her. She withdraws her hand; a moment later, the Zippo scoots across the table and stops in front of CB.

"Nice trick," CB says.

Joan frowns. The Zippo rises into the air, hanging in midair in front of CB. Suddenly the top pops open, and a tiny orange flame appears.

CB stares at the Zippo floating in midair. He passes his hand over the lighter, under it, and finally plucks it out of the air and stuffs it in his pocket. "Not a trick."

"No," Joan says, "not a trick. Not the way you meant, anyway."

"What do you want?" CB looks at her guardedly. He's suddenly glad that he can see four different ways to make it to the door before she has a chance to get out of her chair.

"I want to help you," Joan says.

"I'll be fine." CB doesn't believe it when he says it, and the expression on Joan's face tells him she knows he's lying.

Joan leans forward and puts her hand over his. He likes the way that feels. She squeezes his hand, just a little, then says, "I've been where you are right now. I can help you."

"I don't know what you're talking about," CB says.

"Don't play stupid. You're not. You're a little lazy, maybe, but even if you haven't admitted it to yourself, you know *exactly* what I'm talking about. You haven't been the same since your fight with Plague, and you don't know how to cope with it."

CB doesn't reply. He looks down at the table.

"Look, CB..." Joan looks around the room, then leans in further and lowers her voice. "You've been drinking a lot this week."

"Says who?" CB glares at Joan, voice sharp. "And how is it your business? I never met you before today."

"Says Billy," Joan says.

"You know Billy?" CB says incredulously.

"Yes, I know Billy! Everyone who comes here knows Billy! He's one of the bouncers! He's worried about you. He thought I could help. And I can."

CB pushes her hand away, pushes out his chair. "Thanks for the concern, but no thanks."

CB's ears buzz, he feels lightheaded, and the room spins for a second. He grips the table to keep his balance. "*I **can** help you. Let me help you.*" His eyes widen. His hand immediately covers his mouth. He's the one who spoke, but they weren't his words.

Joan looks apologetic. "Sorry. I needed to get your attention."

His fists clench. He imagines launching himself across the table—a very specific move that involves tucking into a roll on the table itself, and lashing out with his legs, striking her full in the face, sending her toppling backward in the chair. In that instant he's positive he can do it. He sees her eyes widen, and she tenses slightly.

"I'm trying to show you that I can help."

CB fights back the urge to fight. He stands, fists still clenched, and backs away from the table. "We're done talking."

"Let me help you," she says.

"No. Don't... don't ever do that again."

He wants to run, but he forces himself to walk to the door, threading his way around a sudden influx of people who have decided to arrive late. It looks like the band will get a full house for its second set. He steps to his right to avoid a group of five, then steps left sharply, forcing the next group to split up to pass around him, and a moment later he's managed to redirect the incoming traffic so that there's a wall of people between himself and Joan.

He steps out of the club into the cold night air, and looks around uncertainly. Where to? There are really only two directions: out of Little Dresden, taking him back into the rest of the city, or deeper in. It's safer to head back to the city, but it's a longer walk. And if Joan tries to follow him, it'll be easier to catch up.

"Right," CB mutters. "Deeper in." He fumbles for his cigarettes—only four left—and lights one as he walks deeper into the burned-out landscape of Little Dresden.

PART THREE: LITTLE DRESDEN, JANUARY 6, 1984

Little Dresden is the way it is for a number of reasons, but the biggest is that it has a reputation for being destroyed by metahumans. Once upon a time it was just another part of the East Village, with all the baggage that came with it—thought of, primarily, as a haven for beatnicks, hippies, artists, and other unsavory people. But in the 70s it bore the brunt of some of the most vicious fights between metahuman hero and villain groups. Eventually people stopped trying to rebuild, and simply moved away. New York City gave up on the neighborhood, and the neighborhood became a wasteland of empty, crumbling buildings. 8BC is the first legitimate business to open there in at least six or seven years.

No one knows why Little Dresden was the focus of so much fighting, but it left its mark. Standard procedure for rescue services was to wait until the fighting was over before sending in personnel and equipment, a tactic learned the hard way after a criminal who went by the handle "Backbreaker" tried to use a fire engine as a *club* against Liberty. It wound up collapsing the building the firemen had hoped to save. The building still has a piece of the fire engine in it, as far as anyone knows, buried under a ton of bricks.

Only the outer edge of Little Dresden has working street lights. The further in you go, the darker it gets, until the only light comes from whatever fires the inhabitants have decided to make for themselves—mostly in the form of burning trash cans set along the road, where the homeless and squatters gather to talk about whatever it is they talk about. CB doesn't actually know.

There's a thriving squatting community in Little Dresden. A number of groups have staked out various buildings for their own use, fixing them up as best they can. CB hears that some of them are almost bona-fide homes— no electricity or plumbing, but with oil lamps, wood-burning stoves, and outhouses. Turn of the century living right in the middle of the most modern city on earth. But there are other parts of Little Dresden where you just don't go: parts that are claimed by very dangerous people. Drug dealers, mostly, but there are whispers of worse things. Terrorists, psychopaths, even the occasional rumor of a metahuman villain in hiding. Most people stay away from that part, even the homeless.

That's where CB winds up.

He isn't walking with any particular direction in mind, and he isn't paying attention to where he's going. He can't shake the memory of Joan's words coming out of his mouth. What bothers him most is how utterly natural it felt. It wasn't until after he'd spoken that he realized what happened.

Mind control. That had to have been mind control.

If he had more distance from the event, he might be amused that his revulsion over the way Joan offered to "help" has driven all thoughts of pool from his mind entirely—the very thing he'd been trying to achieve all night. But CB isn't in the mood for analysis at the moment. He's trapped in the horror and the disgust of the realization that Joan casually reached out into his brain and made him her mannequin, without so much as breaking a sweat.

It isn't until he finishes his last cigarette that he finally looks up and realizes where he is. He swears softly, and looks around uneasily, trying to get his bearings. It's futile—he's never been in the part of Little Dresden you're not supposed to be in, primarily because he agrees with the reasons you're not supposed to be there.

The sky is overcast. The glow from the rest of the city seems oddly muted here, and doesn't do much to light the sky at all. There are no fires burning in trashcans. He stands in the middle of the street, ankle-deep in snow, and can only barely make out the outlines of buildings. He has no idea where he is, or where he needs to go in order to get out. Everything looks the same... that is to say, everything looks like nothing at all.

He stands completely still, listening intently. He doesn't hear anything, but the hairs on the back of his neck stand straight up. He feels like he's being watched. He squints, willing himself to peer through the darkness, but his eyes aren't adjusting.

I need light. I need the moon.

All at once the clouds part, the moon shines down, and he can see. He blinks in surprise at the sudden change, but he's grateful. The light is weak, but he can see the buildings clearly now. That's good.

"Well, well, well. What do we have here?"

CB spins around. He sees a group of people about half a block down the street. He can't make out who they are—all he sees are dark silhouettes.

"I gotta give you credit. You got a pair, coming to find me all by yourself. And how the hell did you know I was here? I haven't even unpacked."

CB finally recognizes the voice. He forces himself to sound casual, even dismissive. "Oh, hey. It's Plaque, right?"

"Very funny. Look, boys, we got ourselves a race traitor *and* a comedian."

His "boys" don't respond other than by spreading out across the street. CB looks over his shoulder and sees more silhouettes fanning out behind him. He's surrounded.

There's no way this isn't going to hurt.

"You interest me." Plague's voice is easygoing, almost friendly. "You're the only guy I know who doesn't get sick when I want him to. That makes you one of a kind. Maybe when my boys are done with you I'll cut you open to see what makes you tick. See if you have a mysterious extra organ, or something like that."

"No need," CB says. "I can already tell you about the organ I have that you don't. It's called a *brain*."

The easygoing, friendly facade drops immediately. "Go get him, boys."

Immediately the other silhouettes crouch, their arms rising into formal, defensive positions. They look like extras in a Kung Fu movie.

"Ninja skinheads?" CB laughs in spite of his situation. "*Seriously?*"

"Kill him!" Plague screams. "I want to hang his corpse on my wall!"

CB abandons his smart-assed comeback when it becomes clear that the "ninja skinheads" are taking their leader very seriously. They rush him en masse, shadowy figures flowing toward him like a silent, deadly wave. The only sound comes from the crunch of snow beneath their boots.

He's playing pool again. All of a sudden he's lining up shot after shot after shot, all in the blink of an eye, option after option presenting itself to him. But they're useless. He can't pull them off. He's too weak. He's too slow. He's too clumsy. He can't bend like that...

Seriously, why would I ever consider trying to move like that? I'd break something halfway through. It doesn't make sense.

Too many ideas, all of them ridiculous. His head is killing him, and in moments the skinheads will be killing him as well.

He hears a sharp intake of breath behind him. He turns. A lone skinhead has broken ahead of the rest. His arm is drawn back, he's inches from CB, and that fist is going to *hurt*. CB instinctively jerks back, and in a moment of panic he feels his back leg lose traction. The world spins, he falls, twisting, just managing to land on his hands and knees instead of on his face. The skinhead grunts in surprise, tries to stop, slips, and trips over

CB's hunched form, falling face-first onto the snowy street...

...and in that moment, the possibilities end. He smiles. "Thanks, crazy me," he says. He doesn't try to stand. He looks at the fallen skinhead next to him, grins, and winks.

Somewhere in the distance, CB thinks he hears a small popping sound.

The fallen skinhead rolls away from CB and gets to his feet just as the others close in. It's bad timing on his part: he stands just as two of his comrades try to step over him, and they crash into him, propelling him forward. CB rolls out of his way, and the skinhead smashes head-first into a third, closing in from the other side.

CB doesn't waste time admiring the folly. He's busy.

He crouches in the snow, one hand on the ground for balance. The snow is freezing, and he isn't wearing gloves. He tries not to think about it. The other skinheads are slowing down now, because they're not completely stupid, but CB launches himself toward the closest one he can find, aiming for the knees. It's not a graceful move—nothing like what he saw Liberty do when he was fighting that weird fire thing six years ago. It's ugly, and clumsy, and if he saw someone trying to do it he'd probably double over laughing. But it works: he smashes into the skinhead's knees, and while it doesn't actually hurt the guy, he can't keep his balance in the snow. He falls; CB rolls out of the way and kicks out backward, hitting the shin of another.

That kick hurts. Unfortunately, it doesn't make him fall.

The skinhead swears angrily, and kicks back, hitting CB in the back of his thigh. It's only a glancing blow, but he's wearing steel-toed boots. That hurts a *lot*. CB grunts and forces himself to roll away, putting himself in the path of another, who trips—which is good—but winds up landing *on top of him*... which is very, very bad.

CB and the skinhead swear simultaneously. CB struggles to push him off, but the skinhead locks an arm around his neck, then stands, hauling CB up with him.

"Got him," the skinhead says, sounding smug.

Smart skinhead. *Strong* skinhead. CB's vision is swimming. He can't breathe. Someone slams a fist into his stomach, and suddenly he can't breathe *even more*. A fist hits him full in the nose. He hears something crunch, and his face goes numb. Another fist to the jaw, and his head snaps back. His ears are ringing. He vaguely hears taunting, but he can't make any of it out.

So much for playing pool.

CB struggles to get free of the arm. He feels his captor rumbling in laughter—he can't hear anything at this point, but he knows what that is. He grimaces, and tries to dig his fingernails into the skinhead's arm. That just makes his grip tighten. Fists keep pounding into his face, his stomach, his ribs... occasionally someone knees him in the groin, which is usually followed by what he assumes is a round of laughter.

Eventually the guy holding him lets go. CB drops to the ground, suddenly able to breathe. A moment of relief is followed by the defeated realization of what's going to happen next. They surround him, and they start kicking. They're all wearing steel-toed boots, and they're all kicking *hard*. He can feel his bones breaking. It doesn't hurt as much as he thought it would, which he thinks is probably a bad sign.

Suddenly he wishes he were back in the club, still talking to Joan. He wonders if she was actually on the level—if she was really trying to help him. He won't find out now.

"Do you want to live?"

He can't actually hear himself talking at this point, but he can feel his mouth moving, and he hears it in his mind. The kicking stops; apparently he spoke *very clearly*, and they weren't expecting that.

"Just nod yes or no."

It's Joan. It has to be. He can't speak on his own, but he forces himself to nod.

"Good." He feels himself speaking out loud again. *"I can't take them all on. I can help, but you have to do whatever it is you do, and you have to do it now."*

CB tries to pull himself up, but the most he can do is twitch on the ground. He shakes his head. He can't do it.

"You have to!" He can feel himself shouting at the top of his lungs. His vision clears slightly, and he can see the skinheads backing up and milling around nervously. His head buzzes, his body goes numb, and all of a sudden his body jerks up, his arms push himself off the ground, and he's sitting upright on his knees. It hurts, God it hurts, but he does it. He feels himself screaming, and he can see the skinheads backing away slowly in alarm.

"You can do this!" He's essentially shouting at himself, and for a moment he feels a strange kinship with some of the homeless crazies he's seen wandering Times Square at night. *"I can't make you move if you really can't move. I don't care if it hurts, do what you have to do to live!"*

He actually heard himself that time. His voice is hoarse and shrill. He sounds more like a screeching parrot than a human being.

"It's that bitch!" That's definitely the voice of Plague. "Come out where I can see you, so I can kill you proper!"

"*Properly. Asshole.*" CB feels his head turn to look at a semi-splotched shadowy figure standing behind the rows of other splotchy shadows that he assumes are the gentlemen who were kicking the crap out of him seconds before. That must be Plague.

"You! Take your boys and find her! You know where to look!" Plague is livid. He's lost all pretense of self-control now. CB's vision clears more, and he can see the man grabbing one of his people by his flight jacket, shouting into his face, then shoving him away roughly. About a third of the skinheads move off, scanning the rooftops.

CB hasn't moved since Joan propped him up on his knees. He sees Plague turn to face him.

"As for you," Plague snarls, "*I can't stop hitting myself!*"

Plague makes a fist and smacks himself in the face.

CB frowns. He's pretty sure that wasn't where the conversation was going.

"*Why do I keep doing this? Why do I keep hitting myself? I just can't stop doing it!*" Plague continues to punch himself in the face, over and over again. His nose is bloody now, and his cheek is starting to bruise.

"God damn it, when I find that bitch I'm going to *poke myself in the eye!*" Plague pokes himself in the eye. He staggers back, covering his face with his hands, shouting in wordless agony.

"*No wait, I have a better idea.*" A look of undisguised panic settles over Plague's face as he sees his hand make a fist and rise up in front of him. "*I wasn't using this anyway...*"

His fist slams straight into his own crotch. Plague bends over in wordless agony. Even CB winces.

"*Hurry up, OK? They're going to find me soon, and then I'm going to be—shit! You're on your own. Back when I can.*" CB hears himself talking this time. His voice sounds better. The world seems steadier. If he's going to do *anything at all*, it's going to have to be now.

How did he do it last time? He saved Sin's life. He stopped Plague's gun from firing. How? Suddenly the world starts spinning again, too fast for him to focus. He can see Plague writhing on the ground, trying to speak, his people crowded around him, trying to see if he's OK. Off in the distance, above and to his left, he hears other skinheads shouting in challenge and alarm. Nobody's paying any attention to CB at the moment. There has to be some way he can use this.

Now would be a great time to play pool, he thinks, but he's not getting anything. He sees little pieces of things, but he can't put them together. It's not working.

"Leave me alone!" Plague snaps, shoving off one of his men. "She's trying to save that asshole's life. She can't control us all. So kill him, then focus on killing *her*."

The skinheads turn to face CB. Suddenly, he's the center of attention again.

Damn.

CB sets his jaw. Fine. If whatever it is that's been tormenting him all week wants to cut and run right when it would be most useful, there's nothing he can do about that. But he's not going to roll over and die. He struggles to his feet—it hurts like hell, his ribs are screaming at him, but he shoves all that aside and stands up.

"Fuck you," he says. "Give it your best shot, assholes." His voice, his words: this time, nobody's talking for him.

The skinheads spread out, advancing cautiously. They aren't going to be tripped up by slippery snow this time. CB doesn't care; he doesn't want to trip them. He wants to hurt them. He wants to hurt all of them.

And then, all at once, the world snaps into place, and CB moves.

The skinheads are being cautious; he isn't. He leaps across the snow, body outstretched, launching himself at one of the bigger ones—he recognizes him as the one who put him in the chokehold earlier. The skinhead's eyes widen in surprise, and he takes a hesitant step back, but he doesn't expect CB to be able to move like this—he probably doesn't expect CB to be able to move much at all.

CB's face twists into a snarl as the fingers of his left hand close around the skinhead's neck. The skinhead grabs CB's arm, and CB immediately reaches out with his right, grabs a wrist, and twists, shifting his weight and pulling hard. The skinhead falls forward; CB uses him as a counterweight to flip around and propel himself, feet first, into the face of the guy standing next to him. CB hears a jaw break. The skinhead shouts in agony, then crumples to the ground, passed out from the pain.

A tiny voice in the back of CB's mind is urgently trying to tell him that what he just did was completely impossible. That voice is ignored. CB lands on his feet, crouches, and catches a third skinhead's fist. He pulls, letting the momentum of the blow carry Number Three forward, then twists sharply, breaking his arm. The man yells in pain. CB lets go, delivers a quick elbow to the ribs, then turns to face Number Four, dodges to one side, and knees him in the gut. He half-turns to grab Number Five, and throws him over his shoulder into Number Four. They both collapse in the snow.

The tiny voice in the back of CB's mind reminds him that he has broken ribs, and there's no possible way he should be able to throw a man over his shoulder with broken ribs. The voice adds that it doubts CB could do it even with his ribs intact.

"Shut up!" CB snarls, then drives his fist into the solar plexus of Number Six. Six doubles over, the wind driven out of him, and CB smashes his knee into Six's face. As Six collapses to the ground on his hands and knees, CB steps on his back, launches into the air, and kicks skinhead Number Seven in the face as hard as he can.

CB is also wearing steel-toed boots. It's not a pretty sight.

Seven falls backward, blood spraying everywhere. Number Eight immediately turns his head to the side and steps back—he has blood in his eyes and he can't see.

In a matter of seconds, seven skinheads are down, and an eighth is blinded. CB spins to face the rest.

"Volunteers! I'm looking for volunteers!" There's something strange about his voice. He knows it's his, but he doesn't quite recognize it. It sounds threatening. The remaining skinheads seem to agree: they turn around and run away.

"No! God damn it, come back here, you fucking cowards!" Plague is up now, and apparently in control of his own body again. "I'm going to kill each and every one of you! I swear it!" He turns back to face CB.

CB tenses and waits.

Plague studies CB carefully. He's calculating his odds, and even after what CB managed to pull off, he thinks Plague's odds are probably pretty good. A moment later both CB and Plague turn in surprise as they hear a strangled yell coming from a nearby rooftop, then hear a heavy, wet thud. A skinhead is lying in the snow in front of one of the burnt-out tenement houses, motionless. A second later they see a dark silhouette on the roof of the tenement, and see the silhouette deliberately leap off the roof, utter a sudden cry of terror, and then hit the ground like the first. And then it happens a third time.

CB turns back to face Plague. "I think they found Joan."

Plague narrows his eyes. "This isn't over." With that he turns and runs off, deeper into the ruins of Little Dresden, disappearing from sight.

CB looks on impassively as two more skinheads add to the growing pile of bodies on the ground. A minute later someone peers over the edge, down at the scene below.

"CB." It's Joan. "Are you OK?"

"Uh..." CB looks around him, and is suddenly aware of a dull ache in his chest that is steadily growing stronger. "I'm alive. But I think I'm going to be in excruciating pain in... oh shit."

CB sinks to his knees as he suddenly feels every ounce of pain he should have felt during that fight but didn't. The tiny voice in the back of CB's mind is repeating *I told you so, I told you so* in a sing-song manner and sounding very smug. He tries to scream, but the best he can manage is a soft whimper.

"Hold on!" Joan says. "Just hold on..."

CB tries to hold on, but he's not entirely sure what that means right now. He falls backward, which turns out to be less helpful than he hoped, and he manages a strangled yell as his ribs remind him, once and for all, that they are genuinely broken. The tiny voice continues singing *I told you so, I told you so...*

"Hey."

CB sees Joan's blurred face leaning over him. "Guh," he says.

"Hey, it's OK, you did pretty good back there, all things considered. I'm going to get you out of here, OK? Are you ready to get out of here?"

"Uh..." CB tries to remember how to talk. He feels it should be easier than it is. "I don't think I can walk."

"You don't have to," Joan says. "You just have to trust me. Do you?"

CB thinks it over.

"God damn it, CB, make up your mind, *now*."

CB tries to laugh, but can't. He nods weakly.

Blurry-Joan relaxes a little. "OK. I'm going to take you to get help. It's going to hurt a lot at first, but you'll pass out. After that everything will be OK."

"What do you—"

"Shut up," Joan says. "You'll find out. Sorry."

She places both hands on his head, one hand over each temple, and closes her eyes. White-hot pain races through him, his brain tries to scream, and then—thankfully—he passes out.

PART FOUR: LITTLE DRESDEN FREEDOM HOUSE

CB opens his eyes to see sunlight streaming in through an old, dirty window. He's lying on a mattress, wrapped in thick wool blankets. The air is cold against his face.

"Welcome back."

He's in a small, bare room, with cracked plaster walls and plywood subflooring. The doorway is an empty doorframe with a heavy curtain hung in front of it to give the room a little privacy. Standing in the doorway is Joan, wearing an army jacket, blue jeans, and thick boots.

"Back where?" CB's voice is a little hoarse, but it doesn't hurt to talk. That's a good sign.

"Our squat," Joan says. "Little Dresden Freedom House."

CB closes his eyes and tries to think. "That's the anarchist one, right? The one that never throws parties."

Joan smirks. "We're not a frat house."

"Right..." CB sits up, realizes he's not wearing any clothes, and hastily pulls the covers up around him. "Uh... how did we get here?"

Joan finds his modesty amusing. "We walked." She walks into the room and sits down at the foot of the mattress.

"I really don't remember that," CB says.

"I told you you'd pass out," Joan says. "And I did apologize. Ari was super pissed, but it was the only way I could think to get you here. I wasn't going to be able to carry you, and I wasn't going to leave you alone, either."

"Who's Ari?" CB asks, feeling more than a little lost.

"I am." A thin middle eastern man pushes aside the curtain hanging over the doorway and steps into the room. His long black hair is pulled back into a tight ponytail. He has a rough beard that is very thick at his chin and gets thinner and wispier the farther it travels up his face. "I'm sort of the doctor around here. And I'm not sure you should be sitting up."

"I feel OK," CB protests.

"Three broken ribs, two fractured ribs, multiple concussions, a broken nose, cracked jaw, and a fractured hip," Ari says crisply. "Among other things. I'm not sure how you even managed to sit up, but you need to lie back down right now."

CB looks at him blankly. "I feel fine."

Ari frowns, then looks at Joan for the first time. "What happened to the splint on his arm? And the bandages on his chest?"

"I took them off a few hours ago," Joan says. "He didn't need them any more."

"He didn't *need* them?" Ari doesn't shout, but he's obviously angry. "How would you know he didn't—nevermind. Of *course* you knew."

Ari steps into the room and kneels on the floor next to CB. "I'd like to check for myself, if you don't mind."

CB looks from Ari to Joan. Neither one of them says anything else. Joan stares off into space, deliberately not looking at anyone.

CB shrugs. "I guess."

"Just tell me when it hurts," Ari says, and begins his examination. A few slightly embarrassing minutes later, Ari shakes his head in bewilderment. "I guess I should have believed her."

"Yeah," Joan says, "you *should.*"

"Well I don't understand it," Ari says to CB, "but I'll take it. You looked like a horror show Friday night." He looks directly at Joan this time, an unreadable expression on his face. "I guess if she found you, I shouldn't be that surprised."

Joan doesn't reply.

Ari stares at her a second longer, then sighs heavily. "Sorry, Joan. I'm just not used to it, and it's hard to get past it." With that he walks out of the room, pulling the curtain closed behind him.

Joan stares at the curtain for a moment, mutters "asshole," then turns back to CB.

"Ex-boyfriend?" CB asks.

"What? No. Fuck off." Joan almost smiles. "No, he just doesn't like me."

"Why?"

Joan stares at him steadily.

"*Three guesses,*" he hears himself say. "*First two don't count.*"

CB frowns. Joan looks away. The scars on her chin look much brighter in the light. Almost like purple lightning bolts tattooed on her face.

"Sorry," she says.

"...it's OK," CB says, not sure if he means it. "Just... please don't do that again."

She nods. "Sorry about Friday. I thought it would help."

"How could you think that would *help*?" It comes out a lot stronger than he means it to. "Sorry. But it, uh... freaked me out. A lot."

"Yeah," she says. "Well I thought it would let you know that you weren't alone, you know? I mean, when I started my trip I was really freaked out until I met Roland. But he had to practically throw me across the room one-handed before it actually got through to me that we were on the same wavelength."

"Trip?" CB frowns. "Like, what, acid?"

Joan closes her eyes and counts to three. "This is not your fault," she says finally. "You sound like an idiot, but I started in the middle. So let me start at the beginning. You're a metahuman. So am I. Billy figured out what was happening to you because he's a smart guy, and he came to me because he knew what I was, and thought I could help."

"OK," CB says. It's the only response he can manage at the moment.

"When I saw you on Friday I figured you already basically knew what you were, you were just freaking out over it. That's why I did the lighter trick, to show you I was like you. But it didn't register, so I did the brain thing. That... was a really bad call."

"I'm a metahuman." He's not asking a question.

Joan nods. "You get it now. I thought you got it Friday."

CB shakes his head. "I just thought I was going nuts."

"Yeah," Joan says, "I can understand that now. Whatever it is you do, it's weird. Not bad weird, but crazy weird. I mean, I was kind of busy at the time, but I saw a little of what happened when it finally kicked in... you were... I don't know. Nobody does that in real life. Plague's goons actually stopped trying to kill me for a second, just to watch what you were doing. Thanks for that, by the way, it made the next part a lot easier."

CB remembers the figures jumping off the roof and shudders slightly.

"What were you doing, exactly?" Joan asks. She looks at him shyly, as if she's asking him to reveal something painfully intimate.

CB frowns. "I was... playing pool. I don't know how to explain it."

"Obviously," Joan deadpans. "Don't worry about it. I have friends who can help you deal with it. Roland, I mentioned him, he's one. He's the one who helped me. But there are a few others. We're a family, and we want to help."

"How?"

"Talk to Roland," Joan says. "He's better at explaining than I am. He can figure out how you tick, and help you get a handle on it. Control it."

"Yeah?" CB narrows his eyes. "What's the catch?"

"No catch," Joan says. "We don't do conscription. It's better for everyone if you get a handle on what you can do. Safer, you know? I mean, I won't lie—Roland will talk about what we're about, because it's *important*. But if you're not interested... well, if I had a dollar for every punk rocker who wasn't an anarchist I'd be a goddamn capitalist."

"So you guys are... what? A team of some kind?"

Joan nods. "Something like that."

"Huh," CB says, grinning. "Little Dresden has its own team of anarchist villains..."

"*No.*" Joan's voice is so hard it makes CB flinch. "I know you were joking, CB, but this isn't a joke. We're *heroes*. We're the reason Plague and his army of Neo-Nazi assholes hasn't run wild over New York City. It's dangerous, and we get hurt, and sometimes we die, and nobody knows because nobody gives a fuck what happens in Little Dresden any more. But we do. Don't ever forget that."

"OK," CB says. "Sorry..."

A short, uncomfortable silence follows.

"Do you have costumes?" CB asks.

Joan laughs. "You're a rat bastard."

"Well? Do you? Are they spandex?"

"No! Shut up!"

"I'm just saying, the right costume can clear up this whole hero/villain misconception, so if you haven't considered it you should. I recommend lots of red, white, and blue stars."

"Oh, you are such an *asshole*." Joan's eyes sparkle with mirth. The room feels a lot more comfortable.

"And glitter," CB adds. "It's very hard to look at someone wearing a red, white and blue costume with lots of glitter and think 'now there's a really evil and scary villain!'"

"Are you going to meet Roland or not?"

The question hangs in the air.

"Just talk?"

Joan nods. "Just talk. No strings."

CB doesn't reply. Joan sits there, still smiling, waiting patiently for his answer. Somewhere in the back of his head he feels something familiar stirring: the faintest tickle of whatever it is he does getting ready to *play pool* all over again. That's coming back, and he still doesn't know how to deal with it. If he doesn't figure it out, it's going to drive him crazy.

Joan wants to help. He believes that now. And if Roland helped her, maybe he can do the same for him.

"I don't know," CB says. "Can I get dressed first?"

Joan's smile slowly turns wicked. "I'll think about it."

PART ONE: SKY COMMANDO

David Bernard hoists his duffel bag over his shoulder as he stands in front of the main entrance and tries to work up the courage to go inside. He takes a moment to look at the letters stenciled into the glass: SKY COMMANDO UNIT on the top, AUTHORIZED PERSONNEL ONLY underneath. He remembers when this door was just an ugly metal slab with no markings at all. When the entire program was secret, and no one was allowed to talk about what they were doing in the condemned firehouse the locals were expecting to collapse in on itself any day.

Four years. Is that all?

He stares at those stenciled letters and tries to remember the first day he walked through the old doors into the chaos on the other side. The old days. Only four years. Stupid to even think like that, but he can't help it. He can see his reflection in the glass, but it's only a featureless silhouette. An outline only, nothing inside.

Only four years.

David sets his jaw, digs his key card out of his jacket pocket, puts it up to the reader, and when he hears the click pulls the door open and steps into the lobby.

It's not the same lobby. There wasn't really a lobby in the old days. They used to jokingly call it the "contamination room," because you'd step out of the comparatively clean environment of New York City and step into a world filled with the mess of engineering: wires and hydraulics and oil and ozone and metal shavings and fumes coming from solvents that probably shouldn't have been used in enclosed spaces. That was when they were still trying to put the suit together, when nobody knew who they were, and even the people who were sort-of footing the bill were looking for a reason to ignore them completely.

It's different now. Sky Commando is the crown jewel of the New York City police department, and with success comes *funding*.

The carpet isn't exactly posh, but it looks nice enough, and the air conditioning is a welcome relief from the humidity outside. The receptionist's desk is one of those curved "L" models that they use on movie sets when they want to show a lobby that looks high-tech. It's ridiculously large for one person. Style over substance.

"Heya Lieutenant." Benny's on duty this morning. He smiles amiably at David over thick-rimmed glasses. The florescent lights shine off his bald head. "You're lookin' a lot stronger today."

"Thanks." To the casual observer David appears to be the picture of health: a clean-shaven man in his late twenties, short, light brown hair, sharp blue eyes, and an ease about him that suggests excellent physical fitness. A more practiced eye will notice that his eyes blink a little more often than is normal, and that his movements, while fluid and graceful, are also slow and deliberate. A very practiced eye might notice the slight tremor in his hands while they are at rest, and his tendency to shift his weight ever so slightly from one leg to the other, as if he weren't sure of his footing.

"Seems we missed out on all the action last night," Benny adds.

"Did we?" David lets his duffel bag fall to his side as he walks over to the doors that lead to the main complex.

"You didn't hear about Forrest?" Benny sounds vaguely surprised. "It's been all over the news."

David stops and turns to stare at Benny blankly. "*What's* been all over the news?"

"You really don't know? Well damn. Martin Forrest and his family were attacked last night by some kind of paramilitary group."

David feels his jaw go slack as he gapes at Benny in astonishment. "*What?*"

Benny nods. "Armed to the teeth. I gotta wonder if it's the same group that hit Liberty... I mean, it's a hell of a coincidence, right?"

"That's what I get for trying to leave the job at the office," David says.

"Hey, don't knock it," Benny says. "It's better than sitting up alone at night, listening to the police radio while you finish off a bottle of Scotch."

"I hate Scotch," David says.

"So do I," Benny says, "but I keep buying it."

All the unit offices are on the ground level. His "office" is a slightly-larger-than-average cube in the "upscale" cube farm near the Captain's office. There aren't many people in at the moment, and the quiet is a little unnerving. The Captain's door is closed, the light is off. She isn't in yet. He looks across the room and sees the rookie's cube is also empty—but her purse is sitting on her desk.

She's here. She's probably upstairs.

He takes the stairway. Elevators bother him. It's funny—he has no problem getting himself sealed in an armored suit that would smother him alive if the life support systems failed, but lately elevators make him feel trapped.

It's probably the concussion.

A short jog up to the third floor—just to prove to himself he can do it without breaking a sweat—and he steps into the hangar. The hangar is the last remnant of the chaos that engulfed the building four years ago: it still smells like ozone, metal shavings, and solvents that probably shouldn't be inhaled. It's also full of sound: engineers are shouting to each other over the sounds of drills and metal saws, and a group of men and women in grimy jumpsuits huddle around something off to one side of the space. It's a side project, he knows that much, but he also knows he's not going to understand it no matter how many times one of them tries to explain it to him.

One or two of the engineers look up and wave as they see him. He nods back, but his attention is drawn, as always, to the center of the hangar. There, standing on its pedestal, is the suit. Half again his size, silver and blue steel, the most advanced tech the NYPD has ever had at its disposal, and the pride of Skylar Industries.

He stares at it in silence for a moment, taking it in, once again transported four years back, when he saw it for the first time. It was cruder then, but he still thought it was a work of art. And it kept getting better.

"Davey!"

David breaks out of his reverie and notices the people standing near the suit. Samuel Vicks is the chief engineer for the Sky Commando Unit—and, as it happens, the man who brought him into the program. He's a stout, balding man who nonetheless insists on sporting a long gray ponytail that falls down to the middle of his back. Standing with Samuel are the rookie and a few of the other engineers. The rookie has her jaw set, and her dark skin is covered in a sheen of perspiration. That means they were arguing, pretty heatedly from the look of it, and she wasn't giving an inch. David chuckles to himself and walks over.

"I can't work like this," Sam complains as he closes the gap. "She keeps telling us to fix things that don't exist!"

"It exists," the rookie insists. "There's a wobble."

"None of our simulations show a wobble," Sam says. "Come on, Officer, it's gotta be in your head."

"The hell it is." There's that jaw again. "Simulations aren't the same as flying. It doesn't feel like the thrust is being distributed evenly. There's a problem."

Sam turns to David. "Davey, help me out here. I can't fix what isn't there."

David shrugs. "If the pilot says there's a wobble..."

Sam sighs and turns back to the rookie. "Fine. We'll look it over. It means taking the suit offline. At least a day."

The rookie frowns. She doesn't want to give up a day of being able to fly it. David doesn't blame her.

"Fine," she says reluctantly. "Just get it fixed!"

Sam grins ruefully, then starts giving orders as the engineers prepare to take the suit apart.

"That must have hurt," David says to her.

The rookie shrugs. "Thanks for backing me up. There *is* a wobble."

"I believe you," David says. "C'mon rookie, I'll get you some coffee."

She frowns again. David never offers to get her anything. Then she shrugs and follows him into the "ready room"—the room where they usually have mission briefings before one of them gets bolted into the suit and flies off into the city.

The ready room is a kitchen. When they first moved into the building the kitchen was one of the few rooms that was fully functional, so they left it intact. There's an industrial-sized coffee maker set up next to the sink, with bins of powdered creamer and various kinds of sugar—real and otherwise—set next to it. David opens a cupboard over the sink and pulls down two mugs.

"What's going on, Lieutenant?" The rookie sounds cautious and concerned.

David concentrates on pouring coffee into the first cup. "You're going to have to start calling me David, Alishia."

The rookie stares at him. David never uses her first name.

"You feeling all right, Lieutenant? You're making me worry. I think maybe you got thrown through that wall a little harder than we thought." She says it playfully, but there's an edge to it. She knows why she's been flying every patrol for the last month.

"Funny you should mention that," David says. "I failed my physical."

He turns, cup of coffee in hand, and sees her staring at him in shock, concern, horror... and hope. And he can't fault her for it.

He holds out the coffee. "You'll have to treat it yourself. I never did figure out your specific mixture."

She takes the coffee, hands trembling. David turns back to the pot and pours the second cup.

"I have to concentrate to pour a cup of coffee," David says. "It took me a week and a half to get the coffee in the damn mug. I have headaches. Food tastes funny—I drink my coffee black now. Weird, right? Thing is, I'm in no shape to fly. I've known that for a while. I was just hoping I'd recover faster..."

"Will you?" The rookie's voice is quiet. "Recover, I mean."

"Probably. That's what they tell me. 'Probably.' Not the most reassuring word in the English language, but it's better than 'probably not.'" David raises the cup and takes a sip. It's strong and bitter, and he likes it. He still doesn't understand that part. "But I won't recover fast enough for it to make any difference here. I'm done. You're Sky Commando now."

Warring emotions play over the rookie's face, then she sets her jaw. "I don't want it like this."

"Tough," David says. "It's the only way anyone's ever gonna get the spot. You know the drill—we recruit young because even in the suit we're going to get hurt. We're going to get hurt more than any professional athlete will. When I came in they gave me six years on the outside. They didn't factor in a drugged-out nutjob using a bus like a baseball bat to knock me through a cinderblock building. We're only human—we only bounce back so many times."

The rookie's jaw is still set. Her eyes flash defiance.

"God damn it, Alishia, I *can't do the job*. I can barely pour coffee! Do you really want to put civilians at risk by putting me in a two-ton walking robot suit with rockets strapped to it?"

The rookie glares, but she shakes her head. "No. I don't want that."

"Of course you don't want that. That's why you're in the program."

They brood in silence a while.

David finishes his coffee, sets his mug down on the counter, and turns back to face her. "I'm out today. I pack my stuff and go home. There's no point in hanging around, and one thing they made sure of was that we get a hell of a pension. So I finished my coffee, and now I'm going to make the rounds, say some goodbyes, clear out my desk and go home. You are going to go back into the hangar and make damn sure they fix the wobble. Sam's a great guy. Don't let him push you around. That goes double for the Captain. I'll take a bullet for her, but don't let her tell you how to do the job. At the end of the day it's your ass on the line."

Alishia Webb looks down at the ground. "OK," she says.

David sticks out his hand. She shakes it firmly.

"Good luck, David," she says.

He forces himself to grin and claps her on the shoulder. "You're gonna be a hell of a Sky Commando, Webb."

And then it's done. The torch is passed, and David isn't a hero any more.

PART TWO: SCRAPPER JACK

Jack hoists the crate off the truck and carries it into the back of the warehouse. The other guys are straining to carry theirs, but it's nothing to him. The only real inconvenience is that it's *awkward*—the crate blocks his view of the ground right in front of his feet—and he has to try to at least *pretend* it's heavy. That's the tricky part: until he sees other people trying to lift something, he has no way of knowing exactly how heavy it is for the average tough guy... to him, it's not much different from raising his arms. His trick is to make a show of not showing it. It's a pretty simple expression: he squints a little, presses his lips together, tightens his jaw, and that's it. It's the "I'm too macho to complain about how heavy it is" look, and it always works.

"So that's why I think it's the Mob."

Jack sighs inwardly and tries to remember that he mostly likes hanging out with these guys. They've been talking about the attack on the Forrest house in Brooklyn all day, and they haven't said anything new since 9:30 this morning.

Eddie does most of the talking. Eddie always does most of the talking. He's a short, wiry redhead who doesn't look like he could lift a beer can, let alone haul cargo. Turns out he's one of the strongest guys in the group— next to Jack, of course, but that doesn't count—and not only is he strong, he doesn't shut up. Jack likes him, but he gets tired of hearing him talk sometimes. Like today, for example.

"I mean, think about it." Eddie cheerfully drags a crate out from the truck, and somehow manages to carry it off despite his arms being barely long enough to grab the sides. "The mob, if they want you dead, they don't just kill you. They kill your family. They go after everyone you've ever loved! Am I right? I mean, of course they'd try to do Liberty's family. Ain't that right, Blackie?"

Jack grunts noncommittally.

"That's what I thought. You don't fuck with the mob."

Thirty seconds later Eddie declares that he's changed his mind, and that it was definitely the "commies who did it." And so it goes for hours. Eddie blames the mob, the commies, Iran, the Reichstaadt, the D.E.A., aliens, Mexican drug lords, and the Russian Mafia before he comes back to the Cosa Nostra. By the time lunch finally rolls around Eddie has started to mix and match groups, imagining an intricately coordinated joint operation of co-conspirators. And at the end of each tortured train of logic, Eddie beams proudly, shouts "Ain't that right, Blackie?" and Jack grunts noncommittally. Then a few minutes later Eddie does it again.

Lunch is half an hour of blissful silence—Eddie is too busy stuffing his face to enlighten them further. The only interruption comes when Theo, one of the new guys, asks him why everyone calls him "Blackie."

"Black Irish," Jack says.

Theo is a college kid who's working the summer to save up for his next semester. Jack admires the dedication—he works hard and seems to be legitimately saving his money—but he's a little worried about how little Theo actually seems to know. The phrase flies right over his head, and all Jack gets is a vacant stare.

Jack points to Eddie. "Red hair. Regular Irish." Then he points to himself. "Black hair. Black Irish."

"Oh, right." Theo looks embarrassed. "Sorry, man."

Jack shrugs.

"How did you get your scar?" The question comes out in a jumbled rush, and Theo flushes scarlet as he asks it.

Jack scratches at the long scar running down the length of his left cheek. "Prison."

"Oh..." Theo licks his lips nervously. "Uh. Cool, man. Hey, I gotta go make a call..."

Everyone laughs. It's no secret that Jack did time, but nobody really talks about it. Getting the new guy to "ask Blackie about his scar" is a game they never get tired of playing.

After lunch Eddie launches into his crazy conspiracy theories again. By the time they punch out Eddie is convinced that Liberty was killed by North Korean agents using the Mafia as a front, and they attacked the Forrest house in order to convince the Freemasons that the Illuminati were behind everything. At this point Jack's pretty sure Eddie's bullshitting just to see how far he can take it. For some reason that doesn't bother him as much.

Some of them stop off at Rick's Bar and Grill after quitting time. There's a game on the TV, so their usual boisterous conversation is set aside as the avid sportsmen wander up to the bar to shout at the screen. Jack orders a burger and fries and wanders off to a booth to eat in peace.

At least, that was the plan. Eddie slides into the opposite bench and stares at him, a funny kind of gleam in his eye.

"Got a second, Blackie?" Eddie leans forward conspiratorially, his voice low, the hint of a grin on his face.

Jack puts down his burger and takes a swig of his beer. He shrugs.

"Look, I might get my ass kicked for this, but I can't help it. I gotta know, and it's *killing* me. So if I'm gonna die, I figure go down swinging for the fences, right?"

Jack looks at Eddie questioningly.

Eddie shakes his head. "Man of few words, you are. Are you sure you're Irish? Never mind, I get it, but I gotta stick my neck out anyway. Do you know? About Liberty, I mean. And the Forrest house. Do you know who did it?"

Jack tenses, just a little bit. Eddie notices and for an instant Jack sees panic in his eyes. But the panic is pushed aside, and Eddie leans in closer. All Jack sees now is curiosity. A burning curiosity.

Jack likes Eddie OK, but Eddie's problem is he's smart. His other problem is that he's almost fearless.

"Why would I know?" Jack asks.

"The man speaks!" Eddie grins wide. The fear is still there, but now it's a rush, and Eddie is riding it to the end. "Look, Blackie, your life is your business, but just because the other guys haven't figured out who you are doesn't mean nobody can. You never take a sick day, you have that pretty scar on your face, and you lift those crates like they're nothing at all. I figured out who you were your first day on the job. The sun rises in the east, it sets in the west, two plus two is four, and you're 'Scrapper Jack' Barrow, the man who crippled Mach for life."

Eddie is keeping his voice low—he clearly isn't trying to tell the world. But the fact that he knows bothers Jack. He doesn't know why: he never bothered keeping his identity secret, exactly. He certainly never wore a mask, and it's not like that scar is ever going away.

Jack takes a bite of his burger and chews slowly, watching Eddie the entire time. Eddie starts to sweat—he probably thinks Jack is trying to decide whether or not to kill him. But he doesn't break eye contact, and he doesn't say anything else. He just waits.

Ballsy. Jack's gotta give him credit for that.

"Since day one, huh?"

Eddie relaxes a little. "All right, it took me the whole week to be sure.

But I was almost convinced day one, yes."

Jack takes another drink. "And you haven't told anyone." He doesn't bother hiding the skepticism in his voice.

Eddie raises his right hand. "On my mother, Blackie. I don't know why a guy like you wants to work a shitty job like this—and I'm dyin' to know why—but I figure you have your reasons. I promised myself never even to bring it up... and I kept that promise till now, and I gotta say, Blackie, it was not an easy thing to do."

Jack smiles slightly at that. He can imagine Eddie going crazy sitting on something like that. "If I ever find out you told anyone I'm going to do a lot more than break your legs."

Eddie's bravado falters slightly. "Yeah, well, I imagine you could do quite a bit more than that. But I got be clear on this, Blackie, because I don't want you thinking I'm more than I am. I won't volunteer it, but I'm not made of stone. If the police were to lean on me hard enough, I imagine I'd crack, just like anyone else. And there are other groups who lean harder. And I'd crack faster. And there's some out there, well, I wouldn't even wait for them to push."

It's a frank, honest assessment, and Jack's not going to kill a man for admitting he has a breaking point. "As long as you don't go volunteering it, or trying to turn me in for a reward. Because I promise you that will blow up in your face. Big time."

Eddie laughs. "Fuck, Blackie, you don't go turning in the neighborhood hero for money."

Jack raises an eyebrow.

"Oh yeah, all us kids wanted to be you. Tragic story, screwed over by the man, sent up the river because a hero was a royal prick... you were the stuff of legends! Local boy fighting against the odds, and all that. And here you are now, sitting right in front of me. And fuck me if you don't look a day older than I do."

Jack snorts, takes a bite of his burger, then shrugs. "Also, don't ever call me Jack."

"I've been calling you Blackie since the first day haven't I? Why stop now? It'd be like calling my mother by her first name." Eddie frowns. "Well, no, not really. That's a bad example. But you know what I mean. Now will you answer my question? It's all I can think about, so it's all I can talk about. And I get the feeling it's wearing a little thin."

Jack actually laughs at that. "That's an understatement."

"Well?" Eddie leans in even closer. "Come on, throw me a bone. You ran with a lot of the guys who'd want to take him out, right? Hell, you fought him before, right? You might be lying low, but you gotta know something about how things work on that side."

It's not like Jack hasn't been thinking about it, and he's actually kind of relieved there's someone he can talk it over with. He washes down his burger with his beer, then reaches for the ketchup to drown his fries.

"It depends on how much things have changed," Jack says. "Back in my day, nobody would dare to touch Liberty unless he was on the job. That goes double for his family."

"Really?" Eddie looks perplexed. "Why? I mean, seems like the best time to take him out would be during his down time."

"It would," Jack agrees. "But Liberty was a special case. He won World War II, you know? Germany had an army of blonde-haired, blue-eyed monsters ready to roll over the world and Liberty took 'em all on. Some of the old-timers on our side were veterans. Some of 'em actually fought alongside him. So there was that initial professional respect."

"Yeah, but most of them are gone, right? I mean, is it some kind of mafia code of honor thing that just kept going?"

Jack nods. "Sort of. The original guys were strictly nine to five. They didn't go after a guy in his downtime. The thinking was you go toe to toe, you slug it out, and let the better man win. They weren't friends or anything, but there was professional respect. Some of the newer guys felt the same way, and some were big-name enough to make sure everyone fell in line."

Eddie looks confused. "How'd they do that?"

"They made an example out of anyone who didn't."

Eddie nods slowly. "Oh. Yeah, OK. Right."

"Anyway, the guys I ran with? They were old school. When it came to Liberty, at any rate. They wouldn't go after him like that, and they wouldn't go after his family. But there were some groups who would have, maybe. Political groups. That half-assed theory you were spouting off about the North Koreans makes more sense than anything else."

"I was just bullshitting."

"I know, but it makes more sense. Most of the guys who do stuff for politics don't exactly have what you'd call a code of honor." Jack stares off into space, frowning thoughtfully. "The Forrest house doesn't make sense, though. I mean, Martin Forrest was a cop. He put a lot of guys in jail, and I could see someone wanting to get revenge for that, but nobody he collared would hire soldiers to do him."

"Curveball and Regiment were there," Eddie offers.

Jack shakes his head. "That doesn't make any sense either. If I knew either one of them were going to be there, I'd be going in with more than just soldiers. I don't care how well trained they were."

"So... that's it?" Eddie looks disappointed. "That's all you know?"

"Sorry Eddie. I've been out of the game for a while. And I want to keep it that way," he adds pointedly.

Eddie throws up his hands. "Sure, Blackie. No problem. I just wanted to know."

"What are you ladies doing over there?" Jack turns toward the voice. One of the other guys at the warehouse is staring at them with a drunken smirk plastered over his face. "Are you holding hands?"

"Naw, Rick," Eddie calls back. "We were just wondering when the Sallys on your team were gonna put their purses away and start playing ball!"

The bar laughs raucously. Eddie grins, winks at Jack, then heads up to the bar. Jack finishes his fries, pays his bill, and heads home.

PART THREE: OVERMIND

It's a short walk to his apartment—a dingy little efficiency on the fourth floor of a fire trap that the city never condemned because it assumed it already had—and Jack's tense the entire way. When he made his arrangement with Celona he didn't exactly try to hide his identity. He wasn't in the business any more, he didn't want to be disturbed, and Mr. Celona saw to it that as far as anyone was concerned he was otherwise occupied and no longer on the market. But Pasquale Celona has been dead for three years, and Jack has no interest in entering into any kind of arrangement with his son. If Eddie was smart enough to figure out who he was, then anyone who knows he's still around can probably find him, if they put any effort into it.

All the way home he tries to tell himself there's no reason to believe it'll ever come to that. He was never one of the masterminds—he was always the muscle. At one point in time his muscle was in high demand, but he's not the guy people think of when it comes to plots and schemes. *There's no reason anyone would track me down because of this*, Jack thinks, but he can't convince himself it's true. Eddie thought he might know something because he was connected, once upon a time. It's a reasonable assumption to make, and if Eddie made it, others will too.

Might be time to take a vacation.

It's hot and muggy, more humid than usual, and it smells like it might rain again. The rain is starting to annoy him, and he finds himself thinking the desert might be a nice change of pace. It's a shame: the warehouse isn't the greatest job in the world, but he's had worse. The guys he works with aren't exactly the cream of society, but he's worked with worse. And his apartment is a crappy little hole in the wall in danger of burning to the ground any day now, but he's definitely lived in worse. There's nothing great about poverty, but when you're almost impervious to the harsh conditions that come with it you can get along much better than most. It's a quiet, low-key life. He likes that.

His apartment building is only five stories high and it doesn't have an elevator. He walks up four flights, listening to his footsteps thud on the soft, slowly-rotting wood stairs, and when he emerges onto the fourth floor he stops cold. His pulse starts racing, he feels his hands curl into fists, and he tenses in anticipation. He smells smoke; not just any smoke, but smoke from a very specific brand of cigar. He only knows two people who smoke that brand, and he's one of them.

He exhales slowly, forces himself to relax, forces his fists to unclench. No point in running now. Not from him.

He unlocks his front door, walks through the door, says, "Hello, Artie," and heads straight for the refrigerator.

A low, affectionate chuckle comes from the direction of his couch. "Hello, Jack. It's been too long."

Jack opens the refrigerator door. "Beer?"

The smell of cigar smoke swells for a moment. "No thanks. But don't let that stop you."

"I wasn't," Jack says. He takes a bottle from the top shelf, pops the cap off with his thumb, swings the refrigerator door shut, and turns to face his old boss.

Jack's apartment doesn't look *furnished* so much as it looks *scavenged*. The efficiency is organized into three basic areas; the wall with the stove and kitchen sink has an old, dented refrigerator with a missing icebox handle, and a few cupboards which hold mostly plastic cups and plates. The gas stove has a brick wedged under one corner to keep it from wobbling on its three remaining feet. A card table with two folding chairs serves as a dinner table, though in reality all it does is hold bills and junk mail. The wall with the front door has a small bookcase, which supports an even smaller TV. No cable, but Jack has an HDTV converter and antennae so he can get his fill of useless TV programming. The couch, actually a cheap two-cushion loveseat covered in cracked green vinyl, is placed directly across from the TV. Two milk crates and a plank of wood serve as a makeshift coffee table, and a folding TV tray sits to the right, serving as an end table. The wall with the door to the bathroom has an old army cot—Jack's bed—and the wall opposite the door has a few dirty windows that overlook the alley below. One opens onto a fire escape that Jack is fairly certain won't support his weight. Cardboard boxes full of Jack's clothes are stacked in one corner of the room.

In the middle of it all, sitting placidly on the cheap vinyl couch, sits Artemis LaFleur. Overmind. One of the most dangerous criminals in the world. He is also, after a fashion, one of Jack's closest friends.

It's complicated.

He's taken the form of an older, distinguished-looking man, with a full head of silver hair and glittering green eyes. He's dressed in a dark, elegant three-piece suit, complete with a silk handkerchief in his suit pocket, and an almost blindingly white dress shirt with French cuffs and silver cuff-links.

Jack doesn't know if this is his natural form, but he's sure it's the one Artemis prefers to wear. His formal look—the one he uses when he's making a public appearance, or dealing with flunkies—is far more imposing, and a lot more difficult to talk to.

Jack drags one of the folding chairs over to the "coffee table" and sits, setting his beer down on the plank of wood. "So you're not wearing the helmet, the armor, or the cloak. This isn't a business call."

Artemis puffs on his cigar and doesn't answer. The cigar is rolled from a particular tobacco leaf that Artemis bred himself. As far as Jack knows he's the only one in the world who grows it.

"At least, it's not about *official* business."

"It's been too long, Jack." Artemis sounds a little wistful. "Most of the people I work with these days aren't able to keep up."

"I can't keep up either," Jack says. "I just know that when you don't say anything, it's usually because I said something wrong."

Artemis laughs. "As usual, you sell yourself far too short. You're quite adaptable, Jack. A trait I have always valued."

Jack takes a drink and sighs. "Can we not do the dance, Artie? I've been trying to keep a low profile for years, and it's not encouraging to see the Mastermind of Crime sitting in my apartment, talking about old times. I don't want to play the game any more."

"What *do* you want?" Artemis tilts his head to one side and looks at Jack thoughtfully. "Go straight? Become a 'hero?'"

"Just live," Jack says. "Put in an eight-hour day, have a beer after work, go home, and watch TV. Or not. Maybe read a book. Maybe see a movie."

"The quiet life." There is a hint of derision in the old man's voice.

"Hey Artie," Jack says, "why don't you take your opinions and—"

"Apologies." Artemis looks around the room and frowns. "I'll admit, Jack, I don't understand this. I'm a man who believes in the value of understanding the motives of everyone around him, and this... is not the man I know. You are not given to a lavish lifestyle, I understand that, but... why do you live in squalor? You could have so much more. You could *be* so much more."

"I have my reasons."

Artemis nods. "That, I believe. I don't know what they are, but I don't doubt you have them. And so I apologize."

"Fine," Jack says. "So why are you here?"

"To ask a favor."

Jack narrows his eyes. "What kind of favor?"

"A very complicated and dangerous one," Artemis says. "One that will very likely force us to make unpleasant and difficult alliances. I'm about to do something very dangerous, and believe me when I say I need your help."

"What are you going to do?" Jack asks, curious in spite of himself.

"I'm going to find the people who murdered Liberty," Artemis says. "I'm going to find them, and I'm going to destroy them."

Jack isn't sure what to make of it. "I see," he says finally.

"I am not a particularly good man, Jack. This isn't something that, I think, surprises you very much. I do what I must to build a better world, but I am not a man who *represents* a better world." Artemis broods over the glowing tip of his cigar, watching the ash slowly build up on the end, until in a sudden, swift motion he knocks the ash into a cheap tin ashtray sitting on the TV tray. "Our approaches to the future couldn't have been more different. Incompatible, even. I see the world as it is and break it, in order to build something better. He saw what the world *wanted* to be, saw what it was, in those few instances when it lived up to its ideals, and moved it forward. He *was* a man who represented a better world. I hope you aren't offended when I say he was the most remarkable man I've ever met. One of the few I admired and respected."

"No, I get it," Jack says. "Most of the guys we know would have to admit respecting him a little. That doesn't mean he wasn't a pain in the ass."

Artemis laughs. "Yes, he was indeed. If you'll indulge an old man changing his mind, I believe I would like a beer."

Jack grunts, gets a second beer from the refrigerator, pops the cap with his thumb and hands it to Artemis.

Artemis raises the bottle in a toast. "To the pain in the ass."

Jack raises his in return. "So who did it?"

"That's just it," Artemis says. "I have no idea."

Jack raises an eyebrow.

"Hard to believe," Artemis agrees. "When I first heard of his death I was furious, of course. Times have changed, mores have changed, but enough of us are still around that I was certain we could maintain some of the old codes. That one, at the very least. But here's the interesting thing, Jack: it wasn't any of us. Of that, I am *absolutely certain*."

"What do you mean?" Jack asks. "That doesn't make any sense. Had to be some outfit."

"I immediately conferred with some of the other groups with which I maintain terms. Groups that still supported enough of the old codes that I was confident of their cooperation. We can find no one in any of our communities who had any knowledge of it. So I began to investigate other avenues, using my contacts in various world governments to determine if it was a political matter."

"Yeah?" Jack leans forward. "What did you find?"

Artemis purses his lips in annoyance. "Nothing. I found nothing at all. I found nothing in a way that leads me to suspect I was *intended* to find nothing. I told Curveball as much the day of Liberty's funeral."

Jack's eyebrow goes up again. "You met Curveball at the funeral?"

"The viewing, actually. A short conversation. He did not seem happy to see me." Artemis appears vaguely amused by the memory.

"Big shock, that," Jack says. "How's he doing?"

"Hasn't aged a day," Artemis says. "Still angry at everything, I imagine. More so now than ever. Still looked like a drawn weapon in a room full of sheep, even in that rumpled suit. I offered him my card. He took it. He didn't commit to using it, but at some point I believe he will."

"You think he's investigating Liberty's murder."

"I'm convinced of it," Artemis says. "That evening, a disturbance was reported in Liberty's apartment. There were signs of a fight. Only hours later, Martin Forrest's house is attacked by a large force of highly trained and woefully unprepared soldiers of unknown origin, only to be repelled— quite forcefully—by Curveball and Regiment. And now, according to my sources, Curveball is nowhere to be found. That is less than twenty-four hours after our meeting."

"He does know how to stir the pot," Jack says.

"He does indeed," Artemis agrees. "But I believe he is getting in over his head. And while it may seem strange to you, Jack, I have come to believe that Liberty's death is more significant than I first thought. How can an organization with the resources to murder Liberty exist while managing to evade my detection entirely?"

Jack nods. "I see what you mean."

"The circumstances surrounding Liberty's death are ridiculous. No mere mercenary would be able to assassinate him, no matter how well trained or prepared. It defies logic. There's more to this story. Because of my regard for him, and because I will not allow a group to operate in the secrecy this one apparently enjoys, hidden from my sight, I will see to it that the people responsible are exposed and destroyed."

"So," Jack says, "personal *and* professional."

"Quite. And I need your help for this."

Jack sighs. "Yeah. OK, I'm in."

"Thank you, Jack." Artemis smiles warmly. "I appreciate it."

"What do I do first?"

"Hmmm. Yes." Artemis reaches inside his jacket and produces another cigar, offering it to Jack. "First, we smoke. It's really been too long. After that I need you to contact your... brother."

Jack takes the cigar. "Well. I guess I see why you came here first."

Artemis laughs.

PART FOUR: CROSSFIRE

"For a factory that was shut down by the EPA, it sure gets a lot of traffic." Street Ronin stands on the roof of an old warehouse two buildings down from the factory in question. He puts down his binoculars, turns to the other two men standing with him, and shrugs. "I saw Mauler, but I don't know if the others are there. Mauler's kind of hard to miss, though."

"Leave Mauler to me." Vigilante rolls his right shoulder, then his left. Limbering up. "Greg, you need to find where they're keeping the 'cargo.'"

Red Shift nods absently. "No problem. You gonna keep it together tonight?" He asks the question lazily, but there's an edge to it.

"Yes." The annoyance in Vigilante's voice is obvious.

"Just wanted to know how to plan the rest of my evening." Everything Red Shift says comes across as easygoing and laid-back. He's the most low-key speedster Street Ronin has ever met. Either that, or he's the most amazing actor Street Ronin has ever met.

"God damn it, Greg—" Vigilante stops short, takes a breath, and forces himself to calm down. "It's been pretty bad lately," he admits.

"Glad you noticed," Red Shift says. "Worried about you, Chief."

"You're dying too much," Street Ronin adds.

Vigilante nods. "Pushing too hard," he says. "But it got us this address. And damned if we're not taking Darius down tonight."

Street Ronin checks his rifle and his pistols one last time before going in. "Alive?"

"Preferably," Vigilante says. "But we're not the good guys."

We're the guys who get it done. That's the second part. It's always been the second part, for as long as they've been working together. Street Ronin and Red Shift nod, almost in unison.

"Try not to get killed, Tommy," Red Shift says, slapping Vigilante on the back. "You're always so *grumpy* after."

Vigilante chuckles. "Yes, mother."

"Target priorities," Street Ronin prompts.

"Yeah..." Vigilante thinks. "I'll focus on Mauler. If he's the only one there, then Greg finds the cargo and takes down anyone on guard. Hector, you'll be taking out anyone else."

"Sure," Street Ronin says. "That's the easy scenario. What if the whole crew is there?"

"Earsplitter got tagged by Sky Commando a few weeks back. She's in the Pit now. Or should be. I didn't hear about any breakouts. If Flicker and Target are there... well, Greg, you've got Flicker. Hector might get a lucky shot off—"

"Doubt it," Street Ronin says sourly. "Too fast."

"That leaves you, Greg. Hector, if Target's there things will get really messy, because he'll probably kill the cargo out of spite. And if we're taking on all three, that'll give Darius a chance to bolt."

"If the whole gang is there we're screwed," Red Shift says, "but best bet is you and Hector take 'em on first, while I take down the goons. I'll have a few seconds before Flicker notices."

Vigilante thinks it over. "Yeah. That's a better plan. Hector, that means you and me, we go in first. Greg doesn't come in until we can assess, then he can either target goons or go for the cargo, however it goes."

"Sounds like a plan," Street Ronin says.

Red Shift laughs. "You always say that. You never say if it's a good plan."

"We never have good plans," Street Ronin says.

Red Shift laughs again.

"Visors down," Vigilante says. "Time to fight."

Most heroes and villains have unique costumes that are intended to reflect their individuality, their strengths, their weaknesses, or some kind of theme that reflects their basic nature. Some groups adopt costumes that are similar—variations on a theme—but they still adopt personal touches. Crossfire's uniform is intended to be identical. The reason is simple: in their costumes, Vigilante, Red Shift, and Street Ronin look essentially the same, which makes it that much harder for them to be identified out of costume.

A very observant person might notice that Street Ronin's skin is slightly darker than the others, or that Red Shift's hair is light brown, while Vigilante and Street Ronin have almost coal-black hair. But they are roughly the same size, and wearing the body armor they appear to have roughly the same build. With the visors down no one can see the color of their eyes.

The uniform is Street Ronin's design: black, snug-fitting, reinforced with armor over all the vital organs. A yellow, stylized target sits over the left breast, but other than that, there are no markings. Their visors almost look like ski goggles: the faceplate is a dark, glass-like lens that covers almost a third of the face. It does more than provide anonymity: it has UV and IR displays, as well as the secure comm channels they use to coordinate their actions. The original design had the visors attached to a ski mask, to obscure the faces completely, but Vigilante found the ski mask was too easily twisted around in close combat, and too difficult to readjust. Now a thick elastic strap keeps the visor over the face, and a simple tug repositions it as needed.

Vigilante looks out at the old factory, clenching and unclenching his fists. "Sentries still there?"

"Hold on." Street Ronin pushes up his visor and takes out the binoculars again. He reminds himself to try to add a zoom setting to the visor display. "Yeah. Same three. One fell asleep."

"Take 'em out quiet," Vigilante says.

Street Ronin goes over to the big gun sitting on its tripod. It's the size of a machine gun, but it's not. It's large because it uses a magnetic field to propel iron wedges through the air with the power of a high-end hunting rifle. It's a little unwieldy, but it has the advantage of being silent. He turns on the generator and waits for the whine to stabilize before looking through the scope and lining up his first shot.

He pulls the trigger. The gun makes a soft buzzing sound, and a sound similar to a release of compressed air comes out of the nozzle.

"One."

He pulls the trigger again.

"Two."

He pulls the trigger again.

"Three. All down."

"Going in," Vigilante says, and leaps off the roof, flying through the air in a high arc until he lands with practiced precision in front of the main entrance. Street Ronin hears the sound of metal being torn apart.

"He's in," Red Shift says.

"My turn," Street Ronin says. "Can you pack everything up for transport after I'm down?"

"Yep," Red Shift says.

* * *

The grapple gun is already lined up for the shot, and a moment later it shoots through the night, embedding into the factory wall. Street Ronin pulls down his visor and when the line is pulled tight he attaches the harness and jumps. It takes ten seconds to cross the length of it. He nearly falls flat on his face when he lands. Angle was too steep—he needs to be more careful. *He* can't instantly heal a broken leg.

He unhooks his harness and unslings his rifle. The front door to the factory is gone, and so is most of the doorframe. Vigilante made quite an entrance.

Then his comm link crackles to life. "We got all four! It's a tra—"

The wall beside the door explodes outward as Vigilante flies out into the street and slams into the wall of the building on the other side. He leaves a man-sized indentation in the concrete. A high-pitched keening noise emerges as an armored form flies out after him, followed by a sonic boom, and Street Ronin staggers, his head throbbing in agony from the sound. He grits his teeth, reaches into a pouch on his holster and shoves an earplug into his left ear.

Vigilante jerks forward, forcing his upper torso out of the indentation, only to be knocked back into it as the keening noise stops, and the air in front of the armored figure's outstretched hand ripples and warps as waves of compressed sound slam into his chest.

Earsplitter isn't in the Pit.

Street Ronin hears a bellowing roar, and more of the wall explodes as the massive form of Mauler races across the street, his huge fists balled up and raised back. Mauler gains size and mass—Street Ronin has no idea where he gets it from—and he's addicted to a particularly nasty designer drug that increases his natural ability while simultaneously making him absolutely, 100% bat-shit crazy to boot.

That's two. There are two more.

Target's a normal human, so he's going to keep his distance. They have a little time before he makes his move. Flicker, however...

Something smashes into him, hard, knocking him to the ground and sliding him back nearly ten feet. Street Ronin's vision whites out for a second, and as it clears he sees Flicker, his crooked, rictus grin plastered permanently to his scarred face, as he grabs Street Ronin's rifle and rams the butt into his stomach. The armor does its job—the blow stings, but doesn't incapacitate. Flicker looks disappointed, then runs off, running around the corner of the building, moving so fast he looks like he's an actor in an old movie.

Street Ronin doesn't bother to get up. He rolls over, draws both pistols, sits up and starts firing at the other end of the building. It's a long shot, but he knows Flicker is coming back around. Maybe he'll get lucky.

Flicker's foot smashes into the back of his head. Street Ronin slumps over, his last conscious thought *the bastard doubled back.*

He *hates* not being a metahuman.

* * *

"We got all four! It's a tra—"

The sound of the wall exploding is ambiguous—that could have been Vigilante—but the keening sound isn't. Earsplitter is a nasty piece of work, and her sonics do very inconvenient things to Vigilante's organic armor. Red Shift is off the top of the building in the blink of an eye, and before he's past the first building he's already supersonic. He hears windows shatter— that's what you get for not using SoneX glaze—and moments later he's past Vigilante, Earsplitter, and Street Ronin, through the broken doorframe, and in the factory, looking for targets.

He sees Mauler but leaves him be for the moment. He needs to find Flicker—Vigilante and Street Ronin haven't had much luck against him in the past. He catches a glimpse of him streaking toward the back of the factory, but before he can give chase he notices Target, wearing strange, bulky goggles, aiming a large caliber gun at... nothing in particular. It looks like he's getting ready to shoot the wall.

In the the space of seconds Red Shift tries to figure out what he's trying to do. Target isn't a metahuman, he's a highly-skilled mercenary with a knack for invention and a nasty, creative streak when it comes to tactics. He's essentially Street Ronin, or at least his evil clone. That's the thought that brings it all together: Street Ronin is pressed up against the other side of that wall, and Target doesn't intend to shoot it, he intends to shoot *through* it. If that gun can shoot through a wall, it can probably shoot through their armor. Red Shift changes course, and when he sees a ripple around Target's form—a telltale sign that his force field is active—he pushes himself to go faster. They collide a half a second before Target is ready to pull the trigger.

All speedsters have ways of coping with the hostile environment created when they run at high speeds. When Red Shift moves past a certain speed, he generates a force field that protects his body from turbulence and drastically reduces friction. He's well past that speed when he collides with Target's force field: when Target flies across the room, slams into the far wall, and slides to the floor like a sack of potatoes, Red Shift feels almost nothing at all.

"That was a lot easier than I expec—"

Red Shift is standing completely still when the bomb goes off under him. The first flash of light causes him to jerk away from the source, and the movement saves his life—it allows his body to generate the force field, which protects him from the brunt of the blast.

It's not enough to keep him conscious. He passes out before he hits the ground, which, on some level, he appreciates.

* * *

"We got all four! It's a tra—"

Mauler hits him dead on, and the next thing Vigilante knows he's sailing through the air into the night sky, only to hit a wall so hard he winds up embedded in it. A second later he's in agony as waves of sound beat mercilessly against him, threatening to shake him apart. Vigilante knows he's in trouble, but he keeps losing consciousness before he can do anything about it. That's one of the reasons he knows he's in trouble.

Earsplitter's sonics *hurt*. They do something to his skin that breaks down his invulnerability much faster than he can heal it back up, and it's reached the point where Mauler's fists are doing some real damage. Each blow strikes with enough force to shatter bone—bone that is repaired seconds later when his healing kicks in, but those seconds are spent with his consciousness circling the drain.

When Flicker joins in it gets worse. Flicker hits hard and fast, blow after blow concentrating on one spot on Vigilante's side until he feels his ribs break. This is bad on many levels: first, it just adds to the hurt. Second, if Flicker is here, that means Street Ronin and Red Shift are out of the picture.

He hopes they're all right.

As much pain as he's in right now, he's not particularly worried about himself. Vigilante is the byproduct of a scientific experiment gone completely awry: twelve years ago he was used as a test subject to try and duplicate the powers of someone his captors called "Patient Zero," a villain who possessed enormous strength, invulnerability, and regenerative abilities. He got some of the strength, and a strange derivative of the invulnerability, but what surprised everyone—including himself—was exactly how much farther they went with the regeneration. He heals at a molecular level. He was disintegrated once; it took him four months to come back from it. He doesn't stay down, which is why they're spending so much time trying to keep him as damaged as possible.

The sonics are shaking his armor to pieces now, and Mauler starts hitting him in the face. His vision is swimming, he can feel swelling somewhere. Flicker is starting to work on the ribs on the other side of his chest. Now they're snapping like twigs, and breathing is an excruciating ordeal.

The car that flies through the air and hits Earsplitter straight on is an unexpected development. But it's a welcome one: her sonics are no longer shaking his armor apart, and it hardens almost instantly. Flicker curses as his blows no longer have any effect, and Vigilante feels his ribs knitting back together. Mauler is still pounding on him, oblivious to any change, but he yelps in surprise when Vigilante is finally able to catch a fist with both hands, twist hard, and force him down to one knee.

Vigilante's vision is still a little blurry—eyes take longer to heal than other organs—but he can see enough to know that someone else has entered the fight. He works his right leg free and kicks Mauler in the side, sending the giant sprawling backward. He works his left leg free, then he's standing on his own feet again, feeling pissed.

"Abort!" Earsplitter has chosen the better part of valor. Vigilante hears her fly off, then sees Flicker blinking and weaving out of sight. Mauler gets to his feet and glowers at Vigilante, but a second later he turns, leaps high into the air, and bounds out of sight.

That was a sudden and unexpected change in fortune. His vision clearing at last, Vigilante sees a rough-looking man wearing a white t-shirt, faded jeans, motorcycle boots and a leather jacket staring at him. A long, jagged scar travels down his left cheek.

Jack Barrow. Scrapper Jack. Patient Zero himself.

"Hello Thomas," he says.

"Hello Jack," Vigilante replies.

They stare at each other warily for a moment.

"Thanks," Vigilante says, somewhat unwillingly.

"Let's find the others," Jack suggests.

They find Street Ronin sprawled on the ground not far from the fighting. Red Shift is in the factory, covered in debris and a fine layer of pulverized cement powder. Both are out cold.

"What are you doing here?" Vigilante asks. "I don't mean to sound ungrateful, but it's a hell of a coincidence."

"No coincidence," Jack says. "We were looking for you."

Vigilante tenses. "We?"

"Don't play dumb. Look, Thomas, you were set up by the dirty cop you were going after. He knew you were on to him so set up a trail that would lead you here. He also called the police, they'll be here soon."

As if on cue, Vigilante hears the faint sound of sirens in the distance.

"We need to talk," Jack says.

"About what?"

"Liberty. And Martin Forrest."

Vigilante looks at Jack thoughtfully. "We have a safe house half a mile from here. Help me get these two back there and I'll hear what you have to say."

"Thanks," Jack says.

"This better be good."

Jack shakes his head. "It ain't good, Thomas. It's a mess. And it's going to get a lot worse."

PART ONE: OFF THE GRID

The Farraday City bus station smells of desperation steeped in false hope and empty promises. CB steps off the bus, reaches for a cigarette, sees the NO SMOKING sign, and mutters something rude under his breath. Jenny is arguing with the bus driver, who doesn't want to open up the cargo bin to let them get their stuff.

"Destination on your ticket is Jackson," the driver says. He's a short, fat man with a thick mustache that, in marked contrast to the rest of him, is waxed and meticulously groomed.

"Don't worry about it," CB says.

Jenny narrows her eyes. "I'm not leaving my bags behind. There's equipment—"

"—we're not leaving anything behind," CB says. "We'll get everything in a couple minutes." He scans the terminal carefully.

Jenny looks around, noticing her surroundings for the first time, and sniffs the air. She frowns, and moves closer to CB. "What are you looking for?"

"Not what," CB says. "Who. There we go."

CB sets off purposefully across the terminal floor. Jenny has to hurry to keep up with him.

"We leave in twenty minutes!" the driver calls out after them.

Farraday City is many things to many people: for the very rich it's a paradise, catering to every whim at exorbitant prices, with the added promise of no paparazzi dogging your every step. If you're a corporation it offers tax-free, low-regulation commercial zones that let you get away with practically anything—as long as you don't do anything to embarrass the city. If you're in the middle class—at least, in the upper part—it's quite possible to live a safe, comfortable life, as long as you choose your neighbors carefully and don't attract the attention of the wrong people.

If you're poor, you're screwed.

There's an event horizon in the social strata of Farraday City, a line that, when crossed, offers no hope of return. That line is *poverty*, and once you're in, there's no getting out. There's *literally* no getting out.

The dirty little secret of Farraday City is that the poor aren't allowed to leave. Anyone can get in, but if you don't own a car there's no practical way to get out. The city has a bus station, a train station, and a shuttle service that goes to and from the nearby airport, but the use of each is strictly regulated by the city: a city ordinance that exists officially to prevent debtors from skipping town and reneging on their financial obligations gives the city the right to screen every person attempting to purchase transportation out, and the right to prevent them from doing so until any outstanding debts are accounted for.

Technically all you need to leave the city is a valid ticket. Practically, getting that ticket is next to impossible if your name winds up on any of their lists. People who find out they're on a list spend most of their lives trying to get off it, and the net result is they usually wind up being put on more lists.

The couple CB is walking toward is sitting on one of the benches near a ticket terminal that won't be open for another hour. The look on their faces is enough to tell CB this isn't the first time they've been here, trying to work their way through a bureaucracy that was specifically designed to screw them over. They haven't quite given up, but they're close: someday soon, after yet another failed attempt to get a ticket out, one of them will be approached by a man who says *I hear you're having some problems with City Hall. I think I'm in a position to help. I just need you to do something for me first...*

And that will be the beginning of the end.

They look older than they probably are; fear and hardship have added lines to their faces that wouldn't be there in a better place, during better times. But they're not beaten yet. They still have a chance.

"Trying to leave town?" CB asks.

The man and the woman look at him abruptly. Their eyes harden. The man grips the woman's hand tightly. "I'm not interested," he says. "And neither is she."

"Good for you," CB says. "You know what, screw the sign, I'm smoking anyway." He pulls out a cigarette and fumbles with his lighter. "They didn't let me smoke on the bus—I expected that—but I thought at the very least they'd let me smoke here. Farraday City. You know?"

Neither of them answer. They're trying to figure out what CB's game is, and whether it's going to lead to violence.

CB raises his hands, trying to look disarming. "Look, I'm not making the rounds. I've got a simple offer. It's not specifically safe, but it gets you out of this hellhole today. In the next fifteen minutes."

No response.

CB gestures to Jenny, who's standing off to one side looking confused. "The two of us have some, ah, 'friends' who think we're going to Jackson, Mississippi."

Jenny nods silently.

"For reasons that are none of your business we've decided to stay here instead. Take in the sights, start some trouble... but we don't want them to know that just yet." CB reaches into his trenchcoat pocket and pulls out their ticket stubs. "If we leave here and nobody gets on, the driver's gonna call it in to his dispatcher—or, uh, whatever the bus drivers call it—and suddenly our departure is on record. We don't want that. So we'd like the two of you to give Jackson a try. It isn't perfect, but it's better than here."

The woman's eyes widen as she realizes the tickets are real. The man scowls. "Right," he says. "You want us to meet your friends in your place?"

"Uh... no," CB says, "I *really* don't advise that. But here's the thing: they know what I look like, and *I don't look like you*. They're going to see a bunch of people get off a bus, but they're not going to see me, so they're not going to do anything about it. Simple, no fuss, and you get out of this shithole before it's too late."

A glimmer of hope—just a glimmer—shines in the man's eyes. "Are you on the level?"

CB shrugs. "I'm not doing this out of charity. I already told you my angle. And there aren't any guarantees, I guess, but buddy, you don't look anything like me and she doesn't look anything like my friend."

The man and the woman look at each other.

"Tickets," the woman says. "Let me see them."

CB immediately offers them to her. "Smart lady. They're real. The boarding part has been torn off, but it's still in transit so you can use it to get back on."

The woman stares at the tickets intently, then hands one to the man. "Thank you," she says.

"Bus leaves in fifteen," CB says. "If I were you I'd get on *right now*."

"We don't have any—" the man starts to say, but the woman cuts him off with a shake of her head.

"It doesn't matter," she says. "Nothing we own is worth passing this up."

The man nods, they both stand, and CB leads them over to the bus.

The driver is sitting in his seat, scowling at them. He nods curtly at the two new passengers, and glares at CB and Jenny.

CB smiles at the man as if he didn't have a care in the world. "How about opening that side compartment? We'd like to get our luggage now."

The driver grumbles, then climbs out of the bus, fishing for his keys.

* * *

It's mid-afternoon when they leave the station. The sun beats down on the grimiest urban squalor Jenny has ever seen. The only pictures she's ever seen of Farraday City have been of the uptown area, and it always looks immaculately clean, modern, metropolitan. Uptown is an area City Hall cares about. The Greyhound station is not.

The streets are covered in trash. The walls are blanketed in graffiti—not the artistic kind, just crude tags everywhere. There aren't any cars parked on the street except for a few taxis that look like the wheels might fall off at any moment. The buildings are old and dirty: pool halls, bars, two-bit casinos, and yes, strip clubs and brothels. Neon signs are everywhere, announcing the names of the establishments: *Mike's*, *Larry's*, *The Dirty Pool*, and the ever-classic *Girls Girls Girlz*.

Jenny is traveling light—just her laptop case and two smaller bags—but she wishes she were carrying less. CB's army bag slings conveniently across his back. Her laptop case slings across her shoulder, but the other two bags, small as they are, have to be carried. She feels more exposed with her hands full. There aren't many people outside, but the ones who are look like predators. She feels like she's being sized up as she follows CB down the street.

She hurries to draw up alongside him, then asks "Where are we going?"

"Not too far," CB says. "A block and a half that way." He points. "Here, let me take one of your bags."

"Thanks," Jenny says. "I think—"

"Got anything expensive in this?"

"No," Jenny says, "it's just—"

"Good." Suddenly CB stops in his tracks, turns, and swings the bag behind him with all his might. Jenny turns, startled, and sees the bag impact against the side of another man's head—a thin, bony man who looks like he was taken from central casting at a B-movie about Vegas: slicked hair, jewelry, cheap but flashy clothing.

The man stumbles to one side as his hands reflexively go up to shield his face. CB kicks, hard: the sole of his boot connects with the man's kneecap, and Jenny hears a sickening *crack* as the leg bends unnaturally. The man sinks to the ground, screaming.

Something dull gray drops to the sidewalk in front of the screaming man. CB takes a step to one side and kicks—the gray thing skitters across the street and disappears into a gutter. Just as it disappears beneath the far sidewalk Jenny realizes it's a revolver.

"Just broke your leg," CB says conversationally. "And your gun is currently unavailable."

The man snarls.

"Also," CB adds, "if you reach for the spare you have tucked in the small of your back, I'll break your other kneecap."

The man stops reaching.

"A man in your condition is at a serious disadvantage in this part of the city," CB says. "I recommend finding some place to lie low for a while. I'm pretty sure you have colleagues who would love to get a leg up at your expense. So to speak."

The man looks at CB in a mixture of hatred, pain and fear.

"Right," CB says, then turns away. He and Jenny don't take two steps when suddenly he turns again, flinging the bag at the thug who has, apparently, decided to reach for his spare—a snub-nosed revolver—after all.

The bag hits the hand holding the gun, causing the shot to go wide. CB kicks his wrist, and the gun flies out of his hand. The man screams and holds his wrist, his hand pressed tight against his chest.

CB ignores him, walks over to the gun, and picks it up. Jenny looks around nervously. A few seconds ago she thought the block looked empty. Now it looks completely deserted.

"What are you going to do?" she asks.

"What I told him I'd do," CB says. "I'm going to break the other kneecap."

The man tries to speak, but all he can do is gag in pain.

"I wish you wouldn't," Jenny says.

CB glances at Jenny, sighs, then turns back to the man lying on the ground. "She's new. You got that part right. You got every other part *dead wrong.*"

The man starts to whimper. CB snorts in disgust, puts the revolver in his pocket, picks up Jenny's bag, and walks off briskly. Jenny hurries to catch up.

"Is this the best way to disappear?" she asks nervously. "Doesn't this kind of thing attract attention?"

"This kind of thing happens all the time," CB says. "If he's connected it might be a problem. I'm pretty sure he isn't."

They walk one and a half blocks without running into anyone. They stop in front of a grimy but solid-looking building with the sign FAIR DAY PAWN sitting over the display window. Jenny can't see much in the display window, because it's caked with dirt. Both the window and the door have heavy iron bars over them.

"Here we are," CB says. He holds the door open as Jenny steps through, then follows. An electronic chime sounds from the other end of the store.

The pawn shop is cluttered. The walls are lined with glass shelves, and all the shelves are locked. The shelves are stocked with watches, cell phones, jewelry, tablets, iPods, video cameras, DVD players, silverware—anything someone might think of pawning for money appears to be on display. The center of the room has larger items—musical instruments, some furniture, a few jackets and coats. The register is set in the far corner. Behind it sits a large man with shoulder-length hair and a thick, light-brown beard. He wears thick-rimmed, untinted glasses and a light yellow t-shirt with a picture of a moose printed on it.

"Heya Carl," CB says.

"CB," Carl says. He stares straight at Jenny. "Who's your friend?"

"A *friend*," CB says, emphasizing the word very distinctly.

Carl nods absently. "I won't shoot her, then. What do you want?"

Jenny stares at Carl uneasily.

"I need to talk to Elliot," CB says. "He in?"

Carl shakes his head. "Back soon. You can wait in the office if you want."

"OK," CB says. "If anyone asks, we're not here."

"Right on," Carl says.

CB motions for Jenny to follow. He walks around the counter, through a door in the far wall. As Jenny walks by Carl she notices the back of the counter is lined with plate metal, and that a shotgun and two pistols are mounted within easy reach from the cash register.

The office has two desks, a bench and an extra chair on one end, and a workbench with an assortment of tools on the other. CB sits on the bench. Jenny chooses the free chair.

"Carl's OK," CB says.

Jenny shudders.

"He's a vet and he has that thousand-yard stare you always read about but never see. Elliot—that's his brother—says it's PTSD. But he's a decent guy."

"What's he doing here?" Jenny asks. "The way you talk, there's nothing decent about the place."

"There isn't. The place is lousy. The people in it are kind of a mixed bag."

"Got that right," a voice says. CB and Jenny look up. Standing in the doorway is a thin, short man with long, curly black hair, graying in streaks. His face is lean, clean-shaven, and weathered. He wears the same kind of thick-rimmed glasses Carl does. "For example: here we are in Farraday City, and there's a God damn cape sitting in my office."

CB grins. "Heya Elliot. Jenny, Elliot Grady. Elliot, Jenny. No last name at present."

Elliot grins, showing slightly yellowed teeth. "Interesting. What's up?"

"How's my special project?"

Elliot's eyebrows shoot up over the rims of his glasses. "Well, it's mostly ready. You moving in?"

CB nods. "We need to go off the grid," he says. "And I need a modification. Communications stuff, mostly. Jenny's going to need some extra equipment—she'll give you a list after she sees what we already have."

Elliot nods slowly. "So, what's this? Phase two?"

CB shakes his head. "Something else came up. Can't talk about it yet."

"Christ," Elliot says. "Well, I'll need a few hours to get it all turned on, then you're good to go."

"What are we talking about?" Jenny asks. "Some kind of secret bunker?"

"That's right," CB says. "My very own underground lair."

"... wow," Jenny says. "That's actually kind of cool."

"That's not the cool part," CB says.

"What's the cool part?"

"It has cable."

Jenny shakes her head. "Nobody has cable any more, CB. That's not even close to cool."

CB frowns. "It isn't?"

"No," Jenny says, "it isn't. Cable companies are money-grubbing monstrosities who charge you way too much money to deliver five hundred channels, and most of them are worthless."

"Huh," CB says.

Jenny rolls her eyes. "Honestly. Sometimes I forget you're a hundred years old. Then you pull a stunt like this. 'It has cable.' You might as well brag about it having Internet access."

"It doesn't have Internet access," CB says.

Jenny stares at him incredulously.

Elliot looks from Jenny to CB and tries to suppress a grin. "I guess that's going on your list?"

"Yeah," CB says sourly. "I guess so."

PART TWO: PRODIGY

PROJECT PRODIGY: CASE FILE 47793-A
(OVERVIEW/SUMMARY OF INVESTIGATION)

Peter Raphael Travers, Lead Investigator

- OVERVIEW -

Shortly after 9/11 a government initiative called PRODIGY attempted to create a Federal registry of metahumans who could be called in to respond to national emergencies. PRODIGY initially did this by co-opting the Federally-sanctioned metahuman groups operating under the Civilian Deputization Act, but eventually announced their intention to forcibly register all metahumans operating on U.S. soil. I was assigned to PRODIGY during the creation of the Office of Homeland Security, the precursor to the Department of Homeland Security, and the realignment, consolidation, and coordination of all Federal agencies that followed. My first assignment was to coordinate the transition of Federally-sanctioned metahuman groups in the Northeast as they were integrated into the PRODIGY program. This was not a popular decision among the groups, and I spent most of my time trying to convince them not to disband. As noted in field reports at the time, I was having particular difficulty dealing with the New York City Guardians of Justice.

During the time of PRODIGY's formation the Guardians were operating at a reduced capacity. They had lost a core member during an off-world incident (see file 43352-C supplemental, hero name GREY FALCON, and additional briefing on the alternate timeline known as WASTELAND).

At that time, the members were GLADIATOR (ROBERT THORPE, team leader), LIBERTY (ALEXANDER MORGAN), REGIMENT (ROGER WHITMAN), and CURVEBALL (NAME UNKNOWN).

Reaction to the transition was so varied it was clear the group would splinter. LIBERTY was willing to comply with the directive even before Congress passed the law that gave PRODIGY's registry legitimacy. GLADIATOR refused to have anything to do with PRODIGY or the registry, to the extent that he funded the creation of an artificial island in neutral waters to act as the fully independent headquarters for Thorpe Industries. REGIMENT was opposed to the registry but stated he would comply when Congress made it mandatory. CURVEBALL reacted with immediate hostility, attacking me during a heated confrontation and then immediately going into hiding (see medical report on TRAVERS, PETER R in attached supplemental file).

As a result of the attack, CURVEBALL was immediately classified as a rogue metahuman and placed on the villains list.

A few months later, the apparently disbanded Guardians of Justice attacked a PRODIGY facility in Northern California. In the aftermath of the attack, it was discovered that PRODIGY's metahuman registration was a cover story for the project's true purpose: to breed semi-sentient clones of metahumans that could be controlled remotely using technology similar in concept to the remote drones used in Afghanistan. The Guardians destroyed PRODIGY's prototype cloning facility, PRODIGY was dismantled, and the upper echelons of the program were arrested and charged with conspiring against American citizens.

Shortly after this final action the Guardians of Justice disbanded.

- SUMMARY OF INVESTIGATION -

Unknown to anyone at the time, the apparent splintering of the group and the perceived acrimony between the individual members was premeditated, coordinated, and intended to further the group's own investigation into PRODIGY and the program's true purpose...

PART THREE: LEARNING FROM THE PAST

"Can I have my laptop back yet?" Jenny shifts restlessly on the couch, watching CB read.

"Still reading," CB says.

"Why?" Jenny doesn't bother keeping the annoyance out of her voice. "What's the point? Weren't you one of the ones who actually brought them down?"

"Sure," CB says. "That was a fun plan. We played it perfectly, too. I mean, everyone expected Alex to be the good soldier and for me to go rogue. Nobody expected Robert to build a mechanical island floating in the middle of the ocean and declare it a sovereign nation, or for Roger to get pissed and threaten to break both Robert's arms. They played the press, and the government, and PRODIGY like pros. But we weren't part of the investigation afterward, so I never saw how far it went. I never got to see any of these attachments that actually name names. Now shut up and let me read."

Jenny sighs, looks around the safe house, and sighs again. She's bored, and the novelty of being hidden from the world has long since worn off.

Elliot Grady claims it was a rich man's fallout shelter, once upon a time. She can believe it—it's as comfortable as a large, windowless box can possibly be. Six rooms, all on the small side but well furnished. Two bedrooms, a common room, a bathroom with a shower, a small kitchen, and a room set up with Jenny's computer and some perimeter security monitoring equipment.

"I never understood the island thing," Jenny says. "Why would Gladiator need a floating island?"

"Wouldn't," CB says. "Thorpe Industries found it awfully convenient, though."

"I don't see that either," Jenny says. "It seems like it would be a money pit."

CB looks up from the laptop. "Can't say anything about that part, but it probably would have been more expensive not to build it and move there. Thorpe Industries was about to be sued out of existence."

Jenny's eyes widen. "What? Why? I never heard anything about that."

"Think about it. The Gladiator armor is proof of concept not just for cold fusion, but for *miniaturized* cold fusion. Not to mention energy efficient force fields, high-density lightweight polymers, ridiculously advanced sensor tech, and that energy gun he had coming out of his arms. Add to that, he invented the medical tanks they'd always stick us in after a fight. And he inherited Gray Falcon's anti-gravity technology after... after he died. He has all this *stuff* that could change the world forever—for the better—and he made it clear from the beginning that he wanted to make it available to the general public. All these companies out there that are essentially competitors in name only, along the lines of 'hey, we build things, too'—they were going to become irrelevant as soon as any of that tech hit the market. There's no way they were going to take that sitting down."

"What could they do about it?" Jenny asks. "I mean, too bad for them, right?"

"Well a bunch of them got together and started suing Robert for violating their patents."

Jenny frowns. "Patents of what?"

"That's what I asked, first time I heard about it. And Robert said they were just trying to force him to reveal how everything worked."

"I thought you said he wanted to make it available to the general public," Jenny says.

"He did," CB says. "But he wanted to make money off it too. He's not really an open source kinda guy. He figured he'd keep exclusive rights on the tech for ten years then release it to the world. His competitors pulled every dirty trick they could think of to keep him from selling any of it, and the legal tricks worked. He was barred from ever selling any of the technology in his Gladiator suit on the grounds that it might have infringed the copyrights of one of these other companies. Which is bull, but since Robert wasn't going to reveal any of his secrets to prove it, there wasn't much he could do about it."

"But that's not right!" Jenny protests. "The advances in computer technology alone could—"

CB laughs. "Robert is probably the smartest man in the world. His only competition is Overmind. Maybe. But it didn't matter how many circles he could run around Microsoft when it came to designing software, he didn't stand a chance against them in the business world. Or in the courtroom."

"Let me get this straight," Jenny says. "The reason we don't have rocket suits and regeneration tanks is because a bunch of companies successfully sued him in court by claiming *they thought of it first*?"

"Pretty much," CB says.

"But that's stupid," she says.

CB shrugs.

"And that's why he has a private floating island in the middle of the ocean."

"No," CB says, "that happened because all those companies *then* petitioned the government to *force* him to reveal how his technology worked. And they were going to do it, too. Using the PRODIGY laws."

Jenny falls silent again.

"Now, can I get back to this? I have a lot of homework to do..." CB turns his attention back to the laptop, and starts to read.

And so he reads.

And reads.

And reads.

And reads.

The USB drive Travers gave CB has a lot of material on it. Jenny is interested initially; she was in high school when the PRODIGY conspiracy was uncovered and was more upset by the fact that "Uncle CB" had disappeared and been classified a villain than she was by the thought that metahumans were being conscripted by the government. The files are interesting, and she guesses there's probably something useful in them, but once is enough for her. Not for CB: he reads them over and over again, looking for any minor detail that he might have overlooked on his last pass, hoping that some shred of information might give him something to work with.

Jenny starts to wonder if they're ever going to get around to cracking the encryption on her great-grandfather's file. That, she suspects, will have all the *really* important information.

She stares at her jacket, thrown over a chair in front of a security monitor, and sees the edge of her smartphone sticking out of a pocket. She grabs the phone, sits down and begins prying off the back.

"What are you doing?" CB doesn't bother to look up.

"I'm disabling the phone part of my phone," Jenny says. "Taking out the SIM card and doing a few other things to keep it from accidentally making emergency calls. That way it can't connect to the cell network, so it can't be tracked by cell phone towers."

"It also makes it sort of useless as a phone," CB points out.

"Sure," Jenny says. "So? It's still a handheld computer. It's more powerful than the desktop computers that were around ten years ago. And I've got some apps on it that might come in handy. Custom ones."

CB looks up, regarding her thoughtfully. "Good idea."

Jenny gets to work. She removes the SIM card first, then rummages through one of her bags to retrieve the tool kit she uses for small electronics. She carefully makes a few physical alterations to the phone, reassembles it, and plugs it into a nearby outlet. She spends the next hour making sure the phone is off and can't be inadvertently turned on.

"Did you and mom have a thing?" she asks suddenly.

"What?" CB looks up, surprised. "Did your mom and I what?"

"You know," Jenny says. "Have a thing. I mean, neither of you talk about it, but whenever I see you guys talk there's... subtext."

"Ah," CB says. "Yes, there is definitely subtext."

"Well?"

CB actually looks uncomfortable. "Yes. Yes, we have a history. We had a... *thing*. Before your dad was in the picture. *Not after*."

Jenny clamps her mouth shut. That was going to be her next question.

"It ended, and your dad came into the picture, and I like your dad a lot, so that was a good thing all around." CB turns his attention back to the laptop.

"How serious?" Jenny asks.

"Do you really want to know the answer to that?" CB asks.

"I asked, didn't I?" Jenny says crossly.

CB sighs, closes the laptop lid, and turns to face her. "Fine. Yeah it was pretty serious. As serious as I get, anyway. I don't know how serious that is compared to other people. I don't focus well on... people..."

He trails off, frowning. For a moment Jenny thinks he looks terribly sad. Then, as quickly as she sees it, it's gone. "I always called her 'Lois.'"

"Because she was a reporter?"

"Because she kept getting into trouble," CB says, laughing. "I told her she was only doing it to get my attention. Which, for the record, she never denied."

Jenny tries to picture CB dating her mom. She can't quite manage it.

"It pissed Alex off something fierce, too," CB adds. "Despite the fact that he liked me an awful lot, he in no way felt I was worth the attentions of his granddaughter."

Jenny laughs. "Really? Did you ever fight about it? Did he forbid you to see her?"

"Well... yes, actually. Juliet and I had been together for a few months, and he took me aside and told me that I'd better, and I quote, 'respect her, and treat her like a lady, or we would have more than words.'"

"Huh?"

CB smiles slightly. "He meant 'no sex.'"

"Oh..." Jenny giggles slightly. "What did you say to him?"

"I said 'too late.'"

Jenny stares at CB in shock. "You did *not*."

"I sure as hell did. And then Alex hauled off and hit me harder than I've ever been hit *in my life*. When I woke up he was standing over me apologizing."

Jenny wants to laugh, but she's not sure it's appropriate. "What happened? You shook hands and that was the end of it?"

"No, I kicked that son of a bitch in the nuts as hard as I could."

Jenny laughs outright.

"When he could breathe again, it was *my* turn to apologize. And that bastard *kicked me through a window*." CB grins ruefully. "It was just like the old days. Only, I could fight better, because he'd been training me."

"And you could hex him," Jenny adds. "Or whatever you call it."

"Hex is close enough," CB says, "but no, I was never able to hex him. Never worked on him."

"Why not?"

"Dunno," CB says. "Never understood it. It just wouldn't work... which was very inconvenient back when I was a bad guy. I could hex something he was trying to use—make a pair of handcuffs malfunction, for example—but I could never get him to trip over his own two feet, or pull a hamstring, or anything like that."

"So you and great-granddad were having a fistfight because you told him you were having sex with my mom."

"Yeah," CB says, "that just about covers it. And it only stopped because we fell through a skylight into a Bar Mitzvah."

"Shut. *Up*."

"I shit you not. We were fighting on a building that was under construction. Like the James Bond movie... well, like many James Bond movies, actually. Point is, it was all steel girders and sub-flooring. We're grappling, I slip, Alex decides he doesn't actually want me *dead* and he grabs my wrist. So there I am, dangling over the edge of this building, your great-grandfather the *only thing* that's preventing me from falling to my death, and does he pull me up?"

"...yes?"

"*Hell no,*" CB says. "No. He lets me *dangle there* and proceeds to *lecture* me about the proper way to show respect for a woman. So I pull myself up with one arm, lock my legs around his neck, and jerk upright—unbalancing him— which pulls us both off the goddamn building."

Jenny shakes her head, grinning. "That doesn't seem very smart."

CB grins back. "I wasn't known for 'smart' back then. I was known for 'interesting.' Besides, I'd already figured out how it was going to go. There was netting under us for... something. I don't know what. But I angled us to it and we hit it, just like I wanted. Only... the net didn't stop our fall. It snapped, we rolled off one side and crashed right through the skylight of the building next door. Right into that Bar Mitzvah."

Jenny laughs, and can't stop laughing.

CB waits for the laughter to die down, then adds, "They were pretty surprised."

Jenny breaks into another fit of laughter.

"The father was *brilliant,* though. He took it all in, then stepped right up and introduced us as if he'd planned the whole thing. And Alex rolled right along... he apologized for the entrance, and explained we'd been fighting a villain, which is why we were late. The kid was *floored.* It was great. We hung out, danced a little, had some drinks, chatted with the family a bit, excused ourselves and went home."

"That's *amazing,*" Jenny says, then frowns. "You're not making this up, are you?"

"Nope," CB says. "True story."

"Does mom know that story?" Jenny asks.

"*Hell* no," CB says. "That's way too complicated to explain to your girlfriend."

"I guess," Jenny says doubtfully. "So, what, great-granddad was OK with you and mom after that?"

CB's face clouds, then he sighs. "No."

"Why not?" Jenny leans forward. "What's wrong? Did he say something else? Did you break it off with mom?"

"No, I didn't break it off," CB says. "It's complicated."

"I'm sorry," Jenny says. "I'm prying too much. I'll shut up."

"No... it's OK." CB doesn't look like it's OK. His eyes are unfocused; he stares off into space, remembering something that happened a long time ago. He fumbles with his cigarettes and sticks one in his mouth. He picks up his lighter and toys with it, flipping the top open, then closed, then open, then closed. "Alex didn't really object to me personally. He objected to something none of us had any control over."

He lights the cigarette and inhales. The cherry glows bright red. Jenny frowns and fights back the urge to cough. She considers protesting—the ventilation down there is terrible—but she isn't sure CB will hear her.

"Alex was a great guy, you know?" CB keeps playing with his lighter. Open. Closed. Open. Closed. "He was little too damn smart for his own good, and I didn't like hearing all his good advice, but... he'd seen a lot. He saw history happen, over and over again. He saw what history did to people."

CB leans back in his chair and closes his eyes. White smoke streams out of his mouth as he sighs again, almost sleepily.

"We had one more conversation that night."

PART FOUR: FLASHBACK, NEW YORK CITY, 1988

They're both laughing, and they're both a little drunk: Alex's nose is red, CB weaves and staggers as he attempts, unsuccessfully, to prove how sober he is by walking a straight line. It rained at some point during the party. They hadn't noticed, despite the holes in the skylight, but the asphalt is wet and water pools in puddles all over the uneven road. They're taking a shortcut home in a neighborhood that, until very recently, would have been considered unsafe. It's safe now, and the two of them have something to do with that.

It's a good feeling.

"I just found another piece of glass," Alex says, pulling it out of his sleeve. "I'll probably keep finding them for the next month."

CB thinks about it a moment, then snickers. "I can see it now. You'll be fighting Terror Prime, and he'll be giving one of his 'now you will know the face of terror' speeches, and then he'll stop and say 'Liberty, aren't you LISTENING TO MY FIENDISH PLAN?' And you'll say 'sorry. Found some glass. Bar Mitzvah. Long story.'"

Alex laughs, doubling over, and CB laughs with him. Everything is good again, and the *relief* of everything being good again makes everything funnier than it has a right to be. They turn down an alley and stumble through, still laughing, until they come to a pair of empty dumpsters where the alley opens up into a side road.

"Hey, CB hold on a minute." Alex speaks easily, but there's something in his voice that makes CB stop, turn, and squint. Alex is still smiling—he doesn't look angry—but he also looks serious.

"What?" CB asks suspiciously.

"We need to clear the air, is all," Alex says. "Tonight was bad. I'm sorry about that. It was my fault. But we can't just leave it like that."

Suddenly CB feels tired. "I don't want to fight again, Alex."

"I don't want to fight either," Alex says. "So let's not. Let's talk. Honestly. No dancing around words, just coming flat out and laying it all on the table. OK?"

CB smokes the rest of his cigarette as he decides whether or not to answer.

"Fine," he says. "Look. Juliet... I really like Juliet. I mean, I don't know how to explain it, but she does something to me and it's not lust. You want to call it love, I could live with that."

"Really?" Alex sounds surprised. "You don't throw that word around much."

"Yeah," CB says. "I mean I get it, right? I'm not exactly a paragon of fidelity. But I do respect her, Alex. She's funny, she's smart, she's strong-willed, she doesn't let people push her around... she's her own person. I respect her, and I don't want to hurt her."

"I'm glad to hear that," Alex says.

"But I'm also not you," CB continues. "I wasn't raised by your parents. I don't have your values. I'm not going to become a choirboy just because you think this is awkward. Which, to be fair, it is. I wish it weren't. So what do you have to say about that?"

The end comes out as more of a challenge than he wants, but CB doesn't back down from it.

Alex sighs. "Got another cigarette?"

"Do I have another cigarette," CB mutters. "Who are you talking to?" He fishes through the pockets of his trenchcoat until he pulls out a pack, fishes one out, hands it to Alex, then tosses him his lighter.

Alex catches the lighter without looking, lights the cigarette, then holds it out for CB so he can light a new one as well. "Turns out I knew that kid's grandfather."

"What kid?" CB asks. "Oh, the Bar Mitzvah kid? Really? From the war I guess."

Alex nods. "He was at Dachau when we came in."

"... oh."

"Yeah. We're the same age. Sixty-eight years old."

CB shifts his weight uneasily. "You're holding up better than he is."

"I remember him, actually," Alex says. "I talked to him, way back then. His name is Issac. He's sixty-eight years old, and I'm sixty-eight years old."

CB doesn't reply. He never knows what to say when Alex gets like this.

"Did you ever meet Marie? I don't think you ever did. She died of cancer before we met professionally." Alex has a strange gleam in his eyes. It's intense, and angry, and... desperate.

"No," CB says. "Alex Junior told a few stories. I've seen her pictures on your wall. She was really pretty."

"She was fifty-nine years old when she died. I was sixty-one. Alex Junior was thirty-eight. Juliet was fifteen. Alex is forty-five now. He's forgetting names, dates. They tell me he has Alzheimer's. He's going to slowly lose his mind."

CB just stares at the ground.

"Do you know what it's like watching the woman you married—who is two years younger than you—grow old, while you don't? Oh, I look older than I did when we got married. But only a little. And my body? Just as healthy. *Healthier.* Do you know what that does to a marriage?"

CB clears his throat. "I imagine it was pretty rough on you."

"Forget about me!" Alex says. "Think about her! Every year she got older, and I didn't. I was *abandoning* her! She had to deal with all the aches and pains and limitations that people just have to learn to accept... but I never did. She got sick and died from something that I will *never, ever* catch. I grew older, I guess, but I grew *different.* She died before I did, but she was already a widow."

"Alex..."

"She never said anything, though." Alex is pacing now. "Not a word. She was an amazing lady, CB, and we kept pretenses up right until the very end, because *damn it all* we really *did* love each other. So we pretended I wasn't different. We pretended. But at some point she stopped going out in public with me. She didn't want people to see us together. I looked like I could be her grandson. It horrified her."

CB leans against one of the dumpsters and waits.

"And Alex Junior... damn it. My own son looks like he could be my father. You know he told me once that when he turned thirty he considered blowing his brains out? The only reason he didn't was because he couldn't do that to Toby and Julie. But whenever anyone ever saw us in public, they always asked if he was my older brother. He was the *baby*, CB. His sister is two years older than he is."

"Look, Alex, I'm sorry," CB says. "Really. I don't know how to relate, but—"

"The thing is," Alex interrupts, "is that when you're this way, you watch the world change. And that's hard. I thought World War II would be the war that made sure concentration camps never, ever happened again. We'd exposed it to the world, and we'd learned our lesson, and we'd make sure *never again.* And it didn't happen. You see the world change, and you make the same mistakes, but it's *worse*, because everyone stops being shocked about it. That's hard to take. But that's not even *close* to watching the people you love change in a way that you *can't*... and you know eventually you're going to lose them. Because you don't change, CB, you stay the same.

Maybe not forever, but long enough so that it doesn't really matter..."

Alex stops talking. He's staring at CB, eyes wet, breathing ragged, on edge in a way that CB has never seen him before.

"What does this have to do with me and Juliet?" CB asks.

"Because you're like *me*, God damn it, CB you're *just like me!*" Alex hits the side of the dumpster, hard. CB jumps away quickly; the side of the dumpster buckles under the blow. "You're not getting older."

"What the hell are you talking about?" CB demands. "Of *course* I'm getting older. I get older every year."

"Don't be an idiot," Alex snaps. "I first met you in 1976. You've aged since then, sure. But you're twenty-eight now, and you look exactly the way you did four years ago."

"Alex, that's because it was *four years ago*," CB says. "Most people don't look much different between twenty-four and twenty-eight."

"Most people don't *have your job*," Alex says. "Send a soldier off to war, he comes back home looking older. Put a boxer in the ring for four years, have his face smashed in non-stop, week in and week out, he looks older in four years. You know the average career length of a villain? Four months. Four months, then they're in the Pit and they never come back."

CB lets that slide.

"Two years is a long time in this business, CB. You were a *veteran* when you turned. Two years on that side, two years on this side, always running, fighting, planning, always on point, never able to let your guard down... I've seen you break both legs, four ribs, your left shoulder, your right wrist, you've had skull fractures, concussions, you were thrown through a windshield, run over by a truck, you've been shot, stabbed, bludgeoned, pummeled... and tonight you dropped through a glass skylight into a Bar Mitzvah, onto a marble floor."

"But I got better," CB says. "I'm fine now."

"That's the *point*," Alex says. "Most guys don't get better from all of that. Guys in the army who got even a piece of that would wind up getting sent home, and they'd probably have a limp *if they were lucky*. The guys I worked with in the old days, the ones who weren't metahuman, or who were but didn't have any physical boosts? They didn't bounce back like you did. The guys who were just really good at what they did, they could last a few years—three or four—but then you'd see it wearing on them. They'd move like old men, even when they didn't look it. And they looked it, eventually."

CB doesn't reply.

"You don't have the right boosts to bounce back the way you do," Alex says. "But you do anyway. You get hurt, break an arm, break a leg, the cast comes off and you're fine. You still move like nothing ever happened to you before in your life—that's not possible for someone who does what you do, CB. Not unless you're invulnerable, like Regiment. Or unless you've been through Project Paragon. But somehow, there you are. You're in the same boat I am, kid. In ten years you're going to look exactly like you do now. In twenty, you'll still mostly look like this. You'll look a little older in the eyes, but you'll still be carded whenever you try to buy beer. Thirty years, forty years..."

"Shut up!" CB shouts. "You're fucking crazy! I'm only twenty-eight, for Christ's sake!"

"And you're going to stay that way!" Alex shouts back. A moment later his control is back, and he lowers his voice. "And what about Juliet? She's twenty-two now. Six years doesn't seem so bad, since you're still basically a juvenile..."

There's a hint of humor in Alex's voice as he says it. CB smirks in spite of himself.

"But let's say the two of you get serious and stay together for ten years, twenty years, thirty years. Think about everything I just said."

CB shakes his head. "This is stupid."

"Don't hurt my granddaughter, CB." Alex is pleading. "If you stay with her, you will. She won't admit it, you won't admit it, but eventually it'll hurt her. A lot."

CB laughs hollowly. "You're making an awful lot of assumptions. How do you know we're going to last that long?"

"I hope you don't," Alex says. "No, don't get mad, CB. I don't mean it like that. I just... I don't want that to happen to you. It's brutal, and it's not fair, and it's cold-blooded, but neither one of you deserves..."

Alex can't finish. He turns away from CB, stares down the alley.

CB flicks the rest of his cigarette into a puddle, watching it drown. "You really think I'm going to age like you?"

"Call it a hunch," Alex says. "Sorry kid. It's not all it's cracked up to be."

"And *that's* what's been bothering you? Not the sex?"

"Well." Alex laughs weakly. "She *is* my granddaughter. And it's not like I've never heard you brag."

"Fair enough," CB says. "Yeah. Fair enough. But it's not like that, Alex. I mean it. It really isn't."

"Part of me wishes it were," Alex says.

They lapse into silence. A car alarm goes off in the distance. Alex finishes his cigarette and grinds it out on the street. "Sounds like someone is trying to steal a car."

"Yeah," CB says. "Or someone is standing too close to the door. Those things are obnoxious."

"Well," Alex says, "I was just thinking how surprised a car thief would be if Liberty and Curveball showed up."

CB laughs. "Let's go. If you think we're sober enough."

"I am," Liberty says. "I burned it all off five minutes ago. As for you... well, some people think you're drunk all the time anyway."

CB laughs again. "Asshole. Let's go arrest a bad guy."

PART FIVE: HIDDEN LINKS

CB sighs and grinds out his cigarette on the table. "We never talked about that night again. My choice. Never talked about it at all until now, actually. I wasn't ready to hear it when he told me, but eventually I understood. Fortunately your mom and I split for other reasons."

"What happened?" Jenny is still trying to figure out how she feels about CB's story. She doesn't remember her great-grandfather being sad about anything. He was always so happy around her, and around Andy... but CB wasn't describing a happy man.

"Well you know the story about how it's hard being married to a cop. Your dad says he lucked out because the only thing your mom had to compare it with is dating a hero, and a cop's life is cake by comparison. I mean Christ, in one year she was kidnapped *fifteen times*. That's more than once a month. 1989 was pretty exhausting."

"So she got tired of being kidnapped?" Jenny wrinkles her nose. "That doesn't really sound like mom. I mean, she wouldn't let that stop her if she really wanted something."

"That was just a symptom," CB says. "The problem was the job. The job always came first. I mean, I adored Juliet, but if there was a hostage situation on the radio or the TV I was out the window pulling on my pants faster than you can—"

"*Pulling on your pants?*"

"Yes," CB says. "That happened once."

"I'm OK with not hearing any more about that." Jenny's cheeks are bright red.

"... right. Well, it pissed her off. Can't blame her. That's the way it was, though. So we split, and she was mad at me for a while. Then she met Marty, who was perfect for her in every way, and a genuinely great guy to boot. She fell head over heels in love with him, and suddenly she wasn't mad at me any more."

"Just like that?"

CB shrugs. "You'd have to ask her for the specifics there."

"That's sweet," Jenny says. "Was there ever anyone else?"

"What, someone serious?" CB grimaces. "Not after. Alex was right. That's... it would be cruel, in the long run."

There's a long, awkward silence.

"Anyway," CB says, "back to homework." He flips up the laptop and starts reading again.

Jenny sighs. The conversation has been far more depressing than she expected.

"Oh, God, my *eyes*," CB moans. He leans back and rubs his face. "I've been looking at that screen too long. It sucked my eyeballs dry."

"It was probably the smoking." Jenny allows a hint of disapproval to touch her voice. "There's no ventilation."

CB mutters something, then stands. "Your turn. I need you to read me the dummy corporations listed in Appendix K. Out loud."

"Oh, come *on*," Jenny complains. "Let me do something useful. Let me try to decrypt great-granddad's email. That probably has everything we need in it."

CB shakes his head. "Something in Travers' report bugs me. I can't put my finger on it."

"Of course it reminds you of something," Jenny says. "*You were there.*"

"Smartass." CB grins appreciatively. "No, something recent. Now quit complaining and read out loud. Welcome to the glamorous life of being a sidekick." He sprawls on the couch, puts up his feet, and covers his eyes with one arm.

Jenny grumbles, then dutifully sits in front of the laptop and begins reading through names of dummy corporations, shell companies, off-shore accounts, contractor agencies...

"Stop." CB lowers his arm, perks his head up and stares at Jenny intently. "Read that last part again."

Jenny sighs, backs up a few lines, and begins to read. "Tertiary Plus, TestLabs, Thorne Industries, Tomorrow Ltd., TriHealth, Twinn..."

"TriHealth!" CB almost shouts the name. He swings his feet to the floor and sits upright, eyes wide. "Fuck! That's too big a coincidence to be a coincidence."

"Hold on..." Jenny scrolls through to the back of the appendix. "It says here that TriHealth was a health insurance company that PRODIGY used as a front for money laundering. A lot of its managers went to jail... but it bounced back. It seems to be a legitimate company now."

"Yeah, it sure is," CB says. "And I ran across that name the night Alex was murdered, when I was investigating a serial killer."

"When you were what?" Jenny asks.

CB fills her in on the bodies at the beach, and his investigation at the Farraday City morgue. "The thing is, none of the victims had anything in common. Nothing that jumped out at me. But now that I think of it, when I was reading through the victim profiles, at least one victim in every group listed TriHealth as their insurance provider."

"Well it's health insurance," Jenny says. "Someone's going to have it, right? I bet one person in every group had Aetna, or Blue Cross."

CB closes his eyes. "Nope. Only two people with Aetna. Hold on. I need paper and pencil."

He walks out of the room, leaving Jenny to stare at the door in mild confusion. A minute later he comes back with a list of names. "Search for these and tell me if they're anywhere in this appendix."

They are. Every name on the piece of paper is also in Travers' appendix. Some are other dummy corporations, others are companies with suspected, but unproven, ties to PRODIGY.

"What are these?" Jenny asks.

"They're the names of other health insurance companies the victims had. Look, this is sort of a long shot, but it's a weird coincidence, and I have a habit of tripping over those. So I'm going to check it out."

"Can I come?" Jenny asks.

"No, better not. Try getting into that encrypted file instead."

Jenny sighs. "At least I get to do something."

"Elliot should be by later with some extra supplies," CB says. "Check with the security cameras before you let anyone in. And only let Elliot or me in."

"Hey," Jenny says, "I'm not stupid."

"I don't know about that," CB says. "You're the one who wanted to come along."

PART ONE: TRIHEALTH, UPTOWN

There's one TriHealth building in Farraday City. It's uptown, which means it doesn't cater to riffraff. It also makes the organization look shadier than it already did. Large companies don't stay large by being naive, and a company that opens an office in Farraday Uptown is doing so because of the advantages the location brings. Some of those advantages look good on a ledger. Other "advantages" never show up on a ledger, or on any official documentation for that matter. Those advantages come with certain *expectations* that are plainly, and occasionally painfully, communicated.

It's not impossible to find an honest company in Farraday City. The downtown business district is full of them—well, it's full of businesses who are willing to pretend they don't know who runs the city because they want the tax breaks, but aren't particularly eager to break the law themselves. That's about as honest as it gets in the city. But uptown—uptown business zoning is reserved for preferred partners.

The TriHealth building is a modern-looking glass-and-steel design. It's not very tall—ten or eleven stories at most—but it's fancy. A long series of steps surrounds the building, putting it up on a pedestal in the middle of the richest, most corrupt part of the most corrupt city in America. The row of revolving doors in the front are recessed into the building, so after climbing up the pedestal to enter, people have to essentially walk *underneath* the building to get inside. It's an interesting psychological effect: it conveys authority, stylishness, and modernity all at the same time.

It's exactly, CB thinks, what you'd want your health care provider to convey.

The lobby is a clean, spacious, well-lit area with a long, polished receptionist's desk facing the door. It travels the entire length of the far wall, ending where the lobby connects to a wide, short hallway with elevators at the far end. The hallway turns a corner and continues on behind the lobby wall. The black marble tile floor gleams and shines to the point that it's almost a mirror: CB can see distorted reflections of everyone in the room. There are cameras everywhere. Sophisticated cameras... more sophisticated, CB thinks, than a health insurance provider would normally justify purchasing. He glances over at the security desk to his left—a much simpler desk than the receptionist's desk, but taller and with a lip at the edge, so you can't see the top. The guard stares down at his desk, apparently lost in thought. CB suspects the guard is probably staring at a bunch of monitors obscured by the desk.

"Can I help you sir?"

CB is standing next to the receptionist's desk. An attractive, well-dressed woman looks at him with a polite and entirely fake smile. CB immediately notices the employee badge hanging off her jacket: it has her picture and the name *Lauren Millany* under it. The outline of a computer chip can be seen in the upper right-hand corner of the badge.

Lauren is trying very hard not to look uncomfortable, but today he dressed for the part, and she's finding it difficult to keep her smile from sliding into a grimace.

He's in his "guy from the skids trying to dress for success" outfit: along with his trenchcoat he's wearing a grimy white button-up short-sleeve shirt with a slightly frayed collar, a bright red clip-on tie that's far too short for his frame, scuffed brown leather loafers and a pair of navy blue work pants with oil stains around the cuffs. The clothes look ridiculous, and the shirt *stinks*—nothing about his appearance says he belongs there.

Of course, the same could be said about his usual appearance, but he's trying to set off a very specific trigger for the upper middle class.

"What?" CB blinks at her rapidly and rubs his eyes in a sudden, slightly frenzied motion. "Sorry? I'm trying to find the lawyers."

"I said, can I help you? Do you have an appointment?" Lauren's fake smile stretches to nearly menacing proportions.

"Uh..." CB looks around, adopting a lost and bewildered expression. The security guard is still staring down at his desk. "The law firm. I think I have a three o'clock?" He starts scratching the back of his head furiously, and whirls around to glare at nothing in particular behind him.

Her smile falters for a moment. "This is the TriHealth building."

CB nods. "Right. I know TriHealth is here but I'm looking for... hold on a moment..." he makes a show of going through his trenchcoat pockets, then pulls out a folded-over piece of paper. He unravels the paper, then squints down at it. "Mueller and Donally? Lawyers? They're here too, right?"

Lauren stares at him blankly. Her smile becomes even more forced. "I'm sorry, sir, but I think you have the wrong address."

CB steals a glance at the security desk. The man is mouthing something. Talking into a microphone, probably.

"No!" CB raises his voice, adding a bit of desperation. "224 45th Street! That's what this says!" He flashes the paper to her, too quickly for her to see anything written on it. "Mueller and Donally at 224 45th Street!"

"Sir, I'm sorry, but there's no one here by that name." The smile is gone now. "This is the TriHealth building, and only TriHealth uses it. If you don't have an appointment, I'm going to have to ask you to leave..."

At that moment two security guards step out of the hallway, move purposefully past the receptionist's desk and close in on him.

CB pretends not to notice. "Stupid!" He smacks his forehead. "So stupid. I should have known. It was too good to be true, I should have known."

The guards aren't carrying guns. They are, however, carrying tasers, and he thinks he recognizes the modifications that were made to them.

"Sir," the receptionist says, "if you'd just step away from the—"

"Do you know how long I've been trying to get a goddamn job in this city?" CB lets his voice crack, just a bit, and focuses his attention on a well-dressed, bearded man wearing John Lennon glasses making his way past the guards, to the hallway beyond. The man quickens his pace while trying to pretend he hasn't noticed anything.

CB turns back to the receptionist. "I'm sorry. My buddy Mitch told me to go here. Some friend, right? I bet he's standing outside laughing his ass off right now."

A firm hand closes on his right shoulder. An equally firm hand closes around his left bicep. CB forces himself to relax and give in—he's in much better shape than the kind of guy he's trying to portray, and while he doesn't expect a receptionist to notice, the security guards might. CB looks to his right, then to his left. They don't look like the typical uniformed rent-a-cops you see in malls and department stores.

"Let's go see if he's there." The guard on his left, a slim black man in his early thirties, has a warm, friendly voice and smiles at him in a fatherly, reassuring manner. The guard on his right, a freckled redhead with a build like a linebacker, has a neutral, businesslike demeanor.

They have employee badges just like Lauren's. The friendly guard's badge identifies him as *Ray Jennings*. The redhead is *Curtis Hagan*.

CB gapes at Ray, keeping his expression slack and confused.

"Come on," Ray says. He tugs gently at CB's shoulder, and CB allows himself to be led meekly out of the lobby, through the double doors, down the steps. It's not until they reach the bottom of the steps that Roy and Curtis let go of him.

"You see this guy Mitch?" Curtis' voice is gravelly. Heavy smoker, CB guesses. Ironic for a health insurance company.

CB looks up and down the street, then stares intently at his feet. "No."

"Well, that was a real rude thing your friend did to you," Ray says. "If I were you I'd let him know exactly what you thought of it."

CB nods sullenly. "I thought you were going to... you know."

"What?" Curtis sounds slightly amused. "Beat you up a little?"

CB nods again.

"There's no need for that." Ray smiles broadly. "This was just a misunderstanding, right? We don't waste our time with misunderstandings. Now if you were to turn around and go back into that lobby and make another scene..."

"Yeah," CB says. "Yeah, I get it. Sorry for the trouble. I... I'm gonna just go."

"I think that's a good idea," Curtis says.

Neither of them move.

"Right." CB walks, keeping his head down, until he reaches the crosswalk at the corner. He looks over his shoulder once—Ray and Curtis are still there. He crosses the street, and by the time he reaches the other side Ray and Curtis are gone.

CB frowns, reaches into his trenchcoat pocket, and pulls out a cigarette.

"Service entrance," he says.

He stays on the opposite street, crossing from block to block until he faces the back of the TriHealth building. There's a cafe on that block, and the window booth is empty. He ducks into their bathroom to change out of the collared shirt—the primary source of the smell—then parks himself in the window booth and orders lunch.

For the next few hours he orders enough to keep his waitress happy and pretends to read the newspaper while he watches the comings and goings of the service entrance. All the trucks that pull up to unload supplies are unmarked, the people flash credentials before being allowed to unload, and everyone involved wears a badge of some sort. It is, CB thinks, an awfully paranoid way to run a health insurance company.

He manages to get the license plate numbers off two of the delivery trucks. He pays for his food, uses the bathroom, then asks the manager if they have a payphone.

The manager is a stout, gruff woman with blonde hair pulled back into a severe bun. "Payphone? What is this, the 80s? Use your cell like everyone else!"

CB sighs, then asks for directions to the public library.

He has to pay for another cab, which aggravates him, but the uptown public library is nice, and the Internet terminals are semi-enclosed. The library is mostly empty at this time of day, so he has plenty of privacy. This is a good thing: it would have been awkward to explain how he managed to get access to the FCPD police network, and even more awkward to explain what he was doing with it.

He runs a search on the first license plate and finds it's registered with a company called Elmuth Shipping. The second license plate returns the same registration. Elmuth Shipping has a local address in midtown.

CB sighs again. He's going to have to hire another cab.

PART TWO: ELMUTH SHIPPING

It's early evening, but not yet dark, when he finally reaches the Elmuth Shipping compound. CB wonders if it'll be as heavily guarded as TriHealth. It isn't. It has security, but prowling around the fence he doesn't see anything out of the ordinary: chain link fence, barbed wire on top, bored blue-shirts not paying a lot of attention to their jobs. The fence is in lousy condition, and there's a section on one side that's come loose from its moorings. It's trivial to crawl through.

That's the problem with conspiracies. You just can't rely on your contractors to hold up their end of things.

There are plenty of trucks parked in the lot, but they all have Elmuth logos on them. He wants the unmarked trucks—eventually he finds them at the far end, parked next to a windowless building, smaller than the main office and very heavily locked. The windows are barred, a metal grate is pulled down over the door, and the grate is padlocked shut. It reminds CB of Elliot Grady's pawn shop.

It's the most aggravating place in the compound to get into, so he figures that's where he needs to look first.

He mills around for a bit, testing the doors of each of the unmarked trucks parked near the building until he finds one unlocked. He opens the door and climbs into the cab, closing the door behind him, then manually turns off the overhead lights. He exits the cab and carefully makes his way to the main office. There are still lights on in that building, but the garage on the side is dark and silent. He tries the office entrance to the garage—locked, but it's an average, commercial-grade doorknob lock. In a few minutes he jimmies the lock and slips into the office. They didn't bother locking the door between the office and the bay.

A few minutes later he finds what he's looking for: bolt cutters and a new padlock. He puts the bolt cutters under his trenchcoat, the padlock in his trenchcoat pocket, and makes his way back out to the smaller building. It's dark now, so it's easier to get around without being seen. At the smaller building he uses the bolt cutters to cut open the padlock: it's every bit as loud as he was afraid it would be, and then some. He quickly retrieves the cut padlock, replaces it with the new padlock—he makes sure it isn't completely closed, just enough to be overlooked in a casual inspection—then hurries to the truck with the unlocked doors and deactivated overhead lights. He slips into the cab, locks the doors, worms his way into the space behind the seats, and waits.

It doesn't take long for a few security guards to show up. He hears one rattle the grate to make sure it's closed, while others go from truck to truck, checking to make sure the doors are locked. CB finds an army blanket stowed under the driver's seat and pulls it out, spreading it over himself as he forces himself to lie completely still. Then he waits and listens.

The guard checking out the grate over the door doesn't go beyond the first rattle, so CB assumes the new padlock didn't do anything inconvenient. He can hear the other guards trying the doors to the trucks around him. Eventually he hears the driver's-side door shake, then the passenger's-side, then sees the reflection of a flashlight through the folds of his blanket as the guard shines it through the window. Then he hears the squelch of a walkie-talkie.

"False alarm." The voice is faint through the truck but sounds distinctly relieved. "I don't know what it was, but everything looks fine over here. We're headed back. There better be pizza left."

CB waits five minutes after he stops hearing the guards before he peers out the window. He's alone again. He grabs the bolt cutters, slips out the passenger-side door, and heads back over to the grate. The padlock has done something inconvenient—it's hanging open. He's grateful Ray and Curtis don't work here—he's pretty sure they'd notice something like that. He stuffs the padlock in his pocket, then pulls at the bottom of the gate. It creaks a bit, and he stops. He starts to inch the gate up, bit by bit, minimizing the sound the gate makes. He raises it enough so he can get at the door lock—a heavier lock than the door to the garage office, but he manages it. The door swings open inward, and CB stoops, steps under the grate, and eases it down behind him. He puts the padlock back on to complete the picture, then steps into the building, closing the door behind him.

It is pitch dark. He fishes out his Mag Lite.

He stands in a single large office complete with a small kitchenette, a beat-up microwave, and an old Mr. Coffee coffee maker. The pot still has coffee in it—about a quarter full—and three plastic bottles of powdered creamer, all open, sit next to it. One large metal desk sits in the center of the room. An old computer, an even older laser printer, and a combination scanner/fax machine all crowd the desktop. A row of old-school metal filing cabinets line one wall.

No windows in the room, but CB decides against turning on the lights: the door, while heavy, doesn't quite seal the frame, and any light that spills through will invite investigation. Still, he sees no reason not to turn on the computer. The computer is *old*—it still uses a square, heavy CRT monitor, which displays the Windows 95 splash logo as old hard disks sluggishly grind into action. It's going to take a while. Time to focus on other things.

The filing cabinets are unlocked and contain personnel files and badges. The badges look like the ones contractors used to get into the loading area of the TriHealth building. This is confirmed in the personnel files: each file lists what businesses the employee has access to, and a number of them list TriHealth. CB studies the badges curiously. Each has a microchip embedded into the card, just like the ones he saw earlier today.

The computer beeps, and CB turns his attention back to the desk, sitting in an old office chair that creaks under his weight. He finds the computer password written down on a piece of paper in the top desk drawer. A minute later the computer loads the desktop, and CB starts looking through its contents.

The computer has Microsoft Office loaded on it. CB opens Excel, then opens the most recently used document. As expected, it's a spreadsheet of shipment schedules, listing both origin and destination points. He sorts the spreadsheet alphabetically by destination and searches for TriHealth, turning on the laser printer with his free hand.

"There." CB sits back in smug satisfaction. He's staring at a list of all the companies TriHealth accepted shipments from in the last six months. He selects those entries, and the laser printer hums to life, printing out only the selected rows. As it starts to spit out page after page of information, CB returns his attention to the filing cabinets and the personnel files.

The last cabinet on the right is locked.

CB frowns. The fact that the filing cabinet is locked probably means there's something interesting in it, but these filing cabinets are serious business, and the locks are much smaller and more complicated than the one on the front door. He's pretty sure he won't be able to pick it, and wonders if he can use the bolt cutters to pry it open. On a hunch, he goes back to the desk and starts rummaging through the drawers. The top desk drawer has a set of keys. The smallest key fits perfectly, and the cabinet slides open.

There are only four folders in the top drawer. CB picks up the first folder, opens it, and whistles softly. Inside is another badge, similar in size to the badges in the other cabinets but black with a red TriHealth logo instead of the nondescript gray. These, CB decides, are VIP badges that give access to other parts of the building.

CB pockets one and closes the filing cabinet drawer. A moment later he sighs, reopens the filing cabinet drawer, takes another badge from a second folder then closes the drawer again.

Once the printer is finished, he folds up the printout and stuffs it into one of his pockets. Then he turns off the printer, shuts down the computer, and waits by the door, listening. Eventually he hears one of the guards wander by, his walkie-talkie emitting short bursts of white noise as he passes. Two minutes later, CB cautiously opens the door and peers out.

No one there. He locks the door, removes the padlock, slides up the fence just high enough to slip under, then shuts everything up tight behind him. Twenty minutes later he crawls out from under the loose portion of the chain link fence and makes his way back to the bunker.

PART THREE: TRIHEALTH, 2 AM

The one thing they aren't doing is wearing all black.

CB is wearing his trenchcoat, old blue jeans, his favorite boots and a black Minor Threat t-shirt that's unraveling around the collar. Jenny is wearing dark blue slacks, a button-up shirt, tennis shoes, and a light windbreaker with large inside pockets. They don't look like cat burglars. This is important, CB explains, because people who dress like cat burglars tend to get picked up by the police on the grounds that they look like they're about to steal something.

"I'm tired," Jenny complains.

"That won't last," CB says. "In a minute you'll be running on adrenaline. And terror. Which makes more adrenaline. You'll be fine."

"I don't understand why we have to do all this covert stuff at night."

CB turns to face Jenny. "Do you *really* not understand that?"

"Fine," Jenny snaps. "I would *prefer* not to understand it because it makes it easier to wish I were asleep in my bed."

"You wanted to come along," CB says. "And unfortunately for you, you convinced me you'll be useful."

They're standing in front of the restaurant where CB spied on TriHealth's service area. This part of uptown is mostly deserted at 2 AM, and all the businesses on the block are closed. That was four days ago, and CB has spent the time getting familiar with police patrol routes in the area. Police will definitely stop two people standing around this part of the city at 2 AM. CB wants to avoid that.

"So what's the plan?" Jenny whispers, more out of nervousness than any need for stealth at the moment.

"We go in and find a computer. Then you search for anything interesting."

"Yes, I'm familiar with the broad strokes," Jenny says. "I was hoping you had something more specific in mind."

"Well..." CB pulls out one of the badges from his trenchcoat pocket. "This will probably get us through the service entrance door."

"And what about security?" Jenny asks.

CB shrugs. "What *about* security?"

"Right... well, if *I* were designing a security system I would set it up so it notified the security desk any time a card accessed one of the doors during off hours. Especially the service area. *Especially* at two in the morning."

CB nods. "Yeah, probably."

"Can you whammy the door so it won't do that?"

CB shakes his head. "Not exactly. That's a little too specific. But what will happen instead is bound to be interesting. Come on."

CB starts walking across the street. Jenny hurries to keep up with him. The closer they get to the building, the more exposed she feels. "Shouldn't we be a little... you know... stealthier?"

"Not really," CB says. "Hold on a moment." He stops at the service door and looks around. A minute later he nods to himself.

"What?"

"Just the one camera," he says, pointing above them. "And that one just went out. Very mysteriously."

Jenny looks at the camera. "It's not a very good model."

"That's why it was so easy to break," CB says. He swipes the ID card through a slot to the right of the door, pulls it open, then begins to walk along the side of the building to the front entrance. "Come on, Jenny. You don't want to be here when they show up."

Jenny follows CB, frowning in confusion. "Why was the camera so average? You said their security was top notch."

"Inside," CB says. "I'm pretty sure you'll be impressed. Thing is, though, this city notices things. Expensive security cameras set up outside, around the building? Every player in this city would suddenly want to know what was so damn important to a health insurance company that they needed to spend that kind of money on security. Especially since they've already got an Uptown location, which means they're on the 'special client' list."

"Security through obscurity is a terrible defense," Jenny says.

"Depends on what you're using it for," CB says. "Anyway, the external cameras aren't a defense exactly. They're more like a con. But trust me, you'll be impressed."

The lobby is lit at night, though dimly. CB and Jenny are pressed up against the last stretch of concrete before the long line of full-length windows leading to the double doors. CB peers around the edge and can see the security desk. It's manned.

"OK," CB says, "hold on a minute."

He focuses on the figure sitting behind the desk, winks, then presses back against the wall.

"What did you do?" Jenny whispers.

"I hexed him."

"But what did you *do*?" Jenny sounds exasperated.

"We'll find out in a second..."

Through the glass they can hear the muted jingle of keys, and the rapid pounding of feet on tile as someone runs past them. CB risks a look, then laughs softly.

"He had to use the little security guard's room. Come on, we don't have a lot of time." CB runs to the revolving doors, slides the access card through the electronic key, then pushes his way through.

The lobby is dimly lit. CB walks over to the security station. "All yours, Jenny."

"Thank you." Jenny ducks around the back of the desk and slides into the seat. "Wow. I see what you mean. Very expensive stuff here. I'm not familiar with the brands, but the design is solid. IR and thermal sensors on the cameras, digital recording of images... I've got the whole ground floor here. Monitors everywhere."

"Where are the other guards?" CB asks. He fingers the half-filled pack of cigarettes in his pocket nervously.

"Looks like they're still investigating the mysterious camera outage," Jenny says. "The ones I can see, anyway—the cameras only cover this floor. They have the back door propped open and one guy is setting up a stepladder. OK, I'm getting started."

Jenny looks down at the security desk. It's a series of touchscreen monitors with a few clear spaces where the guard on duty can place physical objects—like the dirty coffee mug half-filled with the bitterest, strongest coffee she has ever smelled.

"No wonder he had to go," she mutters.

"What's that?" CB looks at her questioningly. "Did you do it yet?"

"No," Jenny says. "Hold on."

She reaches into one of her pockets and pulls out a USB drive. There's a USB port right under the desk, and when she inserts the drive one of the touchscreens flashes a warning message. She nods, pulls out the USB drive, then pulls out her smartphone.

"This will take a little longer." She attaches her smartphone to one of her specialized tethers, then plugs the other end of the tether into the USB port.

CB watches Jenny work. He's familiar with the general process of breaking computer security—that is how he got access to the FCPD's network, after all—but what she's doing is way over his head. It's like watching Robert work, he thinks—she has that same look of concentration that makes her oblivious to everything else going on around her.

He glances back toward the hallway leading to the elevators and—he assumes—to the bathrooms. He wonders how much time they have left. "What are you doing, exactly?"

"Breaking the law." Jenny's voice is dry. "It won't take as long as I thought. Their security system is nice, but someone's a little lax with the patching. Give me your key card."

CB hurries back to the security desk and hands her the key card.

Jenny takes the card and swipes it through a slot at the security desk. One of the screens updates to show the card and the access it has.

"I'm adding privileges now," she says.

"Can you give it everything?" CB asks hopefully.

Jenny shakes her head. "Not from here. I can give it more, though. Also, I made it invisible. No more calling the front desk every time it's used."

She hands back the card back to CB, who looks at it appreciatively.

"One more thing," she says, and starts messing with her smartphone.

"What are you doing now?" CB's gaze drifts back to the hallway.

"You'll like it," Jenny says. "Trust me."

"It's not a matter of trust, it's a matter of *time*," CB says. "That guard won't be out of action forever, and I want to—"

He falls silent as he hears the echo of footsteps coming down the hall. Jenny's eyes widen.

"Receptionist's desk," CB whispers. "Now!"

They throw themselves behind the receptionist's desk just as the guard rounds the corner. A few seconds later they hear footsteps and the jingle of keys travel past them, and a few seconds after that they hear the creaking of a chair as the guard settles back into his post.

CB motions for Jenny to follow him. Jenny holds up her hand, and motions for him to wait.

CB frowns, but waits.

Jenny pulls out her smartphone again, navigates through a few settings menus, then presses something on the screen. She nods once, satisfied, then types something into her screen and turns it around for CB to read.

Cameras won't see us now.

CB raises an eyebrow. Jenny nods. CB grins, then on his hands and knees he crawls along the length of the receptionist's desk toward the hall. There's a little swinging door at the end that opens without making a sound. CB creeps out and around the corner as fast as he can. Jenny follows close behind.

"Let's get to the elevators," Jenny whispers.

"No elevators," CB says. "They ding. We use the stairs."

They make their way quickly down the short, wide hallway and find the stairwell right next to the elevators at the far end. CB swipes the stairwell door with his access card. The light blinks green, and the door clicks open. They both hurry into the stairwell and close the door behind them.

"Well," Jenny says in a more normal tone, "you were right about the adrenaline. And the terror. And the more adrenaline."

"Want to tell me why the cameras can't see us?" CB asks.

Jenny grins and taps the smartphone in her jacket pocket. "Found the network the cameras were operating on. Wireless. Encrypted, but that security station let me figure out how to hook in. So I taught the cameras to recognize my phone. Whenever they sense it they'll go back thirty seconds in their surveillance archives and play that image in a continuous loop. We can go pretty much anywhere in the building without anyone seeing us on camera. Even if they're paying attention."

"Nice work." CB is impressed. "In that case, let's get to Recordkeeping."

"Where's that?" Jenny asks.

"Seventh floor." CB starts climbing.

"How do you know that?" Jenny sounds unhappy at the thought of climbing all those stairs.

"There was a directory posted next to the elevators," CB says.

"And what were you going to do if I hadn't messed with the cameras?" Jenny asks.

"Don't know, to be honest." CB takes the stairs two at a time, forcing Jenny to climb faster. "Try to whammy them one by one, I guess. Improvise. That only works for a little while, though. Your idea is better."

By the time they reach the seventh floor, Jenny is completely out of breath. CB doesn't look winded. He opens the door just a bit and peers through. Then he opens it wider, and sticks his head out.

"Empty," he says. He steps into the hall.

Holding her smartphone out in front of her like a crucifix in a vampire movie, she follows suit.

They walk into a cube farm—low half-cubes cluster around little floor communities, separated by long, wide aisles. CB stands in the middle of the room and looks around, frowning.

"What's wrong?" Jenny asks.

CB sighs. "I don't know where to start looking," he admits.

Jenny points to one of the private offices at the far end of the room. "People who work in private offices tend to have better access. And they're usually pretty clueless about security."

The door is locked, but CB jimmies the lock quickly. The office is fancy, obviously for an executive of some sort. The carpeting is thick and expensive, tasteful reproductions of famous art hang from the walls, and a heavy oak desk sits in the middle of the room. On the desk is a flat screen computer monitor.

CB closes the door behind them and gestures to the computer. "All yours," he says, and plops down on one of the chairs.

"The managers in Recordkeeping do well here," Jenny observes. She powers up the computer. It boots quickly. "Gimmie a sec while I log in."

She attaches her phone to the computer's USB port and runs something. A minute later the login screen disappears, replaced by the desktop.

"I think I have the records database application open," Jenny says. "Tell me what I'm looking for."

"Insurance policy records." CB rattles off a policy number, and Jenny types it in.

"Who is this guy?" Jenny asks.

CB gets out of his chair and walks around the desk so he can look at the monitor over her shoulder. The policy profile shows a picture of a middle-aged man with a mustache. He looks for the name on the policy.

"That's one of the first victims of the Farraday City serial killer I was telling you about."

"I'm saving this to my phone," Jenny says. "Actually, right now I'm saving just about anything I can find to my phone. Assume that whatever we look at now, we'll have a copy to look at later."

"OK," CB says. "Let's try more numbers."

He gives Jenny number after number. Each result returns a policy with a picture, and CB confirms that they're all victims of the serial killer.

"How do you remember all those numbers?" Jenny asks. "Is it from your days with the Guardians?"

"Well. Yes. But I developed the skill earlier than that," CB says.

"When?"

CB hesitates. "The old days," he says finally. "When I was a villain. You tend not to want to leave written records when you're actively breaking the law. We need to figure out what these policy holders have in common."

"They're dead," Jenny says.

"Other than that. Uh... search for the primary care physician for each policy holder. Is that on file?"

"Yeah, it's on file. Hold on." A few seconds later, Jenny clucks in irritation. "Sort of a mixed bag. Three of the victims had exactly the same doctor, but the others have different primary physicians listed."

Jenny types a few more commands into the computer, then raises her eyebrows in surprise. "The doctors are all on the same network."

"Yeah," CB says. "TriHealth, right? Otherwise they wouldn't be on file."

"No," Jenny says, "that's not what I mean. I mean medical group. A third of the doctors even work in the same building. Hold on a moment."

Jenny types, then waits, then types, and finally smiles in grim satisfaction.

"CB, all the victims had primary care physicians that were members of the same medical network. There are two clinics, a private hospital, and four doctor's offices that operate under an umbrella corporation called OmegaHealth."

"I don't think they were listed in Travers' appendices," CB says.

"I don't remember them. I've never heard of them before. But every single victim had a primary care physician in that medical network, and—"

At that moment the computer shuts down.

"*What the hell?*"

A note of concern creeps into CB's voice. "Jenny? What happened?"

"Don't know," Jenny says. She reaches for the power button and pushes it. Nothing happens. "I think I triggered something. I think we might be in trouble."

Off in the distance they hear the elevator ding.

"Ah," CB says. "I thought things had been going too well. Nice to know my instincts are still in top form."

"What do we do?" Jenny asks, panic tinging her voice.

CB reaches into his trenchcoat pocket and pulls out his half-filled pack of cigarettes. "I expect we're going to fight. Then we're going to run. If we're lucky, we're going to fight a little and run a lot. If we're unlucky, it'll be the other way around..."

PART FOUR: CONFLICT RESOLUTION

The elevator door dings a second time. CB and Jenny hear the doors slide open as heavy-booted feet stomp out into the cube farm.

CB lights his cigarette.

"You're going to smoke *now?*" Jenny stares at him incredulously.

"Yep," CB says. "It's kind of a thing." He closes his eyes and concentrates. He feels the world spinning around him.

"What are you—"

"Shh." CB's cigarette leaves a trail of smoke behind it as he cuts off Jenny's question with a wave of his hand. "I need a second."

"We know you're in there." The voice is warm, polite, and fatherly. CB recognizes that voice. It's Ray. "We don't want to hurt you, but if you don't come out with your hands up right now... well, we've been told not to take chances."

The world falls into place. CB opens his eyes. "Jenny, get behind the desk and stay there. This is probably going to get messy."

"Like mom and dad's house?" Jenny asks.

"Could be," CB says.

Jenny gets behind the desk.

"You're running out of time," Ray says.

"OK," CB raises his voice to shout through the door. "I'm coming out. Don't do anything crazy, I'm opening the door."

He opens the door wide and stands just inside the doorway. He doesn't step out yet. He puffs on his cigarette, looking out with an apparent lack of concern. "Hi Ray. Curtis with you?"

"No," Ray says. The "no" is a little louder than CB expects. It doesn't fit with the question. "Curtis is off tonight. He leads a charmed life." Ray plays it off well, but CB suspects the "no" was an order given to some of his men.

They're probably on both sides of the door, waiting for me to come out.

"Luck of the Irish," CB says.

"Oh, no, he's going to be disappointed he missed out on this," Ray says. "He said there was no way in hell you were a tweaker, and now I owe him twenty dollars."

CB can see him now. He's taken a position behind one of the cubes closest to the elevator. It doesn't provide a lot of actual cover, but it does allow him to steady his rifle. The rest of his team is doing the same. He can see four: if there are at least two on each side of the door, that means he's dealing with a minimum of eight armed guards.

"Yeah, bad call on your part, Ray. Never bet against the Irish unless you're a bottle of whiskey."

"Are you going to come along quietly?" Ray asks.

"You know I'm not," CB says.

"Right." Ray sounds a little disappointed. "Well, you were warned."

"You weren't," CB says. "Sorry about that."

He dives forward into the room.

The guards standing at either side of the door are not expecting him to dive. They see a flash of motion and surge forward to intercept, only to crash into each other as CB tucks into a roll and comes up in a low crouch just past them. He lashes back with his foot, kicking one man in his ankle—it twists sharply, the man cries out in pain, and both topple to the ground. The others against the wall—one more on each side, CB notes, making a total of eight—charge forward, and CB breaks into a sprint that takes him up to the center of the first row of cubes. He jumps up and vaults over into the second row just as Ray gives the order to open fire.

bambambambambambambambambam

The first volley of shots miss completely, and the two guards behind him scatter quickly to get out of the line of fire. He's alone in this section of the cube farm, but that won't last. He runs left, crouching low, heading to one of the aisles that cuts across the communities. As he runs past a desk, a glint of metal catches his eye: a stapler. He grabs it as he passes, switches the stapler to his left hand, and as he reaches the aisle he grabs the corner of the last cube, leaning back into a slide.

The cube wall jerks about a foot and a half out from the desk as CB swivels around it into the aisle, then automatic rifles tear it to shreds. He sees a guard in the end cube, two rows down, hastily adjusting his rifle to target him instead of a cheap plastic wall. CB throws the stapler, and it flies through the air, hitting the guard right at the bridge of his nose. Something *cracks*—either the nose or the stapler, he can't tell—and the guard's rifle discharges into the air as the guard staggers back.

The wild shot provokes more blind shooting. CB can hear Ray shouting for the guards to rein it in and pay attention.

CB stays low, keeping out of view. He ducks into the next row down, across the aisle, and scurries across the next aisle and switches rows again. A soldier stands a few cubes away, both to his left and across the aisle to his right.

"Fuck."

He didn't mean to say that out loud: both guards immediately train their weapons on him. He jumps toward the guard on his side of the aisle, getting his foot up on a desk and launching himself off the top of the cube partition wall as both soldiers open fire. The guns *crack* as fire spits out of their muzzles, and he hears a *ztszt ztszt ztszt* as bullets streak past his ear. He feels the world *shift* subtly, and they all miss. A few punch holes in his trenchcoat. He kicks the guard in the face—the steel toe of his left boot hits the guard square in the jaw. There's a loud *crack* followed by a sickening splintering sound as the jaw shatters; the guard spins around and collapses into one of the desks. CB's right foot comes down on the next partition wall and he pushes off, leaping into the next empty row as the air fills with gunfire. He hears another crack, another *ztszt*, and he feels heat streak across his face.

One of the guards actually grazed him. He bets it was Ray.

The second guard runs toward the one CB kicked, sticking his gun over the lip of the partition wall into CB's row. He knows which row CB is in, but he doesn't know specifically where. CB pushes himself under one of the desks to keep out of sight.

"He's in the next row," the guard calls out. "I don't know where."

"Shoot it up!" Ray says.

Suddenly his spot under the desk seems like a colossally bad idea.

bambambambambambambambambam

Gunfire tears through the cubes as CB pushes himself out into the row. The world churns around him as bullets slice through the flimsy partitions and destroy the expensive computers sitting on each desk. CB stands, and finds himself face to face with the guard. The guard's eyes widen in surprise as CB grabs the flat screen monitor sitting on the desk in front of him and smashes it over his head. He falls back, and CB vaults over the cube wall to land on a second guard's shoulders. His legs tighten around the guard's neck as he falls forward, then he twists and jerks. The guard lets out a strangled cry of surprise as they flip over and he smashes into a desk, then goes limp.

It's a lot more difficult to break a man's neck than you'd think from watching movies, and CB didn't pull it off that time. He suspects the guard will be wearing a neck brace for a while.

Three guards appear at the end of the row. CB winks, and to his satisfaction he hears the sound of three rifles jamming simultaneously. He charges. One of the guards throws down his rifle and pulls out a knife, the other two adjust their grips on their rifles to use them as clubs.

The guard with the knife drops into a fighting crouch. CB sees a hot plate sitting on a desk; he grabs it and gives it a sharp tug as the plug yanks out of the power strip sitting behind the monitor. He grabs the plug, wraps the cord around his hand once, and swings the hot plate at the guard's knife arm.

The guard curses as the hot plate loops around his arm and then reels as it smacks him in the face with a wet *thud*. The knife drops to the ground. CB leans into a slide as he pulls sharply on the power cord—the guard yelps in surprise as he stumbles forward, and CB slides past him, grabbing the knife as he passes by. He jabs the knife into the leg of one of the other guards, who screams, drops his rifle, and sinks to the floor in agony.

CB turns to face the third guard. It's Ray. CB doesn't have time to get to his feet; Ray kicks him in the face.

CB's head snaps back; his cigarette flies into the air and lands a few feet away, smoldering on cheap carpet. His face is wet with blood, his vision is a crazy mess of light and color, and he gasps for breath as Ray kicks him again, this time in his gut. CB grunts in pain, then hears Ray draw back for a third kick. He forces himself to act—he manages to grab Ray's ankle, wrap his legs around Ray's trapped leg, and flip him on top of the guard he stabbed. Ray's forehead hits the ground hard. The guard he falls on top of stops screaming. Both lie still.

CB finds himself hoping Ray's OK. In a strange way he sort of likes him.

His vision clears slightly, just in time to see a shadow fall across him. He rolls and twists, just barely missing a boot that otherwise would have hit solidly in the small of his back. He kicks and misses. He rolls again, feeling the floor shake as someone tries to kick him again. Finally CB's vision steadies enough for him to see his attacker clearly—a woman this time.

"I'd rather not fight a woman," CB says.

"Fine by me," she says. She pulls out a truncheon.

CB punches her in the solar plexus. She doubles over, a quick jab to the neck drops her.

"I mean, I *will*," CB says. "I just don't *want* to."

The room falls silent. CB does a mental count and comes up with seven guards down. How many came up? If it was an eight-man team then that leaves...

"Stand down!"

Jenny stands in the doorway of the executive office. The last guard stands behind her, his left arm wrapped around her neck, his right hand holding an automatic pistol against her temple.

CB slowly raises his hands. "OK. OK, we're good, right? You got me. Just let her go."

"Shut up," the guard says. "I do all the talking."

CB shuts up. He looks at Jenny.

Jenny meets his gaze. "Did you get the others?" Her voice is hoarse.

"I said *shut up*," the guard says. He tightens his grip around Jenny's neck.

CB nods.

Jenny relaxes, then she moves: her left hand reaches up to grab the guard's fingers on *his* left hand, pulls, and twists sharply. Something snaps, he screams: at the same time she grabs his gun with her other hand, ducks her head out from under the convulsing arm, twists the gun free from the soldier's right hand...

bambam

...and shoots him in the face twice. The guard falls in a heap.

CB blinks. His hands are still over his head as he looks down at the guard's body, then back up at Jenny.

"What. The. *Fuck*."

Jenny's gun arm is still extended. The gun trembles slightly. "My great-grandfather was one of the best hand-to-hand combatants in the world. He'd been giving me lessons since I was thirteen."

CB lets his arms fall to his side. "Alex was teaching you to fight since you were *thirteen years old?*"

"He said it would help me with boys."

She stares down at the body, face blank. She doesn't drop her arm. The gun still points at the spot where the guard stood moments before.

"Jenny."

Jenny glances at CB. CB nods to the gun. She looks at the gun and frowns. Then she removes the magazine, clears the chamber, and drops it to the ground with a clatter. She turns to face him again. "How exactly do we get out of here?"

"Not the way we came," CB says. "There are probably more guards on their way. Those were the guys they had in the building, but I'm pretty sure a call went out, and I'll bet good money their people have excellent response times."

"So the elevator and the stairs are out?" Jenny asks.

"Looks like," CB says. He kicks the body out of the way and closes the door.

"That's not going to slow them down," Jenny says.

"True," CB agrees. He goes over to the window and looks down. "You know, that looks like a nasty fall."

"I guess," Jenny says. Then she frowns. "Please tell me we're not."

"OK," CB says. "We're not."

He grabs the overstuffed office chair sitting behind the oak desk and throws it at the window with all his might. The window cracks into a spiderweb of broken glass, but it doesn't shatter.

"God damn safety glass," CB mutters. He picks up the chair and throws it a second time. This time an entire sheet of glass is knocked out the window and falls to the ground seven stories below.

"CB, what are we *doing*?" There's more than a hint of panic in Jenny's voice.

"Oh, right," CB says. "You don't like heights. Well, that makes this awkward."

He pulls a loop of high-tension wire out of his pocket, hooks one end to his belt, and loops the other end around a leg of the massive oak desk.

The elevator dings. CB leaps up onto the window and tests his weight against the line. The oak desk doesn't budge.

"Come on, Jenny. We don't have a lot of time. Just hold on tight and close your eyes and we'll get down OK."

"I hate you," Jenny says.

The elevator dings again. Jenny swears, runs up to the window, and throws her arms tightly around CB's neck.

"Close your eyes," CB says.

Jenny shuts her eyes tight.

CB leans back, wrapping the wire around his right arm, using his trenchcoat as padding. He quickly, if awkwardly, rappels down the side of the building. They run out of wire about seven feet off the ground, so CB unhooks it from his belt and they fall the rest of the way. Jenny shrieks a little as they land, but they're unharmed.

"I *hate* you, CB!" Jenny snarls as she dusts herself off. "I hate you so *very, very much.*"

"Later," CB says. "This is the part where we run a little."

Sirens wail in the distance. Overhead they hear the sound of someone smashing in the door to the executive office. Without saying another word, CB and Jenny run off into the night.

PART ONE: FARRADAY CITY SEWER

They run across the street, catty-corner, to the cafe where they started the night. They duck around the building, into a side alley.

Jenny doesn't say anything. CB is worried about that.

The sirens are very loud now. CB hears a squad car stop in front of the cafe. He runs to the end of the alley and stops, scraping about in the dirt and debris until finally, with a grunt, he pulls a manhole cover out of the ground.

"Come on." CB's voice is low. "It's dark, but only for a bit."

"We're going into the sewers?" Jenny keeps her voice low as well, but he can hear her distaste. It doesn't keep her from climbing down, however.

CB hears voices. The police and the guards are coordinating; he expects there will be even more on the scene soon. He sees a brief flash of light at the far end of the alley. He slips into the manhole, and when he's mostly in he wraps his leg around a ladder rung so he can drag the manhole cover back in place with both hands. Just in time: he can hear muffled voices arguing with each other about halfway down the alley.

He climbs down the ladder, fishes out his Mag-Lite, and turns it on.

Jenny is standing to one side, bent over, hands on her knees. She's winded from the running, and probably sore from the improvised rappelling they did to escape the seventh floor. Her eyes are unfocused and remote: that's from something else entirely. CB recognizes it, and he doesn't know what to do about it.

Tonight is the first time she ever killed someone. That's a hell of a first.

He shines the Mag-Lite directly into Jenny's eyes. Her head jerks back and she throws one hand up over her face.

"Damn it, CB! What the hell?"

Crisis postponed.

"Come on," CB says. "Put your hand on my shoulder."

"I wouldn't need to if you hadn't just blinded me," Jenny grumbles.

"Yes you would. Two people traveling with a single flashlight in total darkness? Not as easy as it sounds." CB keeps his voice cheerful. He knows that irritates her, and that's the only therapy he can think of at the moment.

They travel in silence, kicking up dust as they scuff along the tunnel. Jenny sneezes.

"It's awfully dry for a sewer," she says. "I wouldn't think there'd be so much dust."

"It's not a sewer," CB says. "It's a maintenance tunnel. It connects to the sewers, though, and that's where we're going."

"Will they follow us?"

"Yeah, eventually. It'll be too late when they do—I know the sewers a *lot* better than they do." CB forces himself to sound cheerful. He's pretty sure Jenny doesn't want him to sound cheerful, and he needs her to focus on something external right now.

"You're pretty sure of yourself." Her voice is thick with annoyance; CB starts to relax a little. "Have you considered the possibility that you're wrong?"

"Yep," CB says.

Jenny mutters to herself.

"Here we are," CB says. He slows down, and plays his Mag-Lite over the wall in front of them. Set into the wall is a large door. "The sewer awaits. Uh... this is going to smell a bit."

Jenny mutters some more.

The door is heavy, metal, and coated in rust. There's no lock, but it sticks—CB has to tug hard to get it open. When he does, it groans as the hinges protest being called into service. As the door opens, they catch a faint whiff of the sewage on the other side, and it makes Jenny gag. A second later, as the door is thrown wide, the smell overwhelms them, and they both need a moment to recover.

"This is not fun," Jenny says, choking back a wave of nausea.

"Oh, it could be worse," CB says, trying to sound cheerful. "It could be much, much worse. Come on, let's go."

The roof of the sewage tunnel is arched. On the right and left sides are small walkways just wide enough for a full-sized adult. The sides of the sewer are covered in faded, barely legible graffiti. Cigarette butts and discarded bottles litter the narrow walkway and occasionally spill into the sewage that flows languidly on.

They travel for a while, continuing down the narrow walkway in silence, listening to their footsteps echoing off the ceiling—and listening for other footsteps as well.

"I don't think they're following us," CB says. "That's good."

"Where are we going?" Jenny's voice is tight again.

"There's a place down here where we can hole up for a bit. It's out of the way, I'm pretty sure the people looking for us don't know about it. We can use it to—"

"I'm *fine*," Jenny says.

"Well I'm *not*," CB snaps. "I got *kicked in the face*."

Jenny falls silent.

CB leads them deeper into the underground. The deeper they go, the higher the ceilings get, the wider the passages become, until finally she can't really think of them as sewers any more.

"Why is this here?" Jenny asks finally.

"Why is what here?" CB turns down a connecting tunnel, hand trailing along the side of the stone wall. His pace slows as his hand moves up and down over the surface of the wall, probing for something.

"All these tunnels. I don't get it. Farraday City isn't old, but this doesn't seem very modern to me. Shouldn't the sewers be a bunch of underground pipes?"

"Don't know," CB says. "That sounds reasonable, I guess. Except... well, these are the sewers." He stops, puts the end of his Mag Lite in his mouth, and starts feeling around the wall with both hands.

"It's just weird," Jenny says. "I mean, Farraday City might be corrupt, but it's supposed to be *modern* corrupt, right? Rebuilt from the ground up? It wasn't much of anything before the mob moved in."

"Beach resort." The words are muffled with the flashlight in his mouth. His left hand stops moving as his fingers close around something in the wall; he nods once, and his fingers sink into the rock. The wall grinds unpleasantly, then a veneer of rock slides away, revealing a heavy metal door.

CB removes the flashlight from his mouth. "It's also a little strange to find secret rooms in the municipal sewer system. I haven't figured that out either, but right now it's convenient. Come on."

He pushes the door open. Jenny hears a hiss, as if the door is breaking a seal. CB stands to one side and motions for her to step through. She does, shuddering as she steps into the dark room. CB's Mag-Lite flashes across the room briefly, just enough to reveal a cot and a few mats sitting on a stone tile floor.

CB steps into the room after her and pulls the door shut behind them—as it closes, Jenny feels herself start to panic. Then a dim light fills the room—CB is pumping a hand-crank electric lantern, and when the light finally steadies he puts his Mag-Lite back in his trenchcoat pocket.

The room is about the size of a small living room in a cheap New York City apartment. The walls are concrete, but not like the sewer walls outside. They're smoother, and cleaner. *Definitely* cleaner. The floor is a series of colorless stone tiles, so smooth they almost gleam in the lamplight. The air is cooler in here, and it *doesn't stink.*

The cot is a knock-off of the kind she used to see in old war movies. She knows it's a knock-off because MADE IN CHINA is stenciled on the canvas. It looks relatively clean, and it has a pillow and a blanket. Two thick mats, sort of a cross between rugs and pillows, are spread out on the concrete floor.

The sound of grinding stone comes through the door—the stone facade sliding back into place, Jenny guesses—and when it stops, CB slides the bolts at the top and bottom of the door into place, locking it securely. He shrugs off his trenchcoat and collapses into one of the floor rug-pillows, exhaling slowly as he hits the ground.

"You can take the cot, Jenny. Lie down a bit. Get a little sleep. We earned it."

Jenny goes over to the cot and sits on the edge of it. She watches CB as he lies on the floor, notices the caked blood and purplish bruising spread over most of his face. One eye is swollen half-shut.

"CB, maybe you should take the cot."

CB shakes his head. "Too late. I'm not moving for at least an hour. Two, if I can manage it."

"For a hero you get your ass kicked a lot." Jenny smiles slightly.

CB laughs. "Yeah, well. Happened a lot when I was a bad guy, too."

Jenny falls back on the cot and stares up at the ceiling. It's a single, solid slab of concrete. "What is this place?"

"Secret room," CB says.

"Yeah, *thanks.* Why?"

"Already told you I don't know." CB sounds half asleep at this point. "Found it by accident. Then I found two more. Doesn't really look like anyone uses them for anything. I brought the gear—thought it would be useful. Funny thing to put in a sewer, but it's a funny kind of sewer too."

"Do a lot of people use the sewers to get around?"

"Eh..." Jenny can almost hear CB shrug. "Some homeless. Some crazies. Not nearly as many people as you'd think, though. Sewers have a bad reputation—never figured out why..."

They lapse into silence again. Jenny closes her eyes and tries to sleep, but every time she does she sees the man she shot. So she opens her eyes and stares at the ceiling, trying with all her might to force that image from her mind.

"How are you doing, Jenny?"

She turns her head. CB is sitting up, staring at her thoughtfully, looking troubled.

"What do you mean, 'how am I doing?'" She can't quite manage to keep the catch out of her voice.

"You shot a guy in the face," CB says. "Twice. It's traumatic, even when you don't really have much choice."

Jenny sits up in the cot and looks away. Her hair falls over her face, obscuring it from CB's view. When she looks up, her expression is remote and vacant.

"I'm not thinking about it right now," Jenny says.

"You're not?"

Jenny frowns slightly. "I'm *trying* not to think about it right now. I'm compartmentalizing it and repressing it in what is probably a very unhealthy manner, and I will continue to do so until I feel *safe*. When I feel *safe* I will revisit the matter."

"Right..." CB keeps his expression neutral. "OK."

"Damn it, CB, I can't afford to crack up right now." She stares back fiercely, voice trembling.

CB sighs. "Yeah. I get it. Sometimes you have to push all that stuff into the back of your head and not deal with it for a while. But don't do that for too long, OK? It's not good for you. I know guys who did that for too long. They're not well. If you want to talk, I'll listen."

"Thanks," Jenny says. "Maybe later."

"OK." CB settles back on the pillow and closes his eyes. Jenny lies back down on the cot and tries to do the same.

"We actually practiced that move." Jenny's voice is soft, and a little sad. "The one I used in the office. We practiced it *all the time*. He played the bad guy. He had a German Luger—souvenir from the war, I guess—it wasn't loaded or anything, but he said being familiar with the weight of the gun was important. I thought it was funny, mostly, and we always stopped right before I pulled the trigger. I mean, I thought that was where I was *supposed* to stop. I thought the whole point was to disarm your attacker and hold him at bay, force him to back down."

CB doesn't answer.

"He taught me to kill," she says finally. "All this time I thought he was just teaching me to take care of myself. But he was actually teaching me to kill."

She hears CB sigh again. "That's not exactly true."

"It isn't?" Her voice is bitter and angry. "Pulling the trigger was just... it was so *easy*. I almost wasn't thinking about it."

"Yeah," CB says. "You're not supposed to."

"Yes you are!" Jenny sits up in the cot, eyes flashing. "If you're going to kill someone you damn well better have the decency to *think* about it first."

"What's so decent about that?" CB asks. He sits up and stares at her, head cocked to one side, sizing her up. "Lots of people think about killing other people, and believe me, Jenny, it's usually not because it's the *decent thing to do*. Serial killers. Assassins. Tyrants. Whoever is killing all these TriHealth patients, there's been an *awful lot of thinking* involved in that. And all it means is that a lot of people are dead who, as far as we can tell, didn't really do anything to deserve it."

"That's not what I mean," Jenny says.

"The guy who had the gun pointed at your head, now, he *definitely* thought about it beforehand," CB continues. "And he would have pulled that trigger if he thought I was going to do anything other than surrender on the spot. I could see it in his eyes—if I didn't surrender it meant he was going down, and he'd decided if he was going down he was going to take the girl with him."

Jenny doesn't say anything.

"Look, Jenny, there aren't a lot of options when it comes to dealing with a hostage-taker. Either you get the guy to surrender and release the hostage or you take him out before he can hurt the hostage. Taking out the hostage-taker is always a risky play, but if that's your option you have to *commit*. If you hold back it increases the chance he doesn't go down; if he doesn't go down it *drastically* increases the chance the hostage *will*."

"Great-grandfather could have taken him down alive," Jenny says. "He did it all the time!"

"He was a *fucking super hero*!" CB shouts, exasperated. "Are you?"

Jenny looks away from CB, focuses on the corner of the cot.

"I don't know if you've noticed, but we tend to do a lot of crazy shit.

Hell, Roger can actually move *faster than bullets*. We have the *luxury* of trying for the best possible outcome. But unless you've gone through Project Paragon and didn't bother telling anyone, I don't think you can..."

CB trails off, frowning.

"That's not fair," Jenny says. "I know I'm not like him. That doesn't make this any easier."

Jenny sees a blur of metal streak toward her out of the corner of her eye. She jerks back, left hand reaching out to pluck CB's Zippo from the air, only inches from her temple. "Jesus, CB!"

CB stares at her, an unreadable expression on his face. "Good catch."

"What are you trying to do, kill me?"

CB doesn't answer. He's lost in thought, staring at Jenny as if he were seeing her for the first time. The intensity of his gaze makes her shiver involuntarily.

Finally he shrugs. "Sorry. Thought maybe you'd want a smoke. Some people find it helps." He holds up a mostly empty pack of cigarettes.

"I don't smoke," she says, voice thick with distaste.

"First time for everything."

"No. First of all, it's disgusting. Second, we're in a *sealed room*. Last thing I want is to be trapped in a room full of second-hand smoke."

"Just thought I'd offer," CB says. "Can I have it back, then?"

Jenny turns the lighter over once in her hand, then tosses it back to CB. He catches it easily; both lighter and cigarettes go back into one of his trenchcoat pockets.

"Sorry," Jenny says. "I didn't want to do this here."

"It's OK," CB says. "You're going to be OK."

"I don't feel OK," Jenny says.

"Congratulations. You're not a sociopath."

Jenny laughs in spite of herself. "I guess a sociopath wouldn't be having this problem."

"No," CB agrees. "Lucky bastards."

Jenny laughs again.

PART TWO: LAST WEDNESDAY

Martin Forrest shifts in his chair and stares at the young man staring back at him from across the desk. Jason Kline is only a few years older than Jenny—Martin's sure he's a few years shy of thirty—but he has the bearing and confidence of someone decades older.

Warm without appearing invested, professional without appearing detached. It's a hard mask to develop. It's exactly the kind of mask Martin used when he was a cop interviewing a witness. It doesn't bother him that Jason Kline is using it on him—quite the contrary. It's effective, professional, and polite. But it puts Martin on his guard.

"Thank you for coming, Mr. Forrest." Jason speaks with just a hint of a Midwestern accent, almost but not quite swallowed up by years of living in the city.

"I'll answer what I can, Mr. Kline." Martin shifts in his chair again.

They sit in a small meeting room that apparently serves as Jason's office. Jason's laptop, a large, black, impressive-looking device, sits in the middle of the meeting table. Jason sits on one side in a small, uncomfortable plastic chair, and Martin sits on the other in another small, uncomfortable plastic chair. The door behind Martin is open, and he can hear the chatter of people working in a large bullpen—Martin thinks they're called "cube farms" these days.

"I apologize for the surroundings. They're growing pretty fast and didn't know where to put me."

"New hire?" Martin tries to settle back into a comfortable position.

Jason shakes his head. "I'm not actually an employee. Kore Innovations brought my team in as soon as they realized your daughter was missing."

Martin frowns. "No offense, Mr. Kline, but I'm not going to help you interfere with an ongoing police investigation."

Jason raises his eyebrows in surprise. "I don't want you to."

"Then why am I here?"

An expression of confusion clouds his face, then Jason droops forward. The mask falls for a minute, and Martin sees his face crease with exhaustion.

"I'm sorry, Mr. Forrest, I just realized how completely misleading my phone call was." Jason rubs his eyes. "I swear it wasn't on purpose."

"OK," Martin says. "Why don't you just explain everything now?"

Jason hesitates, nods, then asks, "Would you mind shutting the door?"

Martin doesn't mind. He shuts the door; the hubbub of the bullpen quiets to a dull murmur. He returns to his seat and waits patiently.

"Mr. Forrest, your daughter has been working for Kore Innovations for about five months. This Monday she didn't show up at work. Kore Innovations learned that she was missing after surviving an attack on your house by armed soldiers. An attack that involved metahumans."

"I can't tell you any more than what you've heard on the news," Martin says.

"All right," Jason says. "Police investigation. I understand. But let me tell you what it looks like from the perspective of her employer. Jenny has a rather unique set of credentials. Those credentials made it very desirable for her employer to place her in a position where she had access to their most sensitive systems."

"I didn't know that," Martin says.

"That's good," Jason says. "If she told you it would have been a security breach. The point is, Kore Innovations is missing a key employee who had access to a lot of security information. She didn't give notice, she didn't arrange for leave, and they can't reach her by phone or email. At this point they have to assume the worst."

"She's not dead."

Jason looks uncomfortable. "From a security perspective, that's not the worst-case scenario."

Martin stares at Jason blankly. Then he gets it. His jaw sets. "If you're trying to imply—"

"Nothing," Jason says quickly. "I'm saying nothing specific about Jenny. Kore Innovations has a security policy—a policy your daughter helped write, by the way—that states that erratic employee behavior needs to be treated as a potential worst-case scenario."

"Isn't that a little ridiculous?" Martin asks. "Sometimes people have bad days. Bad months. Deaths in the family."

"They do," Jason agrees. "And sometimes they are targeted by mind-controlling telepaths and coerced to steal from people they would never willingly betray."

Martin doesn't reply to that.

"I won't get into the specifics of what Kore Innovations deals in," Jason continues, "but another company in the same field had to deal with that very scenario. It's not the kind of thing that happens every day, but it is out there."

"That didn't happen to Jenny," Martin says.

"What *did* happen to Jenny?"

Martin sighs. "I can't talk about it."

"Can you tell me *anything*?" There is a hint of exasperation in Jason's voice that Martin understands all too well.

"She wasn't kidnapped," Martin says.

"Mr. Forrest, unless you're willing to give me more specific information, I can't take your word on that."

"Why not?" Martin asks, irritated.

"Because you could've been instructed by the police to lie about what actually happened," Jason says. "Maybe the kidnappers warned you not to tell anyone, and the police asked you to play along. Or maybe she's fine, but she's in witness protection because she saw something during that attack that the rest of you didn't. I don't know. What I do know is that Kore Innovations is missing an employee who has access to their equivalent of the *launch codes*."

Martin says nothing.

"Look, Mr. Forrest, no one here—at least, no one that I've talked to— actually *believes* that your daughter is involved in corporate espionage. At least, not willingly. They all think very highly of her. So do I, for that matter. We're colleagues. I've met her at seminars. She's extremely talented, dedicated, and ambitious."

"Then why all this?" Martin asks. "If everyone thinks so highly of her—"

"Because given what we know about her—given the dedication she has shown to her job, that every single one of her co-workers and supervisors have mentioned when I interviewed them, the only way her absence makes *any sense at all* is if she is dead or being held against her will. And you, her father, are telling me that neither of those scenarios is true."

Martin tries to put himself in Jason's shoes. He forces himself to stop looking at it as a father, and to look at it like a cop instead. Jason has a point. If the roles were reversed, Martin would be asking the same questions... and probably pushing a little harder.

"Mr. Forrest, your family has had a very bad week, and I know this isn't making it any easier. I hope that you're right when you say that Jenny's OK. But even if you're right, she's put her career at risk. Why won't she answer her phone? Or her email? If you're telling the truth—and I think you are—then my only conclusion is that Jenny left of her own volition. Could she be suffering from trauma? Post-traumatic stress?"

Martin studies Jason carefully. The young man seems to be studying him just as carefully, searching for any hint of expression that might answer the question for him. Martin can't read anything Jason doesn't already want him to see, and he's pretty sure Jason isn't doing any better.

"The reason I ask," Jason says, "is because there are policies and procedures covering that as well. Jenny is a valued employee, and trauma doesn't invalidate that. If the attack on your home affected her, you need to convince her to get treatment, and to do it in a way that will get it covered by her health plan. That way her employers know what the trouble is, and know it's being managed. They still have to change all the locks, so to speak, but at least they know *why* and they know she's not involved in anything dangerous. Mr. Forrest, that probably saves her job. It definitely saves her professional reputation."

For a second—for a very brief, dangerous second—Martin is tempted to tell Jason what really happened. He steps on that urge immediately. "Thanks for letting me know that. The next time I talk to her I'll let her know."

Jason nods once. "Maybe you could do one more thing." He reaches into his inside jacket pocket and pulls out a business card and a pen. He turns the card over and starts writing on the back. "This is my personal cell and my personal e-mail address. The front has all my official contact information, but... it'd be better if she used these."

Jason holds the card out to Martin. Martin looks at it uncertainly.

"We're not exactly friends," Jason says. "I don't want to give you the impression we are. I know her professionally. We're friendly. I admire the hell out of her work. Consider it a kind of esprit de corps. If you manage to contact her—meet her, call her, anything—let her know that if she contacts me privately we can talk off the record. Try to figure out what we need to do. Give her a few options she might not otherwise have."

Martin looks at the card, mulls it over, then takes it, carefully tucking it into his shirt pocket. "No guarantees."

"Understood," Jason says. "I'll take what I can get. Thanks for coming in."

PART THREE: LAST THURSDAY

The Haruspex Analytics situation room isn't like the boardroom. The boardroom is intended to intimidate; one of its primary functions is to distract people who aren't accustomed to it. The situation room is set up to minimize distractions while accessing information and making decisions. It's a long, narrow room with a long, narrow table sitting at the center. Paneled display screens are set into the walls, and each place at the table has its own computer and monitor, tied into the communications network Haruspex Analytics uses to conduct its various operations, in real time, across the globe. Pizza boxes, soda cans and half-empty mugs of cold coffee are scattered across the table.

Jason sits alone in the room. The only light comes from his monitor and one of the large screens set into the wall. The monitor is flashing a Haruspex Analytics screensaver. The screen is showing a map of the United States, with a line tracing a bus route from southern New Jersey to Jackson, Mississippi.

Missed them in New Jersey.

Missed them in Mississippi.

Jason exhales slowly, eyes closed, as he tries to coax the exhaustion out of his body. They didn't get off at Jackson: obviously they passed their tickets off to two of the other passengers at one of the intermediary stops. They could be halfway across the United States right now, and Jason doesn't even know where to look.

Curveball and Jenny Forrest are officially in the wind.

Jason rubs his eyes and forces himself to his feet. He feels slightly off balance—fatigue makes him clumsy, and he places one hand on the table to steady himself as he stumbles awkwardly out of his chair. He rummages through the pizza boxes until he finds an uneaten slice and grabs an unopened Pepsi from the table, then sinks back into his chair with a grunt.

The pizza is cold. The Pepsi is warm.

It's not the end of the world. The meeting with Martin Forrest went well. He took the business card, which meant Jason has a foot in the door. He'd come up with a few more reasons to have follow-up meetings, strengthen the professional relationship, and in time he might be able to develop Martin as an asset. He'd have to be careful, though: Martin Forrest was an ex-cop. He had plenty of experience dealing with informants.

So it's not the end of the world. There's still a potential in. But developing an asset takes time, and he's not sure how much time they have. He returns his attention to the bus route, and feels his irritation rise. What was Curveball's plan? Did he even have one? He had some contacts on the West Coast—at one point the Guardians of Justice worked closely with the Sentinels of Liberty out of San Francisco—and a few of the original members were still active. Would he try to contact them? Jason has a vague memory of a file suggesting those relationships were strained, but he can't remember where he read it.

A high-pitched beep announces that someone is using an access card to unlock the door. Jason sets what's left of the pizza and soda on the table as two members of his team enter the situation room.

"Told you he'd still be here." Phyllis Tanner is a middle-aged black woman who looks more like a housewife than a security analyst. She smiles at Jason warmly as she sets her purse down in front of her computer.

"Good thing I didn't bet you." Will Davison is a blond, blue-eyed surfer who still gets carded everywhere he goes. He grins good-naturedly as he throws his keys down in front of the computer to Phyllis' left.

"What are you guys doing here?" Jason hadn't expected anyone in for hours.

"Looking for you." Will sits down in his chair. His grin widens. "We found something."

"*Billy* found something," Phyllis corrects. "I just told him where to look."

"Like I would ever have thought of this on my own. Anyway, the point is we *found something*."

Jason feels a faint stirring of hope. Phyllis and Will are an odd pair, but they're one of the most effective teams he's ever worked with. "What did you find?"

"Thought you'd never ask," Phyllis says. She sits in front of her computer and begins to type. Immediately the screen with the map updates to show Curveball's file—not the new one Jason created, but a scan of the old paper file he saw his first day in the boardroom.

"This thing again?" Jason doesn't bother to hide his skepticism. "I thought we all pretty much agreed the file was useless."

"It still is," Phyllis says, "except for this."

She keys in something and the image zooms in until the very top of the page fills the screen. In the upper right-hand corner is a string of numbers followed by the letters "AV."

Jason stares at the string for a moment, then shrugs. "The file number? I don't get it."

"The file number isn't important," Will says. "It's the letters."

Jason frowns. "They aren't part of the file number?"

"No," Phyllis says. "I know that for a fact. In the 80s and early 90s metahuman files were all numbers. Don't ask me why, I don't know why, but that's the way it was. 'AV' stands for 'Abbreviated and Vetted.'"

Jason's frown doesn't budge. "Abbreviated?"

"It's not the whole file, Jason." Will's voice is tight with excitement. "It was one of the terms of his pardon. He was debriefed by the FBI concerning his activities for the two years he was a criminal, and after the debriefing all his official files up to that moment were sealed and a new, 'abbreviated' file was created that excluded most of that information."

Jason's frown changes from *dismissive* to *thoughtful*. "What kind of information?"

"His criminal files," Phyllis says. "Threat assessments, speculations on his powers, known associates, suspected associates, investigations into specific crimes."

One eyebrow inches up. "You have that?"

Phyllis and Will both wear exactly the same self-satisfied grin.

Jason looks from one to the other. "How?"

"When I figured out what 'AV' meant, I started looking into the terms of his pardon," Phyllis says. "When I saw a judge ordered his old files sealed, I knew we could get our hands on the information..."

"...because if a judge orders information sealed," Will continues, "you can put money on someone, somewhere deciding 'hell no,' creating a copy, and hiding it for later use."

"Who had the copy?" Jason asks.

"FBI," Will says. "They were in charge of most of the metahuman stuff in the 80s, before Bush created the FBMA. And there were some players in the FBI who really didn't want the FBMA to happen. Fought hard against it. I figured there was a chance one of them was keeping records. Like Hoover. Turns out it was the head of the New York field office."

"That makes sense," Jason says. "That was his home city."

"And where Liberty flipped him," Will says. "And these files are probably going to be really good intel for us down the road. But that's not the part you want *right now*."

"I'm pretty sure it is," Jason says.

"Listen to Billy, Jason." Phyllis types a few commands into her computer and the map returns to its original view—the bus route from New Jersey to Jackson, Mississippi.

"OK, this is *brilliant*," Will says. He's almost giggling with excitement. "So the files on Curveball as a criminal talk about the crew he ran with. They scattered after he flipped, but there's speculation in the last few files that he tipped them off first, as well as a few reports of him continuing contact with two of them."

"OK," Jason says. "Not sure where this is going, though. The contact obviously wasn't that extensive. Curveball's life was pretty public after he turned hero."

"Until the PRODIGY incident," Will says. "The government started a massive manhunt for him, never found him. Not until the Guardians had taken out the Yuba City cloning facility, but he wasn't hiding then."

"After that," Phyllis adds, "he retired, and disappeared again. Not even the people who cut his check knew how to find him."

"Yeah," Jason says. "I already went down that rabbit hole."

"He's in Farraday City," Phyllis says.

Jason frowns. "We *checked* Farraday City."

"We need to check again. He's *there*, Jason."

"Phyllis, you know I trust you and Billy, but—"

Phyllis rolls right over his objections without batting an eye. "The files Billy found had chatter about Curveball staying in touch with his old crew. There are only two who are called out specifically. One of them, Remote, was linked with him romantically. The last time there was a report of contact between Curveball and Remote, she was in Farraday City. CB disappeared two days later."

Jason stares at the screen, hard. "Not definitive."

"We got more," Will says. "The day Liberty was *retired*, there was a metahuman incident in a town called Silverlane. An armored villain calling himself 'Doctor AEvil' tried to rob a bank there. He and his crew were overpowered by the bank patrons after the entire lobby sprinkler system activated, short-circuiting the good Doctor's armor."

Jason stares at Will levelly. "Doctor *AEvil*?"

"I didn't name him," Will says. "But here's the thing: Silverlane is only three hours out from Farraday City by bus. And immediately after the incident, someone cashed a US Government Abstention of Service check."

Jason returns his attention to the big screen. Phyllis types into her computer, and the route expands until it shows all the official stops, then zooms in on Farraday City. A line travels west from the city to a small dot representing the town of Silverlane. "Interesting."

"We did a little checking," Phyllis adds. "Some social engineering. We were able to confirm that someone has been cashing the same check at that bank every month for the last six years."

"Did you get a description?" Jason asks.

"Sort of," Phyllis says. "The woman I talked to said the guy looked like he was in a rock band."

Jason studies the screen a little longer.

"OK, I buy it," he says. "Curveball was in Farraday City before he came up to New York."

"For at least *six years*," Will adds. "And maybe ten, if we use his reported contact with Remote as a starting point. Six to ten years to develop resources in the city..."

"...all the time keeping a low profile so that nobody knows he's developing those resources..." Phyllis adds.

"And he chooses a bus route that stops there, and he's *mysteriously absent* at his ticket's destination."

Jason nods slowly. "He's in Farraday City."

"He's in Farraday City," Phyllis says.

Phyllis and Will beam at him.

"Good work." Jason speaks briskly, all business, but he's grinning on the inside. "I need to contact Mara. The Board wants him taken care of immediately."

"Do we need to bring in the rest of the team?" Will looks a little uncomfortable. "I was hoping to get some sleep."

"Go home," Jason says. "Sleep. Don't come in till noon, and don't worry about dealing with Curveball—that's not our job. The Board has someone specific in mind for him."

PART FOUR: LAST FRIDAY

It's 6 AM and Doyle is getting ready for work.

He stands in front of the bathroom sink, wearing a pair of brown slacks and a white t-shirt, meticulously shaving. He can hear his wife Clara in the kitchen, making breakfast, his son Doyle Junior in a playpen in the living room, and the TV, turned down low, buzzing with some morning show nonsense in the background.

Doyle finishes shaving, washes his face, then steps out into the hall, making his way to the kitchen. Clara's making pancakes.

"Five more minutes." She looks over her shoulder and smiles. He can't help but smile back.

He wanders into the living room and peers into the playpen to check on his son. He's chewing on a rubber teething ring, playing with his feet.

Doyle's dress shirt is draped over the back of his easy chair. He pulls it on quickly, buttoning it absentmindedly as he loses himself in the shallow banter of the morning TV hosts.

"It's ready!"

Doyle hears the clink of plates setting down on the table. Pancakes, toast, orange juice, coffee. Perfect. Clara is already sitting at her spot, and he stops at her chair, bends over, and kisses her on the cheek before he sits down at his.

"We going out with Bill and Emma tonight?" Clara wipes her mouth with her napkin as she asks the question. "I'll need to get a sitter if we are."

Doyle sighs. "Yeah. I guess we can't get out of it."

"I thought you liked Bill and Emma," Clara says.

"I do. But it'd be nice to spend a quiet night at home. Sitting on the couch, watching TV, changing diapers until Junior falls asleep."

Clara smiles. "You're a softy."

"Guess so."

They eat in comfortable silence, listening to Junior play, listening to the television, but mostly wallowing in the earliness of the morning, letting their coffee gradually lead them out into the day. When he finishes his breakfast, Doyle gathers up the dishes, rinses them off in the sink, and starts putting them in the dishwasher.

"Who are you planning to call to watch Junior?"

Clara gets up from the table and goes over to Doyle Junior's playpen, picks him up, and checks his diaper. "I thought maybe I'd call Emily."

Doyle makes a face. "I don't like her. She keeps inviting that boy over."

"That boy is her boyfriend, and he's great with the baby. He even changes him."

"How can you tell?"

"Well, he does it wrong. But it's sweet that he tries."

Doyle shakes his head and mutters to himself as he loads in the detergent and turns the dishwasher on.

"You'd better get your jacket," Clara warns. "You don't want to be late for work."

Doyle looks up at the time, grimaces, and heads to the bathroom to brush his teeth. He does so quickly, rinses, then stops at the hallway closet. His jacket and tie hang on inside hooks. Clara doesn't like that—she says it wrinkles the fabric—but it's convenient. He fumbles with his tie for a minute, then Clara puts Junior back in the playpen and comes over to straighten it for him.

"Thanks," Doyle says, smiling slightly.

Clara *tsks* good-naturedly, then kisses him.

"I'll be home a little late," Doyle says. "That meeting. So I guess we'll have to leave as soon as I get home."

"OK," Clara says, then goes back to the living room.

Doyle puts on his jacket, smooths out the lapel, and adjusts the cuffs before heading out. He's almost at the front door when he hears the kitchen phone ring.

"I'll get it," Doyle says. "That might be Bill."

"You'll be late," Clara warns.

"It'll be OK," Doyle says. "It'll only be a minute."

He walks into the kitchen and picks up the phone. He and Clara are the only couple he knows who still have a land-line phone in the house. "Hello?"

"Project Recall." The voice on the other side of the phone is male, even-toned, and slightly distorted by the cheap earpiece.

Doyle feels his throat catch. He puts his arm out on the kitchen counter to steady himself. "I'm listening."

"You're being reactivated."

Doyle closes his eyes, and forces himself to take a deep, slow breath.

"When?"

"Immediately."

Doyle forces himself to keep his voice steady. "All right."

"Standard protocols."

"Yeah." Doyle clenches his left fist until his knuckles turn white. "Understood."

The phone clicks as the voice on the other end disconnects. A few seconds later Doyle hears the dial tone. He stands there for a moment, listening to the dial tone, trying desperately not to think. Then he places the phone down.

"What did Bob want?" Clara's sitting on the couch, watching a little TV before she begins her day.

Doyle doesn't answer. He walks over to the playpen and looks down at his son. Doyle Junior has abandoned the teething ring, but he's still playing with his feet.

"Hey there, little guy." Doyle reaches down to pick up his son.

Clara looks over at Doyle and frowns. "What's wrong?"

Doyle rocks his son in his arms, looking at his face, then kisses him gently on the forehead.

"Is Bob all right?"

"It wasn't Bob." Doyle's voice is husky with emotion. He puts his son back in his playpen, then sinks onto the couch heavily, cradling his head in his hands.

"Doyle?" Clara touches his arm, worry plain in her voice. "Honey, what's wrong?"

Doyle clasps her hand tight, presses his face against it. Tears stream down his face, wetting her hand.

Clara looks at him in bewilderment. "Honey, you're scaring me."

"I'm sorry." Doyle takes a breath. He lets go of her hand. "I'm sorry. It's... I just... I'm sorry." He kisses her forehead, gently, the same way he kissed his son.

"Seriously, I'm scared." Clara's voice is tight, her body is rigid. "I've never seen you like this before. What is it? Is it your family?"

"It's a long story," Doyle says. "Long story."

They sit there quietly on the couch for a minute, holding hands. Doyle stares at the TV—not really watching it, just staring.

"I have a past. You know that. I told you there were things in my life I wasn't proud of. You never asked, never pressed. God, I was so grateful for that. The phone... that was my past calling."

Doyle reaches over for the TV remote and turns off the TV. Without the background noise, even as low as it was, the room suddenly feels too quiet.

"When I was... hell, I was a kid, really. I thought I knew everything. Thought I had all the answers. I had a vision of How The World Should Be, and I thought I had the power to make it that way. Having a cause when you're young... that's better than any drug ever invented. Having a purpose. A *crusade*."

He sighs. "It wasn't really my crusade, though. I thought it was at the time. I thought I was a leader, at the vanguard of a wave of change. But all I was doing was repeating words someone else put in my head. I was a stupid little *shit*."

The last word comes out hard, harsh, unforgiving. Doyle's mouth curls in contempt as he remembers his younger self.

"I fought what I thought was the good fight, but it wasn't. I was a chump. A puppet. I fought, and I lost, and I deserved it. And while I was sitting in the ruins, looking at the broken trash heap of my life, sitting in the spoiled carcass of everything I ever thought was true and wasn't, men came to me. They picked me up, dusted me off, and gave me a new purpose. They showed me a new vision of How The World Should Be, and offered me more power to make it that way. And God, I signed on. I signed on so fast..."

He lets go of Clara's hand. He slumps forward on the couch, head bowed, hands clasped as though in prayer.

"I was still a stupid little shit. I *knew*, though. The first time, I guess I can sort of explain it away. I was young and eager and trusting and carried away by words and visions and emotion. I wasn't brainwashed the first time, but I was definitely carried away. But the second time I was bitter and angry and looking for a cause, and I signed on with eyes open, knowing where it would lead. And I was all in. I did everything they asked, I didn't ask questions, I did *everything*."

He laughs bitterly. "And then one day they just stopped calling. Nothing. Months passed. Then years. Years passed, and I never heard a word, and after a while I thought 'hey, maybe they're done with me.' So I tried to move on, you know? I got a job, I made friends. I met you. Suddenly I had this *life*. I *love* this life. You showed me what I could have been, Clara. What I should have been. You and Junior."

His voice hardens. "I'm *still* a stupid little shit."

The room is silent. Doyle can hear traffic outside, the sound of people on the street—this house always had thin walls.

"I thought I could have this. I wanted it, and I lied to myself and told me they'd let me keep it. But when you make a deal with the devil and you've already sold your soul, what do you have left to trade?"

He clenches and unclenches his fists, over and over and over again.

"Your service, is what. Eternal, unending service. Whenever they call. Whatever they say. Wherever the road might lead. I knew that when I signed on. I accepted that."

His voice breaks then, a half-sob, cut short by an effort of will. "*You* didn't though. You didn't know anything about this. I was so goddamn selfish, and I'm sorry, Clara. I really am."

He looks at her, finally. Reluctantly. She's slumped against the arm of the couch, head lolled over to one side, eyes wide open, staring straight ahead. She hasn't been able to move for minutes, now. All she can do is stare straight ahead, unblinking, locked in her own body, drowning in her own fear.

"It's kinda like Lou Gehrig's disease," Doyle says. His voice is gentle. It's the voice he uses when he's putting Junior to bed. "The brain can't make the body do anything any more, so it just sits there, trapped. Only with Lou Gehrig's disease you can still feel everything, right up to the end. I wouldn't do that to you. You're completely numb to everything now. Eventually you'll shut down, and I swear you won't feel it."

He looks away. "Junior didn't suffer. It hits infants really fast. All he did was go to sleep..."

He chokes up again. It takes him a few seconds to recover this time. "It's the best I have, Clara. I'm sorry. Most of the fast ones hurt like hell, and I couldn't do that to you. I know this isn't much better, but it's the best I can do..."

He stares at the ground, unwilling to look at her again. "It'll be over soon. It'll be over soon."

He closes his eyes, listening. Finally he can hear it—a shallow, rasping breath, inhaling, exhaling, inhaling, exhaling... each breath gets shorter, and shallower, until finally it's a series of soft gasps.

And then, finally, silence.

Plague opens his eyes, stands, and smooths out the wrinkles in his jacket.

"I'm late for work."

PART ONE: NEW YORK CITY, SOUTH BRONX

David Bernard stands in line at the corner grocery, awkwardly holding the handle of a plastic basket as it bangs arrhythmically against his legs. The air conditioning is out, and bags of ice line the meat and produce isles, adding to the already considerable humidity. It's uncomfortably warm and damp. David tries to suppress his agitation as he waits his turn.

"And they say they can't fix it until tomorrow..." Nirmala is a small, animated Indian woman with long, glossy hair that falls down to her back. She's owned the grocery for as long as David can remember. "Thank goodness we have plenty of ice! But it's very inconvenient."

The man at checkout makes a noncommittal, vaguely sympathetic noise in the back of his throat as he pays in cash. Nirmala puts his groceries in a paper sack, hands him his change and his receipt, and smiles at him as he leaves. David shuffles up to the counter and unloads his basket.

"David." He likes the way Nirmala pronounces his name. *Dahveed.* It sounds exotic when she says it. "You do not look well. And this food! What are you doing to yourself?"

David smiles sheepishly. He does look a mess: his first few days of retirement were spent sleeping, watching television, and not paying much attention to hygiene. This is the first time he's been outside since he left the Sky Commando unit, and he's not buying anything healthy: beer, potato chips, more potato chips, and... he looks through the contents of his bag and snorts. It consists entirely of potato chips and beer.

"I'm letting myself go this week," David says. "Saturday I get back on the wagon."

Nirmala raises an eyebrow. "Did you lose your job? I see a lot of people do this when they lose their job. They don't usually 'get back on the wagon' by Saturday."

David chuckles. "I didn't exactly lose it. I retired."

"You are too young to retire," Nirmala says, laughing, but her expression falters when she sees the look of regret—quickly masked—that flashes over David's face.

"I got hurt on the job," he says.

"Are you all right?" Nirmala asks. "What happened?"

"I'll be fine." David tries to ignore the trembling in his right hand as he reaches for his wallet. "I got punched through a wall."

Nirmala isn't sure if David is joking. She smiles, nods, and starts to ring him up.

David stares out the grocery window into the street as Nirmala scans each of his items, and tries not to think about the walk back. The beer is technically heavier than the doctor wants him to carry, and he feels a little guilty that he went to the grocery store just to buy a lot of crap. That said, the doctor also doesn't want him to drive, and he figures he's earned a few days of self-pity supplemented with artificially flavored food.

Nirmala tells him the total, which he only half hears. He hands her a credit card and she runs it through. He can hear the modem start to dial, and is amused to find himself thinking of her setup as "old fashioned."

That's when he notices the van drive by the display window—again—and realizes why it's bothering him so much.

It's a black van with black-tinted windows. The tint is much, much darker than the state of New York allows—so dark that David can't even see the driver's silhouette—but that alone isn't enough to make him suspicious. Lots of people tint their windows, and a significant percentage do so beyond what the law allows. This annoys him because it's unsafe, but it's not something he considers criminal activity.

However, this van is tinted *and* circling the block, and now that he thinks about it, it's been doing this at least since he first showed up at the grocery store, and suddenly the agitation he's been feeling in line has nothing to do with the wait, the heat, or the humidity—his instincts are telling him *something is wrong* and he's been trying to ignore it.

He steps away from the counter and walks over to the display window, a large pane of glass that takes up a full third of the wall. The van rolls by again, slowing down as it rolls past the grocery, then speeding up as it passes the grocery and its tiny parking lot, and turns at the end of the block to loop around again.

He reaches for his cell phone, realizes he left it at home, and sighs.

Take it easy. It's probably nothing. Don't be the crazy retired ex-cop, OK? At least give it a few months.

"David!"

David turns to see Nirmala holding his credit card out to him.

"It's finished. I need you to sign the receipt."

David flushes. "Sorry." He takes his card back and hastily signs his name on the paper, making a mess of his last name. Too many loops in

Bernard. He gathers up his groceries—two bags, one in each hand—and is just about to walk out the door when he sees the van roll around again. He puts them back down on the counter and heads back to the window.

"David?"

This time the van turns in to the parking lot, and out of his view.

"Is something wrong?"

David turns back to Nirmala. She looks confused; the other people waiting in line look impatient. He points to the end of the grocery facing the parking lot. "Do you have any windows on that side of the store?"

Nirmala looks at him blankly. The customers shift uneasily.

David points again. "That wall. Any windows? Nirmala, it's *important*."

Nirmala blinks once, then nods. "In my office."

"I need to use your office," David says. "Call the police."

He heads to the other side of the store, his bags still sitting on the counter.

"The phone is in my office," Nirmala calls out after him.

Her office is small, and made to look smaller by the presence of an oversized desk set in the middle of the room. A computer, a phone, and a combination printer/copier fax machine sit on the desk, along with a number of binders filled with schedules, shipments, and balance sheets. Cheap tan blinds cover the window on the far wall.

David squeezes around the desk and peers through the blinds. The van is parked at the far side of the lot, next to an old garage that has apparently been converted into an office building.

He has a very bad feeling about this.

David reaches for the phone, tearing his gaze from the window just long enough to dial *9-1-1*. The phone dials once.

"911 Emergency Services, what's the nature of your emergency?" A woman's voice, professional but a little bored.

"My name is David Bernard. I'm at Local Fresh Grocery in South Yonkers..." He rattles off the address. "I think there's a two one seven in progress in the building across the parking lot."

"A... did you say 'two one seven?'" The woman sounds a little surprised. "Are you sure?"

No, you're not sure, David. It's just a van. Don't be an idiot.

"As sure as I can be from here," David lies.

"All right, David, I'm contacting the police. Can you give me any more information?"

David quickly describes the van.

"Do you have a license plate number?"

"I can't see it. I'm calling from the office in the grocery store, and all I can see is a profile."

At that moment the van's passenger-side door and sliding door open. Three armed men, dressed in black commando uniforms and *combat body armor* get out of the van and head for the office.

David notices the weapons they're carrying. His chest tightens.

"Scratch that," he says. "This isn't a two one seven. This is a code ultraviolet. Make sure you tell the police that: give them my name and say 'code ultraviolet.' Got that?"

There's a moment's hesitation. "David, I'll relay that information to the police. Now I'm going to need you to stay on the line—"

"—no time," David says. "Tell them to hurry!"

He drops the receiver and runs out of the office.

Next to the office is a small loading area where delivery trucks drop off fresh inventory. He grabs a long crowbar leaning against one of the walls and hurries toward the door. He steps out into the parking lot and sees the van, all doors closed once more, idling quietly.

This is stupid, David. They're obviously well trained. You have a concussion.

He has to deal with the van first. Sight lines are terrible—there's no way to stay hidden. He's going to have to use the direct approach, which is probably not going to work.

Too bad I don't have a two-ton battlesuit to wear right now.

His vision blurs for a moment—his rehab doctor told him adrenaline would make the effects of the concussion worse—and he curses under his breath as he places a hand on the grocery wall for balance.

I am going to get myself killed...

No point in trying for stealth. He needs to run. He hoists his crowbar, grits his teeth, and runs as fast as he can, for the first time in months, trying to cover the ground between the grocery and the black van faster than the driver can notice and react. He's a quarter of the way to the van when he hears a low *boom*, feels the ground shudder, and the van *disappears* under a mass of instantly-solidifying foam.

Sky Commando is here.

David recognizes the stuckey as soon as it hits: capsules of some kind of high-tech goo designed to solidify, then capture and distribute force. They're useful restraints, and if you deploy a large one correctly it can even immobilize a getaway car without hurting the passengers. The stuckey slams into the parking lot right next to the driver-side door, liquefying on impact, expanding rapidly as the liquid-form stuckey reacts to air, then hardens again into a thick, solid mass. It lifts the van up on the driver's side, raising the entire van off the ground three feet and tilting it slightly back and sharply to the right. By the time the shell hardens, only the back of the van is exposed.

David stops running and looks up: Sky Commando streaks down from the sky, propulsion systems keening as the sun glints off the sleek blue armor. Not twenty feet from the ground it reverses itself, engines flaring to slow its descent sharply enough to land on the parking lot in a combat-ready crouch.

Webb stuck the hell out of that landing.

"Three more inside," David calls out. He jogs closer.

Sky Commando nods once. A loud series of clicks travel down the length of the armor, then segments pop out and slide away. Webb steps out in her tactical suit—a miniature version of the outer shell, less rugged but better suited for going indoors—and turns to face David.

"Aren't you retired?" The Sky Commando helmet does a lot of voice modulation, but David can hear her amusement and exasperation.

"Three men inside, all armed with military-grade weapons," David says, trying to ignore how stupid he feels standing there holding a crowbar. "Webb—it's the same guys who attacked the Forrest house."

Webb swivels her head to look at—or, more likely, *through*—the building. "Stay here. Backup should be here soon."

David nods. Webb runs into the building. Almost immediately he hears automatic weapons fire, and he hastily moves behind the newly-cocooned van for cover.

Automatic weapons continue to fire sporadically, from different locations. He doubts it'll have any effect. The tactical armor doesn't have the level of protection the full suit does, but it's still hefty enough to repel small arms fire. When he hears the grenade going off he frowns. The tactical armor doesn't do as well with those.

She's got a better shot at walking away from this than you do. If you go in you'll only distract her.

He's a civilian now. He has to let her do her job.

The van *thumps* as someone—the trapped driver, David supposes—kicks the back door. The frame of the van is a little distorted from the stuckey shell, and while the back door is exposed, some of the shell has hardened over the edge, keeping the back door shut. It shudders, snaps, and suddenly the door pops open, swings out three inches, then wedges deeper into the shell.

David ducks around the corner of the van, keeping clear of the door's arc, and lifts his crowbar.

Metal groans as whoever is inside pushes the door out, inch by inch. Finally something snaps, and the door opens wide. David calmly steps around the van and swings the crowbar, as hard as he can, into a very surprised black-clad soldier.

The soldier reflexively brings up his arm to block the blow. It's a natural but unfortunate response: the crowbar shatters his elbow then smashes into the combat armor, knocking him back into the van. David grabs the soldier by an ankle and drags him out. The soldier shouts in alarm as he tries to grab hold of something... the alarm turns to pain as his shattered arm jostles against the doorframe. A few more tugs and the solder falls three feet to the asphalt below, and lands on his bad arm one more time. He passes out from the pain.

David takes a minute to catch his breath, then removes the soldier's ski mask and checks his pulse. He's an older, bearded man with graying blond hair. His pulse is fine.

David goes through the soldier's pockets. He doesn't find any ID—not that he expected to—but what he does find is almost as interesting: a small, black plastic box with an antenna and a single red blinking light.

Yep. That's probably for a bomb.

The soldier has a short-range handheld two-way radio clipped to his belt. David takes it and fiddles with the controls until he finds one of the frequencies he knows the Sky Commando helmet can receive. "Webb, this is David. Alishia, can you hear me? This is *important*."

A few seconds later, David hears Webb's *very exasperated* voice, quite clearly, coming out of the radio. "David, how the hell are you talking to me on this line? I'm a little busy right now."

As if to underscore her words, more automatic fire erupts from the building.

"You're about to be a lot busier," David says. "The guy in the van tried to make a break for it. He had a transmitter. I think it's for a bomb. Whoever's left in the building isn't trying to win this fight. They're just running down the clock."

Webb doesn't reply right away. David can imagine what she's saying to herself right now—she's very creative when it comes to swearing. When she finally replies, her voice is very calm.

"How long, David?"

"I don't know. There's no countdown or anything. Just a red blinking light."

"How do you know what it is, then?"

"It's a red blinking light on an unmarked black box," David says. "Taken in context, there are only a few options. You want to assume it's one of the others?"

"No," she says. "We need to get everyone away. Can you evacuate that grocery? Get them across the street, as far away as you can take them. I'll try to cut the red wire. After I find the red wire..."

"OK," David says. "Good luck." He shoves the transmitter and the radio into his pockets and heads toward the grocery.

He sees the soldier's shadow, thin and distorted on the pavement, holding the crowbar one-handed over its head. The shadow twists, the arm comes down, and David ducks and spins. The crowbar passes over his head, missing by inches. The soldier wobbles in front of him, hunched over from the pain in his ribs, left arm dangling uselessly at his side as he grips the long crowbar with his right. He has to be in excruciating pain—he has to be—but it doesn't show on his face. All David sees is a tightness around the eyes and a clenched jaw. It could just as easily be resolve: the resolve to do unto David what had just been done unto him. Revenge is a strong motivator.

David steps back, tensing, waiting for the soldier to make his play. The soldier steps forward, and when he does David falls to the ground, cushioning the impact with his hands as his legs lash out to hit the man squarely on his extended knee. It doesn't break, but it does buckle. The soldier snarls in surprise and frustration, then collapses onto his side—right on his broken arm, again. His snarl turns into a howl of pain.

David winces in sympathy, but that doesn't keep him from scrambling to his feet and kicking the soldier in the face as he tries to stand. The soldier falls to the ground again, but doesn't stay there. He's still trying to get to his feet.

"Just stay on the ground!" David shouts, and aims another kick at the soldier's face. This time the soldier grabs David's ankle with his good arm, pulls sharply, and David tumbles over. He manages to cover his head, hitting with the side of his arms first, but the jolt still hurts. Searing white light saturates his vision, and suddenly everything feels detached, as if it's all happening at the other end of a very long room.

He tries to sit up, but his arms and legs aren't working right. His vision clears just long enough to see the bottom of the soldier's boot come down hard on his face.

PART TWO: BRONX-LEBANON HOSPITAL

David wakes up because someone keeps shining a light in his eyes. He doesn't like it. He turns his head, mumbling a protest, and sluggishly raises one arm to push the light away. Immediately he feels a sharp pain in his side. He drops his arm and sucks in air through his teeth.

He hears laughter—a low, soft, chuckle—then a woman says, "Well. That's a good sign."

He's in a hospital. He knows he's in a hospital because the sheets on his bed feel too thin and the walls are salmon pink. He closes his eyes for a second, opens them again, and the blur clears up enough for him to see that he's in a private recovery room. A doctor leans over him, her mouth turned up slightly in an amused smile, as she tucks a light pen into a shirt pocket. "Good afternoon, Lieutenant."

David shakes his head. "Retired." His voice is hoarse. He coughs lightly and clears his throat.

The doctor raises an eyebrow. "You're a little young for retirement, aren't you?"

David shrugs. "Yeah."

She stares at him for a moment, shrugs, then goes to the foot of his bed to write something on his chart. "Well, you fooled me. You had quite an escort when they brought you in. Even Sky Commando! Did you know Sky Commando was a woman? I always thought it was a man in that suit..."

David smiles slightly. "Where am I?"

"Bronx-Lebanon. You kept us pretty busy when they brought you in."

David feels a mild surge of panic. "How bad was it? I was already injured..."

"With a concussion, I saw your history. When you came in there was some brain swelling, and we were concerned about that. We put you in a medically-induced coma for twenty-four hours—that helped quite a bit. I'm not a specialist, so I can't say anything definitive, but so far we haven't noticed any signs of permanent brain damage."

David sighs in relief. He feels a twinge of pain shoot down his right side.

The doctor notices him wince and nods. "Unfortunately, you'll have some other issues to deal with that will make your regular rehabilitation even more frustrating. The man who attacked you fractured several of your ribs. None of them are actually broken, but it won't feel nice. With that, and the severity of your concussion, you might want to consider getting a caretaker for a while."

She sees his expression and nods sympathetically. "It's not something you need to think about right now. Right now you should try to get a little more rest."

"What day is today?" David asks.

"Saturday."

David frowns. "You said I was in a coma for twenty-four hours. I went to the grocery on Thursday..."

The doctor smiles. "You were in a coma for a day. Then you slept on your own for a day. You should sleep a little more, OK? I'll have a nurse check up on you in a few hours, adjust your bed to let you sit up if you want to. But sleep first."

David sighs and nods, closing his eyes. By the time the doctor leaves he's fallen back to sleep.

He wakes up a few hours later as the nurse enters the room to check on him. He asks her to raise the bed, and she cranks it up a little—not as much as he wants, but it's better than nothing. He asks if he can watch TV, and the nurse says the doctor won't allow it until the neurologist has seen him. David tries his best not to show his frustration.

A few minutes after the nurse leaves, Alishia Webb walks into the room. She tries not to grin when she sees the look on his face.

"Someone just told you not to do something," she says.

"Officer Webb." David smiles, relieved to see someone he knows. "Nice to see you in one piece. I guess you cut the red wire."

"I cut five," she says. She drags a seat over to the side of the bed and sits down next to him. "And it's Sergeant, now. They promoted me right after you left."

"Sergeant Webb!" David grins at that. "Congratulations. It was a long time coming."

Webb shifts uncomfortably, and tries to play it off. "The bump in pay is nice. How are you feeling?"

"Like I was kicked in the face and ribs," David says. "A lot."

"Speaking of that," Webb says, "the Captain wants me to remind you that you're supposed to be retired."

"Yeah," David says. "I was hoping I'd last at least a month before something like this went down."

"The good news is that I won the pool," Webb says. "The techs owe me a lot of money."

They lapse into silence. The silence gets awkward.

"That building," David says. "Was anyone inside?"

Webb nods.

"Did they—" He trails off when he sees the expression on her face. "Damn."

"Only one victim," she says. "I suppose that's something. If those bombs had gone off there would have been a lot more."

David raises an eyebrow. "What kind of bombs were they?"

"Overkill," Webb says. "The kind that would have left a very big hole in the ground. Definitely ultraviolet-class stuff. That was a good call on your part."

"What were they doing?" David asks. "Was it a suicide run?"

Webb shakes her head. "I don't think so. I think they were planning to motor as soon as they set everything up. But they were expendable. You were right—they weren't trying to take me out, they were trying to distract me until the bombs went off. They wanted that building wiped off the planet."

"Do you know why?"

Webb shifts her weight uncomfortably.

David nods. "I'm a civilian, it's an ongoing investigation. I get it."

Webb sighs. "It's more complicated than that. You said they were the same soldiers who attacked the Forrest house. How did you know that?"

"I recognized the guns," David says.

"But how did you *know*?" Webb asks. She looks tense and worried.

David looks at her blankly. "I read the crime scene reports. Saw the photos. You know—I looked it up."

"Civilians can't access any of that information," Webb says. "David, if you're pulling strings to look into this, you could get in a lot of—"

"I wasn't a civilian," David says. "Webb. It was the first thing I heard about my last day there. I walk in and Benny asks me if I know anything about it. So after I make the rounds and fill out all my paperwork, I have six hours to kill before the shift is over. What do I do? I get on my computer and look up the Forrest case."

"That was restricted information," Webb says.

"I was still technically Sky Commando at the time," David points out. "I had enough access."

"Well ever since we carted you in here a guy from Internal Affairs has been asking questions. He doesn't believe you could have come by that information honestly."

"Then he didn't read my exit interview," David says. "They asked me what I did and I told them I looked at the case. Nobody said it was a problem then. The Captain was there. Ask her."

Webb looks relieved. "Sorry. The Forrest investigation is getting weird. Sky Commando unit isn't involved. At all. We were specifically told to stay out."

David frowns. "Really?"

"Yeah. It got kicked over to the Feds. Not even the FBMA—I know some of those guys, and they're complaining about being locked out too. It's some part of the DHS I never heard of before. So now all of a sudden we're in it again and whoever is running the investigation is *pissed*. They're trying to find a way to kick us back out, and I think they're trying to go after you."

"What?" David shakes his head. "Why me?"

"I told you Internal Affairs is asking questions. It's not just how you got the information. They're asking how you're adjusting to the outside world. If we think you can handle retirement after being in the program for so long. If there's a chance the concussion has impaired your judgment, and made you a danger to the general public."

"A danger to the general public?" David can't keep the incredulity out of his voice.

"They're not my questions," Webb says, slightly defensively. "I just thought you should know."

David sighs, exasperated. Then he starts to laugh. "I have to admit, Thursday didn't go too well."

Webb laughs as well.

Someone clears their throat. Standing in the doorway is a uniformed police officer.

"Sorry to interrupt, Sergeant. It's almost one o'clock."

Webb sighs. "Thanks. I'll be right out."

The uniformed officer nods, then steps out of the room.

"Gotta go," Webb says. "Briefing for something about something."

"Yeah," David says. "Thanks for stopping by."

"Thanks for pulling through," Webb says, smiling slightly. "Take care of yourself, OK? Try to enjoy the quiet life for a while. I know it's not your style, but you earned it, and it'd be good for you."

David tilts his head to one side and looks at her thoughtfully. "What do you mean by that?"

Webb hesitates. "It's like I said. Things are getting weird. And you're more exposed now that you're not in the suit."

"I noticed," David says. "My ribs want to thank you for stating the obvious."

"Not just that way," Webb says. She looks out the door and frowns. "I mean politically. You're a civilian now. That makes you exposed. Be careful."

She leaves the room before David can think of anything to say. He sinks back into his pillow and stares at the ceiling. "That was weird."

"She's just worried about you," a familiar voice says. A slightly overweight, balding man in a cheap brown suit stands in the doorway, smiling pleasantly at him. A rolled-up newspaper is tucked under his arm.

"Pete Travers," David says. "Didn't expect to see you." He waves him in.

Travers takes two steps into the room and leans against the wall, looking relaxed and unconcerned. "I heard about your post-retirement adventure and wanted to stop by. Make sure you were OK. So you seem to be having a difficult adjustment period."

David snorts. "I hear a lot of people are concerned about that."

David likes Travers. More than that, David *trusts* Travers. They've worked together a lot in the last few years—Sky Commando is part of the NYPD, but the program was frequently involved in the kind of stuff that turned into "multi-jurisdiction operations." They'd have to coordinate with the FBI, the ATF, the Federal Bureau for Metahuman Affairs... and Pete Travers, as the New York coordinator for the Department of Homeland Security, would be the one who had to make sure everything went smoothly. He was fantastic at his job.

Travers shrugs. "It's not an unreasonable concern. When you're in a high-stakes, adrenaline-heavy job—and your job definitely qualified—it's hard to go into the quiet life. Even when you enter it with the best intentions. It makes some people go crazy."

"It's only been a week," David says. "It doesn't make people go *that* crazy."

"It can, for some," Travers says. "But we both know that's not you. That said, I know you better than some of the others asking the same questions..."

Something in his voice catches David's attention. Travers' demeanor hasn't changed—calm, genial, pleasant—but his eyes are sharp and hard. Unhappy. David is immediately reminded of a hostage situation he had to deal with a year and a half ago, when one of the hostages had been ordered to tell the police that everything was fine, nothing was wrong, it was all a big misunderstanding. His daughter's life was on the line, and he put everything he had into making it look like nothing was wrong. It was a good performance, very convincing. But the whole time he was talking to Sky Commando he was trying to tell him something else.

Travers takes the newspaper out from under his arm and puts it on David's chest. "I know what it's like to have a concussion. Ten years ago, due to an *unfortunate misunderstanding*, Curveball broke my jaw. As it turns out, he also gave me a concussion. Not as bad as I hear yours is, but I still had to go through recovery. One of the things I always hated was that they wouldn't let me watch TV, and they limited the amount of time I had to read. I got very picky about what I read because of that. I wanted to make sure it was good. I think you'll like this."

David unrolls the newspaper. It's called *The Weekly 832*. The text is too small to read—it swims in front of him, going in and out of focus so rapidly it makes him dizzy. As he unfolds the paper, a USB thumb drive spills out and lands on his left shoulder. David picks it up and looks at it curiously. He glances at Travers, who shakes his head and puts one finger up to his lips. *Don't ask.*

David nods thoughtfully and closes his hand around the drive. It disappears from sight.

"I really missed watching TV," Travers sighs. "Did you know that the only way I ever see a movie these days is if I catch it on TV? Network TV, that is. I don't have cable."

David stares at Travers in surprise. "At *all*?"

"Don't like it," Travers says. "Anyway, a few nights ago I saw a movie I'd never heard of before. It was released in the 90s and I didn't even know it existed until this week. That's how bad I am at seeing movies. Big-name cast, too. Mel Gibson, Julia Roberts, Patrick Stewart."

"I remember when that came out," David says. "I was in high school."

Travers shakes his head. "I didn't need to hear that. Anyway, fascinating movie. Parts of it bother me, though. The bit where he has a newsletter that's full of crazy conspiracy theories, but there's one article that's actually true so they try to kill him for it—why didn't they just kill him outright? The only way it makes sense is if they never knew he existed in the first place, only found out about him just before it was too late, and they had to act fast."

Travers points at the newspaper. David raises an eyebrow.

"It's an amusing piece of fiction, I guess. I prefer the one where the lawyer learns that the government is tracking everything he does, all the time." Travers casually looks around the room, then glances at him meaningfully.

"Right..." David keeps staring at the paper. Occasionally the text comes into focus long enough for him to catch a few phrases. What he reads doesn't impress him—it's standard nutjob conspiracy stuff. "I remember that one, too. Will Smith, Gene Hackman. The NSA essentially bugs his house, his work, even him. I don't remember why. Something about a corrupt politician?"

"Something like that," Travers says, nodding affably. "Funny that both those movies were made during the Clinton administration."

"Yeah," David says. He rubs his eyes, pushing back the pain in his ribs as he moves his right arm, and tries to get the words to stay in focus. "Well, thanks for the reading material."

"Sure," Travers says. "I hope it helps you pass the time. Anyway, I have to go. Take care, David."

Travers leaves, closing the door behind him. David returns his attention to the newspaper. His focus is improving, and after a minute of effort the text finally comes into focus enough for him to read the articles. He settles back, trying to figure out what it was about this paper that Travers found significant.

Thirty minutes later he's checking himself out of the hospital against medical advice.

PART THREE: SOUTH BRONX, MORRISANIA

David sits in a window booth in a small, run-down diner, trying to eat a cold cut without throwing up. It's not that the food is bad; he can't tell if it is or not. Everything tastes like cardboard. The problem is that his doctors warned him he needed to stay in the hospital to recover, and his body is sparing no effort to tell him that they were right.

It's mid-afternoon. There aren't too many people in the diner, but the ones who are stare at him furtively when they think he doesn't notice. He looks a mess: his entire face is a splotchy pattern of bruises, his hair is greasy and unwashed, he hasn't shaved in days, his hands won't stop shaking, and he can't focus on anything for more than a few seconds without his vision blurring. His cane, a simple metal crook with a rubber tip at the end, sits on the table in front of him because he can't get it to lean properly—he keeps knocking it over, and when he has to bend down to pick it up his ribs hurt like hell.

The good news is he doesn't look like a cop. It's not good to look like a cop in Morrisania—the cops in the local precinct have a reputation for corruption, not entirely undeserved, and they aren't very welcome. Morrisania has become, unofficially, one of the safest towns in New York... and the people who keep it that way consider the local police part of the problem.

David grew up in the South Bronx, and moved back after he got out of the service and joined the NYPD. It's changed a lot over the years—it's a far cry from the desperate, arson-scarred, crime-ridden wasteland it was in the 70s—but it's still not entirely *safe*. There are still dangerous parts, areas where people just don't go if they can help it. For a long time, Morrisania was one of those areas. When he was a kid Morrisania was one of the "bad places" that you stayed away from at all costs.

It still has one of the highest crime rates in the city, but statistics can be deceptive. Vigilante justice is illegal, and it doesn't matter to the city if it comes from armed citizens taking the law into their own hands or masked metahumans doing the same thing. The two groups who keep Morrisania safe are, technically, criminals. Anything they do to keep the peace is, statistically, criminal activity. But if the crime statistics were broken down, Morrisania would look very different: "Gang activity" is high, "destruction of property" is high... and every other type of crime is very, very low.

As a cop David was technically obligated to treat both groups as criminals. As Sky Commando, he often had to prioritize levels of threat, and he found it difficult to justify arresting people who had arrived to *help* him. Over time he developed a strong but unofficial working relationship with one of the two groups, the Bastions.

The other group is Crossfire. His relationship with them is a bit more complicated.

A shadow falls across his table. David looks up and sees a tall black man staring down at him in surprise.

"Lieutenant?"

Curtis Dupree is the leader of the Bastions, and goes by the name "Brother Judgment." He's a telekinetic, a very strong one, and a moderate telepath as well. He's tall and quite thin, almost gaunt, giving him a slightly cadaverous appearance. Long, thin dreadlocks are pulled back into a loose ponytail that falls down his back. He wears a dark suit, a gray silk tie, and a black trenchcoat that almost reaches the floor. Despite all those layers he appears completely unaffected by the heat.

David squints up at him and nods in greeting. "Hello Curtis. Sorry to drop in like this."

Curtis stares at David for a moment, says "It's OK" to the room at large—to the visible relief of everyone else in the diner—then slides into the bench opposite his. "What the hell happened to you?"

"Oh, it's a long story," David says, then taps his right temple with his index and middle finger.

Curtis nods slowly, closes his eyes, and concentrates.

What the hell happened to you?

David grits his teeth, exhaling sharply. A spike of searing pain shoots through his mind, and he almost passes out. Curtis' eyes widen in alarm, and David feels him retreating from his mind. David shakes his head quickly. Curtis looks at him uneasily, but stops.

Mental communication is difficult when only one side is telepathic. Curtis tried to explain it to him once, but most of it was lost on him: because the non-telepath can't read thoughts, the telepath has to use a mild form of mind control to tell the recipient what to remember "hearing." It only works when there's a certain level of trust between the people having the "conversation," and it's difficult to use when the brain is damaged. Unfortunately, that's what a concussion is: brain damage. In David's case, he hopes it's temporary, but he's pretty sure this isn't helping him recover.

Sssorrrry Curtis. I'm being fffffffolll... folll... folllowwed. Tthhhey are probably *lllllllllllllll… lisstenning.*

Curtis frowns. *I can barely understand you. What happened?*

David tries to focus on the word "concussion" but he can't. Finally he thinks back to his last memory before the concussion. *Bus. Wall. Pain.*

He tries to grin. Only one side of his mouth goes up. "I had to retire. I'm not on the job any more, Curtis. My replacement is good people, though. I think you'll like her."

"Sorry to hear it." Curtis keeps his voice neutral as his gaze drifts over to the diner window.

He's trying to find my tail.

"So what are your plans?" Curtis asks. *Why did you come here? You should be in a hospital. I didn't think you were stupid.*

David laughs. "Sleep. Watch TV." *Nnnnot my ffff… ffffrst choice. Nnnneeed to talllk to Crrrosssfirre.*

Curtis narrows his eyes. The Bastions and Crossfire are allies. They've worked together more than once to keep Morrisania safe, and they've gone out of their way to help each other even in situations where their goals weren't necessarily the same. David's relationship with Crossfire is significantly more complicated: last year they were officially declared a "terrorist cell" by the Department of Homeland Security because they started focusing on public officials accused of corruption.

David spreads his hands placatingly. *Nnnot a cop annnymorrr. Immmportant!*

Sweat rolls down David's face. He closes his eyes and rubs the bridge of his nose with his trembling hands. His head is killing him. The process is excruciating, and the effort is taking almost everything he has.

Curtis looks back out the window, thinking it over. David doesn't blame him for being cautious: David's relationship with Crossfire isn't nearly as good as it is with the Bastions. The Bastions are vigilantes, but they're focused on protecting their neighborhood, and they're careful not to go too far. Crossfire—Vigilante, Street Ronin, and Red Shift—declared war on something years ago, and they take the word "war" seriously.

David has worked with them, and he's squared off against them, depending on the situation at hand. Lately they've been targeting public officials suspected of corruption, which means that lately, David's been squaring off against them more often than not.

Immmportant, Currtis. Forr thhem.

Curtis studies David carefully, then makes a decision. "OK. Wait here. I'll set it up."

David sighs in relief. "Thanks."

Curtis gets up. "He's a friend of mine," he says, looking over his shoulder to the guy working the counter. "Take care of him, OK?"

"Sure," the man says.

Curtis nods once to David, then walks out of the diner. David watches him through the diner window, trenchcoat billowing out behind him, until he turns the corner and disappears from view.

The man behind the counter coughs nervously. "Can I get you anything?"

"Glass of water," David says. His voice shakes. His hands are shaking even harder than they were when he came in. "And a straw."

The worst part of the wait is wondering who is following him and why. The government? The soldiers? What do they want, and what will they do to get it? If it's the government, they might be content to follow him and leave it at that. If it's the soldiers... he decides to move to a table away from the window. He chooses a small table with two chairs next to the bathrooms, out of the way with a good view of the room.

David waits.

The afternoon crowd comes in. The customers are all black and Hispanic, and when they see the beat-up white guy sitting by the bathroom they all have the same reaction—they look over to the guy behind the counter, relax as they get the "he's all right" nod, then ignore him completely. Morrisania residents have adapted to strange events rather well—when they see people running away, they run away as well. When the guy running the diner just shrugs and nods his head, they stop worrying about it. After a while David starts to relax, sinking into the murmur of background chatter as the regulars order their meals and talk about their day.

The door jingles and the murmur falters. David glances up to see that a new customer has taken a seat at a table near the door—a clean-shaven, young-looking black man wearing a gray sweatshirt and sweatpants. His nose is buried in a book, apparently oblivious to everyone else. They aren't oblivious to him, though—the conversation among the regulars is quieter. They look uneasy.

David tenses. The regulars don't know this guy. They don't know him either, but someone they know told them not to worry. Nobody in the room can vouch for the new guy.

He keeps his eyes down, nursing his water. It could be a coincidence. He decides to find out.

He stands up abruptly, swaying as he steadies himself against the wall, and makes his way to the bathroom, deliberately leaving his cane on the back of his chair. It's a short walk, but he has to keep his hand against the wall the entire way to keep himself from falling, and by the time he gets there his side hurts so much he wants to throw up. The bathroom is single occupancy only: a sink, a toilet, a paper dispenser, and a small window where the outer wall meets the ceiling. It's open, providing the room the only ventilation it has.

On a better day, David might be able to work the pane off the window and climb through it. There's no way that's going to happen today.

He locks the door, then uses the opportunity to throw up in the toilet. That hurts, too, but he feels better once he's finished. He cleans himself up, unlocks the door, and makes his way back to his table.

The guy by the door is gone.

David settles back into his chair and waits. A few minutes later the guy comes back, looks directly at David, then returns to his chair and his book.

"You OK, man?" The guy behind the counter looks at David, concerned. "You look really rough."

"I'm having a bad day," David says. "Can I get another glass of water?"

"Want something stronger?" the man asks. "You look like you could use it."

David thinks back to the doctor lecturing about the things he should and shouldn't be doing. Alcohol was solidly in the "no" column. *On the other hand, I'm doing pretty much everything else in that column...*

Reluctantly he shakes his head. "Water's fine."

The door bangs open again, and once again Curtis steps into the diner. The room quiets momentarily until Curtis gives a general nod, then conversation returns to normal. David sighs in relief as he makes his way to the table.

The man with the book stares at Curtis, then at David. He's frowning.

Curtis sits down in the other chair. "Ready?"

David nods.

"OK." He pulls a cell phone out of his trenchcoat pocket and quickdials a number. "Hey! You ready yet? Got it all worked out?"

Curtis listens to something on the other end. "Hold on, I'll check." He stands, walks over to the men's bathroom, and opens the door. "Yeah, all clear."

The man with the book has abandoned all pretense of reading. He stares at Curtis openly, a puzzled expression on his face.

David feels something pulse, hears a low *whumping* sound, and a moment later a Hispanic man with shoulder-length hair walks out, grinning wide.

"Hey Boss," he says cheerfully. He looks over at David. "That the guy?"

"The man himself," Curtis says. "David, this is Manuel. He's new."

Another one of the Bastions. David nods in greeting. "Hi. Hope you don't mind if I don't get up."

"Don't bother, man, I got it covered." Manuel is short and compact, built like an acrobat or a dancer. He moves like one, too—every motion easy and fluid. He wears a red tank top, black cargo shorts, cross trainers and athletic socks. Unlike Curtis, he's sweating profusely.

He sits down at David's table and looks him over. "Heard about you," he says, flashing him a flawless smile. "You look like someone chewed you up and spit you out."

The man's cheerfulness is infectious, and David feels himself trying to smile in return. "I'd say you should see the other guy, but the truth is he probably looks better."

"Yeah, I hate those fights. Grab the table. One hand on each edge. OK?"

David look at the man quizzically.

"Like this," Manuel says, and grabs the table firmly, one hand gripping each side as if he were getting ready to lift it.

David does it. Manuel notices the shaking in his hands and frowns.

"Hey," Manuel says, "this is gonna work, OK? But it will probably hurt like hell."

"What exactly are we going to do?" David asks.

"Just hold on to the table," Manuel says, then closes his eyes. "Don't let go for anything. And get ready. Five, four, three, two, one—"

The entire world tips violently to his right. David cries out in alarm, gripping the table with all his strength as the diner spins around like a cyclone. Everything goes black for a second, then white, then the world spins back into view...

... and they're not in the diner any more.

PART FOUR: CROSSFIRE SAFEHOUSE

David spends the first few minutes throwing up on the floor. It's not the same floor—the cheap vinyl tiles of the diner have been replaced with cool, slightly grimy concrete.

"Are you OK?" Manuel sounds worried.

"No," David says, and takes a deep, ragged breath.

"Sorry the trip was so rough. I'm not used to pushing around that much mass."

David nods wordlessly as he tries to pull himself together.

The table and both chairs are there—wherever "there" is—and so is David's cane. The part of David that isn't preoccupied with being sick is impressed. Teleporters are rare, and the ones he's familiar with can't carry more than a fraction of their own body weight when they travel. Manuel managed to move himself, his chair, the table, David, David's chair, and David's cane.

"I'm not cleaning that up," someone says. It's an easy-going, laid-back voice. David can't see who it is—he's focusing intently on a single spot on the floor—but he's pretty sure it's Red Shift.

He's in a large, square garage, completely empty except for the chairs and tables from the diner. While it's empty, it doesn't look abandoned—there's no dust, and the concrete smells strongly of motor oil, coolant, and cleanser. Three of the walls have garage bay doors, three to a side, and each bay door is paired with a hydraulic lift. The fourth wall is solid concrete with a door in the middle. The harsh, bright light of fluorescent ceiling lamps fills the room. There are no windows.

David, Manuel, and the table are in the exact center of the room. A few feet from the door is Crossfire. They're in uniform—the black combat suits with the stylized yellow crosshair over where the left breast pocket would be—but they're not wearing their visors.

This is David's only advantage, probably the only reason they agreed to meet with him. He's seen them without their masks before, and even though they haven't always been allies, he never told any of his superiors what they looked like.

Vigilante stares at David impassively, arms crossed, dark eyes searching for something. He's a little over six feet tall and built like a construction worker—not the bulging muscles of a professional weightlifter, but the solid mass of someone who spent years doing hard labor. No callouses or scars, though, and his dark hair has no trace of white.

"Any landing you can walk away from..." His voice is hard, but there's a little humor in it.

"I haven't tried to walk yet." David coughs one last time, spits, grabs the back of his chair and struggles to his feet. Manuel offers him a hand, but he waves it off. He grabs his cane off the back of his chair and leans against it heavily. "Thanks for agreeing to see me. I know it's a risk."

"Not as risky as it could have been. Thanks Blink." Street Ronin nods to Manuel. He's about the same size and build as Vigilante—in many ways, they look like they could be brothers. But Street Ronin's face displays every consequence of his profession: it's full of long-healed scars and fresh bruises. He looks like he was knocked around recently: a cut below his left eye is closed with tight, professional stitching, and the right side of his face is heavily bruised. His dark hair is starting to show traces of premature gray.

David turns to Manuel. "Blink?" Crossfire likes to keep things professional—they almost always refer to people by their handles, even if they know the person's real name.

Manuel shrugs. "I don't really like it, but I had to think of something. I'll make it work."

"I'm just surprised it wasn't already taken." Red Shift is a little thinner than his teammates—he's built like Manuel, like an acrobat, which has the odd effect of making him look both shorter and more fragile.

Manuel grins. "Curti—I mean, 'Brother Judgment' did a web search against the registry a few months ago. Last guy who had it died, so technically I could have registered if I wanted. But hey, we're mavericks, right? If someone wants to sue me for it they can try. I don't care. Anyway it's kind of a stupid name. I wanted 'Massdriver,' but everyone keeps telling me that's a gun."

"It *is* a gun," Street Ronin says. "Anyway, thanks for the help. We can take it from here."

Manuel's smile fades. "There's not going to be a problem, right? I mean, I guess you guys have a history."

Vigilante shakes his head. "No problems here, Blink. If we weren't willing to hear him out we wouldn't be here."

Manuel nods slowly, then turns to David. "Well, that's my cue. Don't do anything to piss these guys off, OK?"

"I'll be OK," David says, shaking Manuel's hand. "Thanks. Tell Curtis I owe him."

"Sure." Manuel grins. "I'm pretty sure he already knows that, though."

David feels a pulse of energy surround the man, hears the *whumping* sound, and then in an instant he's gone.

"Neat trick," Street Ronin mutters.

David turns back to Crossfire and wobbles a bit. "Thanks for seeing me."

Vigilante nods. "Why *are* we seeing you, Sky Commando?"

"I'm not Sky Commando any more," David says. "Retired, on disability. I'm a civilian now."

Vigilante, Street Ronin and Red Shift trade glances.

"Why?" Vigilante asks.

"Fight with Rampage," David says. "Knocked through a wall. Technically I haven't been Sky Commando for months. This week just made it official."

"Concussion?" Street Ronin asks. He doesn't heal like the other two—he has a better idea what the ramifications of that are.

"Yeah," David says. "And on Thursday I stumbled into something that didn't exactly help my recovery. That's what I want to talk to you about."

"OK," Vigilante says. He keeps his voice neutral. "We're listening."

"Right," David says. "OK. Background first. Do you know a guy named Pete Travers?"

"He's a Fed," Street Ronin says.

David nods. "DHS specifically, though he was part of the FBMA before that. At some point during the last year he decided I knew more about you guys than I was letting on. He let me know he knew, and also let me know he wasn't going to make an issue out of it."

Vigilante, Street Ronin and Red Shift trade glances again.

"That's a little hard to swallow," Vigilante says.

"I can't make you believe me," David says, "and I'm not going to try. Just hear me out and take it from there."

Nobody says anything, so David continues. "After Crossfire was officially classified as a terrorist group, Pete started doing things to minimize my involvement with the task force they set up to take you guys down. I couldn't stay completely clear of it, but I was never in a position where I had to admit that I knew what you looked like. And I never volunteered it. I was relieved, but I thought it was odd for Pete to stick his neck out like that."

"It is," Vigilante says.

"Well that leads up to Thursday. You guys know a paper called *The Weekly 832*?"

Red Shift laughs.

"I'll take that as a yes," David says. "I'd never heard of it till today, but apparently I live pretty close to it. My local grocery shares a parking lot with it. And on Thursday, as I was getting groceries, it was attacked."

He wobbles again, and grabs a chair with his free hand for support. "They were the same soldiers who attacked Martin Forrest's house. They murdered the publisher and tried to blow up the entire building."

Vigilante looks interested in spite of himself. "Same guys? You know this?"

David shrugs. "The weapons are distinctive. It's either the same group or the same supplier. Same group makes more sense to me. What doesn't make sense is why they'd go to the trouble to go after this guy. The paper's a joke. The publisher was a whack job who was convinced the United States secretly surrendered to Germany during World War II, and that the government has been secretly controlled by shadowy Nazi Overlords ever since."

"The guy was a loon," Red Shift confirms. "I actually met him once. Took a lot of drugs. Muttered to himself all the time. He was pretty harmless, though. It's not like anyone ever believed him."

David reaches into his pocket and pulls out the front page of the newspaper, unfolding it and smoothing it on the table. "It's a 'broken clock is right twice a day' thing. The Weekly 832 was going to publish something true—something about you guys. I'm pretty sure Travers thinks it's the reason these mystery soldiers attacked."

"Conspiracy Theory," Red Shift says, walking up to the table to see the article.

"I liked that movie," Street Ronin adds, and moves to the table as well, followed by Vigilante.

"It's called 'Metahumans Wage Desperate War Against Shadow Government,'" David says. "Not a gripping title. But the first paragraph. Read the first paragraph."

Red Shift leans over and peers at the circled paragraph. "'Most heroes are oblivious to the true powers that control our lives, but three New York

City metahumans have waged a private war against the dark forces that have made every important decision since 1944. The Weekly 832 has learned that not only are these grim warriors united in their struggle against these forces, but two of them were also products of them—victims of a secret test program, the continuation of Project Paragon, later referred to as 'MK ULTRA,' and then even later as PRODIGY. They were used as test subjects in an ongoing effort to create a secret army of metahuman slaves...' Holy shit. That's definitely us."

"That's what I thought," David says. "I don't know how much Travers knows about you guys. I think he actually knows more than I do. He has a lot more resources, and he's been working on that Task Force ever since it started up. But what *I* know—at least, what I *think* I know—is that you guys started this for a very specific reason. One person, or one group. Someone who's been experimenting on people."

He looks at Vigilante for confirmation. Vigilante doesn't reply.

"The article says 'three metahumans,'" Street Ronin points out. "I'm not a metahuman."

"Same difference," Red Shift says. "You might as well be."

Vigilante picks up the newspaper and looks it over. "Yeah. It's probably about us. Why would these soldiers care? And why would a Fed want us to know?"

"Why are they calling you terrorists?" David asks.

Vigilante's jaw tightens. "I'm not going to debate tactics."

"I'm not debating tactics," David says. "You already know I think you go too far. That's not the point. It wasn't your tactics that put you on the No-Fly lists, it was your choice of targets."

"He's got a point," Street Ronin says. "There wasn't nearly as much heat when we were focusing on criminal organizations. It wasn't until we started dealing with the dirty bureaucrats and politicos that we became a threat to national security."

"Odd coincidence, that," Red Shift agrees. "It's almost as if we made someone angry."

"String it together: these guys attack the Forrest house. Some agency takes control of the investigation and kicks out everyone else involved. Then these guys attack a newspaper about to print a story about you. You're classified as terrorists because you're going after corruption in the government..."

Street Ronin smacks his forehead. "It's all the same guys. Vigilante, all this time—"

"Yeah," Vigilante says. He stares at David thoughtfully. "You think Travers is sending us this information because he doesn't trust his people."

"I know Pete Travers," David says. "He's as honest as they come. If he's trying to get this information to you, it's because he's convinced you're right, and he thinks some of the people he's working with are dirty."

Vigilante drops the newspaper on the table. "A lunatic who publishes a newspaper isn't much to go on."

"I was getting to that," David says. "It's not the only thing Travers gave me."

He reaches into his jeans pocket, takes out the thumb drive, and puts it on the table. "I don't know what's on it."

Everyone looks at the thumb drive in silence.

"You're in this now," Vigilante says.

"Yeah," David agrees.

"You're in it on our side. The ugly side. It doesn't matter who was following you—if you're right, it got back to these guys. And if they really are connected to the ones we've been going after, they'll kill you. They'll call you a hero, they'll give you a really big funeral, probably even put it on TV…"

"Like they did with Liberty," David says quietly.

Vigilante nods once. "No proof though. Not yet."

"I want in," David says. "I can help. I can't fight, but I can help."

Vigilante looks to Street Ronin, who nods, then at Red Shift, who shrugs. "You're not going to like who we're working with."

David considers that. "Maybe," he says. "But this isn't about liking people, is it? If we're right, some of the guys I do like are dirty."

"Yeah," Vigilante says. "OK. First things first. You're not fit for much of anything at the moment. Let's get you cleaned up. We have access to some tech that's a little more advanced than whatever your doctor has."

"OK," David says. "What then?"

"Then the fun starts," Vigilante says. "Then we read you in."

PART ONE: JACOB K. JAVITS FEDERAL BUILDING

The New York offices of the Federal Bureau of Metahuman Affairs take up four floors of the Jacob K. Javits Federal Building in the Civic Center district of Manhattan. Peter Raphael Travers' office is on the 28th floor—the lowest of the four—and it's small compared to most of the others. Technically he should have moved up to a much larger office in the Department of Homeland Security floors a decade ago, but so much of his work is with the FBMA it didn't make sense to move him out of his old space. Travers doesn't mind. Once upon a time, before computers were standard business equipment, the office might have been a little cramped. Now it's more than adequate: large enough for his desk, his chair, two guest chairs, and a file cabinet with an old coffee maker sitting on top of it.

Travers leans back in his chair, sipping his coffee while he stares at the monitor, and frowns as he considers the report on display. *It's going to be a rough week.*

His desk phone rings. It's Sally, the unit receptionist.

"Agent Travers, Agent Henry is here to see you. With... others." Sally sounds nervous.

Travers raises an eyebrow. "Send him in."

He opens the bottom drawer of his desk and pulls out a small vial of liquid, which he quickly opens and pours into his coffee. He's topping off his mug when the door to his office opens, and Agent Phillip Henry, leader of Division M, steps into the room looking pissed.

"Hello Phillip," Travers says. "Coffee? Fresh pot."

Agent Henry is a tall, thin, dark-skinned man, younger than Travers but possessed of an existential weariness that makes him seem older than he is. He's dressed in an expensive black suit, white shirt, and black tie. He's wearing black sunglasses. Travers finds the ensemble ridiculous—he looks like a stereotype brought to life—but he forces himself not to smile. It's not actually Henry's fault. It's the sunglasses that do it, and he wears them because he's courteous.

Agent Henry steps into the room without saying anything. He's followed by two more agents, a man and a woman, both wearing dark suits. Travers notices they're armed. Henry isn't, but that's irrelevant.

Travers looks at the three of them, sits down in his chair, takes another sip of coffee, and sighs. "Close the door."

Agent Henry nods curtly. The man to his left turns and closes the door. The woman to his right just stares at Travers. She's tense—not frightened, but on guard.

Travers looks from her, to Agent Henry, to the man returning to Henry's left, then back to Agent Henry. "What's this about, Phillip?"

Agent Henry hesitates. "I have orders to bring you in."

"Are you arresting me?" Travers asks, keeping his voice mild.

"No." Agent Henry shifts uncomfortably.

"Well," Travers says, "we're currently in the New York office of the Federal Bureau of Metahuman Affairs. I'm already 'in.' We could go up five floors to the DHS offices if you like, but I don't see how—"

"David Bernard," Agent Henry interrupts. "What is your involvement with him?"

Travers shrugs and takes a long drink of coffee, wincing slightly at the bitter, metallic taste. "When he was Sky Commando I worked with him a great deal. A few days ago he very heroically involved himself in an incident that would have caused the deaths of a great many civilians if he had not, injuring himself in the process. Yesterday I visited him in the hospital, told him he'd been put under surveillance by his own government, gave him a newspaper and a USB thumb drive full of useful information, and wished him well."

As a general rule of thumb it's useless to lie to Agent Henry, and Travers doesn't bother to try. Henry's reaction is priceless: his mouth goes slack and hangs open as he rocks back in stunned silence. The woman to his right blinks in surprise, and the man to his left looks at the others as if to say, "Did he really just say that?"

Travers takes another sip as he turns his monitor around so they can see the report. "Strange world we live in. This kid literally sacrificed his body when he was on the job, then selflessly put himself in danger *again* when he stumbled into a situation that he was able to tie back to Liberty's assassination... and our first response is to invoke the Patriot Act to search his house and put him under warrantless surveillance."

Agent Henry recovers from his surprise. "I'm not at liberty to—"

"Agent Henry," Travers says, voice soft, "*shut up.*"

Agent Henry falls silent.

"At least we didn't classify him as a terrorist," Travers continues. "That would be beyond insulting. But Title XI can only be invoked when dealing with a metahuman threat. Bernard no longer has access to the technology that would qualify him as a metahuman under Section 1125. He doesn't wear the suit any more, Phillip, and you're thorough enough to have known that before issuing your orders."

"You don't know everything," Agent Henry says.

Travers waits expectantly.

Agent Henry shakes his head. "Not going to happen. But what you did—"

"Was in direct violation of DHS and FBMA protocol," Travers cuts in agreeably. "And, I'm quite certain, a violation of my oath as a Federal officer and of at least three laws. Oh, and I'm pretty sure it was in violation of my security clearance as well. I've been a naughty boy." He swigs down the last of his coffee and sets the empty mug on his desk.

Agent Henry grits his teeth. "What you did was aid and abet a *suspect* in a *criminal investigation*. We know a *lot more* about him than you do—"

"No you don't," Travers says. "You *invented* a lot more about him, I'm sure. But it's a pack of lies. I'll do you the courtesy of believing that you genuinely believe it's necessary for the public good, but in order for me to do that it also means I have to believe that you're an idiot. I'll do you another courtesy and hope that it's a temporary condition."

"I don't have time for this," Agent Henry says, almost growling the words. "Agent Collins, please restrain—"

Travers' foot kicks the back of his desk hard enough to crack the faux veneer, depressing the hidden trigger with a loud click. Instantly the three fire sprinklers in the room go off, spraying everyone and everything in it. It's funny how nobody ever commented on them—nobody in his right mind would put three fire sprinklers in an office that small. Most people don't notice things like that, and the few who do tend to think nothing of it.

Travers faceplants onto his desk as soon as he's hit with the spray, but he had his coffee. A moment later he stands up, weaving unsteadily, and looks at the three agents collapsed on the floor in front of him. He looks at his door warily. Still closed, nobody coming in. The trigger locked it as well as deploying the neurotoxin, so he has some time.

"Don't worry," Travers says, voice quavering slightly from the effort. "It's non-lethal. I try very hard not to kill. You should regain the ability to move and speak in an hour, I think."

He arranges each agent out on the floor so they're resting a little more comfortably. It's a tight space, so it's not ideal, but it's better than the positions they were in before. When he's finished he kneels over Agent Henry and removes his sunglasses.

"Look at me," Travers says.

Agent Henry can move his eyes, but they're not tracking very well. Travers slaps his face, very lightly, and moves his index finger around in front of it until the eyes focus.

"Look at me," he says again.

Agent Henry looks at him. A moment later, Travers feels the compulsion lock in.

Agent Henry is a metahuman. At a very basic level, he can tell whenever anyone is lying to him, or is telling him the truth, but whenever he makes eye contact, the subject is *compelled* to tell the truth—the entire, unvarnished, often painful truth. He can't control it, which is why he wears sunglasses.

"I don't know where you stand in this," Travers says simply. "I've always considered you a decent man, but if you're as deep into this as you appear to be, then you're either an accomplice or someone giving you orders has figured out how to lie to you and get away with it. I'm going to hope it's the latter. I hate being wrong about people..."

He sees Agent Henry's brow furrow slightly. That's all he can do.

"That said," Travers continues, "I have been wrong before, and I expect I will be again. So whether you're a traitor or a dupe, listen to me *very carefully.*"

Agent Henry watches him.

"I am not a traitor," Travers says. "Everything I did for David, and everything I'm doing now, is in service of my country. It also, I might add, lines up perfectly with the scope of my responsibilities and the purpose of my department, though the lengths I find myself going to in order to meet those responsibilities probably qualify as *above and beyond the call.* That's not me bragging, Agent Henry, that's me *complaining.* I have spent my life doing whatever I can do to protect my country from her enemies. You know that pledge? 'External or within?' Well lately they haven't been external, and that makes me *very, very angry.*"

Agent Henry's eyes widen just a fraction. Travers is telling him the truth—at least, the truth as he understands it. He can't do anything else.

Travers places the sunglasses back over Agent Henry's eyes and coughs apologetically. "I'm going to leave now. I won't be exiting through the front door, because you might have other agents placed out there. I'm... actually glad you can't see how I'm going to leave. Not because I want to keep anything from you, just because while it would look spectacularly dashing if someone like Curveball were trying this, it's going to look awkward and painful when I do it."

He sighs, goes over to his filing cabinet, and opens the bottom drawer. He pulls the harness out from the back and steps into it as quickly as he can manage.

"Right."

He pulls up the blinds and starts working on the window. It takes five minutes for Travers to pry it open, and by the end of it he's gasping and sweating profusely. It's not supposed to open, of course. It took him an entire weekend to switch the old one out and the new one in. He almost fell to his death in the process, and it's now clear he didn't exactly do it right. Finally the window swings open like a miniature glass door, and a warm breeze blows into the room. The sounds of traffic going across Duane Street can be heard faintly, twenty-eight stories below.

He opens the bottom drawer of his desk again and pulls out the zip line. He hums softly to himself as he sets the base of it up against the base of the window and fastens it firmly in place with the attached tool. When it finally locks in to the bottom sill, the firing mechanism is pointed exactly where it's supposed to be—just above a ledge running around the Ted Weiss Federal Building. He checks again—just to make sure—then fires. The zip line streaks across the distance, burying itself in the stone, right on target.

He clips the safety harness onto the zip line, then awkwardly heaves himself over the window. He looks down, regrets it, then sets his jaw.

"Yeah," he mutters, "definitely a rough week." He jumps.

For a brief moment he's falling, terrified. A moment later the safety harness jerks sharply, and the next thing he knows he's sliding down the line, across the street, toward the other building, terrified. It feels like it's taking much too long, while at the same time he's certain he's traveling much too fast. He hits the far wall much harder than he expected; he feels his right knee pop as he tries to cushion his impact with his legs. Muscles tear and burn, and he topples sideways as his right leg gives, hitting the wall with his hip, then his shoulder, and then his face.

Travers hasn't been a field agent for a very long time. He hurts, he's bleeding, his head is throbbing, and his ears are ringing. He dangles from the zip line for a moment, reeling from the shock of the impact, then adrenaline and will force him to find his feet, open his eyes, and take stock of his situation.

He's on the ledge.

He looks down. A few people have gathered on the sidewalk, staring up and pointing.

He reaches up to unhook his harness from the zip line and feels a sharp pain in his right shoulder. He grunts, fumbles with the release one-handed, and almost falls backward when it finally disconnects. He curses, steadies himself, then steps to his left until he stands in front of a full-sized window made of safety glass. With his left hand he reaches up to a small indentation in the stone next to the window, then pushes hard.

The window clicks, then opens smoothly inward.

Travers looks back down, weaving unsteadily. More people have gathered on the sidewalk.

He grins, waves once, steps through the open window, and disappears.

PART TWO: CROSSFIRE SAFEHOUSE

Street Ronin sighs, rubs his eyes, and leans back in his chair. His computer has been analyzing the files from a USB thumb drive for the last hour, and it's boring.

He and Red Shift have been in the safehouse Tactical Room for most of the night, trying to piece together all the information they received from their new partners. He's tired; Red Shift is bored. As far as Street Ronin knows, Red Shift doesn't sleep.

"You know how TV shows always have computers showing you a search in progress? Like, they have a graphic of a file being put next to a graphic of another file, and then big blocky letters say 'no match,' and then it does it again?" Street Ronin reaches for his coffee, sees the mug is empty, and frowns.

"Yep." Red Shift takes the empty mug and sets down a fresh, full one. "Almost as dumb as the bomb always being disarmed three seconds before it goes off."

"You're a *saint*," Street Ronin says, grabbing the mug gratefully.

Red Shift snorts. "No saints in this neck of the woods. Except maybe the cop."

The cop is the latest addition to the ragtag group working with Crossfire to figure out who murdered Liberty and why. He'd been a pretty well-known hero—an armored hero that went by the name Sky Commando—until an injury forced him to retire before he turned thirty. It's his USB thumb drive they're examining.

"He's not a saint," Street Ronin says. "He came here."

Red Shift shrugs. "Saints eat with sinners all the time. Wash their feet, even."

Street Ronin's computer *dings* as a pop-up window alerts him to a match. Relieved to have something to do, he tabs over to view the report.

"What's that?" Red Shift asks, more out of boredom than interest. When Street Ronin doesn't answer, he looks over, then raises an eyebrow at the expression on the man's face. "Found something?"

Street Ronin stares at the screen for a moment, then takes a breath. "Yeah. Hell yeah, I got something all right. Look at this."

He moves out of the way to give Red Shift a clear view. In half a second, Red Shift has memorized everything on the screen and parses through it mentally. He stops on a name. His eyes widen in shock. "Holy shit."

"Yeah." Street Ronin opens up a new terminal window on the screen and starts typing in commands. "I need a little time to see where this goes. Then we need to tell the others. Meeting in an hour?"

Red Shift nods and heads to the door. "I'll tell Vigilante."

* * *

David Bernard shifts awkwardly in the chair, trying to find a comfortable position and not quite managing to settle in. His IV—an almost-constant fixture since his arrival at the safe house—bumps against his shin, and he has to grip the IV stand to keep it from toppling over and ripping out of his arm. That's already happened twice today.

"We're not used to this kind of crowd," Red Shift says, almost apologetically.

The Crossfire Safehouse is a blend of cutting edge technology and secondhand furniture. Crossfire doesn't skimp on tools—their computers are far beyond what the NYPD has at its disposal, and the "bare bones" medical station set up in the spare room has things in it that would make any hospital envious. The furnishings, on the other hand, look like they were *scrounged*. Folding chairs, card tables, futon couches and milk crate shelving makes everything look more like a college dormitory than a base for one of the most dangerous vigilante groups in the country.

David sits on an old wood folding chair in the upstairs apartment's living room, waiting for everyone to gather for the urgent meeting Red Shift and Street Ronin are organizing. He grips his IV stand in one hand while he eyes the cup of coffee Red Shift just set down on a small card table in front of him. Coffee is one of the things he isn't allowed to drink—caffeine is apparently bad for a concussion.

"It's OK to drink it," Red Shift says.

David looks at him dubiously. "That's not what my doctor told me."

"Your doctor didn't have access to that." Red Shift points at the IV drip. "How are you feeling?"

He's the least dangerous-looking of the trio: he has an easygoing demeanor and always seems to sport a relaxed, friendly smile. Relaxed, affable, almost *lazy*. For a man who has been clocked at speeds exceeding Mach 12, he seems perpetually at rest.

"Lousy," David says. "But better than when I first got here. I'm still pretty clumsy, but the headaches are gone. I can focus now. I don't feel like I'm going to throw up all the time. Still a solid bruise from top to bottom, though."

"A few more days of meds and you'll be out of the woods," Red Shift says. "Drive, drink beer, run, lift weights, the whole nine yards. You won't be at a hundred percent, maybe seventy-five, eighty tops, but that's pretty good considering where you were."

David looks at the IV drip thoughtfully. "What the hell is in that thing?"

"Trade secret," Red Shift says. "Something Street Ronin and I cooked up to help him bounce back faster. It's designed specifically for him, and I had to dilute it to get it to work for you, so it's not a perfect fix. Also if you take a drug test in the next few months you're going to test positive for opiates. So... don't take a drug test."

A *tsking* noise draws David's attention to a small, ramshackle futon at the other end of the room. David glances at the elegantly-dressed white-haired man and tries not to frown. Artemis LaFleur—Overmind—seems completely at ease among the shabby furnishings, even though his suit looks like it's more expensive than anything else in the building, including the electronics.

LaFleur meets David's gaze and bows his head slightly in acknowledgment. Other than the initial round of *very awkward* introductions, they haven't spoken. David is still trying to come to grips with the fact that he's working with one of the most dangerous criminal masterminds in the world. And, if Vigilante is to be believed, that LaFleur is doing so for at least partially altruistic reasons.

Red Shift glances at LaFleur, pulls up a second folding chair, and sits down next to David. "Strange days."

David nods, still eying LaFleur warily.

"And," Red Shift says, "they're about to get stranger."

Twenty minutes later they're all assembled, and Street Ronin is setting up a projection system for his presentation. Overmind and Scrapper Jack— an old-school villain David had honestly thought was dead—sit on the futon, David and Red Shift sit on the wood folding chairs, and Vigilante sits on an ottoman upholstered in cheap yellow vinyl.

The presentation system consists of an oversized flat screen monitor, a computer, and a tablet Street Ronin holds as he faces the group. He swipes across the surface of the tablet, and the monitor blinks once, displaying a list of names David doesn't recognize.

"All right," Street Ronin says, "let's get started."

Everyone waits expectantly.

"I've been working with three sets of data and a few fundamental assumptions," Street Ronin says. "We know that last week a newspaper that was about to print an article about us was attacked by armed soldiers. We know, thanks to David Bernard, that they appear to be the same type of soldiers that attacked Martin Forrest's house the morning after Liberty's funeral. We're currently operating under the assumption that both events are connected to Liberty's murder."

Three blue circles display on the monitor, one labeled *Liberty*, one labeled *Forrest*, one labeled *Weekly 832*. The three circles are grouped in a triangular pattern in the center of the screen, with blue bars connecting all three together.

"We know that the *Weekly 832* was about to print an article about Crossfire—an article that specifically mentions PRODIGY. We know PRODIGY was an illegal government project that attempted to clone metahumans in order to turn them into... well, essentially into remote-controlled drones. It's more complicated than that, but from what I understand it would have been a catastrophic failure, resulting in the creation of rampaging mindless *things* with the ability to level the entire West Coast in a matter of days. It was dismantled ten years ago, and at least officially, all the responsible parties are in jail. We also know that Pete Travers gave David a thumb drive full of files related to his investigation into PRODIGY, which he apparently intended for us to have."

A green circle labeled *PRODIGY* displays on the right screen, with a green bar connecting it to the *Weekly 832* circle.

"Finally, we know that when Overmind attempted to use his government assets to look into the Liberty assassination, the responses he got—or, in some cases, the lack of responses—caused him to suspect that all his assets were compromised. He gave us a list of those assets, where they were placed, and an extensive profile for each one."

An orange circle labeled *Overmind Assets* displays on the left screen, with an orange bar connecting it to the *Liberty* circle.

"For the last few days I've been searching for common points of reference between the data we have, looking for connections and relationships that might not be immediately obvious. I've also searched through public records, looking to see if there's anything hidden in plain sight. What I've found is... interesting."

The monitor blinks again. Framed in the monitor is a picture of a handsome, clean-shaven man in an expensive navy blue suit. His hair is perfectly cut and combed to one side, mostly dark with a touch of gray at the temples. His dark eyes are warm, intelligent, and kind. His smile is friendly but dignified, showing perfect teeth.

Tobias Alexander Morgan, Junior Senator of New York. Liberty's grandson.

David stares at the picture in shock. He looks at the rest of the room—everyone looks just as surprised as he feels, even LaFleur.

"Are you sure about this?" Vigilante asks quietly.

Street Ronin takes a breath. "Ten years ago, when the PRODIGY incident broke, *Representative* Morgan was serving New York's 20th district. He sat on the House Oversight Committee, and was one of the congressmen involved in the investigation after PRODIGY was brought down. He also sat on the House Intelligence Committee, developed very strong ties with key members of the NSA, and has maintained those ties ever since. Fast-forward to his Senate campaign: he ran primarily on health care reform, of all things, and sits on an advisory board for a health insurance company called TriHealth Services."

"What's significant about TriHealth?" David asks. "Other than a conflict of interest, I guess."

"It was one of the businesses PRODIGY used to launder its money," Street Ronin says. "Other than that it seemed to be a legitimate business. It had so many real customers that the Federal government stepped in to run things for a while after all its corporate managers were hauled off to jail. Four years ago it finally won back its independence, so to speak, and returned to operation as a fully independent, for-profit operation."

"I have a hard time believing this," LaFleur says, shaking his head. "I dislike the Senator immensely, but you're suggesting he's involved in the murder of his own grandfather. Tobias Morgan is vain, narrow-minded, self-serving, manipulative, and occasionally cruel. He is also cautious, intelligent, principled, and utterly committed to his ideals. On top of that, his grandfather was one of the few people he seemed to have any genuine regard for. It doesn't make any sense."

"He currently sits on the Senate Homeland Security and Governmental Affairs Committee, which serves as oversight for the Department of Homeland Security. As of last week, the DHS took control of Liberty's murder investigation, forcing every other involved party out." Street Ronin shrugs. "All I have are connections, but it's significant that he's connected in some way to every aspect of this. His relationships with key personnel in various intelligence communities gives him access to your spies. He was involved in the initial investigation of PRODIGY, and sits on an advisory board for one of the businesses involved in the affair. And through his committee he has access, via the DHS, to the murder investigation."

"Too many connections," Vigilante agrees. "We need to look into it."

"Where?" Red Shift asks. "Do we search his office? Do we head to DC?"

"I don't believe that's necessary," LaFleur says. "If he is involved in this conspiracy—which I'm still not sure I believe—he will want to keep any information about it separate from his day-to-day work. Where does he live? His primary residence?"

Street Ronin checks his tablet. "Albany."

LaFleur sighs. "It's a bit farther than I'd like, but—"

"I can be there in fifteen minutes," Red Shift says.

PART THREE: SKY COMMANDO UNIT

Sergeant Alishia Webb sits in the Sky Commando Unit briefing room and shifts uncomfortably under the enigmatic gaze of the man in the suit and sunglasses sitting across the table.

"Miss Webb—"

"*Sergeant*," Alishia says firmly.

The man nods once. "My apologies. Sergeant. Thank you for taking the time to talk to us."

Alishia's gaze drifts over to the man's left, farther down the table, where the rest of his group—two men and three women—sit listening patiently. Their expressions are professionally blank, betraying nothing. Alishia's Captain sits across from them, on her side of the table, arms folded. Her expression is professionally neutral. The Captain, among her many other talents, is good at wading through the shark-infested waters of local and federal politics in New York City, so Alishia isn't surprised to see her poker face.

"There's no need to thank me," Alishia says, keeping her voice dry. "When the Captain tells me to do something, I usually do it."

Usually. Alishia sees the Captain shift slightly out of the corner of her eye, and imagines the right corner of her mouth curling up into an almost-smile.

"Sergeant Webb," the man begins again, "I understand this is abrupt and probably insulting. However, this is a matter of national security. We appreciate your cooperation."

Alishia doesn't reply.

The man stares at her a moment longer, sighs, then says, "My name is Agent Phillip Henry. I work at the Department of Homeland Security, and we're concerned about your predecessor."

"You're one of the assholes who kicked us off the Forrest investigation."

Agent Henry nods. "I am *the* asshole who kicked you off the Forrest investigation."

"And you're investigating Bernard." She doesn't bother to disguise the hostility in her voice.

"No," Agent Henry says. "I'm trying to *find* him."

Alishia frowns and glances at Captain Lloyd. Her poker face is still up, Alishia can't read anything. She looks back at Agent Henry. "What are you talking about?"

"David Bernard has been missing since Friday." Agent Henry stares at her impassively, his emotions hidden behind the dark glasses. "He checked himself out of Bronx-Lebanon Hospital—against medical advice, for the record—and was last seen in the company of an unregistered metahuman vigilante who calls himself 'Brother Judgment.' No one has seen him since."

Alishia pushes back a nagging worry and shrugs. "I guess it's his business."

"I guess it *isn't*," Agent Henry says. "As I said, this is a matter of national security."

"National security," Alishia says, trying and failing to keep the scorn out of her voice. "You expect me to believe that—"

"I don't *care* what you believe," Agent Henry says. He's tense; he leans forward for emphasis. "I have a legitimate and lawful reason to find David Bernard and you have a professional obligation to help me."

Alishia glowers at him.

"For what it's worth," Agent Henry continues, "I think he's being used. But we are certain that, intentional or not, he has passed on classified information to foreign hostile powers—"

"*What?*" Alishia is out of her chair. "That is the *stupidest*—"

"Do you know Peter Travers?"

The question is so unexpected that it stops Alishia cold. She sits back down in her chair. "Yes."

"This morning Agent Travers confessed to telling Mr. Bernard that he was under Federal surveillance. He also confessed to passing on sensitive information. We believe Travers has manipulated Bernard into passing that information on to an unknown, hostile third party."

Alishia shakes her head. "Travers? That's insane. There's got to be—"

"Immediately after confessing to these acts," Agent Henry says, "he used a neurotoxin to incapacitate the agents sent to apprehend him."

"I... find that hard to believe," Alishia says.

"So do I," Agent Henry says. "And I was one of the people he attacked."

Alishia doesn't reply. She's trying to process this information. She's not sure she believes this guy, but she's also not sure why he'd lie.

Agent Henry frowns, then looks over his shoulder at the other agents sitting to his left. "We need to vet her and read her in."

"There's no reason to vet her," Captain Lloyd says.

Agent Henry sighs. "You know there is."

Alishia looks at the Captain. "Vetted for what?"

The Captain sets her jaw. "You don't have the authority."

"Not without your permission," Agent Henry agrees. "It is my hope you will give that permission."

"Permission for *what*?" Alishia says, raising her voice just a little.

"We're going to have to go through channels first," one of the other agents protests.

"No we won't," Agent Henry says. "She's Sky Commando."

Alishia's eyes widen. "You're using the *Patriot Act* on me?"

"Sergeant Webb, I am *trying* to put you in a position where you will understand what's going on," Agent Henry says. "In order to do that I need to use a metahuman ability that will compel you to speak the truth. It will only be for four very specific questions."

"You're a metahuman?" Alishia asks.

"Yes." Agent Henry sighs and rubs the bridge of his nose. "Sergeant. Under normal circumstances I would be required to fill out paperwork and get a judge's authorization before I could use an ability that would compel you to tell the truth. Until I use that ability I cannot officially verify that you are not a security risk. I am under strict orders not to read people in unless it have been officially verified that they are not a security risk."

"I see," Alishia says. "Well. That puts you in an awkward position."

"Fortunately, your role as Sky Commando allows me to invoke Section 1125 under Title XI of the Patriot Act in order to expedite matters in an emergency. Which is what this is, Sergeant. Captain Lloyd will serve as a witness on your behalf, to ensure that I ask nothing inappropriate."

Alishia thinks it over. "Fine. Let's get this over with."

"Very good." Agent Henry takes off his sunglasses. "Please look me in the eyes, Sergeant."

Alishia meets his gaze. He has green eyes. A moment later her gaze locks into them, and she feels her muscles tense involuntarily.

"I'm going to ask you four questions," Agent Henry says. He looks uncharacteristically apologetic for a Federal agent. "Four yes or no questions. If you answer yes to any of them, I may ask a follow-up question for clarification. Bear in mind, Sergeant, that I don't have the power to force you to speak. Anything you say to me, for as long as we maintain eye contact, must be the truth—but you can remain silent, and although it feels difficult to do, you can also break eye contact at any time."

Alishia takes a deep breath.

"First question," Agent Henry says. "Are you now or have you ever been involved in a conspiracy against the United States of America?"

"No," Alishia says.

Agent Henry nods. "Second question: are you in any way involved with the person or people responsible for the murder of Alexander Morgan, also known as Liberty?"

"No," Alishia says.

"Third question," Agent Henry says. "Are you involved in a conspiracy to cover up or otherwise impede the investigation into Liberty's murder?"

"No," Alishia says.

"Final question," Agent Henry says. "Do you suspect anyone you know of being involved in a conspiracy to cover up or otherwise impede the investigation into Liberty's murder?"

"Yes," Alishia says.

Agent Henry raises an eyebrow. "Interesting. I have a follow-up question. Whom do you suspect of being involved in a conspiracy to cover up or otherwise impede the investigation into Liberty's murder?"

"You," Alishia says.

The other agents laugh quietly. Agent Henry's mouth twitches once, then he puts his sunglasses back on. "That's fair enough."

He looks at Captain Lloyd. "I have no objections to reading her in." He turns to the other agents. "Agreed?"

The other agents murmur their assent.

Agent Henry turns back to Alishia. "Sergeant, have you ever heard of Division M?"

Alishia shakes her head.

"We're the metahuman branch of the Department of Homeland Security. We're not like the FBMA—we don't specifically monitor and respond to metahuman threats. We *are* metahumans."

"Okay," Alishia says. "What brings you here?"

"The attack on the Forrest residence has convinced us that whoever was responsible for Liberty's murder has influence in the local enforcement community. By 'local' I am including the local Federal branches involved in the investigation as well as the NYPD."

"Seriously?" Alishia looks at him in disbelief.

"Seriously. The Forrest residence was supposed to be under surveillance the night they were attacked. Someone disrupted the surveillance schedule. If they hadn't, law enforcement would have been on the scene much faster than it was."

Alishia nods slowly. "Someone created a window."

"Yes." Agent Henry shakes his head and lets out a quick hiss of frustration. "It was someone at a high level—someone who had access to that schedule. But we don't know who, and we don't want to tip them off that we're looking for them."

"I get it now," Alishia says. "That's why you took over the investigation the way you did. You wanted everyone to think that the Feds were moving in to take charge, in a typically insulting fashion, in order to make sure the mole was frozen out without knowing why."

Agent Henry nods. "We are bringing people back in where we can, but it's slow going. Captain Lloyd was brought in last week. We wanted to make vetting the Sky Commando unit a priority, but this business with the new attack, and now Bernard and Travers... well, it complicates matters."

"David isn't dirty," Alishia says.

"Maybe," Agent Henry says. "You know him better than I do. But if you were to tell me that Peter Travers was going to do what he did today, I would have laughed you out of the room."

"Neurotoxin?" Alishia asks.

"Deployed from the sprinklers. He'd obviously planned for this moment for a long time."

This is crazy. Alishia sorts through everything Agent Henry said, and that's the only thing she can come back to. *This is completely crazy. It makes no sense.*

But that's not surprising—she doesn't have the whole picture. All she sees are pieces, and the pieces are too different to fit together comfortably. She needs more pieces, which means she needs to investigate. It looks like Agent Henry, for whatever reason, is willing to give her the chance to do just that.

Alishia takes a deep breath. "OK," she says, "I'm in. What do you need me to do?"

PART FOUR: FARRADAY CITY

It's raining in Farraday City. Water courses through the sewers, the sluggish and nearly stagnant waters now rushing like overflowing streams. The water level has risen above the side walkways to the point that water flows over CB's ankles. He can feel the tug of the current slightly. It's inconvenient, and if it keeps rising it might get dangerous.

"OK back there?"

Jenny grunts in reply. Her hand tightens on his shoulder for a moment, and CB feels a stab of pain.

"Easy, Jenny. I might need that later."

Her grip eases slightly, still firm but not uncomfortable. "Sorry, tough guy."

She still has an edge to her voice, but the barb softens it a little. It's encouraging.

"Ten minutes." CB plays the thin, bright beam of his Mag Lite across the walls, noting the markings on the side passages. "We'll be there in ten minutes."

"OK." Jenny's voice is even and strong. "Are you sure this is a good idea?"

"Seriously, Jenny, most people who work with me know better than to ask that question."

"You're *hilarious*," Jenny says. "Answer the question."

"It's risky," CB admits. "The reason I had Elliot activate the safe house ahead of schedule is because I figured the bad guys were going to locate my apartment sooner or later. I don't think they have yet, but I can't swear to it."

"Then why are we going there?"

"I need some stuff," CB says. "I *really* need some stuff, and I get the feeling the window is closing on actually being able to get to it."

"What stuff?"

"Gear. Weapons. Things to keep us alive."

"I like the sound of that," Jenny says. "The 'keep us alive' part, anyway. I can get behind that."

Ten minutes later they emerge from a manhole cover near the boardwalk. The rain falls thick and heavy, and they hear the surf churning in the distance. The cloud-covered sky blocks the mid-morning sun, and the few street lights that still work flicker as if the rain were about to put them out.

They walk two blocks from the manhole cover to the boardwalk, and two more blocks along the boardwalk to get to the apartment. The boardwalk is largely deserted; those who have places to stay are staying inside, those who don't are huddled somewhere else. CB and Jenny are soaked to the bone by the time they get to his apartment building.

It's a squalid, dirty cinderblock building. The glass on the front door is missing; a dirty tarp has been stapled across the frame in its place. The tarp is torn in places, and a pool of water sits right at the front of the lobby where the rain comes through. Whatever the lobby was, once upon a time, it's now a gutted room consisting of graffiti-covered walls and cheap vinyl flooring. It smells strongly of urine.

"Nice place," Jenny says, shivering slightly. Her hair is plastered to her head, her windbreaker and pants heavy with rainwater. Her tennis shoes look like they're in danger of falling apart. She almost looks miserable enough to be a tenant.

"It has its good points," CB says. "Right now I can't think of any. I had a list once."

"It's dry..." Jenny looks up at the ceiling, and frowns at the condensation dripping through. "Jesus, CB. You couldn't do better than this?"

"Could have," CB says. He pulls out a damp pack of cigarettes from his trenchcoat pocket, ignoring Jenny's disapproving glare. "But this was useful. Come on, I'm on the third floor. We'll take the stairs."

They pass by the elevator. It sits open, the bottom sunk a foot below the level of the floor. Both the up and down buttons are lit, and the interior light flickers like a strobe.

Jenny looks at the elevator apprehensively. "Stairs," she agrees.

The stairs are wide and the stair rail is mostly intact. CB takes them two at a time. When they reach the third floor Jenny shakes her head in annoyance.

"You're a *smoker*," she says. "And you're not even winded. How fair is that?"

CB doesn't bother to point out that she matched his pace all the way up and didn't break a sweat.

The third floor stairwell's door has no window. CB hesitates, puts his ear against it, and listens intently. He can hear the noise of everyday life: a few televisions, a few stereos playing loudly, a lot of arguments, some sober, some not. Nothing out of the ordinary. He opens the door a crack, peers through into the hall, then relaxes as he swings the door wide open.

"All clear?" Jenny asks.

"So far," CB says.

The main hall has a cracked, yellowed linoleum floor littered with trash—bottles and cans, mostly, though at the far end of the hall is a small bundle of cloth that may be laundry, or discarded clothing. A trail of fast food wrappers starts at the stairwell and ends a third of the way down the hall. The walls are an industrial shade of gray, cracked, covered in peeling paint and graffiti, and occasionally have chunks gouged out, revealing support beams and an utter lack of insulation. In stark contrast to the apparent flimsiness of the walls, the door for each apartment looks solid and heavy.

CB stops in front of room 313. The first number fell off the door years ago, leaving only a dust-encrusted outline of the first number three on the wood.

Jenny laughs. "Room Thirteen. Seriously?"

CB puts a finger to his lips. He bends over and stares at the seam between the door and the doorframe. He can just barely make out the outline of the slip of paper, still wedged where he put it the last time he left. It's a trick he picked up from watching *The Sting*—one of his favorite movies—and he exhales in relief.

"I don't think the bad guys found this place yet," CB says. "That's good."

He fishes his keys out of his trenchcoat pocket and starts unlocking the door. There are four separate keys for four separate locks, and by the time the last tumbler clicks Jenny is shifting from foot to foot, staring down the hallway nervously.

"Come on," CB says, and steps into his apartment, flicking on the light switch. Jenny follows, exhaling in relief, then stops at the entrance as she takes it in.

"Not what I expected," she admits.

CB closes the door behind her, and goes down the locks, one by one. "What were you expecting?"

Jenny shrugs. "Old food? Towering piles of garbage? This is actually clean. It even *smells* clean."

The furniture is shabby, but not trashy. An old armchair and a repaired love seat sit in the living room, with a nicked and battered wooden coffee table set in front of them and a not-quite-matching end table set between them. An old TV and a beat-up but well-maintained stereo sit on a cheap entertainment system—the kind you get from a drug store, made entirely of particle board and prone to falling apart if it is moved after being put together. A small kitchen, separated by an island, is on the far end.

"No leaks," Jenny adds, looking up at the ceiling.

"One of the advantages of living on this side of the building," CB says. "Make yourself at home. Dry off. I'll get my gear."

Jenny sits down on the love seat and pulls out her phone.

"No calls," CB warns.

"Yeah," Jenny says. "Not going to be a problem. I took out the SIM card on this thing, remember? I want to look through the TriHealth files."

CB nods. "Right. Good idea. Back in a bit."

CB's room consists of a mattress set on the floor, a dresser, one closet, two footlockers and four ashtrays. Band posters litter the walls. He opens his closet, rummages through his clean clothes, and heads back to the living room with a Joy Division t-shirt and a pair of black capri shorts. He drops them on the couch next to Jenny.

"They're probably a little big, but they're dry."

"Capris?" Jenny raises an eyebrow. "Seriously?"

"What? Skaters wear them all the time. Or they used to. I don't know what they do now."

"You *skate*?" Jenny is grinning openly now.

"Shut up," CB grumbles, and heads back to his room.

"Thanks," she calls after him.

He finds the crowbar in the back of the closet, hiding behind an old army jacket that slipped off a hanger and caught on the crook. He leans his mattress against a wall, then spends the next few minutes using the crowbar to tear up the floor. Everything is still there: three metal cases, each the size of a garment bag, stacked neatly on top of each other. He drags the first out and lugs it into the living room. Jenny, now wearing the t-shirt and shorts instead of her dripping clothing, looks up from her phone and stares at the case curiously.

"Gear," CB explains, then goes back for the other two. A few minutes later they're open, the contents of each laid out on the floor.

"Wow," Jenny says. "Is that your old costume?"

CB has never been big on the idea of costumes. While his gear is distinctive, it doesn't have any of the designs or symbols that a lot of other people in the game seem to favor. The black leather trenchcoat is plain, though the segmented armored plates inserted along the back and down the sides make it a little bulkier than normal. The long black gloves—gauntlets, really—are fingerless to minimize the loss of fine manipulation, and have rigid plates set into the back of each hand, coming just past the knuckles. Extra plates travel up his forearm ending in elbow pads. The tactical vest is similarly armored, and has plenty of pockets for various gadgets. The heavy canvas pants also have the segmented armor, and knee pads built into the fabric. The boots aren't nearly as heavy as CB is used to—the armor plates around the toes and shins are significantly lighter than steel.

"It's a bit warm for the summer, this far down south," CB says, "but I think I'm going to want it."

He sheds his shirt and kicks off his boots.

"Hey!" Jenny's eyes widen, and she turns her head away. "How about you do that in private?"

"We will both survive the indignity," CB says. "Tell me about the files. Find anything?"

Jenny stares intently at her phone. "A few things I don't understand," she says. "A few summaries of medical reports that focus on something called TRH. I don't understand that. And then there's this..." She holds out her phone to CB, head still turned away. "It's some kind of test."

"It's OK," CB says, amused. "I'm wearing pants now." He takes the phone and looks at the display. He frowns, then hands the phone back. "The name of the patient... he was one of the murder victims."

"That's what I thought," Jenny says. "Do you know what kind of test it is?"

CB shakes his head, then picks up the tactical vest and straps it on. "Not specifically. It kind of reminds me of a metahuman classification test. It's not, though. The categories aren't right."

"Well, so far all patients in these files have one," Jenny says. "And they're all referenced in one of the TRH reports. Do you know what TRH might be?"

"Nope," CB says. He reaches for the gloves. "A company, maybe? Can't remember a TRH in Travers' report."

"I think it's a medical term," Jenny says. "That's what it looks like in context."

"We'll need to ask a doctor." CB slips on the boots, tugging sharply to tighten and close them.

"You know one we can ask?" Jenny asks.

"Robert," CB says. "Gladiator. It's been a while, but I'm pretty sure he's going to want in on this."

"How do we contact him?"

"Good question," CB says. "He's a pretty solid recluse these days. I don't have a phone number, and he doesn't respond to email that often. Back in the day we all had homing beacons we could activate in a pinch, but I didn't bring one with me. I guess sending an email is our best shot..."

CB's voice trails off into silence. He cocks his head to one side and frowns.

Jenny tenses. "What's wrong?"

CB raises a hand for silence. He hears music playing three rooms down. Televisions in four other rooms. Everything else is quiet...

People. He can't hear people.

"We're in trouble." He grabs the armored trenchcoat and shrugs it on, then empties his old trenchcoat pockets hurriedly, transferring their contents.

"What's going on?" Jenny's voice instinctively drops down to a whisper.

CB shakes his head. "Don't know, but all of a sudden everyone stopped shouting."

He falls silent again. Very faintly, almost hidden behind the sound of the music and the televisions, he can hear a low *thrummm* that reminds him of the sound you hear from an electrical generator—only it doesn't have a specific location. It sounds like it's coming from everywhere at the same time. Then something *oily* slides across his skin. Something burns his blood, something freezes his soul, something cuts into his mind like a thousand tiny razors.

"*Fuck,*" CB snarls.

Jenny stares at him in alarm. "What?"

CB takes a breath and forces himself to stay calm. "You need to run."

Jenny's eyes widen. "Why?"

"Listen to me very carefully. Get your jacket. Go into the spare room next to the kitchen. Open the window, climb out onto the fire escape. Climb up to the roof." CB reaches into his pocket and pulls out the cell phone Travers gave him and his USB thumb drive. "There should be an old extension ladder up there. Extend it, put it across this building to the one next door, crawl across, and drag it onto the other roof after you. Take that building's fire escape down, then get to the pawn shop. Find Elliot. Can you get there on your own?"

Jenny nods. "I think so, but—"

CB hands the cell phone and thumb drive to Jenny. "This phone can be used to call Travers once—just once. Call him, tell him what's going on."

"I don't *know* what's going on," Jenny says.

"Magic," CB says. "They're coming after me with magic. That takes this to a whole new level of bad news."

Jenny stares at him blankly. "Magic? You're kidding, right?"

"Magic is *bad*, Jenny. It's *very bad*. I'm going to give you as much of a head start as I can. Get going."

"But—"

CB cuts her off. "Don't lose that thumb drive. There's another copy on the laptop at the safe house, but Elliot might not be able to get you back there. Tell Travers. He'll help you out."

Jenny glowers, torn between a desire to help and the thought that there might not be much she can do. "Try not to get killed," she says, then runs to the spare room. A moment later he hears wood squeaking against wood, then hears the sound of rain through the open spare room window. He walks over to his door and starts unlocking the deadbolts, one by one.

Try to give her five minutes. Try to give her at least five minutes.

The last deadbolt slides open. CB takes a shuddering breath, opens the door, and steps into the hall.

PART FIVE: ALBANY CITY

The only reason it takes Red Shift fifteen minutes to get to Albany is because he doesn't want to break the sound barrier.

It's not hard for him to run faster than sound—he can run considerably faster if he has to. The problem with breaking the sound barrier is the sonic boom: it's not a one-time event, it's a continuous, window-shattering sound that follows you, a sonic wake, and he doesn't want to attract that kind of attention. Anyway, he doesn't need to go supersonic: 700 miles an hour is more than sufficient to get to Albany.

Interstate 87 is the most direct route. Night running is perfect for stealth: his dark uniform makes it easy for him to be overlooked, especially when he's moving much faster than anyone expects a man-sized object to travel. The night vision enhancements in his visor, combined with the hyper-awareness he has when he's pushing any kind of speed, makes it trivial to avoid traffic, dodge tolls, and generally remain unnoticed.

Senator Morgan's house isn't actually in Albany, it's in Schenectady. Schenectady is usually thought of as Albany's poor cousin these days, full of neighborhoods in steady economic decline, but parts of it have been set aside for the rich and powerful. Senator Morgan qualifies as both.

The house is set on the outskirts of town, a three-story colonial on not quite an acre of land, surrounded by old trees and a tall iron gate. It's much more room than the Senator needs—he's one of those rare politicians who is a bachelor—but he probably describes it as "modest" to his friends.

Red Shift perches on a billboard set on a hill about two miles out from the house, gazing down at the estate through his visor.

"I don't see anyone," he says. "The house is completely dark."

"There may be no one in the house, but I'm pretty sure there's someone on the grounds." Street Ronin's voice comes clearly through his earpiece. "I'm linking up with your visor now. Stand by."

A few seconds later his visor displays a layout of the house and grounds.

"The detached garage," Street Ronin says. "The security detail is stationed on the second floor of the detached garage."

"Are they private security?" Red Shift asks.

"I expect so. He doesn't qualify for a dedicated Secret Service detail. But I also expect they'll be upper-tier professionals."

Red Shift sighs in frustration. "Guys, the easiest thing to do is take them out first, then search the house. That's my vote."

There's a moment of silence, then Street Ronin comes back on the line, sounding vaguely amused. *"Both* the Lieutenant *and* Overmind believe that's a bad idea."

Red Shift almost laughs out loud. "OK, I'd like to know why."

"The Lieutenant thinks anything that results in harm coming to the staff of a US Senator—even the non-lethal variety—will immediately put Crossfire so high up the danger list we'll be spending all our time dealing with that instead of making progress on this," Street Ronin says. "He's probably right. Overmind thinks that taking out the Senator's guards will only tip him off that we're interested in him. He also says if the guards are worth the money the Senator is paying them, one of the ways they establish an all clear is to remain in constant communication with an outside office. If that communication is disrupted it'll trigger a red flag and they'll bring extra resources to bear. He's probably right, too."

"Remember when the bad guys were dumb? No offense to Overmind or Jack. Fine, I need a plan. I don't have one."

"Do a drive-by on the west side, throw the snoop over the fence."

It takes a little under ten seconds to reach the house. Deploying the snoop is the tricky part: it's a small metal globe, a little larger than his fist, and he can't just toss it through the bars as he races by. Something thrown by a man running seven hundred miles per hour continues traveling at seven hundred miles per hour, and not only would it not survive the landing, the noise involved would attract a lot of unwanted attention. Red Shift has to come to a full stop in front of the gate, put the snoop through the iron bars, then set off again before anyone has time to react. All told, he stops in front of the gate for little more than half a second. It feels longer. Ten seconds later he's back on top of the billboard, watching the grounds carefully.

"OK," he says. "Turn it on."

A few seconds pass. "OK, sit tight. I'll get back to you when I find something useful." With that, Street Ronin breaks the connection.

Red Shift lies on his back on top of the billboard and relaxes, waiting patiently for the snoop to do its job. It's a clear night, and they're far enough on the outskirts of the city to actually see stars. He takes the opportunity to enjoy the moment. He doesn't get them often.

"OK, I've got something." Street Ronin's voice returns, businesslike but sounding pleased. "The snoop found the encrypted wireless network the security firm uses. I was able to hack in. I have access to their monitoring station now, and I'm mapping the network. I just need a few more minutes."

"So who are these guys?" Red Shift asks. "Anyone we know?"

"Group called 'Forward Point Security,'" Street Ronin says. "Never heard of them before today. Approach from the back of the house. Over the gate, across the grounds, straight to the back door. You'll need to bypass the lock. Don't worry about the security system. I've got everything looped."

Ten seconds later Red Shift is up to the gate. He vaults over it easily, staring a security camera straight on as he pitches over the top and lands in the grass on the other side. Moments later he's at the back door, quickly working at the lock with tools from his belt. The lock is mechanical, and it's a good one—it actually takes him a minute to get all the tumblers in place. Finally the door clicks open. He steps through.

"I'm inside."

The kitchen is a spacious, open room with a tile floor and marble countertops. An island with a sink sits in the middle of the room. All of the appliances are black and polished chrome. None of them look like they've ever been used.

"This is the tricky part," Street Ronin says. "I have a floor plan of the house—it's the one Forward Point uses when they're monitoring the alarms. Problem is, the floor plan fits the house perfectly."

"That's what it's supposed to do, isn't it?"

"Sure," Street Ronin says, "if you're not storing information about a conspiracy that resulted in a murder of your very famous grandfather in it. If you are, I think you want it kept in a place not accessible to the help."

"Wall safe?" Red Shift suggests.

"I don't think so. He'd need someplace to work. He needs a secret office."

"Right," Red Shift says. "Well, where's the fusebox?"

The wine cellar, like the kitchen, is fully stocked, meticulously clean, and apparently just for show. The circuit breaker box is set at the far end of the room, the only wall not covered with wine racks. It's a large, modern box, and when Red Shift opens it he sees rows of circuit breakers, all clearly labeled.

"You getting this?"

"Yes," Street Ronin says. "Take the backplate off."

Red Shift produces a multitool from his utility belt, and removes the cover and backplate from the circuit breaker box, exposing all the wires as they connect to each circuit.

"There we go," Red Shift says. "A power line that bypasses every single breaker on the panel..." He traces it as it passes its way through the box, notes the wire as it comes out the other end, then screws everything back in place. "We just need to see where it goes."

"Sure," Street Ronin says, "but once it disappears into the ceiling the only way to do that is to—"

"Found something," Red Shift says. "It doesn't disappear into the ceiling. It disappears into the concrete wall, behind one of the wine racks."

He waits a minute to allow Street Ronin and the others to see what he's seeing.

"This is starting to feel a little cliched," Red Shift adds. "Want to put money on one of these wine bottles opening a secret door?"

He starts pressing wine bottles at random. Finally one of them clicks, and the entire wine rack pushes out, swings to one side, and reveals a vault door set into the wall.

"I guess it's a good thing I didn't take you up on that bet," Street Ronin says. "Let's take a look at that door."

It's not an old-school vault door with the large spinning lock set in the center. It has an electronic screen on one side, a thin slot that looks like you could insert something the size of a credit card into it, and a keypad beneath the slot.

"I think we're screwed," Street Ronin says. "Obviously you need to enter a numerical combination to open the door, but you also need some kind of card. The Senator probably keeps that on him at all times."

"Maybe," Red Shift says. "But you know, every time I buy something that needs a key, it always comes with a spare."

There's a wall safe in the master bedroom; it's tied in to the main security system. Street Ronin is able to pop the safe remotely while simultaneously masking the alarm. In the safe is a stack of legal documents, a watch, and an electronic key the size of a credit card.

"OK, we have the key," Red Shift says. "Now we need the number."

"Just put it in," Street Ronin says. "I'll try to hack the PIN through the card."

The key fits into the vault door slot perfectly, and when inserted the digital panel and keypad light up. The digital panel starts counting down from a minute.

"Uh..." Red Shift says.

"God *damn* it," Street Ronin snarls. "Hold on."

Red Shift watches the countdown, tension rising with each second that slips away. At the thirty-five-second mark Street Ronin gives him a number, and he punches it in.

"No dice," Red Shift says.

Street Ronin swears again. Red Shift continues to watch the countdown, wondering what will happen if it reaches zero. At the fifteen-second mark, Street Ronin gives him a new number. This time the countdown stops: the door buzzes, clicks, and swings open to reveal a very small office with a chair, a desk, and a computer.

Red Shift sighs in relief. "We're in."

He can hear Street Ronin laughing on the other end. "Thank our resident mastermind supervillain. Overmind guessed it was either the date he was sworn in to the House or the Senate. It was the House."

"Well let's see what we've got." Red Shift steps into the room, moves around to the front of the desk and sits in the chair. "I'm about to turn it on."

He presses the power button. The monitor blinks on.

"Greg! Get out!"

The urgency in Street Ronin's voice combined with the use of his real name causes him to look up in alarm. He hears a loud *click* echo through the room, and sees the vault door swinging shut with surprising speed.

He moves. His perspective shifts.

The world slows to a crawl as his hyper-awareness kicks in. He's dimly aware of the sonic boom as he vaults over the desk and races out of the room—he can't hear it, but he can feel it forming around him. The vault door is half open, appearing to have frozen in mid-swing. He sidesteps through it with inches to spare, surging across the room and up the stairs into the kitchen. He lowers his head slightly, instinctively raising one arm as he runs through the outer wall at nearly three thousand miles an hour, ripping it to pieces as he bursts free into the night air. He feels heat behind him, the shuddering beginnings of an explosion, but he doesn't turn to look. He gathers speed, leaving a furrow in the grass, then bursts through the iron gate. Twisted bits of iron and brick fly in all directions as he turns and tears down the road, still gathering speed. The sonic boom follows him as he runs, sounding like the unending snap of an infinitely cracking whip. A few seconds later he stops and looks back the way he came. He's miles away now, but he can see the glow of fire on the horizon. He can feel the reverberation of the explosion, even from here.

"Looks like I made someone angry," Red Shift says.

"Jesus," Street Ronin says, relief flooding his voice. "Jesus Christ, that was close."

"I try not to get blown up more than once a month," Red Shift says. "It's inconvenient."

PART SIX: UNHAPPY REUNION

All the lights on the third floor go out.

A few of the lights flicker on, then off, then on, then off, creating a strobe effect as CB cautiously makes his way down the hall to the stairwell. In the brief moments of light, the hallway looks different: the walls seem taller, the ceiling shimmers and rolls like water, and all the while he feels that strange oily, burning, freezing, cutting *power* slide over him. He reaches out to the wall to brace himself, then immediately draws his hand back. The wall is *soft*. It *throbbed* ever so slightly as he touched it, and his fingers are wet.

*Not just magic. This is a **lot** of magic.*

He closes his eyes for a second and reaches out, trying to find the world around him, to pull it together and let it all fall into place, but he can't. The power that surrounds him isn't a part of the world, and it isn't letting the world in. He sways in place as the power gathers. The air around him feels heavy.

At the end of the hall the stairwell door opens. Light streams out from the stairwell—those lights are, apparently, working—revealing a black silhouette standing in the doorway. CB can't see its face, but he can feel the power swirling around it.

"You have my attention," CB says. His voice sounds muffled, like he's trying to talk through a burlap sack. The figure doesn't move.

And then it does: in the blink of an eye it crosses the hall. Strong hands grab CB by the lapels of his trenchcoat, and with a violent, wrenching motion CB slams into the opposite wall.

And crashes through the opposite wall.

And flies into the apartment behind the opposite wall.

CB doesn't feel the initial impact of the wall. The wall is thin, and he doesn't hit any support beams on the way through. He crashes into a green couch in the living room, knocking it over backward, spilling over onto the floor. Immediately he rolls to his feet and into a low crouch, nearly tripping on something lying on the floor. His hand reaches down to steady himself, and quickly draws back when he feels flesh.

The body of an older man, slightly overweight with graying hair and a sparse, patchy beard, lies on its back, wide glassy eyes staring sightlessly at the ceiling. The mouth hangs open; blood and vomit stream down the corners and are caked around the lips.

CB stares at the body. He's seen this before.

Little Dresden. 1984.

The door bursts open, wood splintering to pieces as one sad remnant, still attached to the frame, swings crazily on a single twisted hinge. The figure stands in the doorway, still a silhouette in the darkness, but CB recognizes it now. Recognizes *him* now.

"I hoped you were dead," CB says, voice flat.

"You'll never be that lucky," Plague says.

The oily power surges. Plague leaps through the air, hands outstretched. CB twists in his crouch, then buries his shoulder into Plague's solar plexus. Plague grunts, stumbles, and falls to the ground, gasping.

CB doesn't waste time. He runs out of the apartment, down the hall, to the stairwell.

Five minutes.

The power he senses is coming from Plague. It shouldn't come from Plague. Plague is a mutant. Plague believed absolutely and unshakably in the purity of his own blood, that it was the purity of his blood that allowed him to inflict sickness on almost anyone he wished. The Plague he knew probably didn't even *believe* in magic.

Yeah, well, it's been more than twenty-five years, hasn't it?

Plague steps into the hall just as CB pushes through the door to the stairwell, blinking rapidly as his eyes adjust to the light. Jenny's headed to the roof, so CB goes in the other direction. He's halfway to the second floor when he sees three armed men on the second floor landing. They're dressed like the ones who attacked Martin's house—same gear, same weapons. All three look up as CB leaps down the rest of the stairs and launches himself, feet first, into the chest of the closest soldier.

The soldier smashes into the man on his left; both crash into the wall and slump to the ground, motionless. CB twists in midair, landing on his hands and feet. The third soldier brings his rifle to bear; CB grabs his leg and *pulls* just as the soldier pulls the trigger. The soldier falls back, rifle firing wildly into the air. He strikes his head on the floor and doesn't move.

The door to the third floor stairwell crashes open.

CB grabs the rifle. Looking up, he can see brief flashes of Plague over the tops of the railings as he races down to the second floor. He ejects the old magazine, takes a fresh one from the soldier's belt, and reloads.

Plague is getting closer. His footsteps echo like thunder, the stairs shake with each step, and half a second later Plague runs into view. CB sees him clearly for the first time in twenty-five years.

He's still a bruiser. His dark button-up shirt strains against the size of his arms, and he stands and moves with no trace of infirmity. But he looks *old*. His hair is white, his face droops, the joints in his fingers have swollen in a way that suggests arthritis—despite looking just as tough as he always did, there's no question that time has marched on. The only direct link to the man he was are his eyes: they burn with the same contempt, the same murderous hatred, as they did in Little Dresden.

CB opens up with the assault rifle. Bullet after bullet tears into Plague: leg, shoulder, chest, neck, head. Plague stumbles as the bullets continue to rip through him. CB keeps the trigger down until the magazine is empty, then calmly steps back and watches as Plague falls to the second floor landing with a heavy, wet sound. Blood pools quickly beneath him, and he makes a gasping, gurgling sound as he claws feebly at the floor.

A small voice in the back of CB's head says *that wasn't very heroic*. CB thinks about the corpse in the apartment in his hall, and then thinks about how many other corpses they'll probably find, and decides he doesn't care.

"Goodbye, asshole," CB says.

As if in response the oily power gathers again. Plague's body twitches once, then he pushes himself upright. He stares at CB, his mouth twisting into a savage, triumphant smile.

"Not this time," he croaks.

The wounds on Plague's neck and head close. They close so quickly that it looks more like they're being *erased*. The only trace remaining is the blood, and even that is starting to dry up and flake away. Plague unbuttons his shirt with one arm, and CB sees the wound in his shoulder doing the same thing. Plague shrugs off the shirt, casting aside the blood-soaked cotton, to reveal smooth, unblemished skin.

And runes.

His chest and both arms are covered in a strange, oily script that shimmers silver under the stairwell lights. CB doesn't know what the symbols mean, but looking at them makes him queasy: they're *unnatural*, they bend and twist in ways that writing simply can't do on its own. And the symbols aren't still: they *move on his skin*, scuttling across his chest and around his arms like swarms of insects.

Better part of valor BETTER PART OF VALOR

CB takes two steps off the second floor platform and vaults over the stair rail, dropping into the space between the twisting stairwell until he lands on the platform leading to the lobby. His right leg twists as he lands, and he feels a sharp pain in his ankle. He pushes the pain aside and shoves his way through the door, into the lobby.

Gunfire tears through the lobby as four soldiers open fire from the far end of the room. CB dives, sliding across the dirty floor, as bullets sail over him, ripping through rotting wood and mold-caked plaster. The soldiers adjust their aim, and CB rolls to the side, grunting in pain as bullets hit his trenchcoat. They don't pierce the armor plating, but they *hurt*.

In panicked desperation CB reaches out, trying to focus on the world around him, to find some thread of reality that isn't tainted by the oily mess of power that seems to have displaced everything else. There's almost nothing there, almost... but there—*there*, just out of reach, he can feel the pulse of the world, swirling. It's faint, and it's almost too far away...

He grits his teeth, closes his eyes, and focuses. The world wobbles for a moment, hesitates, then everything falls into place.

CB exhales slowly. Bullets ricochet off the ground around him as the soldiers start to miss. He stands, reaches into a trenchcoat pocket, and pulls out a pack of cigarettes. He twirls the pack in his fingers as he looks at each soldier in turn, then winks.

Every rifle jams at the same time.

"Leave it, boys." Plague's voice comes from the stairwell door. "Take a walk. I got this."

CB can't see their faces, but he recognizes their body language. They don't *precisely* take orders from Plague, and he just told them to do something that directly contradicted someone they *do* take orders from. It's a tough spot to be in. If circumstances were different, he might be inclined to sympathize. He takes a cigarette out of the pack, places it between his lips, and fishes around for his lighter.

One of the soldiers makes a decision: he stands down. He slings his rifle over his shoulder and heads out the door. It's still raining, and the soldier starts to jog as soon as he exits the building. CB finds his lighter, pulls it out, and lights his cigarette, eying the other three. Two more soldiers head for the door at almost the same time. The third, seeing the others leaving, hurries after them.

CB waits until the last soldier leaves the lobby, waits for the door to close, then turns around.

Plague stands outside the stairwell entrance, leaning against the wall. His arms are crossed, and the strange oily runes appear to flow down the length of his arms, to his wrists, and then *jump* from his wrists to his stomach, flow up his chest, and down his arms again. There's no trace of the gunshot wounds at all—even the dried blood is gone.

"New ink," CB says.

"*Old* ink," Plague says. "Older than you or me. Older than time."

CB snorts in irritation as he blows out a stream of smoke. "Oh come on, *Doyle*. Don't start that shit."

"Fuck you," Plague says. "I don't work for you."

"Yeah?" CB flicks some ash from his cigarette. "Who *do* you work for?"

Plague offers a thin smile. "The *real* masters."

"Give me a fucking break," CB says. "You work for, what, the Illuminati now?"

"People who understand power," Plague says. "People who know what power demands. Who understand that sacrifices..." He sways a little, and a brief flash of grief twists his face into a pained grimace. "Sacrifices must be made."

"Like the people in this building," CB says.

Plague shrugs. "Those weren't people. They don't keep people in this part of the city. Just animals."

"Now *there's* the Doyle I used to know," CB says.

"Yeah," Plague says, "here I am."

CB tenses.

Plague moves so fast CB can barely track him. He leaps across the room, the runes on his body glowing brightly as the air ripples around him. CB throws himself to one side, dodging Plague's attack by inches. Plague lands on the ground in a crouch, and with inhuman speed he lashes out again. CB rolls out of the way, feeling a breeze as Plague's fist misses his head and drives deep into the floor, his arm sinking in as far as his elbow.

He didn't use to be this strong.

CB kicks. Plague pulls his arm out of the hole he made in the cement sub-flooring and grunts as a stronger-than-steel-toed boot connects with the small of his back. Plague sprawls on the ground, but immediately gets back up. CB rolls up to his feet and jumps back as Plague rips up a piece of cement from the floor and throws it at him. It misses and crashes into the wall. The wall shudders as cement shatters against cinderblock.

Too strong. You can't fight him directly. He's too damned strong.

"WHY AREN'T YOU GETTING SICK?" Plagues voice rises in pitch to an enraged madman's shriek. "GET SICK, DAMN YOU!"

The runes on Plague's arms are shining so brightly that they look like tiny spotlights roving over his body. The air around him shimmers and swirls as if the oily power is straining to take a visible form. CB's stomach clenches and he stumbles, nearly falling into Plague's kick. He twists in desperation, and the heel of Plague's boot glances off CB's knee. CB shouts in pain. His stomach clenches again, and a moment later he rolls over onto his hands and knees and vomits. His hands are shaking. His head feels hot.

He's getting sick.

Plague smiles, showing his teeth. "Finally. *Finally.* After all these years, I finally get to kill you the way you've always deserved: painfully. Slowly. Helplessly."

CB tries to focus, but the world isn't there. Just oil and sick. He gags, feels his stomach twist, and vomits again.

"I got power now," Plague says. "I paid a hell of a price to get it. I did things..." He breaks off, and through the haze of his own sickness CB is dimly aware of the grief in his voice. "I did things. Killing you won't make it all worthwhile, but you know what? *Not* killing you would make it a *waste.*"

CB's vision blurs. He feels mucus pouring out of his nose and eyes. His hands won't stop shaking.

Plague stands over him, watching him writhe and puke and claw at his face. "You're going to die today, Curveball. You're going to die, then everyone *else* is going to die. Every hero, every villain, every poor metahuman bastard on this planet is going to die. There's not a damn thing you can do about it."

PART SEVEN: LINES OF COMMUNICATION

The rain has picked up since they arrived at the apartment, and the fire escape is so slippery from the mixture of rain and grime that Jenny's first attempt up the ladder is almost her last. Her foot slips, her body twists, and she feels herself falling over the edge. She avoids falling by thrusting the crook of her arm through the top rung of the ladder. She dangles there for a moment, trying not to panic, then manages to get one foot back on the ladder, then another.

She makes her way up the remaining seven floors, then finally pushes herself up onto the roof. The roof is a flat, shallow depression that is currently a pool of filthy water about two inches thick. She grimaces as she hauls herself over the edge of the roof, and grits her teeth as she slogs across the roof, looking for the ladder.

The ladder is stuck, and she has to struggle to get it to extend. Eventually it does, emitting a loud squeak of protest all the way to its full length. Getting it across the building to the one next door—a building of similar height and quality, complete with its own shallow pool of filth on the roof—is considerably easier to do. Crawling across it, however, is terrifying. She clings to the ladder and forces herself not to look down, ignoring the way the ladder shakes and rattles in the wind, and ignoring the way it creaks every time she shifts her weight on it. When she finally crosses she pulls the ladder along behind her. The fire escape is at the far end. It's wider, sturdier, and in much better condition; it's much easier to climb down than the one on CB's building was to climb up.

Once she hits the ground she starts running. For a while that's all she does: CB wanted her away from whatever was in the building, so she focuses on doing that first. Despite the events of the last few days she finds she has more than enough energy for running. She follows the boardwalk for a while, then, suddenly remembering some of the things CB had said about the boardwalk, she abruptly veers inland for a few blocks.

When she finally slows down, she realizes she has no idea how to get to the pawn shop. She knows where she is in relation to CB's apartment, but they got there through the sewers. She needs a map. She doesn't have one. She doesn't know where she is. She doesn't know where to go. And, once again, she's drenched to the bone.

She looks around for a shop, or a restaurant, or even a bar. She doesn't see anything like that. It looks like she walked into a warehouse graveyard: empty buildings, boarded up with shattered windows, large, empty loading bays, graffiti on all the walls and trash everywhere. She doesn't see any people, though, and that surprises her. Based on what CB had told her, she expected to see homeless.

The building to her right looks as if it was gutted by fire, but the roof appears to be intact, and she wants to get out of the rain. She makes her way up a concrete loading bay and walks through the open bay door into a dark, cavernous room filled with debris. She stands in the doorway, shivering despite the summer heat, and tries to decide what to do next.

She has to get to the pawn shop. She has to figure out where the pawn shop *is*. There are only a few ways to do that, and none of them are particularly safe. Asking random passersby for directions is dangerous, Farraday City being what it is. Being *lost*, she assumes, will be interpreted as being *vulnerable*. She doesn't want to deal with that at the moment. The other option is to turn on the GPS in her smartphone—even without the SIM chip, she should still be able to use that. But that's probably a bad idea on an entirely different level. She has to assume that the "bad guys"— whoever they are—will be waiting for her to use something like that. The best solution, she thinks, would be to get on a city bus and ride it until she reaches the terminal. She knows how to get to the pawn shop from there. The problem with that plan is that she'll have a higher chance of running into the police, or into the TriHealth people who are looking for them.

Or she could find a pay phone, call Elliot, and get him to come to her.

She shoves her hands into her jacket pockets. Her right hand closes around the cell phone—the one Travers gave CB. She pulls it out. It's a cheap model, with a flip top and a very basic LCD display. She takes a breath, flips it open, and turns it on.

The phone takes a few seconds to boot. She accesses the address book, and finds a single entry—a New York phone number, no name, no address. She dials it.

The phone rings three times, then she hears Pete Travers' voice on the other end.

"CB, this is not a good time."

Travers' voice is muffled. It sounds like he's outside, which is unusual. Jenny can hear cars driving by.

"Uncle Pete?"

Travers hesitates a moment, then clears his throat. "Jenny?"

"Uncle Pete, we're in trouble. CB needs help. He gave me this phone and told me to call you. I don't know what's going on but he says it's magic and he told me to run."

"Wait, what? Hold on." She hears Travers puffing—he's running. The street noise fades, and when he speaks again his voice is a little less muffled. "Did you say *magic*?"

"Yes."

Travers sighs. "OK. This is... kind of an inconvenient time. Where are you now?"

"I'm in a warehouse..." Jenny says.

"Right, sorry, I mean city. What city are you in?"

Jenny hesitates, torn between caution and desperation. Desperation wins. "Farraday City."

"Really?" Travers sounds mildly surprised. "That's interesting. Um, something happened at the office recently, and I don't have access to as much support as I'd like, but I do have a few options. Hold tight. I can't promise anything. The support may be unconventional."

"I'm not sure what normal support would look like, right now," Jenny says.

Travers laughs a little. "That's fair. Jenny, after we hang up I need you to keep the phone turned on."

"I thought this phone could only be used once safely," Jenny says.

"Don't call anyone with it. Just leave it on."

"OK," Jenny says. "Thanks."

"Don't thank me yet," Travers says. "Stay safe. If everything works the way I want you'll have help soon."

"What if it doesn't work the way you want?"

"Well," Travers says, "then I guess it must be Tuesday."

The line goes dead. Jenny stares at the phone, sighs, then puts it back in her pocket, careful not to shut it off first.

"*Fraulein Forrest.*"

Jenny spins in alarm. She sees the pistol first: a modified Luger, larger and heavier, with an elongated barrel and a larger bore. The man looks about her age, maybe a year or two older, and is dressed in black combat fatigues. He's clean-shaven, his blonde hair is cut short on the sides, slightly longer on top. His clear blue eyes are hard and calculating. He carries himself with ease and confidence; he radiates a sense of purpose that reminds her inexplicably of her great-grandfather.

She tears her gaze away from the pistol and forces herself to look the man in the eye. It is only then that she recognizes him. He's the man from her great-grandfather's security feed. He's the man who murdered him.

"Richter."

Johann Richter, the most infamous metahuman of World War II, smiles politely in return.

* * *

Peter Raphael Travers stands in a New York alleyway, stares at his cell phone, and sighs.

"Shit."

He stares at the ground for a moment, thinking quickly. Then he starts walking deeper into the alley.

"Marty is going to kill me. Assuming no one else does first..."

Travers is no longer dressed in a slightly rumpled, nondescript suit. He's wearing blue jeans—something he hasn't done in decades—and a garish red-and-blue Hawaiian shirt that isn't tucked in. His hair is gone—he's completely bald—and he has a day's growth of beard. It's enough of a change that most of the people who are looking for him who *know* him might not recognize him on a first pass. He carries a camping backpack slung over one shoulder. As he walks farther into the alley, he unslings his backpack and starts tugging at the drawstring on top.

When he's out of view he starts digging through the backpack in earnest. Eventually he finds what he's looking for—another disposable cell phone. He pulls it out, turns it on, waits for the beep, then closes his eyes and tries to remember the number.

He dials.

He waits.

* * *

Vigilante sits in the Tactical Room of the safehouse, monitoring news feeds. The morning news shows—usually reserved for superficially cheerful topics, birthday announcements, and weather and traffic reports—are breathlessly reporting on the explosion that leveled Senator Morgan's Schenectady home.

So far the narrative is that terrorists blew up his house. The press, of course, is trying to find a link between the attack on the Senator's home and the attack on the Forrest Brownstone. The official government statement is that "no information on a link has been proven at this time."

There is video of the destroyed iron gate and the furrow Red Shift created while exiting the house. Thankfully, due to Street Ronin's snoop, there is no footage of Red Shift.

That we know of.

Vigilante sighs, drinks day-old coffee, and tries to figure out what to do next.

"What's the damage?" Red Shift comes into the room balancing four fast food bags on top of two boxes of donuts. He sets them down on a small table next to the computer desk and pulls up a second chair.

"Light breakfast?" Vigilante suppresses a smile. Every time Red Shift pushes the limits of his speed he spends the next few days eating a seemingly endless stream of fatty and sugary foods. What's weird is that it doesn't matter how long he was running: last night he only topped out for a second or two, but it triggered this reaction just the same.

"Well, I had those pizzas when I got back." Red Shift grins good-naturedly as he opens the first bag, unwraps an egg sandwich, and starts wolfing it down.

Vigilante turns back to the feeds. "Nothing publicly tying Crossfire to the Senator's mansion. Not even on the rumor sites. So that's something."

Red Shift nods, his cheerful demeanor changing into a thoughtful, pensive look. "I hate to say it, but I think this is a win for the bad guys."

Vigilante raises an eyebrow. "How do you figure?"

Red Shift shrugs, then reaches for the second bag of food. "If we assume the Senator is working for them, all they need to do is claim that he was attacked by the same group who attacked Martin Forrest. Then they can come up with any fall guy they wish. They get an extra layer of protection because one of their people is now a 'victim.'"

"I agree." Artemis LaFleur steps into the communications center, nodding politely to both of them. "I would, if I were them, use this opportunity to pick a credible target and accuse him—or her—of being responsible for Liberty's murder, the attack on the Forrest residence, and the explosion. I would target someone the conspirators consider a threat, and the performance I would put on for the public would be spectacular enough to justify whatever actions I'd need to take to further my own aims."

Vigilante doesn't like working with villains. From time to time he's worked with heroes, which has its own challenges, but nine times out of ten heroes have the same general goals he does. Villains, by and large, don't— but LaFleur is complicated. His aim, his mission in life, is to save the world from itself. The way he chooses to do this, from Vigilante's perspective, is alarming... but, in very specific circumstances, it makes him easier to trust.

"OK," Vigilante says. "That sounds reasonable. But who would they go after?"

"I can't say with certainty," LaFleur says, "but given how effectively they've neutralized all my contacts in the government, I'm inclined to believe I'm in the running."

Vigilante nods slowly. "I could see that. You're famous enough that the public would eat it up, and your reputation would make it easy to justify all kinds of extreme actions in the name of taking you down."

"It's not really his style, though," Red Shift says, wiping his mouth on a napkin before reaching for the third bag. "I mean, when I first heard Liberty was murdered, Overmind wasn't even in the running to be put on my list of possible suspects."

"Mine either," Vigilante agrees. "But the public would probably focus more on the fact that he's tried to take over the world twice."

"Three times," LaFleur says. "Though the third attempt was, I grant, too subtle to make the news."

Vigilante shrugs. "You see my point. You have a reputation for *trying to take over the world.* You've been out of the public's eye for years. All they have to say is that you've been 'radicalized' and are adopting extreme measures because this time around, you're playing for keeps."

LaFleur smiles slightly. "You don't have to convince me. I'm already taking precautions." Something in his jacket buzzes. He reaches in, pulls out a very expensive cell phone, and looks at the number. One eyebrow shoots up and he frowns.

"Odd," LaFleur says. "I don't recognize this number."

Vigilante tenses. Red Shift stops chewing for a moment, frowns, then swallows his sandwich.

"You want to trace the call?" Vigilante asks.

"Yes," LaFleur says. "I very much do."

"I'll get Street Ronin," Red Shift says. He hurries out of the room.

Seconds later Street Ronin hurries into the room, sits down in Red Shift's chair, and starts typing at the computer furiously. "Hook up the phone."

Red Shift hands LaFleur a micro-USB cable. LaFleur attaches it to his phone, Red Shift attaches the other end to a hub sitting next to the monitor.

"OK," Street Ronin says, "put it on speakerphone."

LaFleur presses a button on his phone. "Yes."

"My name is Peter Raphael Travers."

The room is uncomfortably silent. Red Shift, Vigilante, and Street Ronin exchange uneasy glances.

"I believe you know who I am," the voice continues.

LaFleur takes in the information, apparently unfazed that a Federal agent called his personal phone. "I do."

"I expect you're wondering how I have this number," Travers says. "Let's not get into that. The short version is 'I'm a spy'—the long version is more interesting, but it's long. Instead, I want to talk to you about Curveball."

LaFleur reacts then. His lips thin, he cocks his head to one side, and he stares at the phone intently. His curiosity has been piqued. "Do tell."

"I am operating under the assumption," Travers says, "that you want to assist him in his investigation into Liberty's murder. Do I assume correctly?"

"You do," LaFleur says.

Red Shift looks from LaFleur, to the phone, to Vigilante. Vigilante shrugs.

"Glad to hear it." Travers takes a deep breath. "Curveball is in Farraday City. He is there with Martin Forrest's daughter, and she has just contacted me asking for help. They are, at this very moment, in trouble."

"What kind of trouble?" LaFleur asks.

"Magic," Travers says.

"That's 800 miles from here," LaFleur says. "And searching for anything in Farraday City is... problematic."

"I can't help you with travel arrangements," Travers says, "but the young lady has a cell phone. I can give you the phone number. I can also give you access to a satellite that will allow you to pinpoint the location of that cell phone in a matter of minutes. One-time access, of course—I expect they'll detect the breach immediately, but it should take them at least an hour to kick you off."

LaFleur purses his lips thoughtfully.

"I'm not in a position to help them right now," Travers says, "but just between you and me—and anyone else who might be listening in—if the bad guys want someone dead, keeping them alive is usually a fantastic idea."

LaFleur looks at Vigilante questioningly. Vigilante nods.

"Give me the information," LaFleur says.

Travers recites three numbers—a telephone number, an IP address, and a password—then disconnects the phone.

"He was in the city," Street Ronin says. "But I didn't get him."

"Do we think it's really him?" Vigilante asks.

LaFleur considers the question. "Yes," he says finally.

"Six minutes," Red Shift says.

LaFleur turns his attention to Red Shift. "I beg your pardon?"

"I can be in Farraday City in six minutes. Street Ronin, can you give me a weather report?"

"Six minutes," LaFleur repeats.

"It won't be quiet," Red Shift says. "Someone's going to notice. But I'll get there before they can do anything about it."

"It's clear all the way there," Street Ronin says. "Raining like hell in the city limits, though."

"That'll be fun." Red Shift looks at the boxes of donuts longingly and sighs. "Give me a hand with the rig?"

"Yeah," Street Ronin says. "Vigilante, hack in to the phone, then send the location to his visor."

"Got it," Vigilante says. Street Ronin gets up and leaves with Red Shift; Vigilante moves to his spot and starts typing.

"His rig?" LaFleur asks.

"It's like a ruggedized IV," Vigilante says. "Pumps nutrients and glucose into his body."

"Why?"

Vigilante keys in the last number Travers gave them, and the computer monitor updates to display a map of the United States. Halfway down the Georgia coast is a tiny blinking red dot. "So he doesn't starve."

PART EIGHT: SHOWDOWN

"I would prefer to do this without resorting to force," Richter says. "I have no desire or need to kill you. It is wasteful."

Jenny says nothing. She keeps staring at the gun.

"Do not, however, mistake reluctance for unwillingness." Richter's voice is calm, almost soothing. "I will do what I must. I will reflect, very briefly, on the unfortunate waste of your life, and then I will continue living mine."

She doesn't believe for a second that he's going to let her live. As soon as she no longer serves any useful purpose, he will kill her without a second thought. There's no chance of her doing anything to stop him, either; he and her great-grandfather were about as evenly matched as they come. She doesn't have a chance. That said, she isn't going to just shrug her shoulders and surrender.

She forces herself to look at Richter, pushing back the anger she feels when she sees his face. She keeps her expression neutral, and when she speaks her voice is calm and even-toned.

"What do you want?"

"I want very little," Richter says. "Your cooperation, for a time. I represent certain parties who desire information. Give us that information and all will be well."

He's lying, of course.

"Bullshit."

Richter's expression doesn't change. "You have a coarse tongue."

Jenny crosses her arms stubbornly. "You murdered my great-grandfather. I'm pretty sure I know what's going to happen to me, whether I cooperate or not. Since I'm not going to get what I want, I don't see why I should cooperate."

Richter's expression hardens. "Don't try my patience, *girl*. You are not worth the effort it would take to subdue."

"Do what you have to do," Jenny's voice is tight with barely-contained anger. "Pull the trigger. Quit wasting my time."

Richter shrugs slightly and raises the pistol so the barrel is pointed at her head. "Goodbye, *Fraulein Forrest*."

Jenny stares down the barrel of the pistol and sways slightly. She feels dizzy and lightheaded, her heart is racing, and all of a sudden she is hyper-aware of everything around her: where she's standing, where Richter is standing, every piece of rubble on the floor, every disturbed patch of dirt. She notices, for the first time, that the wall on the other side of the warehouse has collapsed inward, as if a wrecking ball had smashed into it. She notices how far away Richter is standing from her. Her instincts scream *move! Run! Fight!*

It's useless, she thinks. Richter outclasses her, physically, in every possible way. He's faster, he's stronger... but what the hell.

She sees his finger tighten on the trigger. She drops to the floor. The gun roars, the sound amplified by the echo of the empty building, but the shot goes over her as she rolls toward him.

He is surprised by her response, but not overcome by it. He's seen enough desperate people performing desperate acts that he knows how to adjust to them. He steps back, calmly adjusts his aim, and prepares to fire.

Jenny twists onto her left side and throws something—a handful of loose change taken out of her jacket pocket. Quarters and nickels and dimes fly into Richter's face. He swears in German, his free hand involuntarily rising up to shield his eyes. Jenny rolls to her left and springs forward, launching at Richter's legs.

The change scatters harmlessly across Richter's face. Richter's hand drops. Cold fury shines in his eyes. He kicks at Jenny the way he might kick a dog. His boot races toward her face; Jenny intercepts it and manages to deflect it just enough so that it hits her shoulder. Pain lances down her side, but she keeps her grip on the leg. A moment later she twists, wraps her legs around his, and pulls, toppling him to the ground.

It's hard to say, at that moment, which of them is more surprised.

Richter grunts as he hits the concrete floor. His pistol slides across the floor, disappearing beneath a mound of trash and rubble near the loading dock entrance. He rolls to his feet, apparently unfazed by the fall. His expression—in fact, his entire stance—has changed. He's cautious, now. Calculating.

Jenny isn't sure what happened. She expected to be dead by now, and she isn't, so she decides to make the most of it and save her questions for later. She gets to her feet and crouches low, a stance she remembers from one of her great-grandfather's lessons.

Richter kicks again. Immediately Jenny brings up her arms to block. The kick is weak; it was a feint. Jenny almost doesn't notice the left hand striking at her unprotected side. She half-turns, lets the blow glance off her ribs, then jabs at a spot just under Richter's left arm. His right blocks, his left pushes her away, and Jenny feels herself flying across the room.

She flips in midair and lands on her feet.

*...I did **what**?*

"You keep secrets, *Fraulein*." Richter circles around to the side, measuring her up. "Even from yourself, I think."

Jenny's heart is pounding so hard it feels like it will burst out of her chest. The air tastes sharp. She feels giddy. She grins fiercely and clenches her fists.

The ferocity of her attack forces him back, step by step. Blow after blow, each blocked, but each time a blow comes closer to landing home. Finally one strikes home—a sharp jab to his side. He grunts, takes another step back, and her foot connects with the side of his knee. He staggers, but manages to block the next three blows.

And then Richter relaxes.

Jenny presses her attack, but each blow is countered immediately, completely, almost without effort on his part. And each blow he delivers in return requires more effort to block. Finally she stumbles, and his fist smashes into the side of her head, sending her spinning. He kicks her in the stomach, hard, and she flies back, hitting the floor, hard, gasping for breath.

Jenny scrambles to her feet, trying to breathe, willing her eyes to focus. By the time they do—by the time she can do anything at all—Richter has retrieved his gun.

"You surprise me, *Fraulein Forrest*," Richter says. "I did not expect you to be one of us."

She tries, and fails, to think of something to say.

"I feel enormous sympathy for you, *Fraulein*. I do." Richter's voice has returned to its calm, almost soothing tone. "To taste so briefly of that nectar. Had you the time to hone your skill, you might have beaten me. But now... now you have become a liability."

She's not going to be able to close the gap again. Richter is too far away.

"Shut up," she says. "Just do it, and be done."

She stares at him defiantly. Richter pulls the trigger. The gun echoes like a cannon. Jenny sees a streak of red.

Nothing happens.

Wind whips through the warehouse, dirt and debris fly in every direction. Jenny covers her ears as she hears a loud boom and the sound of glass shattering. She hears Richter shout in alarm, then hears the crackle of energy as the smell of ozone mixes with the dirt, dust, and rain. The wind dies down immediately, and Jenny hears someone else—someone American—swearing.

"He got away," she hears the voice say. "Teleport. Have I mentioned I hate teleporters? Uh, maybe don't tell Blink I said that."

Jenny wipes her sleeve across her face and coughs again. She can see a little—the dust isn't thick, it's just everywhere. The silhouette of a man stands framed in the loading bay door.

"Who the hell are you?" She coughs once more and tenses, preparing for the worst.

The silhouette turns to her. "Jennifer Forrest? You can call me 'Red Shift.' Agent Travers sent me."

Jenny frowns. "Red Shift? Crossfire? He sent *Crossfire?*"

The air clears enough that she can see him. He's dressed in a black uniform—a body suit with armored plates stitched into it. A yellow, stylized crosshair sits over his left breast. A harness that looks like a plated web belt is strapped over his chest, whirring softly. A visor that looks like a solid sheet of mirrored glass covers most of his face—except for his mouth, which is smiling slightly. He holds out his hand—sitting in the palm is a twisted lump of metal.

*He caught the bullet. He actually **caught the bullet**.*

"He was a bit pressed for time," Red Shift says.

Jenny picks the deformed bullet out of his hand and turns it over in her own. "So was I. Thanks."

The smile warms a bit, then turns into a frown. "Where's Curveball?"

Jenny's relief disappears. "He's back at his apartment. On the Boardwalk. I don't know what's going on over there, he just said it was magic and told me to run."

Red Shift nods. "Right. Where's the Boardwalk?"

"It's a little more complicated than that," Jenny says. "I'll take you. Or... you take me. I'll point."

Red Shift hesitates. "It's not a very dignified way to travel," he says.

"Just watch your hands," Jenny says, "and we'll get along fine."

* * *

CB isn't throwing up any more—his stomach is too empty for that—but the dry heaves won't stop. He's completely incapacitated at this point. He hasn't been able to do anything meaningful for minutes, and Plague is content to lean against a wall and watch him suffer.

"I'll admit it," Plague says. "I was worried at first. It never worked on you before. Everyone else in the room would be two steps from the grave, and you'd just stand there, laughing at me."

The satisfaction in his voice is unmistakable. The resentment doubly so.

"But things *changed*. Somebody made me an offer I couldn't refuse..." Plague's voice trails off. "So I didn't. And they made me better."

"They... rebuilt you..." CB's throat burns with bile. "Made you... stronger. Faster..."

Plague walks over to CB, staring down at him calmly.

"Yeah."

He drives the heel of his boot into the small of CB's back. CB yells, voice breaking and falling off into a high-pitched squeak.

"But I cost a lot more than six million dollars, asshole."

"You're... just... a pawn..." CB gasps.

"No shit." The boot comes down again, this time into his side. "Of course I'm a pawn. You think I don't already know that? Power comes with strings. It *always* comes with strings. They made me better. There were conditions. That's *life*. I'm a pawn and I'll play my part. I either make it to the other end of the board, or someone tips me over..."

Plague kneels down, grabs CB's hair, and pulls up sharply. He looks at CB's face: eyes unfocused, jaws slack, sweat and mucus covering his face. "I don't think you're going to be the one, though. You don't have a lot of time left."

"You can't... kill... everyone..." CB can barely speak.

Plague laughs. "We can. We *really can*."

Plague lets go of CB's hair. CB's forehead smashes into the floor with a *thunk*. He doesn't cry out.

"Not long now." Plague walks back to the wall and leans against it, looking bored. "A few minutes, I think. After that, I don't know. I'm hungry, maybe I'll get some—"

The wall explodes inward as something tears through it in the blink of an eye. The building *rocks* from the impact—bits of cinderblock bigger than a fist go flying everywhere. Plague starts to turn toward the noise, surprised, when a shimmering red blur streaks directly toward him. A second later the blur stumbles, falls, and slides across the floor. Red Shift curls up into a ball, holds his stomach, and starts to retch.

Plague's initial shock wears off. He turns to look at Red Shift and smirks. "Your backup didn't last as long as you did. Nice trick with the wall, but..."

That's when Jenny punches him right in the face.

The force of the blow knocks him clear off his feet. He falls on his back, grunting in surprise from the impact. The runes on his chest and arms flare up for a moment, and he sits up.

That's when Jenny knees him in the jaw.

His head snaps back, his jaw shattering on impact. He screams in pain, and scurries away from her crabwise. When he's far enough away, his eyes narrow and he starts to concentrate. The runes in his torso flare again, and the room fills with oily, sickening power.

Nothing happens. Plague, his face covered in blood, screams in frustration and pain through his shattered jaw. He closes his eyes, balls his fists, and the runes on his chest and arms flare so brightly he looks like he's on fire.

Again nothing happens. When Plague opens his eyes, the only thing in them is fear.

He runs. He's not nearly as fast as Red Shift, but he's fast. He runs through the shattered wall and he runs down the boardwalk, shouting in pain and terror as he does. Almost immediately the oily power fades. In a second, Red Shift pushes himself off the floor and moans quietly.

Jenny kneels down next to CB. He's a mess, but he's breathing regularly. She presses her hand against his forehead. He doesn't have a fever.

"CB?"

CB's eyes flutter open, focus on Jenny, and he frowns slightly. "Did you...?" His voice is dry and cracked. He coughs once, tries to clear his throat, chokes, and coughs again.

"Don't try to talk," Jenny says. "We need to get you to a doctor."

CB shakes his head. "It'll be OK." He can talk now, though not more than a whisper. "If he doesn't hang around long enough to kill you, you bounce back pretty fast. Help me sit."

Jenny grabs his shoulders and hauls him upright. CB looks around the lobby and sees Red Shift climbing to his feet.

"You're a little out of your usual stomping grounds," CB says. His voice is much stronger now. He almost sounds conversational.

"I'm slumming," Red Shift says. "Are you in your *uniform*?"

"I thought it would help," CB says.

"Did it?"

"Not as much as I'd have liked." CB tries to get to his feet. Jenny slings one of his arms over her shoulders. He leans against her and gets his bearings.

"Travers contacted us," Red Shift says. "Said you were in trouble. Gave us the location of the phone Miss Forrest used to call him."

"Looks like I owe Pete again," CB says. "Jenny."

Jenny looks up at him. "Yeah?"

"Did you just kick Plague's ass?"

"Yeah," Jenny says.

"Well. Thank God somebody did." CB can stand on his own feet now, and walks over to the hole in the side of the building. He looks at Red Shift, looks at the door next to the hole, and shakes his head. "Let's get out of here. There are still some soldiers around, and I think this is one of those rare instances when the police are actually going to show up on the boardwalk. Red, we have a safehouse in the city. Coming?"

"Sure," Red Shift says. "But I'm going to need to stop for breakfast first."

* * *

Street Ronin sips his coffee, waiting impatiently for his computer to finish its work.

Red Shift's trip to Albany had not gone well. The only thing they learned was that the mysterious computer in the mysterious secret room had been booby-trapped. That suggested there had probably been something on it worth learning, but that door had shut. And then blown up, rather spectacularly.

Red Shift's trip to Farraday City went much better. Miss Forrest and Curveball were both alive, and they were all rendezvousing at a safe house Curveball had set up somewhere in the city.

That left them with one success and one failure—the scales are balanced. Street Ronin is hoping to add a little more weight on the success side.

Red Shift's visor recorded everything in the Albany mission. Just before the bomb went off, it had recorded a brief flash of information from the computer monitor—the self-test the computer performed during a cold boot to make sure all its basic components were working properly. The image was only there for a moment, and it's not very clear, so Street Ronin is running a few filters to make the text on the screen easier to read.

He looks at the image again. It's getting close to legible. He can almost make out a few of the words and numbers.

A shadow falls across the monitor. Street Ronin turns to see David Bernard standing in the door.

"No IV today," Street Ronin says.

David nods, walks over to the empty chair to his left, and sits. "Red Shift said I could take it out this morning."

"Feeling better?"

"Yeah," David says. "It's a little scary how much better I feel. I won't be boxing any time soon, but... this is amazing."

"Better living through biochemistry," Street Ronin says. "It's pretty much the only reason I'm still in the fight."

His computer beeps, and an image of the Senator's monitor appears on the screen.

"There we go," Street Ronin says. "Let's see if we can find anything interesting."

David and Street Ronin both lean forward, looking at the image carefully.

"There," David says, and points.

"What?" Street Ronin squints. "What are you looking at?"

"Not sure," David says. "That's usually where the computer reports what kind of BIOS it's running, and the company that created it. I don't recognize the company, though."

They stare at the name for a minute.

"Haruspex Analytics," Street Ronin says. "Who the hell are they?"

WRITER'S NOTES

The thing about working with a conceit is you can get awfully attached to it, even if nobody else cares. A conceit is different from a concept or a theme because it doesn't actually have to be closely married to the core content of whatever you're creating. It's a lot closer to an affectation because it can be trivial and shallow and, if you're not careful, it can actually detract from your work by coming off as gimmicky. But they can be really, really fun.

The conceit for Curveball is that it's a story that wants to be a comic book. You can look at the cover of each issue and see what I mean. You can notice I call each episode "issues" and see what I mean.

There's also a lot of stuff I try that might not come across as effectively: I chose the average length of each issue (between 8,000 and 10,000 words) because I thought that was long enough to capture the feel of a traditional story arc as told in each issue of a comic book. I chose to write in present tense because I noticed that, traditionally, narration boxes in comic books are written in present tense. These decisions had an effect on the way I wrote the story, and I'm mostly happy with my attempts at present tense narrative, but I don't know that they actually add anything substantive to my conceit.

But I love that conceit. Curveball is a story that would have been a proper comic book if I had the kind of artistic talent necessary to pull it off. Viewing the project as a "comic book, only without the pictures and a slightly overwhelming bag of words" has helped me focus on the project in ways I usually find difficult. And at the end of issue twelve, when I realized I'd written enough words to fill a somewhat-longer-than-average novel, I figured there needed to be a Year One compilation. Which is what you're holding now.

But what to call it? I need to stick to my conceit, after all.

My first thought was to call it, with tongue firmly stuck in cheek, a "graphic novel." But it turns out that's not what you call these things. It was something of a surprise to me—when I bought Preludes & Nocturnes back in 1989 or 1990 I called it a graphic novel, and so did just about everyone else I talked to. Turns out it's officially described as a "trade paperback," which is a little confusing because in the world of novels that's just a description of the size of the pages and how it's bound. Technically, that might also be true in the world of comic books, but at least informally it's become shorthand for "a compilation of multiple issues of a comic book bound into a single book."

So to summarize: I call this series a "prose comic." I used to call Preludes & Nocturnes, and other books like it, "graphic novels." With that in mind, this would be a graphic novel, if my prose comic books were real comic books, but since they're not the print version is just a "trade paperback." However, and this is significant, since the official term for this kind of thing in the comic book world seems to also be "trade paperback," it all works out in the end.

Try not to think about it too much. The important part is I've satisfied my conceit.

Thanks for reading!

C. B. Wright (http://www.curveball.xyz)

ABOUT THE AUTHOR

Writer, former musician, occasional cartoonist, and noted authority on his own opinions, C. B. Wright's weakness for tilting at windmills has influenced every facet of his adult life. He enjoys reading and writing fiction. He also enjoys writing about himself in the third person. He refuses to comment on whether writing about himself in the third person also qualifies as fiction. He currently lives in Alabama with his wife, daughter, dog, and his overpoweringly large ego.

ABOUT CURVEBALL

Curveball is an ongoing story published monthly as web fiction, then through retailers in eBook and paperback formats.

http://www.curveball.xyz

ALSO BY AUTHOR

Curveball Year Two: That Which Does Not Dream (eBook, Trade Paperback)

Pay Me, Bug! (eBook, Trade Paperback)

www.ingramcontent.com/pod-product-compliance
Lightning Source LLC
Chambersburg PA
CBHW070533260626
47161CB00002B/357